RUN

*

Senator Gorman: tough, ruthless, ambitious, had set his sights on the White House. To keep in the headlines, he was waging a well-publicised war on the Mafia. He had a star witness: Joe Bono, a key Mafioso, ready to reveal the organisation's secrets to Senator Gorman's Congressional Committee. It looked good.

Then; trouble. Joe Bono murdered.

But the Senator announces that he has another witness, a witness whose identity he is keeping secret. A witness who is in hiding abroad. An experienced private detective, Peter Congdon, is engaged to fetch the witness, a girl, and smuggle her back into the United States.

Secrecy is vital, but even so, the Senator seems incapable of discretion. Mafia agents track Congdon. Time and again he succeeds in losing his pursuers—but never for long. As the chase moves across Europe, Congdon begins to realise that the Senator is playing a very devious game.

Hillary Waugh

Run When I Say Go

ARROW BOOKS

ARROW BOOKS LTD
3 Fitzroy Square, London W1

AN IMPRINT OF THE HUTCHINSON GROUP

London Melbourne Sydney Auckland
Wellington Johannesburg Cape Town
and agencies throughout the world

*

First published by
Victor Gollancz Ltd 1969
Arrow edition 1971

Made and printed in Great Britain
by The Anchor Press Ltd.,
Tiptree, Essex

ISBN 0 09 005250 1

SATURDAY 1:30–3:00 P.M.

Peter Congdon leaped down the steps of the dusty dull-red Pennsylvania Railroad coach and started up the platform, overtaking the scattering of other passengers with long, swinging strides. He crossed the concourse, gathering his coat against the chill November draught, dodged a tow motor pulling a mail wagon, and went through the doors into the near-empty vastness of Washington's Union Station.

It was one-thirty on a Saturday afternoon and only a handful of people were there, most of them workmen re-setting waiting-room seats. Peter looked around without pausing, went past the show-case model of a 1968 canary yellow Dodge and into the great hall where the ticket windows were. He stored the attaché case he carried in one of the lockers behind the posts and sat down at the nearby lunch counter to order a hamburger and milk shake.

To anyone watching, he was only another good-looking, youngish man stopping for a snack, a man impeccably dressed in a charcoal grey suit, a dark tweed topcoat, and a sedate, narrow-brimmed off-black hat. In New York he would have passed for a banker, probably on the executive rungs of Morgan Guaranty. In Washington, D.C., he looked like someone connected with the government, possibly a subcommittee attorney.

Actually, Peter Congdon was an employee of the Brandt Detective Agency in Philadelphia, a world-wide organisation whose boss, Charles F. Brandt, required, among other things, that his employees dress like New York bankers or subcommittee attorneys. Looks might not make the man, but they helped build organisation prestige. And the hamburger-milk shake was for more than the satisfaction of an appetite. It enabled Peter to kill time waiting for a three o'clock appointment and it gave him the chance to make sure that no one was watching an impeccably dressed, good-looking youngish man stopped for a snack.

He spent twenty minutes at the lunch counter and killed the rest of the time getting his shoes shined and browsing through the paperback bookstore beside the restaurant on the opposite side of the waiting room. When the station clocks said two-thirty, he went outside.

Across the way, looming above the bare-limbed trees, the Capitol dome gleamed pristine white against a clean, bright azure sky. Peter had never been inside the Capitol and, in fact, had only seen the dome on three other occasions, all from the same vantage point—the entrance arches of Union Station—but he still only gave it a cursory glance. He fancied himself as patriotic as the next man—if he stopped to think about it—but he wasn't much for monuments and he'd been around too long to retain ideals. It was a cynical world and he expected presidents to be vilified and senators to be censured.

A line of black and tan cabs was stretched in front of the station and he climbed into the first one, giving the uniformed attendant a dime. 'Twenty-two hundred and fifty Kalorama Road, Northwest,' he told the driver and lighted a cigarette. When they swung into Massachusetts Avenue traffic, he sat back, opened the ash receptacle, and crossed his legs like a company executive making himself comfortable in his personal limousine.

'Twenty-two fifty Kalorama?' the driver said as he

pulled up at the first traffic light. 'That's where Senator Gorman lives. Edge of Georgetown. Kind of, anyway. You a reporter?'

'No. Why?'

'I just took a reporter out there. You're the second fare in a row to the same address.'

'The senator's a popular guy.'

'He's not as popular as he ought to be, if you want my opinion. There are plenty of people who hate his guts. And I don't just mean guys in the Mafia either. I mean guys like that reporter. And guys who are big in government too. You may not believe that, but I know what goes on in this town. I truck a lot of wheels in this buggy and I hear what they say.'

'What's the reporter's beef?'

'He doesn't think he's sincere. He thinks Gorman's only investigating the Mafia to build himself a reputation. He thinks Gorman doesn't give a damn about the Mafia, he thinks he's making all that noise about them to get to be President. President of the United States, no less. He figures he's laying the groundwork.'

'That sounds kind of far-fetched.'

'Yeah, well he's not the only reporter who thinks that. You'd be surprised. They talk about how Kefauver got a vice-presidential nomination and Joe McCarthy wielded almost as much power as Eisenhower himself. They think he's after some of the same. They think he's picked himself an issue and is trying to make it hot stuff.'

'And what do you think?'

'You want to know what I think? He's a good man trying to do a job. Me and my wife, we've been for him ever since he showed us how much the Mafia causes all our problems—I mean, how it controls all the crime and dope and prostitution and a lot of the big businesses and the Communist party in America and everything. I mean he really opened our eyes. And when his star witness got murdered, I guess that proved it all right. That's the kind of thing we're up against. And anybody else but Gorman would've had to fold up that committee after that happened. But not him. He's no quitter. He's got nothing to fight with and he's still fighting.'

Peter knocked ashes off his cigarette. 'Then you don't think he's trying to be President?'

'Well, I don't figure he'd knock back the job if it was offered to him. I mean, if you're in politics, I guess you'd like to be President. Me, I wouldn't touch it with a ten-foot pole, the mess the world is in. But Gorman? Sure I think he'd take it. And he'd do a job too. But he's not trying to use the Mafia to get there. No, sir. I think it's like he says. There's a cancer in this society and he's got his finger on it. Hell, you don't really think, if he was trying to be President, he'd be investigating the Mafia, do you? Do you think it makes him look good to haul in a lot of Mafia big shots and have them show up with a battery of attorneys and do nothing but plead the Fifth? And then the one real witness he's got, the one Mafia guy who's willing to sing, gets murdered, where does that leave him? And even if he hadn't been killed, what would it get Gorman? Look at Valachi. He sang like a bird but that didn't end crime in these United States. And it didn't promote anybody into the White House either. Hell, I can't even remember who headed that committee.'

'But everybody knows Gorman's heading this one.'

'You want my opinion, that's because he's a grade-A patriot. Maybe there're a lot of big shots and intellectuals who hate his guts, but there're a lot more people, who don't get heard, who figure Senator Gorman is just what this country needs, and wish we had a few more like him. And I'm one of them.'

Kalorama, N.W., was a quiet street off Connecticut Avenue better than a twenty-minute ride in heavy

Washington traffic. It was a narrow street with cars parked solidly down one side and the senator's house was on the corner of Twenty-third, across from the Royal Thai Embassy. It was a large, attractive Georgian building, constructed of old brick, with high first-floor windows and a pillared front stoop. A blacktop driveway along the side led to a parking area in the rear with a three-car garage in matching brick. The drive and the rear were also filled with cars and, in front, a white-gloved policeman handled the traffic.

'Well, that's the place,' the driver said, stopping short of the policeman and opposite the drive. 'Looks like quite a party. You want to tell me what's going on?'

'I don't know what's going on,' Peter said, getting out.

'Neither did that reporter,' the driver said sadly. 'Ninety cents is the tab.'

Peter paid and tipped. He crossed over, squeezed between cars at the kerb, and went up the short walk to the stoop. The bare branches of careful plantings framed the large slate flagstones, the wood trim of the house was painted an antique olive cream which gave it a mellower, older effect than the customary white. The front door was a dark green with brass fittings, unlatched and slightly ajar. On it, tacked under the doorknob, was a plain white card with 'Walk In' typed on it. Peter followed the instruction.

The entrance hall inside had wide-planked flooring, a broad staircase, and a plethora of drinking, talking, and laughing people, nearly all of them men. The wallpaper was white with a stripe design. There were some pictures, a gold-framed bubble mirror, a reception table with a silver salver and two vases of flowers on it, and several chairs. White double doors on the right were closed. A matching pair on the left were open and it was through these, in and out, that the gentlemen and occasional woman of the press flowed, their hands occupied with punch glasses and snacks, their tongues busy with the in jokes and chit-chat that had no meaning for those outside the fraternity.

'Hats and coats under the stairs,' a short, plump man with a tall rye and water told Peter as he entered. 'Or give them to Sam.'

'Thanks.' Peter edged through the throng holding the hat so it wouldn't get crushed, using his other arm to protect his shoulder holster against discovery.

Under the stairs, a pipe rack on wheels was already full of coats, with a surplus thrown over the top. Others lay at random on the floor, some folded, others not. A felt hat, kicked into the hall, had already been trampled.

Peter removed his own coat, folded it, and placed it and his hat in the best remaining spot he could find. One man close by was telling another about what a third had reported regarding women in Saigon. Peter squeezed past and worked his way back to the open double doors. Three reporters there were speculating on the purpose of the party and one said, 'Whatever it is, Gorman sure as hell can't beat a dead horse much longer.'

In the large drawing room beyond, two Negro waiters in spotless white jackets handed out spiked punch or the hard stuff itself at a long white-clothed table by the two front windows. Another long table opposite held enough trays of snacks to feed a family of five for a week, but they and the alcohol were disappearing fast before the attacks of the forty or fifty reporters gathered for the occasion.

Peter got in line for the punch and said to the waiter who served him, 'Where would I find the senator?'

The man showed him a smile of teeth almost as white as his jacket and said, 'I dunno, suh. In his study, mos' likely. I reckon he'll appear when he's ready.'

Peter accepted the punch glass. 'Where would I find his study?'

'He's not to be disturbed, suh. Just help yourself to what we got here and make yourself at home. He'll be along presently.'

Peter nodded without comment. Behind him a reporter said, 'You must be new on this beat. Gorman only gets interviewed when *he* chooses, not when you choose.'

Peter said he got the idea and moved away, across to the tidbits that still remained. Apparently this wasn't a party to butter up Washington reporters; this was a press conference, Gorman style, and the senator was waiting for the propitious moment to make an entrance. Well, Peter decided, it wasn't up to him to rock the boat. He tried to look as much like a reporter as he could and settled down in a corner with his glass of punch for the wait.

SATURDAY 3:30–3:50 P.M.

It was half an hour before a slender and bustlingly efficient young man with slick hair, delicate features, and plain glasses pushed his way into the room and lifted a hand containing a sheaf of papers. 'May I have your attention, gentlemen? The senator would like to see you now. Will you step across the hall, please?'

The young man led the way out and a general exodus got under way. A few countercurrents were set up as a scattering of newsmen made a final onslaught on the available liquor supply, but, for the most part, the trend was general and obedient. Senator Robert Gerald Gorman was not the most notable and most newsworthy member of the Senate, but he had carved out a sufficiently large niche for himself over the months of his subcommittee's investigation of the Mafia for the press to play the willing scribe. Gorman was strongly liked and just as strongly hated. One did not feel neutral about him. One only felt strongly—and this kind of reaction, shared by reporters as well as the public at large, made him good copy. And when good copy spoke, newspapermen were quick to listen.

Peter moved with the middle wave and the thin-faced secretary impatiently and arrogantly waved them towards the room across the hall, whose doors were now open.

The room was similar to but deeper than the one supporting the popular food and liquor tables. Again, the furniture had been removed and rows of folding chairs had been set out, stretching from a small desk at one end all the way to the windows at the other.

Behind the desk was a door into the rear section of the house and through this door, as the seats began to fill, came the senator with a folder of papers. He was in his mid-forties, a balding man with black hair greying at the temples and a week too long around the ears and neck. He stood an even five-ten and his build was paunchy but not yet fat. He was vigorous, he showed a beard line even when freshly shaven, he had narrow eyes and a way of smiling that kept the eyes from showing it. His laugh was an uncertain giggle but it was seldom heard. He didn't joke very often and when he did, it usually wasn't in front of the press. Senator Robert Gorman was not buddy-buddy with newsmen. He never had been one of the boys, and since his discovery of the Mafia conspiracy he had conducted himself with even greater aloofness. He was on a separate plane, a

Cassandra-like prophet who warned but was not heeded.

He was a senator midway through his second term who had, until recently, remained virtually unknown to the public at large. Now, however, though he did not command the attention that the big public figures got, his name was nearly as well known. He was chairman of the Senate subcommittee which, under his aegis, had taken up the cause of investigating the Mafia. Now he spoke from loftier levels and the arrogance of his tones had increased accordingly. Now he ordered rather than requested, now he told rather than informed. Now he was the embodiment of anti-Mafism and his life was devoted to the organisation's destruction.

To his enemies, he was an arrant opportunist and a potential danger to America. To his followers, his anti-evil stance made him, by definition, pro-virtue, and he was his country's patron saint. To the press, he was good copy.

The seats filled with reasonable speed for newspapermen, the most irreverent of all humans, but many preferred to stand along the walls or sit on the window ledges. Peter took a position just inside the doors and heard one man mutter to another, 'I'll bet he picked now just to make us miss the football games.'

The reporters got themselves assembled, their notebooks out and their pens and pencils ready. Senator Gorman, meanwhile, ignored them while he looked over papers, sorted, laid things out just so, and consulted with an aide who was setting up a tape recorder.

Then, at the exact moment when all the visitors were settled and sufficiently expectant, the senator, displaying a remarkable sense of timing, looked up and surveyed the situation. His young secretary, still with the sheaf of papers, was standing in the open doorway, legs spread, the papers held in both hands in front of him, looking quite like a Nazi storm trooper out of uniform.

Gorman took it all in. He leaned forward, bracing himself on the table with his fingertips, and steadfastly regarded the people in the room. Again his timing was shrewd and he spoke at the exact moment of maximum expectancy. 'There is,' he began sonorously, speaking to no one in particular, 'in this country and in this world, a conspiracy of evil. Its slimy tentacles reach from the dark regions of sin and subversion into the light of truth and honour. Its corrupting influence is apparent in every walk of modern life until even the halls of Congress are not safe. I do not have to tell you its name. You know its name. It degrades and despoils, and what it cannot corrupt, it threatens, and what it cannot threaten, it kills.'

He looked down at his papers briefly and then at the assembled corps of press men. 'And what can be done against this conspiracy? What is the one weapon the Mafia fears? Exposure is what the Mafia fears. Names is what the Mafia fears. The finger, ticking off the account of their evil. That is what the Mafia fears. This committee. That is what the Mafia fears. The spotlight and the publicity we on my committee direct on the Mafia and their degrading practices. That is what they fear. That is why they come before us in fear and trembling, hiding behind their high-priced attorneys, hiding behind the honest intention of the Fifth Amendment to the Constitution of the United States. That is why we on the committee get threatening notes. That is why we get anonymous phone calls. Because they fear exposure. And that is why they killed Joe Bono.

'All right.' He was almost perfunctory about it. 'They thought when they killed Joe Bono they killed the investigation. They thought when they killed Joe Bono they left us with no one inside the Mafia who could tell us their inner secrets.' He paused, and intoned, 'This investigation is going on. We will not be stopped by threats. We will not be intimidated by murder. We will pursue this dragon of evil. We will slay this dragon. We will expose its workings to the world. And I mean we will document the case, stonc by stone, step by step, name by name. They thought Joe Bono was our only witness. They are wrong. They are terribly, terribly wrong.'

He paused there to let the little ripple flow through the crowd, and then he stepped in on it and went on. 'Joe Bono is not the only person in the world who can expose this dirty stigma on the face of man. He is not the only witness who can name the names, date the dates, and place the places. The Mafia thought they had won when they killed Joe Bono. Well, the Mafia will tremble in their boots tonight and from this time on. Because we have another witness. And when this witness takes the stand, the Mafia will be rocked to its foundations.'

Gorman stopped there and looked around grimly, but there was the tinge of pleasure in his eyes. The newspapermen had been impressed. Really impressed. At the same time, the secretary moved forward. He handed Peter one of the papers he held and advanced to the front row to start distributing the others. Peter glanced at the short paragraph and saw that it was a virtual copy of the statement the senator had just made.

There was momentary silence in the room and then one reporter said, 'Can you give us the name of this witness, Senator?'

Gorman smiled a little. This was the way he liked it, an eager press begging for crumbs. It hadn't been like that since Bono died. 'Not on your life,' he said. 'That's top-secret.'

'Is he a member of the Mafia?' another asked.

Gorman permitted one of his characteristic giggly chuckles. 'Did I say the witness was a "he"?'

'It's a she then?'

'Did I say it was a "she"?'

'Senator,' put in another, 'are you trying to say that the sex of the witness is top-secret too?'

Gorman smiled at that and relented a little. 'I guess the sex of the witness doesn't have to be classified material. All right, I'll let you in on a little secret. The witness is female.'

A stir swept over the room. Notebooks were flipped open, seats were shifted, brief undertones were heard. The sex of the witness was at least as exciting as the fact of the witness.

'Does the Mafia know about her?" came a question like a shot.

Gorman chuckled. 'If the Mafia didn't know, it does now.'

'Can we take it that the Mafia already knows?' asked a serious voice. 'In view of what happened to Bono, Senator, can we assume you would not make public the fact you have another witness if the Mafia did not already know that witness existed?'

Gorman smiled a little. 'I think that's a fairly safe assumption to make.'

'Does the Mafia know who the witness is?' came from across the room.

Gorman's grin became almost malevolent. 'I hope not.'

'Is she a wife of one of the Mafia members?'

'I can't tell you any more than that she's a female.'

'Is it Bono's wife?'

'I plead the Fifth.'

Everybody laughed and the next question still had the end of the chuckle in it. 'Are you prepared to say that it is *not* Bono's wife?'

Gorman was still chuckling himself. 'I'm not prepared to say anything on that subject at all.'

A man in the back said, 'Can we quote you as saying,

Senator, that the Mafia is aware that a witness exists and that she's a woman, but the Mafia does not know what woman?'

'No. You may *not* quote me as saying anything like that at all. The Mafia has not been taking me into its confidence of late as to what it knows and does not know.'

There was more laughter but it was a surface reaction. The questions and answers were deadly earnest. 'You're pretty certain they know you have a woman witness, are you not?'

'I don't have any comment to make of that.'

'Senator, you said earlier that they did know.'

'And I just said I'm not a mind-reader. The Mafia doesn't tell me anything and I don't tell the Mafia anything. But I am telling you—and the Mafia can make whatever it wants out of it—that I've got a witness who can blow the whistle on their whole operation and that witness is female. Who she is, where she is, and when she'll appear is something you aren't going to learn and the Mafia isn't going to learn until I produce her.'

More questions followed but they were tacks and traps devised to get more information out of the senator. Gorman, however, was an old pro in that field and he had a courtroom background to boot. He had given the reporters what he had intended to give them and it was a game from there in, a game they all knew would end in a stalemate but one both he and his questioners could enjoy playing.

It was an alien field to Peter Congdon and he soon lost interest. He slipped out and crossed the hall to the drawing room, but the punch bowls, the bottles and glasses, the hors d'œuvres, and even the tables had been cleared away.

SATURDAY 4:00–4:25 P.M.

The press conference lasted only five more minutes and Peter was waiting by the door when the reporters came crowding out. There was talk as they made their way to the piles of coats and hats behind the stairs and the voices were excited and impressed. Gorman's secret witness would vie with Vietnam for the headlines and the questions she raised held equal fascination. 'It's a cinch the Mafia knows what he's told us,' one man said. 'You wouldn't catch Gorman giving them free information a second time. Not after Bono.'

'Then he must have a pipeline,' another answered. '*That's* the story I'd like to get.'

'And that's the one we won't get—even off the record.'

They swirled and eddied, jamming the hallway, the coat-and-hatted ones pushing their way to the front door, the others bucking their way to the racks. Peter waited until the stream out of the conference room thinned, then moved against it, edging his way inside. The senator was at the desk talking with three of the newsmen as he gathered his things. He was sober and serious, like a professor after a class that had gone well, but a busy professor who didn't have time to ponder how the class had gone.

Peter moved up to the fringes and waited his turn, listening as the senator reminded one reporter that Joseph Bono had had a $100,000 price tag on his head, set there by the Mafia when it was learned he would testify, and that was why secrecy was so important in the case of the new witness. Any leaks as to her identity or whereabouts could endanger her life, and surely the reporter could understand that. The senator turned to Peter. 'You got a question?'

'I'll wait till the others are through, sir.'

Gorman turned away, answered two or three more questions and told the men they could have more information as soon as it was safe to give it. When they departed, he finished putting his papers back into the folder and glanced at Peter with shrewd, penetrating eyes. 'Now, you wanted to see me?'

'I believe you wanted to see me, Senator. I'm from the Charles F. Brandt Detective Agency.'

Gorman gave him a quick second look and his eyes narrowed. 'Oh, yeah. The man from Brandt's. What's your name?'

'Congdon. Peter Congdon.'

'Congdon, huh? All right, Mr. Congdon, you got some identification with you—some credentials? But not here.' He nodded at the last of the men leaving the room. 'Let's go find someplace private.' He turned and led the way through the rear door into a small panelled music room, out of a side door into a back hall and up a narrow flight of stairs to the second floor. A few steps down a green-carpeted corridor brought them to the senator's study in the rear corner of the house. It was a spacious room looking out on the side at the Thai Embassy and in the back upon the garage and the modest grounds of the 150′ × 150′ lot. Included was a grape arbor, some fruit trees, a picnic table and goldfish pond, all made private by a shadow fence, the fence being in turn hidden by protective plantings. It was a private house that was extremely private.

The study itself was panelled in dark mahogany, carpeted with burgundy pile, furnished with comfortable leather chairs and couch, a large mahogany desk, sparsely filled bookshelves, and three tiers of file cabinets behind the door. Orange rectangles of light gleamed on the side panels where the lowering sun pierced the rear windows.

The senator switched on the overhead, went behind the desk to draw heavy curtains, turned on the desk lamp and laid his papers on the blotter. 'Now then, Mr. Congdon,' he said and held out his hand.

Peter showed him his Brandt's identification card bearing his photograph, signature, his vital statistics and, on the back, his thumbprint. He followed that with a letter of introduction from Brandt to Gorman which he laid on the desk top.

The senator studied the card and read from it. 'Age thirty-one, hair brown, sex male, eyes brown, height six feet no inches, weight a hundred and eighty-five.' He studied Peter and sucked a tooth. 'I guess it looks like you.' He returned the card, read the letter and dropped it back on the desk. 'All right,' he said. 'It looks like you're it. You get here in time for the party? You get something to drink?'

'I did. I also attended some of the conference.'

'Good. I guess you got the general idea then. Have a seat, Mr. Congdon.' He indicated the green-leather facing chair and opened a drawer in the desk to remove a quart bottle of Old Crow bourbon and a pair of highball glasses, which he stood on the leather top. 'You like a drink?'

Peter, sitting, shook his head. 'Not on duty, sir.'

'Yeah. Good point. Well, if you change your mind . . .'

He poured himself two inches of the amber fluid and sat down in his swivel chair. He regarded Peter thoughtfully for a moment, took a small sip from his glass and set it down without letting go. 'How much did Brandt tell you about this job?' he said.

'Nothing at all, except that I was to see you at three o'clock this afternoon here. He said you'd tell me what I had to know.'

'Just as well,' he said, and sat up. 'You know about the

work of this subcommittee of mine? You been following it in the papers?'

'I know you're investigating the Mafia.'

'And that's all?'

Peter crossed one leg over the other but he still kept his back clear of the chair. Brandt didn't like his agents lounging on business calls any more than he liked them drinking. 'I believe one of your witnesses was murdered before he could testify. There were quite a few headlines about that.'

'Yeah,' he said. 'The press played that part up all right. So there it is. Our witness got murdered. Joe Bono. One of the real big ones. And he was willing to talk. And they shut him up. You know anything about Bono?'

'I understand he was in the Mafia.'

'That's right. In it but not of it, if you get what I mean.'

'I don't.'

Gorman took another small sip of uncut bourbon, savoured it for a moment and swallowed. 'I got to brief you then. Without going into a long history of the organisation, it was originally formed by Sicilian families, and their descendants are what is the Mafia today. The descendants form the hierarchy. They rule the Mafia. They organise, they control, they run the operations. And only they become the Dons. The rest of their gangs are outsiders and only God knows how many there are all over the world. God, and maybe that guy Bono they killed. Those outsiders are all kinds—smart, dumb, thieves, cutthroats, lawyers, anything. But none of them can get to the top in the Mafia. In fact, nobody who wasn't born into it can get much of any position of leadership. You follow me?'

Peter said, 'Yes. It's like a family business.'

'Yeah. That's what it is. A family business. And, like

any family business, Mr. Congdon, it has the exceptions. Once in a great while you get an outsider coming along who's exceptional. Like Al Capone. He wasn't a Sicilian. He was a Neapolitan. But he was also a genius. I mean in the field of organisation and development. He was so good that the Mafia even deferred to him most of the time. He couldn't become a Don himself, as I told you, because he wasn't born to it, but he could pretty well decide who would be.'

Gorman had another sip of bourbon and set the glass down. 'Joseph Bono was another. Like Capone. He was even Neapolitan, the same as Capone. And he was good. Not so good as Capone, but good. Bono was good enough so that he went a hell of a lot farther in the organisation than most outsiders. The trouble was, so far as Bono was concerned, it wasn't far enough. He was sore that he couldn't crash the innermost circle.'

Gorman titled his chair back and clasped his hands behind his head. 'Now let me tell you this. One of the reasons for this closed system the Mafia's got is because of their training. The Mafia settles its own quarrels. It metes out its own justice. You never see the Mafia turning to the police for help. No matter what happens, no matter what internal trouble they may have, no matter who gets killed, the Mafia and their wives keep their mouths shut. I guess, if you've been following what's been going on in my committee, that's pretty obvious. They all hide behind the Fifth Amendment.'

The senator made a face at the thought and had another little drink. 'That, you might well understand,' he went on, 'is one of the reasons why no one else can get top leadership positions in the Mafia. They only trust their own. Capone, for instance, didn't have the emotional stability they require of themselves. Bono couldn't be trusted not to talk. And the more embittered he became, the more willing he was to talk. And he was high enough up so what he had to talk about was important.'

Gorman tilted back his chair and reclasped his hands behind his head. 'We heard about this, of course. When we started our investigation and began questioning and probing, we got the word he might be persuaded to open up. If he was going to blow the whistle, he wanted the biggest soapbox he could get and this was it. So we dickered through our intermediaries and got him to see things our way. We got it all set up but, of course, the Mafia didn't like the idea. They didn't want him to talk.' Gorman's face grew bitter. 'Unfortunately—for the good people of this country—the Mafia got to him before he got to us. And they did a good job. I suppose you read about that. They left him in the trunk of a stolen car, hands and feet tied, half his head shot away, four other bullets and fifty ice-pick wounds in the rest of him.'

Peter nodded. 'I heard.'

'Yeah,' Gorman said sourly. 'That got good coverage all right. That got more space than anything our committee's been doing. O.K., you got the picture so far?'

'I've got it.'

Gorman had another little sip and leaned back again. 'I guess that's a pretty easy story to follow. Well, you heard my statement to the press. Now you know we've got another witness. A female witness this time. And I guess now you know why you're here.'

Peter shook his head. 'No, sir, I don't.'

'Come on, Congdon. You're supposed to be a smart detective, aren't you? You mean you can't figure that one out?'

'I don't see much point in guessing about it. I'd rather have you tell me.'

Gorman put one foot on the desk and a corner of his mouth twisted. 'All right, Congdon, I'll make it short and sweet. Your job is to bring the girl to us, all in one piece, safe and sound.'

'I see.'

'Now don't tell me you couldn't guess that was what I was going to say.'

'No, sir, I couldn't. I didn't have any idea what you wanted me to do.'

'You surprise me, Congdon.'

'You surprise me, Senator. Or maybe I'm just not familiar with the way Senate committees operate. I expected that the girl would be under the protection of government agents.'

'Oh, when she gets on United States soil we'll have plenty of government agents taking care of her. Right now, however, she doesn't happen to be in this country.'

'But we have federal agents in other countries.'

'Who? What? You mean the CIA? That's espionage. This isn't their department at all.'

'How about Treasury men? Dope smuggling is their department and I gather the Mafia controls the dope racket.'

'Yeah, that's right. Only we don't happen to have any control over the Treasury men.' Gorman put his foot down and came forward in his chair for another sip of bourbon. There was only one inch left in the glass now. 'That happens to be the province of the damned executive branch of the government and, as you may have noticed, Congdon, this investigation doesn't happen to be very popular in a lot of places.' He looked up at Peter, his eyes narrow. 'You get a load of the press this afternoon? I got them sitting up and taking notice for a change. I might even get back on page one of the papers tomorrow with that story of a new witness. But those damned reporters are so busy filling up their rags with stories about Vietnam or hippies or black power or credibility gaps, they don't have sense enough to take a look where the real stories are.' He shook a finger. 'But there'll come a day, Congdon. They'll learn one day where the real power lies. They'll find out who holds the whip hand. And they'll come to heel. You can bet your bottom dollar on that one.' He shook his head. 'It's the Mafia, Congdon. It's the root of all evil and it's the evil we're going to root out. You and me and this woman you're going to bring home. And then we're going to see what we're going to see.'

He glowered and leaned into the light. 'You know how columnists snipe? No, I guess you don't. You don't get your name in the paper that much. Your reputation isn't at the mercy of some guy second-guessing you behind a typewriter. Well, they snipe at me. We might as well be frank about this because if you don't know it, you probably will, and you'd better hear the facts from me rather than a lot of rumours from some of those smart boys trying to attract readers through character assassination.

'There're some columnists who have all but come right out and suggested that this whole investigation is a sham. I've got my enemies, Congdon. When you're in public life and are trying to do a job and are controversial, you're going to have enemies. I've got mine. And one of the things my enemies say about me is that the whole purpose of my investigating committee is not to investigate the Mafia at all, but to build my and the committee's reputations.'

He sat straight and looked Peter hard in the eye. 'That's bullshit, and you better believe it's bullshit.' He leaned forward and pointed a finger. 'You let me tell you something. If reputation was what I was after, I could get myself a hell of a lot more reputation just making one big speech about our conduct of the war in Vietnam. Either attacking it or defending it, it doesn't matter. I could get more headlines for myself talking about draft-card burning or the race riots last summer, or by introducing a new law making the possession or use of LSD a federal offence. That's if I was after headlines.

'But what does that mean? The war in Vietnam's going to end someday—somehow or other. The day will soon be on us when Stokely Carmichael will be as dead an issue as Malcolm X. But the cancers that cause the wars, the problems that produce the Malcolm Xs and the Stokely Carmichaels, they'll still be with us.

'Ride the streets of Harlem some night. New York isn't my state, thank God, but investigation is my job, and there's the place to go. Harlem. And you'll see them there, the drug addicts, out in the streets. Everyone you see is an addict. They're all out. They're looking for fixes or they're looking for the money to buy a fix. And where do the fixes come from? The Mafia. And who does the money go to? The Mafia. Your sister becomes a prostitute? The Mafia's behind it. You lose your shirt gambling? The Mafia. It's the Mafia that controls and promotes the cancers of our society. They run the dope rings, gambling, prostitution, pinball machines, juke boxes—you name it and, if it's evil, the Black Hand is in it up to the wrist. No wonder there are riots in this country. No wonder there's crimes in the streets. People say I see a Mafia man under every bed. They think I exaggerate. Well, I don't. I only see what's there, what other people can't see because they're looking at the surface things. They see society's sickness without seeing the cause.'

Gorman relaxed, had another swig of bourbon and tilted back his chair. 'You get the idea, right? Well, a lot of people in this country don't. And that's why we aren't using the T-men. My committee doesn't control the Treasury Department. I can't order those men to do Senate work. And those who do control the T-men aren't responsive to my committee's needs. So we hire our own men to do our own work and that's where you and the Brandt Agency come in. You and I are going to throw a new witness into proceedings and when we do, Vietnam is going to take a back seat and my committee is going to be the hottest thing in Washington. We're going to be in the driver's seat. And then I'm going to remember who's been my friend and who's been my enemy.'

SATURDAY 4:25–4:45 P.M.

Senator Gorman grinned at Peter and his eyes gleamed with anticipation. 'How does that appeal to you, Congdon? You want to be part of something big?'

Peter said quietly, 'I want to do the job you've hired me for—whatever it is.'

'Whatever it is, eh? Well, I'll tell you what it is. Your job is to be escort and bodyguard for our Miss X. You will go to her whereabouts in Europe and bring her back here.' Gorman's face was set and serious now, the black eyebrows pulled together over the narrow eyes. 'I need not caution you that if the Mafia knows what you're doing and can stop you, they will. You know what they did to Joe Bono. Well, they'll try to do that to anybody who's willing to blow the whistle on them. Your job is going to be dangerous and I'm going to warn you it can be very dangerous.'

He leaned his elbows on the desk and pointed a jabbing finger at Peter. 'Now the reason we hired your agency to do this job is because it's the kind of large organisation that has the contacts and manpower to handle it. Your Mr. Brandt has been told the nature of the job and you are the agent he picked to do that job. I specified that the man have no wife and family. The Mafia will stop at nothing to keep this witness from testifying and that includes reprisals against innocent women and children and I don't want a man going out on this assignment who might throw our prize witness to the wolves because of a threat to his near and dear. You're supposed to be single. Are you single?'

Peter nodded. 'I am.'

'And are you willing to run the risks? I don't want anybody going on this job whose first thought is going to be his own skin. If you aren't absolutely sure of yourself on that score, I want you to back out now, before you're given any secret information. The man who undertakes this mission carries my total trust. That trust cannot be violated.'

Peter said, 'I was warned there would be danger. I understand all that.'

'And you're prepared to go through with it?'

Peter smiled slightly. 'Mr. Brandt would not have spent the train fare on me if I were going to back out.'

Gorman nodded. 'All right, that's what I want to hear. Because—and you'd better understand this—when you go on this mission, you carry the future of our country with you. This woman is our second chance to expose the Mafia and break up their organisation. But if anything happens to her, it's the end of the investigation. There is no third witness.'

Gorman sat up then and took a good swallow of the bourbon. 'All right,' he said and poured another inch of liquor into the glass, 'you're our man. You got any questions so far?'

'I've got a lot of questions, Senator.'

'All right, shoot.'

'First question. Exactly how much does the Mafia know?'

Gorman tilted back. 'They know there's a girl who's willing to talk.'

'They don't know who she is or where she is?'

'They know *what* she is, perhaps. They may even know who she is. What they don't know is where she is.'

'And what is she?'

'One of Joe Bono's girl friends.'

Peter eyed the senator. 'You mean Joe Bono told *all* to his girl friends?'

'Don't make the mistake of thinking this is any ordinary girl friend, Congdon. This was a particular mistress. This was somebody very special to him.'

'More special than his wife?'

'Far more special. This woman he kept in luxury in a large villa, staffed with servants, outside a large European capital.' A corner of Gorman's mouth twisted. 'You want to see some proof?'

'If you've got it.'

Gorman took out his key ring and used a tiny key on the end to unlock the left-hand top drawer of his desk. He removed a small jewel box. 'Take a look at this,' he said, opening it and pushing it across the desk.

On a small red-velvet pad there lay a gold disc the size of a nickel, inlaid with diamonds forming the letters JB. Attached to the rear of the disc were two tiny gold links, a stirrup-shaped piece and a fine gold shaft shaped to go through one side of the stirrup, through the lobe of a woman's ear, and fasten to the stirrup's other side. It was a handsome, but heavy and masculine earring.

Peter lifted it out for examination. There were tiny markings scratched on its back but they required either a jeweller's loop, better eyes or better light than Peter had to read them. He set the glistening object back in its case and pushed it across the desk again. 'That's supposed to prove something, I take it?'

'That proves plenty.' Gorman lifted the earring and gazed at it fondly before replacing it in the box and locking it back in the drawer. 'What would you call it?'

'It's an earring now, but something was cut off the back. It wasn't originally an earring.'

'Yeah.' Gorman nodded. 'You're a detective after all. That piece of jewellery—and I've got papers to document all of this—and another just like it were originally made as a pair of cuff links by Martin Feinwick, a noted craftsman in Chicago. This was done on the order and to the specifications given him by Frank "Midge" Rennie. You know who he is, don't you?'

'No.'

'And that goes to show how much trouble my committee has getting proper coverage in the press. Everybody in the country ought to know that name. Because Frank Rennie is one of the top men in the Mafia. So what do you think of that?'

'I suppose I'm impressed.'

'And you damned well should be. Because those cuff links were given to Joe Bono at a forty-fourth birthday party for him back in nineteen sixty-one. Those cuff links were a little token of appreciation and affection. About eleven thousand dollars' worth.'

'And he later gave them . . .'

'That's right. He later had them made into earrings for this mistress. She sent this one to me to validate the story—her story. And, like I say, it does because we've got a deposition from Feinwick himself authenticating the piece. But you can see it does more than just tell us she's who she says she is. That earring validates what she's got to tell. You said, would Joe Bono tell all to some woman? That earring says yes. That earring says she's no ordinary woman. She was so special he gave her—he had made over for her—something that must have been one of his most prized possessions. The woman who possesses the mate to this earring can blow the lid off the Mafia!'

'She can, but why would she?'

Gorman gave him his cruel, twisted smile, 'Vengeance, Congdon. Vengeance. They killed Joe Bono to keep him from talking. And I mean the very people she knows all about—the people she entertained in that villa, people she listened to, talked to, heard all about from Bono himself, who they were, what they did, and how they did it. They killed him and she's going to make them pay for it. And you and I, Congdon, are going to see to it that she does.'

Gorman's malicious smile broadened in contemplation but Peter remained unsatisfied. 'You say the Mafia knows the witness is Bono's mistress? And she entertained them? Then they must know her name. They know *her*.'

Gorman shrugged. 'That's probably true. Bono had other mistresses, and that might throw the Mafia off the track, but we'd better figure the Mafia is on to the right mistress. We're working on the assumption they know who this mistress is. But where she is is another question. And that's the question they don't know the answer to. I don't give a good God damn what else they know about this witness, just so long as they don't know how to find her.'

'And why wouldn't they know that?'

'I assume that's a rhetorical question and you know the answer as well as I do. And that answer is that this particular woman does not intend to suffer the same fate as her lover. She made sure she changed her name and address before getting in touch with my committee.' He took a sip of bourbon. 'Any more questions?'

Peter permitted himself a short laugh. 'I've only just begun. If this girl is in Europe, why didn't she come here first before letting the Mafia know what she was going to do? This way . . .'

Gorman waved him off. 'Now you're getting into the inconsequential details. That's got nothing to do with the matter at hand.'

Peter said politely, 'I'm afraid I have to be the judge of that, Senator. It's a dangerous mission, as you pointed out, and . . .'

'Sure it's dangerous, but I'm the one who knows what those dangers are. I know . . .'

Peter's voice was quiet but it was insistent and cut the senator off. 'I once knew a World War II pilot,' he said, 'who got hired by one of the South American countries after the war to train pilots, test-fly planes, things like that. And I always remember him telling me how, one time, this country he worked for bought some old PBY's from the United States. Four mechanics worked two days getting one of them tuned up and then told him it was ready. So he said to them, "O.K., get your chutes and get aboard." They said "Us?" and he told them that any mechanic who worked on a plane he was going to test-hop had to fly in it with him. The upshot of that was, those mechanics went back to work on that plane for four more days.'

Gorman gave his giggly chuckle. 'Heh, heh. Yeah. Very good. That's a good story.'

'Yes, and it made a lasting impression on me. That pilot's dead now. But he died in bed. He didn't die in an airplane. And that's a fact I keep in mind. Right now, Senator, you're like those mechanics and I'm like that pilot. Only I can't make you fly with me. I've got to take this trip alone. But if that's the case, I'm going to have to be the one who decides what I need to make the trip a safe one.'

Gorman's eyes narrowed. 'Yeah. Well, sure. That's absolutely right. Nobody could disagree with you on that.'

'So I want to know why this woman didn't come over to the United States before letting the Mafia find out her plans.'

'Yeah. Well, as I said before, this doesn't have anything to do with the job of getting her and bringing her over here.'

'That's your opinion, but I happen to want to know. And it's my neck, right, Senator?'

Gorman's eyes narrowed still further. 'Sure it's your neck,' he said with a certain, ill-concealed hostility. 'So you want to know? So you don't trust me? That's all right. We've got to work together, whether you trust me or not. And I trust you. That's one thing I want you to understand. Regardless of what you think about me, I trust you.'

'All I want to know is . . . Or is it supposed to be some secret?'

'No. No secret. You want to know about this woman? It's very simple. She wants asylum in the United States. You're talking about why didn't she come over here? There're immigration problems, in case you didn't happen to think about that. She wanted certain conditions. She figured we could give them to her. We can. It wasn't easy, but we worked it.'

'What things did she want?'

'Well, hell, God damn, you know. She wanted to come to the U.S.—under the immigration quota, able to become a citizen. And money. And, of course, protection. The Mafia has a long memory and, if she puts them on the spot, they're not about to forget it. She wanted to make sure she's going to be safe.' Gorman's mouth twisted. 'She knows how to drive a bargain. She got her money's worth out of that earring. Don't worry about that. She'll give us what we want, but she's made sure she's going to get what she wants. Money, protection, and citizenship.'

'She seems to have more than revenge on her mind.'

'Oh, she's shrewd. She's no cheap broad, I can tell you. She's got something to sell and she's making us pay for it. She aims to take good care of her future. But, you've got to remember this. I don't give a good God damn about her motives. I'm only concerned with her information. If she can crucify the Mafia, she can have gold toilet paper in her bathroom and I'll buy it for her. But that's not what this is all about. You and I have only one object—to make sure that she tells us—and the world—everything she's got to tell!' Gorman glowered. 'Any further questions?'

Peter wasn't put off. 'Yes. How did the Mafia find out about her plans?'

Gorman gave his crooked smile. 'Like those reporters, you talk like you think I get invitations to their secret councils.'

'All right, here's another question. The reporters asked it downstairs and you ducked it. But I want an answer. How do you know the Mafia found out?'

Gorman scowled. He looked at his blotter. He looked, narrow-lidded, at the ceiling. He picked up and killed half the remaining bourbon. Finally he said, 'You're asking for confidential information. If I tell you this, it doesn't go beyond this room. Is that understood?'

Peter was quick in his reply. 'It'll have to go to my boss. Mr. Brandt does not like his agents keeping secrets from him.'

'To your boss then. That's understood. But no one else!'

'No one else.'

Gorman nodded and pursed his lips. He sat forward in his chair and leaned his elbows on the desk. He ignored the bourbon glass and something about the way he did it said it was deliberate. His eyes, now, were even narrower.

'All right,' he said. 'You want to know the worst. Did you read about a private detective named William Clive recently? His body was found in a roadside ditch outside Washington, hands and feet bound, half his head shot off.'

'I don't remember it.'

'It probably didn't get much play in the Philadelphia papers. Anyway, there are no clues. The police are investigating Clive's background, what cases he's had, what enemies he's got. They're not getting anywhere. You want to know who killed William Clive? The Mafia, that's who.'

Gorman waited but Peter said nothing. Gorman gave him his twisted grin. 'You don't act surprised at my knowledge. I'm sure if I made that statement to the Washington police, they'd think I was seeing the Mafia under every bed again. The fact is, he was killed by the Mafia because he was secretly working for us.'

'He was my predecessor?'

'Yeah, you guessed it. You still want the job?'

'I've been assigned to this job. I didn't have to take it. I did.'

'Well, you ought to have better success. You're cool. I don't think Clive was cool enough.'

'What happened?'

Gorman sipped the bourbon again. He scowled and worked his mouth. 'Well,' he said, 'it went like this. We got this communication, this wire, from this witness—Bono's mistress—wanting to know if we'd be interested in her testimony. Wires went back and forth and she produced the necessary evidences to convince us she was bona fide. Also, she mentioned enough names of high-up Mafia men to tell us her testimony would be almost as valuable as Bono's would have been. So we met her terms. And the first thing we thought about after that was protection for her. Because we don't want anything happening to her before she testifies like what happened to Bono.

'At that time, understand, nobody but us knew she was defecting. But she'd changed her name and address before getting in touch with us and that gave us something to worry about. After the Mafia kills Bono, you can damned well figure they're going to keep an eye on Bono's friends, especially someone as close to him as this mistress. In which case, her suddenly disappearing is going to put them on the alert. So even if they didn't know where she'd gone to hide, or what name she was using, we could be damned good and sure they'd be watching for her to try to get to the United States. So we didn't want her making the trip by herself, no matter what kind of a disguise she tried to use. And she didn't want to make the trip alone either. That's one of her conditions. We've got to give her protection before she takes her first step.

'So we interviewed some private detectives and we hired this guy Clive to do the bodyguarding. And the next thing we know, we read in the papers that he's dead.' Gorman cleared his throat. 'Nobody knows what happened, who did it, or why. But our group has its own theory. The way we figure it, the Mafia got onto him. Don't ask me how. Maybe they're watching us and took notice when we started interviewing detectives. Maybe Clive made a slip somewhere. Anyway, it's our guess the Mafia started tailing Clive, that Clive tumbled to the tail and jumped him. At least we can't see any other reason for their grabbing and killing the guy before he could help them. So we guess the tail wasn't alone, Clive was beaten down and kidnapped, made to talk, and then slain so he couldn't tell us about it.

'Like I say, that's theory. We don't really know what happened, except his office wasn't broken into and we figure, if he'd refused to talk, they'd have ransacked his office to find out what we'd hired him to do for us.

Anyway, whether he talked or not, we have to work on the assumption he talked. Fortunately he didn't know the witness' new identity and address. We weren't so dumb we were going to give him that information before he got to Europe. But he did know what he was going for. He knew, in short, what you know, or what you'll know by the time you leave here.'

Peter nodded and said, 'I see.'

'So,' Gorman went on, 'now we've changed our tactics. Before, we were after secrecy and figured a small detective agency would give us that. Now, figuring the Mafia knows what we're up to, we've decided our maximum safety lies in a large organisation like Brandt's. And, since we've got to assume the Mafia tumbled to Clive through having spies keeping an eye on me and my committee, I had you come here to the house like a reporter coming to my press conference. That's why I told Brandt I didn't want his man coming out here carrying a suitcase or anything bigger than a notebook. That's the way I figure to throw the Mafia off the track.'

Gorman polished off the rest of the liquor in the glass and licked his lips. 'One thing you better understand, though. Just because I figure we've thrown the Mafia off the track doesn't mean we *have* thrown them off the track. So you may find yourself being followed like we figure Clive was followed. Even if you think you aren't, assume you are and act accordingly. If you are followed, it will mean the Mafia knows your mission. Presumably they will not interfere with your getting to the girl. I don't think you'll be in any danger until you reach her—unless you make the mistake Clive apparently made and start tangling with the people who are following you. After you get to the girl, then it's a different matter. That's when I hope you know how to take care of yourself. Or, more to the point, of her.'

Peter said, 'I guess that takes care of most of my questions. What comes next?'

Gorman tilted back and put his foot on the desk once more. 'We're going to work the same arrangement we set up with Clive. The vital information is the girl's name and her whereabouts. We are not going to let you know this until the last possible moment. The programme is as follows: you will fly to Rome as soon as possible . . . Ah, how much time, by the way, will it take you to get ready?'

'However long it takes to collect my bag and get to the airport.'

'Oh? Well, that's too soon. We haven't picked up a reservation for you yet. There are also arrangements to be made at the other end—word to the girl and all that. And tomorrow is Sunday. It'll be impossible to get hold of certain people tomorrow. Count on two days. Take in the sights in Washington, say good-bye to anybody you want to say good-bye to. Have yourself a good rest.'

'All right. Then I board a plane for Rome. Then what?'

'I have a contact in the American Embassy. I will give you his name and address at the airport when you board the plane. When you arrive in Rome you will call him at the embassy. You will, under no circumstances, go there yourself. You will only talk to him on the telephone. When you do, you will identify yourself by a phrase which I shall also give you at the airport so that he will know you're the one he's to meet. This is information Clive had when the Mafia got him, so we can figure they know a contact is going to be made at the embassy. That's why you're not to go there. It's to protect his identity. And the secret phrase is to keep him from making a mistake and giving the information to the wrong party. Just in case the Mafia finds out who the contact is.'

Gorman grinned his twisted grin. 'I guess this sounds like a lot of cloak-and-dagger crap to you, but I've had a lot of experience with the Mafia and things have got to be done that way. We're playing with fire and one guy's already been burned.'

Peter smiled dryly. 'Don't apologise, Senator. It's my neck. I want all the safety factors in the book, including one you're overlooking.'

'What's that?'

'I don't want you waving bon voyage to me at the airport. If the Mafia is watching you, it might give them ideas about me.'

'Don't worry about that, Congdon. The Mafia doesn't watch me when I don't want them to. I can shake them anytime.'

'Just the same, I can tell you that's the kind of thing my boss won't permit.'

Gorman scowled and his voice took on a sharp note. 'Your boss doesn't run this committee. Now pay attention. When you identify yourself to your contact at the embassy, he'll arrange a meeting. At that meeting you will produce a letter signed by me which I shall give you before your departure. He'll have a carbon copy of that letter. When you match letters, he'll give you an envelope which will contain the girl's name, her address, her picture, and the password to identify yourself to her with. Your job will be to get to the girl as fast as possible once you get that information. Then you book passage back on the first available plane and let me know your time of arrival. I will have a police escort or FBI men on hand to meet you. When the girl is delivered into their hands, your job is done.'

Peter said, 'Do you plan to meet the plane, Senator?'

'That depends on when it arrives. Why?'

'I'd hate to hand the girl over to the Mafia, disguised as policemen.'

'Then I'll be there.' He sneered a little. 'That is, if you aren't afraid the Mafiia will follow me to the airport and take her away from you.

Peter ignored that one. 'One more question. Am I supposed to stay any special place in Washington?'

Gorman nodded. 'Yeah. I've got a suite booked for you at the Shoreham Hotel. It's one the committee has been keeping on a more or less permanent basis for our witnesses. The reservation's in the name of Roger S. Desmond.'

'Roger S. Desmond.' Peter said the name twice. 'All right, I guess that pretty well takes care of things.'

'There's one more thing,' Gorman said. 'These messages are going to have to be in code for safety's sake. Can you make one up that's unbreakable or should I see somebody in the CIA?'

'I can fix you up with onc.'

'When can I have it?'

'In about two minutes.'

Gorman scowled. 'In two minutes? And nobody will break it?'

'Nobody. Oh, I don't mean the government cryptographers couldn't crack it if they had enough messages and enough time, but it'll be perfectly safe for your purposes.'

Gorman removed his foot from the desk and got up. He took some paper out of the middle drawer and beckoned. 'O.K. You hop to it. I'm going to take a leak.'

SATURDAY 4:55–5:35 P.M.

Senator Gorman was gone for ten minutes. When he returned, he poured another inch of Old Crow into his glass and looked over Peter's shoulder. Peter handed him the piece of paper he'd been working on and said, 'There's a sample message. Do you think you could work it out?'

The senator frowned briefly over the letters Peter had written: RAVRN AOGAE FIQZM CINCW UVRYT RSSOP TEVCJ UYJAI RHJFJ ZWQLG KIHXN XLNBV. 'It looks like the kind of code the government uses,' he said and dropped it back on the desk.

'This is much simpler, of course. A slight complication can be added to prevent the recurrence of patterns, which would be useful if there were danger of lengthy messages falling into the hands of expert code breakers or the key falling into the wrong hands. But this version should be more than adequate for your needs. It's easy to code and decode with it, but neither the Mafia nor anyone else is going to make anything out of the messages we send.'

'You can say that again. What's the message?'

Peter got out of the chair and laid another paper on the desk beside the first. 'This is the key. Now see if you can solve it.'

On this paper he had written:

Z	H	P	C	I	S	Q	W	L	T	M	A	X
15	6	22	10	18	23	25	5	2	12	8	17	7
F	J	R	B	D	U	N	Y	G	V	O	E	K
26	14	3	24	13	1	20	11	21	9	4	19	16

Gorman sat down and scowled without enthusiasm at the paper. He got a pencil and approached the message like a recalcitrant schoolboy tackling homework. 'Well, let's see,' he said sourly, and took a sip of bourbon, 'the number for R is three. For A is, uh, seventeen. He continued in dour silence translating letters to numbers, one corner of his mouth twisted in annoyance, and eventually had the string: 3-17-9-3-20 17-4-21-17-19 26-18-25-15-8 10-18-20-10-5 1-9-3-11-12 3-23-23-4-22 12-19-9-10-14 1-11-14-17-18 3-6-14-26-14 15-5-25-2-21 16-18-6-7-20 7-2-20-24-9.

'No what am I supposed to do?' he asked, showing the results to Peter.

'The next step is to convert those numbers into letters.'

'That's what I figured. All right, the third letter in the alphabet is C, the seventeenth is . . . ah . . . ah . . . Q. Q? Hell, that can't be right.'

'No, it isn't. That's just the scrambled-letter-type code, like the cryptogram puzzles they give you in newspapers. Notice the key, Senator. There's a reason why the numbers as well as the letters are scrambled.'

'Yeah? Well don't just stand there gloating. Tell me what it is.'

'All right. The whole thing is very simple. The first letter in every message is the key letter. That tells you where your starting point is. The first letter in this message is R. So R becomes the first letter. Now the number with the next letter is seventeen. If you count seventeen letters using R as the first letter, what do you get?'

Gorman looked up. 'You mean you want me to count it out?'

'I think we ought to practise the code if we're going to use it.'

Gorman made a face. He counted. 'Q', he said.

'No, Senator. You counted seventeen letters *from* R. Count R as the first letter.'

Gorman glowered and did it again. 'S?'
'That's right. Now the next number is . . .'
'Nine. That would take me to . . . R is one. That would be O.'
'It would if you kept R as one, but you'd get too many recurring patterns. Therefore, we move the key letter up one each time. So now B becomes the first letter.'
'All right, I get it. B is one. So the ninth letter is E?'
'That's right.'
'All right, I get it. What's the message?'
'If I may say so, I think you ought to work it out.'
'Why? I catch on. I've got it.'
'But we're planning to use this code on very serious business. I think we ought to practise a little.'
Gorman muttered a four-letter word and killed the rest of his glass. He was really the unstudious miscreant staying after school and resenting every moment of it. He went on, bearing down hard on his ballpoint pen. When he reached the end of the first set of five letters, he looked up glowering. 'R-S-E-N-A? That can't be right.'
'It's right.'
'It doesn't mean a goddam thing.'
'It will. Go on some more.'
The senator continued and his tone got very snappish. 'Now I get T-O-R-X-R. R-S-E-N-A- blank. T-O-R-X-R. What are you going to tell me, that I have to decode this now?'
'No, no. You're getting it. In the first place, you ignore the R. That's the key signature, so to speak. It's not part of the message. In the second place, as you can surmise, the message is arbitrarily broken up into five-letter groups. It aids legibility and conceals the actual number of letters in the words. In the third place, you therefore use the letter X in place of a space at the end of each word.'
'Oh,' Gorman said and cleared this throat. 'This says

"Senator R". I get it.' He even grinned. 'Say, that's not bad. You make this up yourself?'

'I made up this particular pattern. The idea is Brandt's. He uses it with us any time a code is required.'

'Well I guess you're right. Nobody's going to crack this code.'

Peter gestured at the paper. 'Yes . . . uh . . . you'd better finish.'

But Gorman was impatient. He pushed the paper aside. 'The hell with that. As long as I know how it's done, I don't have to do it.'

'The practice is good, Senator.'

'Maybe you think I'm stupid or something. You practise. All I need is the key.' He picked up the paper with the key on it.

'You got a copy of this?'

'Yes, I made a copy.'

'All right, you take care of it, because the messages I send you are going to be in this code.' He folded the paper, got up and tucked it in his pocket.

Peter said, 'The thing to remember is, every time you code a message, decode it again to make sure you haven't made any mistakes.'

'Yeah. Well don't you worry about that. You just worry about the girl. Right?' He picked up the phone and called for a cab. 'Now,' he said in brighter spirits, taking Peter to the door, 'the hotel is just across Rock Creek from here. You relax and enjoy yourself and wait there till you hear from me. As soon as I have everything set up, I'll be in touch.'

Peter turned. 'Thank you, Senator, but I think it would be better if I called you. And from an outside phone. That way we can avoid calls going through the switchboard.'

'Well, well, you're thinking every minute, aren't you?

Yes, sir, I can see you're the man for the job.' He clapped Peter on the shoulder.

'And it might be good if I had your phone number.'

'Yeah. You're right.' Gorman took a card from his wallet and scribbled on the back. He gave it to Peter. 'This is my home phone, this one's my office. My office, should you need to know, is in the New Senate Office Building. Not the old one, the new. But don't you ever show your face around there. I don't want the Mafia to get any ideas about you.'

The cab arrived in twenty minutes and the night was getting black. Senator Gorman put Peter into the back seat. 'Nice meeting you, Mr. Desmond,' he said in parting. 'Always a pleasure welcoming people from my home state.'

Peter said it was good of the senator to spare him a few minutes. He said good-bye and had the cabby take him to 2500 Calvert Street, N.W.

He was not followed so far as he could tell.

SATURDAY 5:35–6:35 P.M.

The Shoreham was a luxury hotel with a capital L, complete with a fountain in the lobby with shifting water patterns operating under shifting coloured lights. The reception desk was an elegant semiellipse off left and the clerk there wrote '306D' on the card Peter filled out using the Desmond name and a make-believe address. He wrote 'Senator Gorman' at the bottom of the card and said, 'Do you have any luggage, Mr. Desmond?'

'I'll have some later.' Peter turned and looked around while the clerk went for his key, but none of the scattering of guests seemed to be paying him particular attention. Two men were reading the posted list of Washington activities but everyone else, guests and employees, was in motion, coming, going, criss-crossing the lobby, or circling past the fountain.

A bellhop took the key and Peter followed him down the hall to mirrored elevator doors in an octagonal shaft. A plump coloured girl took them up to the third level, where four hallways radiated out from the shaft and they went down the long one, labelled D, that connected with a similar shaft and set of hallways on the other side of the hotel.

Room 306D was just past the mid-point break and was a blue and white room, blue for the walls, white for the lamp-shades, the curtains, the spreads on the twin beds. Peter gave the bellboy fifty cents as his key-carrying wage, closed the door as if in for the night, made an entry item in his notebook of the tip and the seventy-five cents he'd paid in cab fare, thought for a moment and put down the dollar-five he'd given the first driver. Mr. Brandt did not pay expense money for anything that wasn't listed and was likely, at any time, to question any item that was listed as to why it was necessary or why it cost that much. Peter could see him raising a sharp eyebrow over a fifty-cent tip to a lad who did nothing more than ride an elevator up and down, walk no more than a hundred yards and fit a key in a door. But Mr. Brandt hadn't been in this particular hotel. Peter doubted there was anybody in the place who knew what a coin less than half a dollar looked like.

He put away the notebook, went to the nearest of the

flawlessly prepared beds and pressed down on the mattress. Soft, like heaven. He sighed, tossed the key on the coverlet, went back through the little hall to the door and looked out. There was no one in sight.

He stepped into the corridor, closed the door behind him, returned to the octagonal shaft, opened a door in the side to the service stairs and went down them to the lobby level. No one saw him there either and he took the side hallway past the snack bar and exited through a side door at the front where the drive curved out to the street.

He stayed away from the cabs, went out the drive and started retracing his path up Calvert Street in the darkness. He turned onto Connecticut and crossed the long high bridge between ridges that gave a bird's-eye view of Rock Creek and winding park traffic far below. Cars whisked by him fast up there and he was the only walker.

On the other side he found a cab discharging passengers in front of the Windsor Hotel. He climbed in, told the driver, 'Union Station,' and settled back. But it was not in the relaxed, casual, company-president sprawl he had used coming out. It was no longer that kind of job.

In the station the first thing he did was retrieve his attaché case. It was the kind young executives carry their homework in. In his, Peter too carried the paraphernalia of his trade, but its nature was quite different. There was a drip-dry shirt like the one he had on, a pair of jockey shorts, a pair of nylon socks, a necktie, a plastic kit containing toothbrush, bar of soap, safety razor, shaving brush and deodorant, a blank notebook, some special envelopes addressed to Brandt which could be mailed, postage collect, anywhere in the world (or at least those parts of the world where Brandt had influence), an extra ball-point pen and two pencils. In another small, efficiently designed box was a jar of fingerprint powder, a tiny brush and a magnifying lens. In a bottom corner, held in place by a clip, was a box of ·38-calibre shells to fit the snub-nosed revolver he wore under his arm. The attaché case itself was made of cow-hide with brass fastenings—Brandt issue to Brandt agents. Unlike the usual such case, it was opened by adjusting the tiny dials of a combination lock.

Rearmed with the case, Peter went to one of the phones on the large posts in the great hall and put in a collect call to Philadelphia to the old man himself at the agency number. He smoked half a cigarette while he waited, watched two people sit down at the snack bar, and even saw somebody buy a train ticket at one of the windows. Then a sharp, familiar voice sounded in his ear. 'Hello, Congdon?'

'Yes, Mr. Brandt.'

'Did the client give you the word?'

'The word and a room—at the Shoreham Hotel.'

'What did you do with it?'

'Checked in and went out the back way. Right now I'm calling from the railroad station.'

'Think anybody's been following you?'

'I'd bet my life they haven't. But that doesn't prove I'm right.'

'Smart boy. I suppose you know what you're up against?'

'I have an idea.'

'Then we don't have to talk about it. Put it in a report and mail it to me tonight. I want to know the details of procedure.' He paused and then added, 'Put it in the office code.' The office code was the same kind of letter-number arrangement Congdon had composed for the senator. Each agent had his own special one, which he had to memorise so no written key could ever be found on him. For the agents, however, Brandt had introduced one additional wrinkle, the purpose of which was to break up recurring patterns. One did not shift the starting point one letter each time as Peter had told Gorman to do. The starting point was shifted anywhere from zero to nine letters each time, according to the digits of the multiplication table derived from the number that went with the key letter.

Peter groaned, as Brandt's agents always groaned when told to code their reports. Writing reports was trouble enough, what with Brandt wanting all the details on the record and in his hands. Coding them and then decoding for mistakes, recopying and checking the copy were added hours of work. While, of course, in the office, Brandt fed the stuff into a computer and the decoded copy came barrelling out faster than he could read it.

But Brandt had no sympathy for agents. 'Don't fret,' he snapped. 'This might be a dangerous bit of business and I'm not taking any chances of leaks. Besides, it'll keep you in your room tonight instead of out on the town getting yourself in trouble. And, speaking of that, stay in your hotel room. Keep out of sight.'

'Which hotel?'

'What kind of a question is that? You know which one. Ours.'

Peter didn't quite groan a second time but he did think of the beautiful room he'd left and the ultra-swank surroundings that went with it—even the fountain in the lobby. 'I was just thinking, Chief. The sen— I mean the client—picked out a hotel that's very convenient. And I haven't been tailed. I think that would be the better place.'

'You go to ours, you damned fool. What do you think I go to this kind of trouble for? And I hope you told the client not to try to call you!'

'I told him.'

'That's one good thing anyway. Don't carry anything

valuable on you. Don't cash any more travellers checks than you need . . .' He started in on a routine of do's and don't's that was standard for any dangerous mission. Peter didn't know it by heart but he'd heard it more than once before. He said softly, 'Yes, Mother.'

'What's that?'

'Yes, Mr. Brandt.'

'Don't be flip with me, Congdon. I'm not talking for my health. You're not such a smart apple, you know. I picked up that slip you just made when you almost forgot to say "client". You aren't so airtight, Mr. Hotshot.'

Peter said, with at least pseudo respect, 'I haven't had your experience, sir.'

'Then you'd do well to listen to me. Keep out of sight. Make any further necessary contact with the client from a public phone booth until time to turn over the merchandise and, at that time, make sure it's to him in person. And don't forget a signed receipt.'

Peter cleared his throat. 'I have to see the client once more, Mr. Brandt. He has to give me certain papers that he doesn't want to release until the very last moment . . .'

'What?' Brandt roared. 'What the hell were you given for brains? Last moment, hah! What does he want to do, stuff them into your hot little hands as you get aboard the airplane?'

'I told him that was out. He's going to have to figure another way.'

'Oh he is, is he? Where did you ever get the idea the client calls the shots? When we take a job we do it our way. Now you let him know that whatever material it's required that he give you he send by messenger or registered mail. His idea of what's cloak-and-dagger isn't my idea of cloak-and-dagger and when this organisation takes on a job, *we* do it. We do it all and we do it our way. You ought to know that by now. I picked you because I thought you had some brains as well as guts. Don't make a monkey out of me. Show you've got some brains.'

'Sorry,' Peter said sarcastically. 'I thought you picked me because I was single.'

'That's great.' Brandt's voice was equally sarcastic. 'I just hope your intellect is as smart as your remarks. Now, if you've got anything else, send it in the report and don't forget, I said code. And I expect it on my desk Monday morning.'

Peter said, with more than a hint of bitterness, 'Roger, over and out.' He fancied himself a good Brandt agent. He considered himself one of the best. He regarded the old man's tapping him for this particular responsibility as a sign that the old man shared his view. Getting raked and cross-raked didn't sit well with him even though he had to admit there was some slight merit in the old man's dissatisfaction. Even so, he hung up scowling, his mouth a hard line. Coded messages and the Emerson Hotel! He had liked the classy atmosphere of the Shoreham and it irked him that he couldn't revel in it—nor cut up a little in the big city. There were a couple of addresses he would have liked to check out. But Brandt had evidently anticipated him there. The job was supposed to be dangerous and he had to play it that way, but all the more reason, he felt, why he should be entitled to a little fun before the thing started. Eat, drink and be merry—only Brandt was no gourmet, no lush, and, in the detective business, he had no sense of humour.

The Emerson Hotel was only a couple of hundred yards away and in view from the station—on the near side of First and D streets, Northeast—and Peter walked over. It was a yellow brick building of modest proportions and the name was on a brass plaque beside the door. Peter did not enter the building directly. He went past and into a parking lot a few yards beyond, where a newsstand operated out of a trailer. He smoked a cupped cigarette behind the trailer and then, since no one had come nosing around after him, he decided it was safe to walk into the hotel.

The lobby was small and paved with large black and white tiles. Ahead was the desk, beside the hall and staircase. On the right, up a couple of steps, a small lounge was furnished with leather couches and chairs in blues, olives and orange. On the left, down a couple of steps, a doorway opened into the cocktail lounge. It was a satisfactory enough place if you hadn't been to the Shoreham, and if you didn't have to code a detailed report to Brandt. To one in Peter's position it was downright depressing.

At the desk he asked about a reservation in the name of Horace Pepper. (The name was Brandt's idea, of course, not his. The old man did have a sense of humour at that, if you could appreciate that sort of thing.)

The clerk checked and said yes, and did Mr. Pepper want a single or a double?

'A single—unfortunately.'

'With bath, television and air conditioning it's eight dollars a day.'

'Air conditioning?' Peter said sourly. 'What does it cost with heat?'

The clerk tried to chuckle. 'We have both heat and air conditioning in all the rooms. And television. But we can take the television out.'

'Don't you dare.'

Peter filled out the card and was given room twelve. The clock behind the desk stood at twenty-five minutes to seven when the clerk rang for the bellhop. Peter said, 'I'll want dinner in my room.'

'Yes, sir. I'll send someone right up. Anything else?'

'Yes. A pint of whisky.'

SUNDAY 9:30–11:35 A.M.

Sunday morning was grey and depressing and Peter Congdon slept late. He ordered breakfast in his room and asked for all the newspapers Washington published on Sunday. Then he removed the 'Do Not Disturb' sign from his door, took down the hanging shirt and socks he'd washed the night before, rinsed out the shorts he'd slept in, and took a shower. It was Brandt's contention that a travelling agent should travel light and no one needed more than two of anything, one to wear and one to carry. In fact, there was a mimeographed sheet issued to agents going on business trips listing the items to carry and a wash schedule to assure their having a clean appearance at all times. Peter had not, however, done more with the wash schedule than chuck it in the waste-basket. He might have to listen to Brandt tell him how to be a detective, but he didn't have to listen to him tell him how to keep clean.

He shaved in the shower, hung his shorts on the bath-tub faucet, dried himself and dressed except for his jacket. That remained in the closet along with the holster and gun. Breakfast, with two newspapers, arrived at half past ten as he was knotting his tie and he settled down to his reading over pancakes and coffee.

Gorman, he immediately discovered, had got himself back on the front pages as predicted. His announcement of a second star witness lent more credence to his investigating committee and made him bigger news. Even so, his headlines were small. Editors could still hardly feel that a Senate investigation of the Mafia rated in importance with the situation in Vietnam, the question of a tax hike, the anti-war demonstrations, nor could they be persuaded to the view that Gorman seemed trying to sell—that the Mafia was at the root of all these things.

It seemed, on the face of it, like a lot of nonsense—Gorman squeezing himself into the limelight of the front page, a pip-squeak among giants. Yet, Peter couldn't help reflecting, he *was* on the front pages and, not too many months ago, Gorman was a total unknown. Admittedly he couldn't compete with the big names in politics. He wasn't up there yet. But he had a ruthless quality that was especially apparent close to, and if he had set his sights on the White House, he could become someone to reckon with. Not in next year's election, of course. The big names were already onstage and the battle for the presidency would be among them. But what of the following election? What would happen in five years? How far along the trail would Gorman come, especially if his new star witness gave him a power base? It was racket-busting that had moved Tom Dewey up. It would be unwise to sell Bob Gorman short.

Who would have thought, five years before, that John Kennedy could make the scene? How had Warren Harding got into the White House? Wouldn't he have been voted 'least likely to succeed'? What about the present incumbent, presumably gunning for a second term? Could he ever have had a first if JFK hadn't used him to promote his own campaign? And who, a year before it happened, would have imagined Harry Truman there? Maybe it could happen to Gorman too—provided that he, Peter Congdon, brought the girl back.

Peter finished his coffee standing in the window, looking out. There was the station to the right, the Capitol to the left, dirt, grass and trees in front, and a smattering of Sunday traffic on the visible streets. It was a quiet November Sunday in the United States capital but it could have been Anytown, U.S.A., as far as appearances went. People seemed to be minding their own business, relaxing on their day off, concerning themselves with family affairs.

He, Peter Congdon, this man in this little hotel, standing, looking through the lace curtains of this room, would soon participate in an adventure which should make headlines. It might, conceivably, even affect the lives of those people driving those cars. If Peter failed in his mission, then Gorman's political star was dead. Yet let him succeed and Peter Congdon might turn out to be a kingmaker.

But the drivers paid attention to the other cars and did not know about the window, nor who was standing in it. Nobody except Brandt knew he was there; not the Mafia, not even the senator.

Peter drained his cup and put it back on the table. If he were going to promote careers, he wished it were anybody but Gorman's. But the choice wasn't his. Gorman was the real promoter. Peter Congdon was only the instrument, just as a detective named Clive had been. And if Peter were to end up a corpse, Gorman would hire another detective. He would sacrifice as many lives as necessary to get that girl. But it wasn't for Peter to reason why, it was for him to put on his coat and go find out how the plan for 'getting that girl' was coming along and what his orders were. He put on his gun and holster, jacket, topcoat and hat, went out of the room and locked the door.

He made his call from one of the booths on the concourse of the station and he did it with a certain trepidation. Peter fancied himself a take-charge guy, a leader type, able even to treat his boss with something of a cavalier manner. But he couldn't get away from the sense that Gorman had manhandled him the evening before, that Gorman was a bull, that he had a goal in mind and he cared nothing for rules of procedure or regulations of behaviour, what was proper or approved. In Gorman's bailiwick, Gorman made the rules and the rules were for himself.

A manservant answered the phone, for Gorman had no wife or family. Then Gorman came on the line and his voice had a maniacal note to it. 'Desmond? Who the hell do you think you are?' It was a scream that made Peter wince. 'Where the hell have you been?'

'Been?' Peter forced his voice to be calm and just faintly querulous.

'Where have you been, God damn it? I've been trying to reach you since nine o'clock this morning.'

Peter said tightly, 'Senator, we agreed it would be best if I called you.'

'You said it. I, like hell, agreed to it. If you think I'm going to sit around when there's business to be done, waiting for the phone to ring, you've got another think coming. Who the hell do you think is running this show—you?'

'I'm sorry, Senator, but my organisation has certain rules of secrecy in matters of this kind which I have . . .'

'I'm the one who pays the bills around here and I'm the one who makes the rules. Now, I want an answer. Where the hell have you been?'

'Getting some breakfast.'

'Don't tell me that. I had you paged in all the hotel restaurants.'

'You had me paged? What kind of secrecy . . .'

'You're damned well right I had you paged. When I want you, I want you on the spot. I told you to stay in your room. Now why didn't you answer my paging and don't tell me you forgot the name you signed in under.'

'No, sir, but I'm sure you know I wouldn't answer paging under the circumstances.'

That stopped Gorman for just a moment. 'You mean,' he said in disbelief, 'you heard the paging and you didn't pay any attention?'

'Senator, I told you. We have rules of secrecy. If you have any question, I'm sure my boss can explain.'

'I'll be taking it up with your boss. And I'll find out if his rules of secrecy include dereliction of duty.'

'Dereliction of duty?'

'I mean not being available in an emergency.'

Peter swallowed. As long as he did the job right, Brandt would back him all the way. But if the client were right and the detective wrong—well, those were things you didn't think about, not with Brandt. Just then, Peter wasn't sure how Gorman would make the story sound to the old man. He said carefully, 'What's the emergency, Senator?'

'The emergency is you—and where you were. I make an ordinary call and suddenly you aren't there and nobody knows where you went. And reporters have been calling and I've been going out of my mind wondering what's going on. I've been worried the Mafia got to you. I've been sweating here wondering how we could have slipped up and how they got on to you and where the leak was. I've been going crazy. And you were out getting something to eat and ignoring my calls!'

Peter lighted a cigarette and tried to be calm about things. 'You can relax, Senator,' he said. 'The group you mention doesn't know a thing about me. Unless, of course, they have a way of listening in on this line. Since I'm doing the calling, and from a public phone, we can assume they aren't listening in, but let's remember that my name is Roger Desmond all the same.'

'And let you remember something too, Mr. Peter Congdon. Your name is what I want it to be when I want it to be. I tell you, you don't tell me. So get that flip tone out of your voice. Now I'm going to tell you what I was calling you about. I've booked your passage. You're leaving here tomorrow night from National Airport at five thirty-five on TWA flight seven hundred. You got that?'

Peter slipped out his notebook and scribbled in it. 'Yes, sir.'

'You'll change at New York to Pan American flight number one-fourteen, leaving for Rome at eight-thirty. You'll arrive at twelve-ten Rome time. That's noon, not midnight. The middle of the business day. Do you understand that?'

'I have it.'

'There's a one-hour stop in Paris but I can't help that. There's no good connection from Washington with the non-stop flights.'

'That's all right. Whatever flight you want.'

'Check out of the hotel at three-thirty tomorrow afternoon. You don't pay anything. Just tell the desk you're leaving and turn in your key. Wait outside under the marquee. My car will pick you up there promptly at quarter of four. While we're riding to the airport, I'll give you the necessary papers and your final instructions.'

Peter said, 'Excuse me, Senator, but we agreed that your seeing me off at the airport would be a very foolish manœuvre, remember?'

'I remember *you* thought it would be foolish. I've decided it won't be at all. Not with me handling it.'

'I'm sorry, Senator, but it can't be done that way.'

Gorman's voice was extraordinary quiet. 'What did you say?'

Peter kept his tone very polite but also very firm. 'I said I'm sorry but it cannot be done that way. You may not see me off at the airport.'

Gorman's voice was still quiet but fervour was building. 'Why you God damned, stinking, son of a bitch.

Do you know who the hell you're talking to? You don't tell me what to do. Nobody tells me what to do and that includes the President of the United States. I hired you to do a job. I am paying you to do a job and when I pay, I say.'

Peter said, 'I'm sorry to disagree, Senator, but you don't pay me anything. The head of the organisation I work for pays me and he's the one who tells me what to do. And he specifically tells me that I am not to go to the airport with you. If you can get him to change his orders, I'll be glad to oblige . . .'

Now Gorman's voice was up, high and loud. 'I've got papers to give you . . .'

'He suggests a messenger.'

'He suggests? He tells? Let you get it through your God damned head, Congdon, Robert Gerald Gorman is chairman of this subcommittee, not Charles Foster Brandt. He does what I tell him to do, and his agents do what I want them to do. I'm the one who knows the Mafia. Not Brandt. I'm the one who's telling you this has to be secret. You aren't telling me. And I'm telling you how secret and how we're going to keep it secret. I'm the one who knows the business. I'm the one who runs the committee. I determine how the money's going to be spent and what our programme is and how we're going to do it. You aren't telling me. And neither is your Mr. Brandt. Do you get that, Congdon?'

Peter kept his voice very carefully under control. Gorman wasn't the first difficult client he'd faced, though he was fast promising to become the most difficult. 'I'm not trying to tell you anything, Senator. I was merely making a suggestion. My boss appreciates the seriousness of this business and he's an old hand at this sort of thing. If he thinks a messenger . . .'

'I don't care what he thinks, or you think, or anybody else in your organisation thinks. If the bunch of you are so stupid as to think I'd entrust top-secret documents to go-betweens . . .! The papers I have for you I'm going to give you in person. That's in person, do you hear? There aren't going to be any slip-ups in this operation because I'm going to handle things myself! I'm the only one they can't buy or threaten and I'm the one who's going to make sure the right papers go to the right person. They'll kill for those papers, Congdon. They'll do anything for those papers. I'm not letting them out of my hands until I put them in yours. That's all there is to it. Do you understand?'

'Yes, sir, but Mr. Brandt won't let me go to the airport with you. Perhaps if you called him . . .'

'I don't have time to call him. Damn it, why must I always have to deal with incompetents? All right, we won't go to the airport together. We'll meet some other place. But not the hotel. I don't want us to be seen together at the hotel.'

Peter didn't like it but he saw no way out. If Gorman wouldn't permit intermediaries, they'd have to meet. Even Brandt would realise that. If Peter refused, Gorman would go to the old man and Peter might then catch hell as an obstructionist. 'No,' he said. 'The hotel would be very bad.'

'A bar would be best. But not the Carroll Arms or Nick and Dottie's or the one in the Emerson. I'm too well known in all of them. We must pick an out-of-the-way place, far from my office.' He thought for a moment and then said, 'Do you know Case's Bar, on H Street, Southwest?'

'Case's?' Peter wrote it down. 'What's the address?'

'I don't know but it's just before you get to Maine Avenue. North side of the street.'

Peter made note and said, 'Are you known there?'

'I've only been there a couple of times and this was long ago. Nobody will know me.'

'All right. I'll assume it's safe.'

'If I say it's safe, you better believe it's safe. Case's bar. At quarter of four tomorrow afternoon.'

'Quarter of four.'

'And remember, that's H Street, *Southwest*, not Northwest.'

'Right.'

'And don't let yourself get followed.'

Peter made a face. 'I'll try not to,' he said politely.

MONDAY 3:45–4:25 P.M.

Two days of inactivity, pent up for the most part in a hotel room, were pretty much more than Peter Congdon could stand. By the time he went through the check-out processes at the Emerson and then the Shoreham and headed for Case's, he was ready to tackle the Mafia single-handedly. Anything for some action.

He had the taxi driver let him off at G Street, Southwest, on the corner of Seventh so he could reconnoitre the area. The scene was quiet residential with no people and few cars. No one had followed him there, no one knew him there. All was peaceful.

Peter strolled up a block and went right on H Street. Another block brought him to the intersection of Ninth and the neighbourhood turned from residential to waterfront. H was an empty, untended street now, the brick sidewalks broken and treacherous. On the left was a small boatyard with cabin cruisers up on racks, a couple of house trailers parked and propped, some protective fencing, and the sound of an electric drill. Ahead, Maine Avenue was busy with through traffic. Beyond it were the facilities of Nash Marine Supplies and, beyond that, the channel waters of the Potomac. Off right, the bridges were loaded with a constant flow of traffic. Off left, planes landed and rose from the National Airport field.

Case's was on the right-hand side of H Street, across from the boatyard and a driveway apart from the Flagship Restaurant on the corner of Maine. It was a square, two-floored building of whitewashed brick with a storm doorway entrance projecting from its face. Iron bars covered the tall first-floor windows and those on the second floor were blocked off. A large neon sign down the front said, 'The Original Case's Bar and Restaurant,' but the sign was not lighted and the building looked deserted, except that the storm door was ajar. Gorman could pick his spots, Peter decided. This was a desolate one and wore a forbidding air even at half past three in the afternoon. You could be mugged and robbed or waylaid and slaughtered, and who would know or care?

Peter checked the drive and parking area between the two restaurants, then returned to the uneven brick sidewalk, opened the storm door of the original Case's and tried the inside door. To his surprise, it opened. He had half expected to have to wait in the tiny storm hall for the senator.

Inside, he found himself in the restaurant part, with the bar through a door on the left. The windows were shuttered and the only light came from a small overhead bulb and the red neon sign which said 'bar'. A deserted reception desk was ahead and the main dining area stretched off on the right, the white-clothed tables waiting like squat ghosts in the darkness.

The bar was almost as dark as the restaurant, but at least it was occupied. The counter was opposite the door and three men, who looked more seedy than salty, were standing at it.

There were tables and chairs along the inside wall and a jukebox at the end which boasted a hundred popular tunes. Its fluorescent glow was the brightest light in the room.

Peter took a seat at the second table facing the door and he didn't like the lay of the land. The customers were near-derelicts, the bartender should have shaved two days ago, and the fat waitress who came to his table should have washed her smock a week before that. In such surroundings, Senator Gorman and the neatly dressed Peter Congdon would stand out like a couple of astronauts at a county fair.

Peter stowed his things on the chair beside him, ordered a mug of beer, and made it last over a cigarette as two more salt-seedy men came in and one of the others left.

At precisely three forty-eight, Senator Gorman arrived, wearing a felt hat with a carefully turned-down brim, a yak-wool overcoat with a mink collar, and a pair of dark glasses. It was not an ordinary costume but the senator's chunky build and jowly face made it look ordinary. He was not, Peter decided at sight of him, the kind of man whose physical appearance attracted attention. It was too average. Even his face was the nondescript type it was hard to remember, though, given the kind of exposure his witness should produce for him, it could become indelibly stamped on the collective memory of a nation's people.

The senator took one look around, then sat down opposite Peter, putting his hat aside and removing his glasses. He was in a better mood than he'd been on the phone and he could even give a chuckle with its giggle overtones. 'How's this for a secret meeting place?' he said.

Peter didn't tell him what he thought of it, other than to say, 'It's dark.' He felt that was safe without being dishonest. 'You take the afternoon off?'

Gorman chuckled again. 'Senate hours aren't nine till five, you know. We're not holding hearings today, so I've been catching up on work in the office.' The waitress came over and he behaved as anonymously as he could. 'Manhattan. What'll you have, Mr. Desmond?'

Mr. Desmond said he'd have a Manhattan too and the waitress went away. Gorman leaned forward on his elbow. 'Now you know what you're supposed to do?'

'Take the five thirty-five flight to Kennedy, the eight-thirty flight to Rome.'

'Yes. Now, in Rome I've reserved a room for you at the Hotel Savoy under your own name. But don't wait till you get there to phone my friend at the embassy. I don't know what his lunch hour is, or whether they have siestas or things like that over there, but don't waste any time. The airport's quite a ways out from the city, I understand. The thing to do is phone him just as soon as you get through customs. You got your passport?'

'Passport and health certificate. Everything but the plane tickets.'

'All right, call him. He's expecting to hear from you between twelve and one. You speak Italian?'

'No.'

'Damn it, how the hell does Brandt expect . . .'

'Don't worry. I'll make out.'

The waitress came back and put two Manhattans on the table. Gorman didn't ask the price but took three dollars out of his wallet and gave them to her. 'Keep it.'

'Gee, thanks.' She went away impressed.

Peter said to him, 'Too bad she doesn't know you. You might have won her vote.'

Gorman chuckled and giggled. 'True, true, and it's with the taxpayer's—her own—money you win it with. That's what politics is all about.'

'Remind me not to pay my income tax.'

'Heh, heh. Well, you're a cool one, Congdon. I can see that.'

'I'm not cool. I'm on pins and needles.'

'Nervous?'

'Eager to get going.'

'Relax. Relax. You like a sandwich or something?'

'I'll get a bite at the airport if I'm hungry.'

Gorman sipped his drink. His part of the adventure was being successfully concluded and he could relax, savour the moment, and draw it out. He could also try to woo the detective again, make conversation, be the friendly type, show an interest in the man. 'You got a gun?'

'Yes.'

'You a good shot?'

'Yes.'

'You don't talk much, do you?'

'Not on business.'

Gorman sipped more of the Manhattan. It was better than half gone. 'How do you plan to smuggle your gun into Italy?'

'I'll wear it in. They don't open your bags at the Rome airport—at least not Americans' bags.'

'You've been to Rome before, then?'

'Once.'

'You there long?'

'Three weeks.'

'You know your way around then?'

Peter snorted faintly. 'Let's say, if you put me in the middle of the Forum, I could find the Colosseum and the

Victor Emmanuel monstros—I mean monument. At least I could seven years ago. I'm not so sure I could now.'

Gorman smiled and shook his head. He meant to draw the man out. 'Oh come now. Three weeks? You must know the city well.'

'I never saw the city. I did get to know certain aspects of a certain girls' school rather well.'

'School? Yes. But to go to Rome and not to see the sights? I don't get it.'

'It's simple. I went there to see a girl whose father put her in school there just so that I couldn't see her. It was the girl not the city that interested me. Or maybe it was thumbing my nose at the old man. Anyway, I wouldn't even have seen the Forum except she dragged me there one Sunday afternoon.'

'But you didn't marry the girl?'

'No, I didn't marry the girl.'

'And you've remained single ever since, dreaming of your lost love. And that's why you're willing to undertake a dangerous assignment like this . . .'

Peter finished his drink and set the glass down. 'You're quite a romantic, Senator. I went to Rome to see her and I saw her. And I decided she wasn't the girl I wanted. She only looked good because she was forbidden fruit. So I came home again.'

'And she's been pining all these years . . .'

'She couldn't have cared less. There were a dozen men to hold her hand before I came and after I left. Let's forget the past, Senator. It's tomorrow that counts.'

'I'm just trying to get your mind off things. What you're getting into isn't something to take lightly, you know.'

'That's right.' Peter looked at his watch. 'It's four o'clock . . .'

'Do you have any questions? Anything at all?'

'No, sir.'

Gorman nodded and finished his own drink. 'If I've seemed short-tempered, Congdon, it's because I've been under a lot of pressure. I hope you'll understand that.'

It was Peter who was feeling the pressure now. A new customer came in, a swarthy man in jeans and sneakers with a grey sweat shirt bearing the faded picture of a sailing ship on the back. Peter looked the man over sharply and the man looked him and Gorman over with equal boldness as he went to the bar.

Gorman enjoyed Peter's nervousness. He leaned forward and grinned in his leering way. 'Don't worry, he's not a Mafia spy. You think I don't know how to cover my tracks?'

'All the same, Senator, I'd just as soon get going.'

'No hurry. I've got my car outside. My chauffeur can take you to the airport. I'll stay behind, of course, since your Mr. Brandt . . .'

'You've got your chauffeur outside?'

'Not outside this place. I'm not a fool. He's down the street.'

'You mean you've got your car . . .'

'How the hell do you think I got over here? You think I walked?'

'Senator, they know your car.'

'But they don't know where it is. I told you I know what I'm doing. The Mafia is afraid of me, I'm not afraid of the Mafia. They don't control me. They don't control the situation around me. When I don't want them to know where I'm going or what I'm doing, they don't know.'

'All right,' Peter said. 'Fine. But let's not push our luck, all right? Just give me the papers and I'll leave.'

'Don't be in such a rush. I feel like another drink.'

'Have one. Have it on me. I'm not walking out with you, Senator. I'm going to leave ahead of you.'

'All right, but settle down. Relax, I tell you. Stop

thinking everyone who walks into this bar is a Mafia agent.'

Peter gave Gorman a tight smile. 'I thought the "Mafia under every bed" was your idea.' He pushed his glass away. 'How about it, Senator? Do you think you can bear to part with those papers now? After all, the code is safe, since you and I are the only ones who have the key.'

Gorman put on his twisted grin. 'The eagerness of youth.' He reached into an inner pocket and withdrew a manila business-size envelope with an airline ticket folder bound to it with an elastic. He glanced around, passed it clumsily under the table and lowered his voice. 'You'll let me know when you're bringing her back so I can arrange to meet you?'

Peter nodded and put the envelope into his inside jacket pocket. 'You can bet on that. My boss wants a signed receipt. Thanks for the drink.' He got into his coat and hat, picked up his attaché case and walked through the door.

Outside, beside the boatyard up by the corner, Gorman's black limousine was parked, a Negro chauffeur reading a newspaper behind the wheel. It was a big car, a shiny car, the only car around. How long did Gorman think he could keep his whereabouts a secret? Peter made a face and turned towards Maine Avenue.

It was colder now and he buttoned the top button of his topcoat and took out leather gloves from the pockets. He thought again of Stephanie and it struck him as strange that he hadn't thought of her for so long. Not until there, with the senator. Even knowing he was going to Rome hadn't brought her to mind.

They sure had had hot pants for each other. Peter was never sure whether that trip to Rome was to show Stephanie's father that no matter how much money he had or how much he ran other people's lives he wasn't going to run Peter's, or whether he was dragged there by the prospect of spending three whole weeks in bed with the girl. That part had been pleasant all right, and certainly they had done little else—the trip to the Forum was only because visiting cousins of Stephanie's made bed out of the question. But that was also the trouble. He found out in those three weeks that going to bed was the only thing you could do with Stephanie. Hot pants was all they had in common and, since it wasn't enough, even that couldn't last. Though nothing was said, they both knew that last night in Rome was the last night they would ever spend together. Yet even that knowledge didn't fan their passions excessively. They did not seek each other frantically and desperately despite the finality of the occasion.

There were a few letters after, but neither was much of a correspondent and that soon stopped. He and Stephanie had started as lovers, parted as friends, and now had reached the stage of hardly remembering the other had ever existed. No, Peter wasn't taking dangerous assignments as a palliative for a broken heart. While many girls could stir him in other places, he was still waiting for the girl who could touch the heart part of his anatomy.

A jet was rising from National Airport as he reached the corner of Maine. It climbed across in front of him, trailing a faint line of dark smoke, and Peter watched as it went past the Washington Monument over beyond the bridges. He started walking in the same direction, then hailed a cab cruising slowly up behind him. 'National Airport,' he said, getting in, casting an automatic glance out the back window and settling down.

National Airport was outside the city and cab fares were by the mile rather than the zone. The driver, however, did not record the figures on his mileage indicator, he only picked up speed a little and went through the short tunnel under the bridges. Nor did he make the sharp left at the light right after the tunnel. He kept straight on Twelfth Street, S.W. instead.

To Peter the turn seemed the more logical path, one that would start him back towards the airport, but he didn't know Washington and the driver did. All the same he sat up a little and took note.

'You going to fly someplace?' the driver asked conversationally.

'That's the general idea.'

'I wouldn't fly nowhere. Not if my life depended on it. Where're you heading for?'

'San Francisco.' The gleaming spire of the Washington Monument was ahead and forty-five degrees to the left.

'That's a long way away.'

'Yeah.' They bridged a railroad track and the cut opened a path between buildings straight to the Capitol itself. That was on the right and Peter had a fix. They were heading towards the Mall.

'Got business in San Francisco?' the driver asked.

Where was this guy going? The airport was behind them. Maybe one had to make a left turn at the Mall.

'My mother lives there,' Peter said, his hand starting to play with the top button of his coat, his eyes darting. They were surrounded by buildings now, moving in moderately heavy traffic.

'My mother died when I was a kid,' the cabby said. He started relating what a fine, sweet woman she'd been. They plunged down a ramp and merged with other cars in a well-lighted, slightly curving tunnel. 'What is this thing?' Peter asked suspiciously.

'This tunnel? I don't think it's got a name. It's one of them shortcuts. They got a lot of them in this town.'

It wasn't a long tunnel and they were quickly at the other end. A red light held them up in heavy traffic at the exit. It changed and they started ahead. 'You married?' the driver asked as they crossed a broad avenue.

Peter saw it before new buidings closed in. The Monument was still on his left but now it was forty-five degrees behind him and, beyond it, in the far distance, a climbing jet was paralleling the taxi's path. Peter knew where they were now. They had just crossed Constitution Avenue and the tunnel had taken them under the Mall. He leaned forward and the top button of his coat was already undone. 'Where the hell do you think you're going?'

'The airport. Didn't you say the airport?'

Peter whirled and looked out of the back window. A large black car with four men in it had materialised behind them. He turned back. 'The airport, I said, and I know how to get there. Turn around.'

'I know how to get to the airport too. Better'n you,' the driver answered. He was in the outside lane now, stopping three cars back at the light on Pennsylvania Avenue. The black car was right behind.

Peter pulled out his gun and moved forward in his seat. 'From here on you're going to do what I tell you, buddy,' he said, 'or I'm going to put a bullet through your ear.' He pressed the muzzle against the side of the man's neck, keeping the gun shielded from view of the adjacent cars.

The driver let out an involuntary cry at the touch of the metal. 'Listen, mister,' he said in terror. 'You got me wrong. I'm just trying to get you to the airport.'

'There's a car behind us, buddy, and you're going to shake it. You get me?'

The cabby nodded and swallowed.

'Because,' Peter went on, 'if that car tries to cause any trouble, the first bullet in this gun goes into your brain.'

'Listen, mister, so help me . . .'

Peter backed off, moving to the side, away from the rear window. He kept the gun low but aimed. 'They're your friends, not mine, buddy. You get rid of them fast.'

'Mister, I don't know who they are, and I can't shake nobody. Not in this traffic.'

'Then I'll tell you how. Pull out of line and move up.'

'Out? Against traffic?'

'*Move.*'

The driver moved. He swung out and an oncoming car swerved and honked. 'I'll get arrested,' he complained as he drove to the corner. Behind, the black car had hesitated but now it was starting to follow.

'Turn right,' Peter ordered.

'The light's rcd.'

'*Turn!*'

The cabby moved into Pennsylvania Avenue traffic, edging carefully, and cut across in front of the two rows of cross-town traffic. The black car was out in the oncoming lanes now in an attempt to close the gap. Then the lights changed. Peter's taxi got clear on Pennsylvania, going around the bus lanes and passenger islands. The black car got hung up in the middle of Twelfth Street as two lines of cars moved across the avenue with the light.

'Turn right here.' Peter made the driver take the next corner, down a street full of parked cars with only a one-lane path for buses open. The sign said, 'Do Not Enter; Buses Only', but there were no buses and the way was clear.

'You're going to make me lose my licence,' the cabby wailed, turning at the end. Peter was at the rear window but the black car never came into sight. 'Keep up the good work,' he said grimly. 'You can do it if you try.'

They came back out of the tiny side street onto Twelfth again. The black car wasn't visible from there. It had finally got around the corner. 'O.K., buddy,' Peter said. 'We're living in luck today. Both of us. Turn left here.'

The driver obeyed but he was wailing. 'You're going to

leave me dead in this town, mister. Jumping lights, going down wrong streets. What if a cop stopped us?'

'How's a cop going to stop you, buddy? He can't put his feet on your brakes.'

The cabby was nearly crying. 'All I was doing was taking you to the airport.'

'Sure you were and you're going to do it yet. You can bet your life on it, buddy.'

'Jesus, I never had a ride like this one.'

'That's right. You thought I was a sitting duck, didn't you? Cruising by so nice and slow. How'd you get onto me anyway?'

'Mister, I don't know what you're talkiag about.'

'Who signalled you, buddy? Somebody in that bar? A guy with a grey sweat shirt with a square-rigger on it?'

'Mister, I swear.'

'Forget it. Just obey all the traffic laws and don't let your friends pick up our traii again. You're nice and safe now. You wouldn't want to spoil that, would you?'

MONDAY 4:50–8:25 P.M.

Peter never saw the black car again. It didn't pick up his trail and it wasn't waiting for him at the airport terminal. He put his gun away when the cab swung around in front of the building and he leaped out on the driver's side as it stopped. 'Buddy,' he said, 'I've got your name, your address and your number. If there's any more trouble,

I'll look you up. Now I'll tell you what you're going to do. You're going to put that cab in gear and roll. And don't ever come back. Get moving. And while you're riding, make up a good story for your friends.'

The driver didn't give him any argument. He shifted gears and took off like a drag racer. The first round was Peter's, but it wasn't the fight.

He checked in at the TWA counter, had a cup of coffee and a hot dog in the Terrace Coffee Shop, and spent the rest of the time until the departure call up on the balcony watching the crowds on the floor below. He hadn't got a good look at the foursome in the black car but they hadn't got a good look at him either. Thus his eye was out for people who looked around uncertainly. He couldn't spot any.

The plane was a DC-9, boarded back of the cockpit through an enclosed ramp. Tourist, where Peter sat, was nearly full and when the plane took off there were no empty seats in his aisle. The man beside him looked innocent enough, but Peter kept the manila envelope in his pocket and devoted his attention to the sight of night-time Washington from the air: the interior spots under the glass roof of the Lincoln Memorial, the orange glow of the Washington Monument and the Capitol, the solid, multi-coloured blanket of lights stretching to the horizon, a shimmering, dancing variety of hues, patterns, and luminosities shifting and passing slowly by for minutes as the pilot held the plane at 4500 feet and flew along the edge of the city.

Then the patches of darkness began to break in, the lights grew fewer and the city was behind them, leaving Peter to wonder when he'd see it again. Or if he'd see it again.

It was the cabdriver, he decided. He'd been Gorman's tail, with the black car and the four men available at the drop of a phone call. And the man in the sweat shirt who came into the bar? Had someone slipped him a five-spot to see what the senator was doing in there? Or had they merely locked onto the only other person besides the senator who was decently dressed?

But Gorman was the real culprit in the matter. He, the expert on the Mafia, so arrogantly sure they couldn't follow him when he didn't want them to. And he'd made another wrong calculation too. He thought the Mafia wouldn't move in on Peter until after he found the girl. Hell, they didn't need him for that. All they needed were his papers. Given the papers, anybody could play Peter Congdon for the guy in the embassy and the girl in the hideout. The game had started the moment Gorman passed the envelope under the table and it was Peter's hide, not the girl's, that was presently up for grabs.

But if the Mafia were after him, there was no sign of it at Kennedy. Peter went by bus around the field from TWA to Pan American Airways and no cordon of thugs materialised. No one even looked at him twice.

In the Pan Am terminal he followed the same tactics as in Washington. He reported to the check-in counter and received his flight data (seat 6A, board after eight at gate eight), and spent the next three-quarters of an hour in the balcony coffee shop, sitting by the railing, sipping, smoking and watching the activity below.

Again nothing special went on. Nobody made inquiries that looked unusual, no people stood out as worthy of study, no strangers hunted out faces. If was just a routine fall evening in an airline terminal, the off-season scattering of people, the casual departures and arrivals that the business of flying had become in the mid-sixties.

He came down from the balcony just before eight, and he was puzzled. Surely he couldn't have thrown his pursuers off the track that easily. They wouldn't have fallen for his casual mention of San Francisco, not when

Dulles Airport was the usual departure point for the West Coast. No, the Mafia could be relied on to cover all angles. They should be after him here, and it bothered him that they didn't seem to be. It bothered him that it was so apparently simple.

Gate eight was at the end of the great glass-walled corridor and a young man and pert stewardess were there to check passengers through at a portable counter. Three people were parting from families by the gateway and little children gazed through the glass at the huge Boeing 707 nosed in close by.

Peter checked in and went through the covered ramp into the forward section of the plane. The 707 was larger than the DC–9 and back in tourist there were three seats in a row on each side of the aisle. He found his own—left-hand side against the window, behind the wing, and six rows from the rear. Only two other passengers were in the compartment with him and their seats were far from his. A stewardess, coming down the aisle, smiled at him and he smiled back. Maybe it was really going to be a piece of cake after all, and wouldn't that be a laugh?

Outside, the weather was not like Washington. It was raw and cloudy and starting to rain. Peter looked out at it briefly, then adjusted his seat and withdrew from his pocket, for the first time, the manila envelope.

The envelope was bulky and well glued and he tore it open without ceremony. Inside there was a sealed envelope with his name on the front, a pencil, several sheets of blank paper, and one sheet bearing the typewritten message: PRMXN TBOUZ BVFCW SGBSY LKTZD CTTLZ HQSSY JLFIL JMQIN VXLSU JTCSD UQHDW KUHFE IHSUD EZIIU GADWR CVUEK AYRRT HLBPR FNIYO KKQKT FPTZT ATOFD SPAMV QGFTO ABFNK TJLIS OHTRU SZNLE KLDOF KWYMU OHNSS RYTYO BBXBN SAGMU XDUSC OFRLW SLCUW CZNXB NTMLX LJWTU DGUDO AOYDX FNKEI GAMOB

KJAKY IEGMO AWLZJ BEBGS ACTCX ADXTQ TEGZM LBUFR IOHOO JMGTB OBDXZ WRCXU EJHOY MLKTQ EZIAN LCULZ PBYYV KMEDZ KQDAT QZMRI ENQVS BJCUS CIFCL BOCUQ TQSLU BHTYA HSWCI JPVWP IWNLG NGCUL PIWEU VFUJC USCIF CLWWJ WUIOC OEDGY VKDXQ NTCAJ MQDBU HMISA VOZGG OGABF NKTJF HJCDW SIJUG ANEPQ HEOAH UVCOI EVKIT WDJDH FGOJV FSOPH ETJPS JMMZ.

Peter looked over the discouraging length of the message gloomily. Gorman should have taken lessons from Brandt who, despite his trick to break up repetitions, still stressed that a coded message should be as brief as economical phrasing could make it and, ideally, should not repeat a word. Even a casual once-over of Gorman's message revealed sequences of KKQK followed by T, BBXB followed by N, WWJW and U, and GGOGA. Already one could guess the KQK's and BXB's and the rest were three-letter words preceded and followed by X's and that in the key one would find K and T, B and N, W and U, and G and A four spaces apart. This didn't mean, of course, that one could crack the message, but the longer it was and the more repetitious, the better the chances. In any case, it was going to be a pain in the neck to decode.

He laid the message on his attaché case on the middle seat and tore open the white, sealed envelope. Inside, on a sheet of Gorman's Senate stationery, was typed, 'This is your matching message, gentlemen,' followed by his signature.

Peter tucked that away in the manila envelope, picked up the message and removed the key from his wallet. Decoding Gorman's not so pithy message was something that had to be done and he might as well get on with it.

He had advanced as far as 'IMMEDIA' when a large, solidly built man in dark trousers, grey plaid jacket, and a yellow silk shirt without a tie appeared at Peter's row, threw an overcoat onto the rack above, and sat down in the aisle seat beside the attaché case. His hair was curly, salt and pepper, his eyes dark and shiny, his jowly cheeks showed the blue-grey of the beard line and the grey plaid jacket was decorated by a red carnation. He looked a well-conditioned fifty. 'Always in and out of planes,' the man said. He turned a grin on Peter revealing a blackened front tooth. 'Going to Paris or Rome?'

Though other passengers had come into tourist, there were still more than twice as many rows as there were people and Peter knew the man had not been assigned to seat 6C. How he had been found out, Peter had no idea, but he knew that the enemy had returned to the fray. Round two was about to begin.

'Rome,' Peter said, answering the man's question in abrupt, unencouraging fashion. He turned a little more into the corner of his seat so the newcomer couldn't see the papers he held. A piece of cake? He hadn't really expected it to be, had he?

He went on with the message, keeping the attaché case and the man's feet in his peripheral vision. 'TE' were the next letters and now it was almost twenty-five minutes past eight and all the passengers were presumably aboard. It was a nearly empty plane that would be making the trip. No more than twenty people were distributed among the more than one hundred seats in tourist.

'Say, that's quite a handsome brief case,' the black-toothed man said. 'Yes, sir, that's one of the finest brief cases I ever saw. You buy it in New York?'

'Macy's,' Peter said without looking up.

'That right? Say, I'd like to get one like that. How much did it cost?'

'A dollar ninety-eight.'

'Yeah?' the man chuckled then. 'I think you're kidding me. That didn't cost no dollar and ninety-eight cents. Not if I know craftsmanship and leather. Hey, I see you got a combination lock on it. Well, say now, that's quite something. I bet you got a lot of important papers in that brief case. Right?'

Peter said abruptly, 'Look if you don't mind!'

The man waved a hand. 'That's all right. No offence. Just trying to be friendly. We're gonna be together for a while. Say, why don't you take your jacket off? I'll put it up on the rack for you.'

Peter ignored the question but he knew what it was for. The man was guessing there was a gun under the jacket and he was prodding. Peter might pretend he didn't know who the man was but the man knew it was pretence. This was a confrontation and the man was probing for weak points, starting to test for advantages. Peter guessed he didn't come from Washington but had been phoned in New York, that the 'Desmond' alias had been found out. And even though Pan American didn't give out its passenger lists, it would be a simple matter to call oneself 'Desmond' and get the information. And now a man was revealing himself and his intentions in order to test Peter. And how many others on the plane were hanging back in the shadows awaiting the results?

'Whatcha doing anyway? Some kind of puzzle?' Now blacktooth was leaning half across the intervening seat, trying to see.

The issue had to be joined. Peter turned his paper away slowly and sat up. 'Buddy,' he said, 'you poke your nose into my business just once more and I'll smash it flat.'

The man's face turned as hard as glass and his voice went harsh and ugly. 'Any time you think you're man enough to try, you better reserve a coffin first. Because that's where you're gonna end up.' He stayed where he was, threatening, daring, his black eyes glittering.

Peter looked beyond him up the aisle. 'Miss,' he said to a stewardess coming down. 'Is this man supposed to have this seat?'

She stopped. 'May I see your ticket, sir?'

He gave her the folder and she said, 'You've made a mistake, sir. First class is up ahead.'

He laughed for her benefit. 'I guess I got mixed up.' He struggled out of the seat, turned and yanked his coat off the rack. His eyes met Peter's and the look in them was deadly. He turned, went up the aisle and through the doorway.

MONDAY 9:15 P.M.–TUESDAY 12:35 P.M.

There were delays of one sort or another and by the time the big plane took off it was quarter past nine and raining hard. The wheels folded up into their wells with a 'chunk' and the climb angle turned steep. City lights appeared briefly, disappeared under the overcast, and for a long time thereafter all that was visible was the red glow of the wing light reflecting off the fog.

Meanwhile, the routine of the flight had been got out of the way. Menus had been passed out, the life-jacket and oxygen demonstrations given, and drink orders taken. Peter, during this, had worked out half the message and he had seen no further trace of the husky man with the blackened tooth and the red carnation.

By quarter of ten he had finished filling out his landing card and been given a martini on the rocks. He removed the arm-rests to give himself a three-seat spread, made himself comfortable and got back to the message again.

The TV screens along the upper racks came to life and a stewardess announced that movie of the night would be *Up the Down Staircase* and earphones, if you wanted to hear the sound, could be rented for $2·50 a pair. Peter passed that offer up with a grim smile. He had work to do for one thing, and he could just imagine Brandt coming across a '$2·50—Movies' item on his expense account sheet for another. 'Where the hell did you go to this movie?' Brandt would roar. 'At the Roxy?'

He put the message aside at ten when dinner was served. The movie had started and he watched the pictures a little, sipped his wine and, cupping his hands against the glass, stared out at the Big Dipper standing on end below the North Star and at the way the rotating light on top of the plane threw red flashes across the wing, faint-bright, faint-bright, like heartbeats.

At quarter of eleven he finished decoding the message and couldn't help thinking of the words Gorman could have saved. 'IMMEDIATELY ON ARRIVAL AT FIUMICINO AIRPORT,' it read, 'PHONE AMERICAN EMBASSY DIAL FOUR SIX SEVEN FOUR AND ASK FOR HERNDON TOLLIVER USE YOUR RIGHT NAME AND SAY MOTHERS MILK IS GOOD FOR BABIES HE WILL SAY DOCTOR SPOCK I PRESUME YOU WILL THEN ARRANGE TO MEET AT WHICH TIME YOU WILL PRODUCE IDENTIFICATION AND HE WILL GIVE YOU AN ENVELOPE CONTAINING THE GIRLS NAME ADDRESS PICTURE THE PASSWORD TO GIVE THE GIRL FOR IDENTIFICATION AND INSTRUCTIONS FOR YOUR RETURN SHE WILL BE EXPECTING YOU GOOD LUCK ROBERT GORMAN.'

Peter read the message twice to digest its contents and got up scowling. 'Mother's milk', indeed! A hell of a thing to have to say over the telephone. Was that Gorman's idea of humour?

He took the sheet with him to the lavatory, tore it into little pieces and disposed of it. He returned to his seat, ordered another martini, wrapped himself in a blanket and stretched out across the seats, using the attaché case and a couple of pillows for a headrest. The cabin lights were out, the movie was drawing to a close, and the only sound was the steady background roar of the jets. Peter made himself relax. The plane was a temporary haven and he should get what sleep he could.

But sleep did not come easily nor stay long. Half an hour after he dropped off, the pilot was on the PA ordering everyone to fasten seat belts. It was only for ten minutes but Peter was three-quarters of an hour getting back to sleep. Then it was half past two and the stewardesses came through, passing out hot towels to start off a new day. The sun was well up by then, glaring with dazzling whiteness on the thick multitude of clouds around them. There was breakfast and the announcement that they were five minutes behind schedule and due at Orly Airport at three thirty-three, which would be nine thirty-three A.M. Paris time. There was also ground fog which might delay them.

They did not land at Orly at nine thirty-three Paris time. They did not land at Orly at all. The ground fog stopped them entirely, shutting down Paris and all European alternates and the plane started circling, waiting for conditions to improve.

Conditions did not improve and the circling grew protracted. Peter found himself hanging in suspended animation, looking on helplessly as the hour and minute hands swept around his watch. The hour hand reached eleven, Paris time, and the plane still circled. Resigned passengers were dozing but Peter could not think of sleep. Herndon Tolliver would be expecting him to call from the Rome airport in another hour and here he was, six miles over Paris and six hundred miles from Rome.

At half past eleven it was announced that the plane

would land in London and Paris passengers would disembark there. A fifty-minute trip followed and, though they left the clouds behind some miles south of the Channel, it was so hazy over southern England that, though they made a complete circle of London Airport, the city itself never came into view. A stewardess, in English, French and Italian, announced that London time was eleven-twenty rather than twelve-twenty, that the temperature was eight degrees centigrade, and she repeated again that only Paris passengers were to get off the plane.

Peter, however, started gathering his things. His plans for Rome had been smashed and he might as well make what he could of the change in landings. Something had to be done about the man with the black front tooth and a country where Peter knew the language was the place to do it. Let him get off the plane in England and, once he shook that man, he'd set a trail the Mafia would never find again.

The plane touched down, braked hard, swung off the runway and taxied to the complex of buildings making up the airport. When it stopped and went quiet and Paris passengers were asked to leave by the front door, only one person in Peter's section got up. Peter watched him go through to the first-class compartment, then rose and followed, carefully leaving his hat, coat and attaché case behind to lull Mr. Carnation into believing he was coming back. Mr. Carnation might even get ideas of examining the attaché case in Peter's absence.

The carnation man was up at the front when Peter came through, sitting on the arm of the first aisle seat making conversation with an elderly couple opposite. It was all very casual and innocent except that nobody could leave the plane without stepping around him. He moved aside for the other passenger and glanced at Peter as if he didn't know him. It was very convincing except that he then looked past Peter to someone in the seats behind and his eyes conveyed a message. Then he was smiling again at the elderly couple and telling them it was his thirtieth crossing and the first time he'd ever ended up in London.

He did not pull aside when Peter reached him, nor did he attempt to block the way. Peter stepped around him and into the little lounge, and a stewardess was there at the door to intercept him. 'Please, sir, all Rome passengers are asked to remain aboard the plane.'

Peter muttered something about phone calls, that they were overdue at Rome. The girl remained desperately adamant. Rome knew all about it. His friends would find out from the airport. Passengers were please to stay aboard the plane.

He let himself be persuaded, not because he couldn't have gone, but because he couldn't have gone alone. A man was behind him now, waiting with him, a tall, thin, morose-looking man with sunken cheeks, dead eyes and a soiled, shabby coat. It was a man Peter had passed coming up the aisle, the man Mr. Carnation had signalled with his eyes. If Peter got off the plane, the man would go with him.

He went back into tourist and down to his seat. If they weren't going to make it easy for him, he might as well get the journey part of the business out of the way and elude the Mafia at the destination.

At least the manœuvre told him a few things. Mr. Carnation wasn't alone. Peter had suspected that much, but now he knew the identity of the companion. And the companion looked the deadlier of the two. Despite his tubercular appearance and the deathlike pallor of his face, his eyes said the death wasn't his. It walked with him but it fell upon others.

TUESDAY 4:10–6:15 P.M.

It was four-ten in the afternoon when the big plane hit the runway at Fiumicino Airport. Four hours had been lost to weather and Peter had spent them in sleepless fretting. It wasn't fear of the two men in the first-class compartment that disturbed him. Known quantities weren't frightening. What bothered him was the upset in plans and pre-game nerves, the sitting, waiting for the whistle to blow. And, of course, the more he tried to sleep, the more he couldn't. Only when they broke out under the overcast and the black belt of an autostrada, a railroad, and pretty farms rose slowly closer, only when touchdown was imminent and Peter quit trying to sleep, did the fatigue hit him. His head was nodding when the wheels touched and he hardly felt the hard braking and the taxiing past the isolated tower in the field to the terminal building and the big tower beyond.

Then it was time to disembark and Peter had to pull himself together. Now the whistle had blown and the game was underway. He tried to shake off the fatigue and giddiness and get his bearings.

Tourist class departed through the rear door, down steps and into a blue and white trailer van drawn up alongside. Twenty-five people got into it with Peter, but Mr. Carnation and Mr. T.B. were not among them. First class got separate treatment.

They rode to the terminal, walked up a ramp over a roadway, and went in through a door on the second level to Passport Control. Peter waited his turn in the passport line, handed over his landing card and the blue-grey passport folder that had never been stamped. It and his smallpox vaccination were less than two weeks old.

The man at the little counter studied the landing card and thumbed through the passport. He did not ask Peter what was in the attaché case nor if he were wearing weapons in a shoulder holster. He didn't even stamp the passport but handed it back and passed Peter through into the main luggage retrieving area.

Surprisingly few people were there—only those from the 707 tourist section—and though Peter looked, he could not spot the two faces of the enemy. No more attention was being paid to him here than in the airports in Washington and New York and it gave him an eerie feeling. He knew he was under surveillance but he didn't know by whom, where, or how many. He could find no signs and it made him wonder if he had been watched with the same effective secrecy in all the other airports.

All right, he decided as he looked around for pay phones and a place to get the kind of money that fit, let them watch. Let the Mafia be as secretive as they wanted. They were playing in his backyard now and the picnic was over. It wasn't Senator Gorman they'd be following hereafter. This was someone who knew the game.

The phones were on the pillars by the exit and the place to change money was at a long booth just outside the building. Peter converted forty dollars' worth of travellers cheques into 24,500 lire and went back to inquire of an English-speaking attendant how one reached Rome and how much.

None of the phones were in use and he took the farthest one, the one that shielded his back the most and provided the best view of passing people. He fed in his money and dialled, but his first call was not to the number Gorman had told him reached the American Embassy. This was a seven-digit number and connected him with a leather goods shop just off the Via Veneto on the Via Liguria. A woman's voice answered with words that Peter took to be the name of the shop. '*Pronto,*' she said.

'Vittorio Del Strabo, please.'

There were a few more Italian words and the woman went away. In another moment a man's voice came on. '*Pronto.*'

'Are you Vittorio Del Strabo?'

The man switched to clear and beautiful English. 'Yes. I am he.'

Peter said, 'The Brandt Agency has a far-flung net.'

'And it catches many fish,' the other man replied. 'You are Mr. Congdon?'

'That's right.'

'Everything has been arranged, Mr. Congdon. I have reserved a room in your name at a *pensione*—the San Giovanni on the Via Emilia. It's moderate in price but very nice.'

Peter repeated the name but didn't write it down. 'Fine and thanks. Is there anything else?'

'Mr. Brandt said nothing specific, only that I am to be ready to help you in any way that you might need. If you are in any trouble, night or day, telephone me. You have my home number?'

'Home and shop, address and phone.'

'If I am not in, whoever answers will know where to reach me.'

'Thanks. I hope I don't have to call on you.'

'I hope so too. I hope your task proceeds without incident.'

Peter hung up, checked, and still no one paid him attention. A few people were picking up the last of the bags, the porters sought to be useful, the loudspeaker kept breaking into the silence with sounds that were unintelligible in any language. Everything was so normal it looked staged.

He tried the embassy number next and a man's voice said, 'Receptionist Breslin. *Pronto.*'

'Herndon Tolliver, please.'

Receptionist Breslin repeated the name and said, 'One minute.' Peter waited and put his hand over one ear as another jumbled loudspeaker announcement echoed through the cavernous room.

Then, through the phone a weary voice was saying, 'Meisel speaking.'

Peter asked for Tolliver and Meisel said, 'He's not here.'

That's what Peter was afraid of. 'When do you expect him back?'

'Tomorrow morning. He's gone for the day.'

Peter inwardly cursed both the weather and State Department employees who left early. 'Where did he go? Where can I reach him?'

'I wouldn't know. There was an economic meeting he had to go to but I don't know where and I don't know when it's over or what his plans were after that.'

'He was expecting me to call. Did he say anything about that?'

'Not a thing about calls, sorry. Just good-bye till tomorrow.'

Peter was tired and irritable. He tried to keep his voice calm. 'Maybe if I tried his home? Would you give me his address and phone?'

'Yeah. Sure. Fifteen Via Cimarosa. Phone—let me see if I can find the number.' There was silence and then Meisel read off six digits as if from a card. 'But I don't think he'll be in till late. I think he said something about a cocktail party.'

'Where? Whose party? Do you know?'

Meisel said in the same laconic, slightly bored voice, 'No, sir, I don't. But if it's important, you can give me your name and number and I'll try to get the word to him to call you.'

Peter made a face. He didn't like the idea of anyone other than the Brandt contact man knowing his whereabouts, but time was important. If he could meet Tolliver tonight, he could have the girl on a plane to the States early tomorrow. He'd have the job done before the Mafia even knew he had started. 'All right,' he said and gave Meisel his name and the San Giovanni Hotel. 'Any time after the next hour. And if he should come back there, would you have him wait for my call at the reception desk? I'll call in as soon as I get to the San Giovanni.'

'Yeah, I'll tell him.'

Everything was still normal when Peter finished with his calls. Nobody looked at him, nobody loitered in odd corners. Peter should have felt lulled, especially when he was so dead for sleep, but he tingled instead. Things weren't what they seemed. They couldn't be.

He went outside and took deep breaths and looked around. It was still light but the beginnings of darkness were starting to creep. As for transport to the city he had a choice of taxis or a waiting, half-filled bus. Peter had had enough of Mafia-controlled cabdrivers. He chose the bus and took a seat at the rear. There, he watched the few who had boarded before him and studied those who came after until the bus started the long drive out of the airport and picked up the road to Rome.

Night had fallen when the bus hit the outskirts of the city and the rain was starting to come down. They went through islanded streets jammed with cars, tiny Nuova 500's, Fiats—the little 600's and the bigger 124's. They crammed the sides, parked cheek by jowl, they crowded the street, moving with the bus. They started and stopped at the lights and, in the free spots, darted about like bugs to the musical squeaks of their horns. Peter watched them all but none looked sinister of purpose. He studied his fellow passengers but they were watching the scenery.

They passed dark, rain-swept ruins on a grassy knoll.

They reached the floodlit Colosseum, circled part of it and turned away, up a hill. It was Peter's first glimpse of the great, decaying arena in seven years, the first time at night, but he didn't turn to look back at its light-hued walls looming above the road behind.

The rain had slacked off to a mild drizzle when the bus pulled in at the air terminal offices in the railroad station. The time was not quite six o'clock and Peter called 4674 again. Receptionist Breslin was still on the desk but there was no Herndon Tolliver.

He bought a street map next and looked up the locations that concerned him. He wasn't happy about the results. The Via Liguria, where the leather shop was, the Via Emilia, where the San Giovanni was, the Via Ludovisi, where the Savoy Albergo was, and the Via Vittorio Veneto, where the embassy was, were the four streets around one small block and all points were literally within a stone's throw of each other, given a reasonably good arm. Well, he had to do what he could.

He went out and climbed into a four-passenger green and black cab, making sure he picked it and not it, him. 'Savoy Albergo,' he told the driver and followed the route on the map. The driver did it right.

When he got out in front of the hotel, a red Simca with two young men in it doubled-parked down the street fifty yards behind. Peter had looked for a car to be following him and that was the one. Now it was time to get rid of it and the men it contained.

He mounted the stones steps and went through the glass doors of the hotel, crossed the lobby and, as he had done at the Shoreham, exited by a different door onto a different street. He walked around an extra block, checking people and cars carefully, then worked his way back to the Via Emilia and entered the San Giovanni at quarter past six to pick up his reservation.

TUESDAY 6:15–10:25 P.M.

The Pensione San Giovanni was a family-type hotel which had at one time been an elegant private home. It rose five narrow storeys on the Via Emilia, wedged flush between two similar buidings. There was an ivy-covered wall in front and a small, semicircular drive that was jammed with cars.

Inside, two tile-floored rooms formed the lobby, with the office and reception desk left, the porter's desk right, beside the door to the dining rooms. Peter signed in with the manager, a young man with light hair and a thick moustache who thumbed through his passport and gave a key to a thin lad in cleaning smock and apron. 'Room fifty-seven,' he told Peter. 'Do you know yet how long you'll be with us?'

Peter said he didn't know. 'Any calls?'

'No, sir, not yet. Ah, the accommodations are half *pensione*. Breakfast and one other meal. Lunch, if you wish, is twelve to two, dinner is seven till nine.'

Peter thanked him and followed the thin lad around a corner to a small marble hall and into a tiny four-by-four elevator with narrow double doors and veneered walls. A mirror and folding red bench were at the back and the day's menus were posted on the side. The car only went to the fourth floor and the boy led Peter down a carpeted hall and up a staircase to reach the fifth. He opened the left-hand door there and showed Peter into a big cream-coloured room overlooking the street. There was a wardrobe cabinet on the right, just inside the door, twin beds against the wall, bed tables with lamps and phone, three chairs, a spare table, and a couple of scatter rugs on the floor. The bath was large and the appointments were at least the equal of the Emerson in Washington.

As soon as he had paid off the boy and locked himself in, Peter sat down on the bed nearest the phone and called the embassy again. It was twenty-five after six now and he got the marine guard and the information that there was no Herndon Tolliver there and the building was closed. He tried Tolliver's home and no one answered. He cursed heartily and went to the windows, yanking on the strap to raise the shutters, parting the curtains and pulling open the windows. It was very dark now and the sky was mottled with clouds. Yellow neon spelled out Capriccio Night Club in a sign on the corner and other lights glowed at street level. Higher up, windows were shuttered and all was black. A car went by and another pulled out from the line at the kerb, but the sidewalks were empty.

Peter smoked a cigarette while he studied the scene. Then he pulled the spare table and a chair over to the beds under the ceiling light, and spent an hour drafting a report to mail to Brandt. In it he detailed his flight and his suspicions regarding the black-toothed man and his slim companion. If anything happened to him, at least the suspicions would be on file.

He called Tolliver's number two more times while he worked but the results were the same. No answer. He finished and checked over the report, put it into one of Brandt's special envelopes, sealed it and took it down to the porter's desk for the outgoing mail.

He ate then, dining on pea soup, Florentine fried chicken, and a carafe of white wine that wasn't very good. He gave the waiter his room number, learned at the desk that no calls had come in, picked up his passport and went back to his room. It was eight-fifteen.

He tried Tolliver's number again, swore and lighted a cigarette. He smoked it lying on the striped coverlet by the phone and pondered what action to take if something unforeseen had happened to Herndon Tolliver. The trouble was, how would he know?

After the cigarette he tried to sleep but he was still too keyed, too eager to get moving. Like the nights before a high-school football game. Sleep had always been fitful then and he was ever sure that his performance on the gridiron would have been better had he had good rest. And how would it be here?

At quarter of ten he decided the hell with it and drew a warm bath. It was then, as he was shedding his clothes, that the soft phone buzzer sounded and he jumped a foot. He sat slowly on the bed and lifted the receiver. 'Hello?'

'Mr. Congdon?' It was a light, airy voice with the hint of cocktails in it.

'That's right.'

'My name is Herndon Tolliver. I received a message to call you.'

Peter couldn't help a little sarcasm. 'I'm glad it finally got to you.'

'Well, I did call the Savoy once or twice during the afternoon. It was supposed to be the Savoy, you know.' There was a brief pause and then the voice said, a little more carefully, 'Is there something you want to say to me?'

Peter made a face. Into the receiver he answered, 'I'm supposed to say to you, "Mother's milk is good for babies".'

Tolliver laughed happily. 'That's right, you are. And I'm supposed to say, "Doctor Spock, I presume." Senator Gorman has a wild sense of humour, don't you think?'

'Bizarre is the word. I understand you have something to give me.'

'Yes. The whatever-it-is arrived yesterday along with

a covering letter and I must say I haven't the vaguest idea what this is all about. He asked me to do him this favour and I can't very well refuse, seeing as how I'm in his debt for my job here. At least, he's my senator and it's supposed to be his influence . . . Anyway, I'm supposed to give you this envelope he sent me, only I can't merely hand it to you. I have to meet you someplace outside the embassy, like a hippie hangout or something, and see if you have a letter like the one he sent me. I hope you have so we can get this business done with.'

'I do.'

'What's it say? Maybe we can cut through all this red tape and I can leave it off at your hotel. I'm really rushed like crazy and . . .'

Peter said, 'I think we'd better play it his way. He's footing the bill and he's entitled.'

Tolliver sighed. 'Well, it does seem a little much. I mean an imposition. But that's the way the senator is. He doesn't care what he does so long as he gets what he wants. Say, does this have anything to do with that investigation of the Mafia he's conducting back in the halls of Congress?'

Peter said, 'Why don't we talk about it in person, Mr. Tolliver? Where can I meet you and how soon?'

Tolliver said, 'Well, you do make it sound very cloak-and-daggerish. Really, I haven't given it much thought. You got a place in mind?'

'Not I. You're the one who lives here.'

'Right in my lap again, huh? Well let's see. You're at the San Giovanni? Where's that?'

'On Emilia Street.'

'The Via Emilia?' He laughed. 'How lucky. It's right around the corner from the embassy. Let's meet at Il Pipistrello. You know it?'

'No. What is it and where is it?'

'It's a night club. On the Via Emilia. A few doors up

from the Capriccio Night Club. You can't miss it.' He chuckled. 'You know what Il Pipistrello means?'

'No.'

'Well I won't tell you until I get there. Meanwhile, you try to guess. But it's the perfect name for the perfect meeting place. It's a real grotto and dark as the Black Hole of Calcutta. Just the thing for this spooky stuff Gorman's got us mixed up in.'

Peter wasn't interested in the symbolism. 'All right, Il Pipis . . . whatever it is,' he said. 'How about fifteen minutes?'

'Oh no, that's out of the question. Make it eleven o'clock. I have to go home and fix myself up a little. Besides, that's where the envelope is. How'll I know you?'

'Look for a dark-haired, sour-faced six-footer in a charcoal suit and a maroon figured tie.'

'I'm five-ten and blond and I'll be carrying a large manila envelope.'

'All right, I'll see you at eleven o'clock. Spell the name of the place for me.'

When he had hung up, Peter bathed quickly, dressed, put his gun on under his jacket, but left his topcoat on a wardrobe hanger and the attaché case on the wardrobe shelf. At twenty after ten he locked the door behind him and went down the stairs to the elevator. In the lobby he gave the key to the night porter and walked out into the damp, cool air to look at Il Pipistrello and see what it was all about. Tolliver regarded the elaborate precautions as more of Gorman's sense of humour but Peter was in the business and he didn't like chances. For a meeting with an unknown person in an unknown spot on a matter with dubious safety factors, it was always wise to be early. And with all the time he had to kill, Peter would be early indeed.

TUESDAY 10:25 P.M.–WEDNESDAY 12:45 A.M.

A small lighted sign on the little red canopy said Il Pipistrello and, in red letters at one corner, American Bar. The black door had a big mock padlock on it and was tended by a doorman. On either side, display cases advertised a performer named Armandino.

Inside, there was a tiny grotto-like vestibule with pseudo rock walls and a barred window. Red-carpeted steps went down behind it into almost total blackness. An arch on the right opened into a room with seats and dime-sized tables against a bar, a band-stand, and a thin youth on it wailing into a mike and stroking a guitar. His face was spotlighted but three other members of the band were almost invisible in the darkness. A boy and girl, wrapped in each other's arms, were dancing in the area in front of the bandstand. Beyond was another small room with more tiny tables, but they were empty. The dancing couple were the only customers in the place.

A second arch opened into a small, rock-walled space on the other side of the bar. There was another counter there, a set of barstools, and the best view of incoming customers. Peter went in and a girl in a black dress on one of the stools said hello. It had been too dark to see her before but Peter wasn't surprised to find her there. It was a clip joint. He should have figured that. 'Hello,' he said, and passed behind her to take the end seat by the whitewashed wall. It was three seats away.

'You speak English?' she said.

'That's right.'

'I speak a little.'

'So I notice.' To the bartender, a big man he could

hardly see, he said, 'Beer.' There was a small light under the bar, there was the spot on the singer, there were a few dim electric lamps, but they had almost no effect on the darkness. The colour scheme was red and black but the effect was only black.

'You're not very friendly.'

'You only say that because you don't know me very well.'

She patted the barstool next to her. 'Come, sit here.'

He shook his head and pointed. 'You come sit here.'

She didn't mind. She moved over. 'My name's Eddie.'

'Hi, Eddie. Mine's Bill.'

'That's a nice name, Bill.'

'What's the name of this place mean in English?'

'This?' She pondered. 'It's a bird. I don't know the name. He's small, with big wings and he hangs upside down.'

'A bat?'

'Yes. Bat.'

The beer was cold and tasted Danish. Peter sipped it and smoked and listened to the constant noise of the combo. The singer did an American number in slow rock, then switched to a song in French. Against the strident, amplified sounds, Peter put his head close and made idle conversation with the girl. She was nice about it. She didn't beg him for a drink.

Two other couples drifted down the steps and through the arch but it was still too early for the crowd. Another girl in a black dress appeared on Peter's side of the bar, conversed momentarily in Italian with Eddie, and was introduced as Angie. She took a seat farther down and was shortly thereafter joined by a plump, balding middle-aged man.

Peter offered Eddie a drink at twenty of eleven and she had a small glass of something that fizzed like ginger ale.

He didn't bother to ask what it was. At quarter of eleven he invited her to dance and they joined four pairs on the floor. Eddie was slender and responsive. She danced close without snuggling. She didn't lay it on and she didn't stand off. She acted as if she liked the man rather than the wallet. It made her very appealing.

But Peter had business. At eleven o'clock he ordered them both another round and began to keep tabs on his watch. 'Many Americans come in here?' he asked, leaning close to transmit against the blare of the combo.

'Quite a lot.'

He lighted her a cigarette and had one himself. She said, 'You are waiting for somebody?'

'Yes.'

'Is she prettier than I?'

He was getting edgy now and he didn't play with that one. 'It's a he,' he said and got off the stool. 'Listen, wait here for a minute and keep your eye out for a man with a manila envelope—a big envelope. You understand? If he comes in, hold him over here. I'm going to make a phone call.'

He dialled Tolliver's home, a number he knew by heart, but, as before, there was no answer. He went back to Eddie and his beer and Mr. Manila Envelope hadn't shown. He lighted cigarettes again and swore under his breath. It was after half past eleven.

'Pretty soon the real band will come in,' Eddie was saying. 'This one is a new band—wanting to start. They play to learn.'

Peter nodded and told himself Tolliver was on his way. He could say it and believe it up until midnight. After that he'd know something had to be wrong.

They danced again but it was different now. She was still close but he wasn't aware of her any more. Eddie could sense the difference and the reason. 'This man who is coming? It is important business!'

He looked down at her fragilely young, faintly lit face. 'Oh? What makes you think so?'

'You. The way you are. I feel it.'

He didn't try to kid her. 'I'm afraid he may have changed his mind and won't come.'

'Would you like to sit down?'

They returned to their seats and Peter paid the bill. The bartender told him it was 6000 lire and Peter snorted as he got out his wallet. It was a clip joint, but good. Well, it was out of the senator's budget and the taxpayers could love the senator. He could see Brandt blow fire, though. Brandt wouldn't believe he needed to spend a nickel in the place. Sit, don't talk, and don't order. Let them try to throw you out. That was Brandt's idea. They wouldn't throw Brandt out, that was for sure. Nobody would dare go near the son of a bitch.

When his watch said midnight, Peter stood up. Eddie said, 'You go?'

'I go.'

'I hope you see him.'

'Thanks, Eddie.' He kissed her on the cheek and patted her on the hip. He waved good-bye to Angie as he passed and she reached out to touch his hand and give him a smile. He appreciated the gesture but, he decided as he went out into the cool night air, it would take more than smiles to tide him over the next few hours.

The Via Emilia was quiet. Cars crowded the kerbs but none were moving and no people roamed the narrow sidewalks. Peter went around the corner to the Via Veneto and caught a cab in front of the heavy barred doors of the American Embassy. 'Via Cimarosa,' he told the driver. 'Number fifteen.' He held up fingers in sequence to total fifteen.

The driver laughed as he pulled down the flag. 'You no speak Italian? You speak English?'

'That's right.'

'Me too. Not many drivers speak English. I speak. I know where you want.'

'I'm glad to hear it.' Peter sat back in the broad, square back seat and lighted another cigarette. He really wasn't interested in the cabdriver's lingual achievements. His concern was Herndon Tolliver's whereabouts and how he could locate them.

The cab moved on up the Via Veneto with the traffic. 'You from London?' the driver asked.

'America.'

'Ah. American. How you like my English?'

'Better than my Italian. How far is this place?'

'Is near.'

They went up through the gate in the old wall, skirted the park on the Via Pinciana past the Galleria Borghese, made a couple of turns on crowded streets, and pulled up at the kerb by the gateway to an entry court of a seven-storey apartment. The building, a solid sequence of dark, shuttered windows, filled the block and, large though this entrance was, it was only a side gate. Just inside were entries labelled Scala I and Scala II. On the right, up four steps, was the door to the *portiere*'s apartment. Farther in were other entries, paved walks and a circular pool.

'How about it?' the driver said. 'This is number fifteen. You know what you want?'

'I know what I want, but I don't know how to ask for it.'

'What you want?'

'An American living here named Tolliver.'

'Come,' the driver said, opening his door. 'We find out.' He took Peter inside and up the steps to the *portiere*'s door, where he rapped loudly. It was opened by a fat woman with grey-black hair in a bun and a mouthful of crooked and missing teeth.

The driver and she swapped machine-gun Italian and a few gestures and she pointed across the way at Scala I.

They went down and over and Peter started looking for name tags on the doors but there were none. 'Up two flights,' the driver told him and led the way. There were two doors on the landing up there and the driver looked uncertainly at them, then knocked on both. No one answered one, a woman answered the other. She was short and stout and smelled faintly of garlic, but she dressed well and looked cared for.

There was a brief exchange and she pointed at the opposite door and shrugged.

'That's where he lives,' the cabbie said. 'But he's out.'

'Does she know where?'

That question was put to her and she gestured ignorance. Her husband, a grey-haired man in shirt sleeves, came out and got in on it. He leaned over the rail and called down to someone below. A door opened and voices came up.

Finally the driver translated. 'They say he went out with some friends.'

'Do they know when?'

A good deal of discussion followed which, translated, meant, 'Somewhere around half past ten or eleven.'

'Do they know who the friends were or where they went?'

A full minute of animated conversation ensued before the driver translated again. 'They don't know his friends. It was three men. He brought them home and went out with them later.'

Peter tried to get a description but it was fruitless. He thanked the couple and went down the stairs again, thanking the others in English as he passed. They thanked him in Italian and they were still talking with each other when Peter and the driver went out the door and back to the cab. 'I a big help, eh?' the driver said proudly when he started up. 'Where to now?'

'I guess the Hotel San Giovanni on the Via Emilia.'

It was a ten-minute ride and Peter's routine check indicated they were not being followed. The driver spent the time delivering a monologue in his kind of English on how great the Americans were and how terrible Mussolini had been for the country. He was after a big fat tip and Peter gave him one, both for his help and because it was soothing letting the talk wash over him without interfering with his own thoughts.

The porter opened the front door for him at the hotel and got his key from behind the desk. Peter asked about phone calls. There had been none, of course.

He rode the elevator, walked up the extra flight and unlocked his door. He didn't know what he was supposed to do next but thought that probably he should go to sleep. He reached for the light switch but he didn't quite make it.

As he turned to grope, something like the roof descended on the back of his head. Peter saw a blinding flash of stars and felt his knees buckle. For a second he thought the wardrobe cabinet had fallen on him and then he realised it was somebody behind the cabinet and he'd been ambushed. What he never knew was when he hit the floor.

WEDNESDAY 12:55–1:10 A.M.

The buzz of the telephone seeped through the darkness of Peter Congdon's consciousness. It wasn't a loud sound but it was jarring and painful to his magnified senses, almost unbearable in its brief but vibrant intensity. He wanted to stay in the never-never land of darkness and it was calling him back to the bitter world of pain.

In the silence following the sound he sank halfway back into that nether world but he could go no further. Other things were impinging on his senses, the feel of roughness against his face, the burr and bleat of traffic, the far-off sound of loud, raucous music.

The telephone buzzed again for three unbearable seconds and he lifted his head, squeezing his eyes shut against the hum. When it died, he let his eyelids part and now comprehension was returning. He was lying on a small rug in a dark room but there was light through the window. Above was the grey of a ceiling. Near to hand loomed the dark shape of a large cupboard.

He thought hard, fighting the searing pain that now seemed localised in his head, and recollection began to come back. This was an hotel room—his hotel room. He had fallen. No, he had been struck. He had come into the room, started to turn, and been hit from behind. That was it. Someone had been behind the corner of that same clothes cupboard. He remembered it now.

He pulled himself up on an elbow and the ache in his head was growing in enormity but it was more bearable when his head was erect. He grasped the footboard of the bed and got to his knees. He tried to climb to his feet but pitched onto the bed and off to the floor against the cupboard. He struggled to his knees again as the telephone buzzed a third time.

Someone was calling him. He remembered now. The phone had been buzzing. He had to answer. It was important to answer. That's what phones were for.

He leaned on the mattress. Where was the phone? There it was, that shadow on the night table a bed-length away. He crawled on his hands and knees till he could reach the receiver. He sat on the floor with an elbow on the bed and put it to his ear.

An excited, almost hysterical voice shrieked, 'Hello, hello? Is that you, Congdon?'

Peter grunted and then said heavily, 'Yeah.' He thought the top of his head was going to explode.

'This is Tolliver. Herndon Tolliver. Can you hear me?'

The name rang a bell. He remembered Tolliver. He could remember nearly everything now. He tried to force coherence into his voice. 'Yeah. Tolliver.' He breathed hard once from the effort. 'Where are you?'

'They grabbed me! They got me in front of my place! When I got out of my car!'

'Who grabbed you?' Peter shook his head, trying to get the punch-drunkenness out of it.

'The Mafia. It must have been the Mafia. That's what Gorman's mixed up with. That's what you're here about, isn't it? I was kidnapped. They kidnapped me!'

'Yeah,' Peter breathed heavily. 'What happened?'

'They wanted the envelope. They threatened me. They knew I had it. They made me give it to them!'

'Envelope?' Peter knew there was something about an envelope in his being in Rome.

'The envelope I was supposed to give you at Il Pipistrello. What's the matter with you? I was kidnapped! They made me give it to them. They would have killed me!'

'Yeah,' Peter said. 'I see.'

'You see?' Tolliver shrieked. 'I'm within an inch of losing my life and all you can say is you see?'

It made Peter's head hurt still more when Tolliver screamed like that. 'Yes, yes, calm down,' he said, trying to make the man stop screaming. 'I understand. Where are you?'

'Way the hell and gone outside of Rome. I must be twenty miles outside of Rome! They took me into my place so I could give them the envelope and then they made me drive with them for miles and miles. That crazy maniac Gorman could've had me killed! What's he mean getting me mixed up with the Mafia? I never did anything to anybody. I'm just doing a guy a favour. How can he ask an innocent bystander like me to stick his neck in a noose like this? He didn't even tell me what was in that envelope! He's a monster! I could spit on his grave. I'm just lucky to be alive.'

Peter's brain was functioning better by the time Tolliver paused for breath. If only the pain would let up a little, he'd be able to think fairly clearly. 'O.K., O.K.,' he said. 'You got kidnapped. Tell me the whole thing.'

'That's what I'm trying to do. What are you, cock-eyed or something? I'm trying to warn you.'

'Warn me about what?'

'Those guys. There were three of them. Two young thugs and an older guy. And they all have guns. They drove me out in the country and opened the envelope and looked at what was inside. Then they punched me and kicked me and wanted me to give them what I knew about the whole thing and I said all I knew was that Senator Gorman had asked me to hold the envelope for somebody. Then they made me tell who. I didn't want to, but those two thugs would have killed me. And they knew anyway, because when I told them your name, the big man knew I was telling them the truth.

Then they wanted to know where you were staying. I didn't want to tell them but they threatened to kill me so I had to. I told them the San Giovanni and then they drove someplace where there was a telephone and I guess they called the hotel. I don't know. Anyway, they decided I was telling the truth and they turned me loose way out on a deserted road miles from anywhere.

'I've been hiking for God knows how long to get to the first phone I could find to warn you. They know where you are, Congdon. Watch out for yourself. They're very dangerous. They'll kill you if you aren't careful. I swear I thought they were going to kill me!'

Peter was fully alert now and the throbbing ache in his head was pushed to the back of his consciousness. There were more important things in life than pain. 'The big man you saw, was he the leader?'

'Yes. He asked the questions. The others did the work.'

'Did he wear a carnation?'

'Yes, yes. He did. You know him?'

'What about the other two? What did they look like?'

'Young, dark. Ugly-looking.'

'That doesn't tell me a damned thing. How were they dressed? What kind of features did they have?'

'They had dark suits on, both of them. They looked like gangsters. Black hair. Black eyes.'

'That still doesn't tell me anything.'

'Je-sus!' Tolliver screamed. 'What do you want? I'm looking death in the face and you expect me to remember details. You might at least have the courtesy to thank me for warning you. Lock your door. They might be coming any minute. If I were you, I'd get the hell out of that hotel. And don't call me any more. I don't have the envelope and I don't know anything. I don't want to know anything. I'm not going to have anything further to do with any of this. I'm going to complain to my superiors. I'm going to lodge an official protest. I'm going . . .'

'Look,' Peter said, 'just be thankful you're all right, that you're not hurt.'

'Not hurt? They gave me a bloody nose and cut my lip. I've got a black eye and a big bruise on my cheek. How'm I going to face people at the embassy tomorrow? I'll be embarrassed to show up.'

'Yeah,' Peter said. 'Well, thanks for the warning. Thanks for going to bat for me.'

'I did what I could. They would've killed me if I didn't tell them where you lived. They'd probably kill me if they knew I phoned you. If you want my advice, get out of town.'

'Yeah. Thanks.' Peter put down the phone and switched on the table lamp, blinking in pain at the sudden light. He pulled himself up onto the bed and sat, holding his head erect. He let his fingers move gingerly over the crown till he felt the blood, some of it dried, some still sticky. That was what he got for telling Tolliver how to reach him. He hadn't wanted to. He knew it was dangerous. He'd done it reluctantly, as a calculated risk, and now he had blown the game.

He felt in his jacket. Yes, his wallet was gone. So was his gun.

He stood up unsteadily and went through his pockets. Everything was gone: his passport, his health certificate, his travellers cheques, the works. On the other bed his topcoat lay torn apart, the attaché case open and smashed. His spare clothes were there but the box of cartridges was missing and so was the fingerprint equipment. So, even, were the special envelopes for mailing Brandt's reports.

Peter sat down again and tried to think. The wallet contained the key to the code. That was what they were after, of course. They'd got the envelope from

Tolliver, which gave them the girl's name and whereabouts, but they couldn't decipher the information without that key. Now they had that too and Peter had nothing. He didn't even have a wristwatch. By the time he got back to Brandt, he wouldn't have a job.

Time was flying. That much Peter could grasp. He pulled the phone onto the bed beside him and lifted the receiver. For a moment he wondered if the porter downstairs was one of the enemy but he dismissed it immediately. The old man had been tricked in some way. Had he known of the ambush, Peter would have read it in his manner. In any case, the question was purely academic. Since Peter didn't even have the lire necessary to use a public phone, he had to put all calls through the porter, no matter who he was. He gave him a number and waited.

A man's voice answered the third ring and Peter said, 'Without bothering to use names, let it be said that the Brant Agency has a far-flung net.'

'And it catches many fish,' the other replied. 'But maybe this time one got away.'

'That's right. I'm at the hotel. How soon can you be over here?'

'Ten minutes be all right?'

'It'll take you longer because I want a few things.'

'Name the list.'

'A car. At least twenty-five thousand lire, a passport, a gun and a box of bullets that will fit it, a wristwatch—if it won't hold you up—and that's about it. Oh yes, a box of aspirin.'

'That's quite a lot of "it," I will say. What kind of a passport?'

'Any kind that's immediately available.'

'Is it for you?'

'That's right.'

'It sounds as if there's been some trouble.'

'There has. Now, how fast can you get here?'

The other man paused. 'Maybe half an hour.'

'I'll try to be outside the hotel. Be careful who sees you. I'd like you to stay in good health.'

The other man said soberly, 'What you're asking for gives me all the warning I need. I'll be right along.'

Peter hung up and lifted the phone again. When the porter answered, he said, 'I want to make a transatlantic telephone call to the United States of America. How long will it take?'

The porter wasn't disturbed by the question at all. 'Not very long, sir,' he said. 'Where in the United States?'

He told him Washington, D.C., and said, 'I'm going to want to speak to Senator Robert Gerald Gorman.' He spelled the name slowly. 'And he'll be at—wait a minute.' He frowned and tried to think. 'What time is it? My watch has stopped.'

'Ten minutes after one in the morning, sir.'

'Yeah, well try him—have the operator try to reach him at his home. That's on . . .' He had great trouble remembering. 'Kalorama Road,' he finally said. 'Northwest.' He spelled that out. 'And if he's not there, try his office in the New Senate Office Building.'

'Yes, sir. What numbers, please?'

Peter didn't have the numbers any more. 'I don't know. The United States operators will have to look them up. Now, one thing. If he's not at either of those two places, find out from whoever answers where he is and get through to him. It's absolutely essential that I talk to him right away. It's a matter of life and death. You understand?'

The porter said very seriously, 'Yes, sir. I understand. That will be fifteen American dollars for three minutes.'

'I forgot,' Peter said. 'Reverse the charges.'

WEDNESDAY 1:30–1:40 A.M.

It only took twenty minutes for the call to go through and Peter spent the time in the bathroom soaking his head under a faucet and trying to clean himself up. He felt slightly nauseous and dizzy when he first bent down but the cool water steadied him and eased a little of the pain.

When the phone rang it was the senator himself on the line, with the operator saying, 'Please go ahead, sir.'

'Congdon?' the senator said. 'What's this? Have you got her?'

'No I haven't got her,' Peter replied tightly. 'Some hitches have developed. Your embassy friend was ambushed and his envelope stolen.'

'That's impossible.'

'It's happened. The Mafia has all the information in the envelope. They also ambushed me and got the key to the code it's written in.'

The senator exploded with a series of four-letter epithets, then said in fury, 'You incompetent bastard, do you realise what you've done? Do you understand . . .'

Peter sat down on the bed. 'Never mind the lecture,' he snapped. 'The point is, the Mafia will crack that code pretty fast now that they have the key. As soon as they do, they'll know who the girl is and where she is and they'll go get her. If you give me that information, maybe I can get to her first.'

Gorman's voice was very near an hysterial shriek. 'You want me to tell you that, right now, over the phone, in plain English?'

'Loud and clear, Senator. This connection isn't very good. I can't hear you well.'

'You call me up, here at my dinner table, all the way

from Rome, and expect me to reveal the most secret kind of information right over the telephone?'

Peter gritted his teeth. 'It's information the Mafia already has. If you don't tell it to me right here and right now, your prize witness is a dead woman. She'll never testify in front of your committee. What's more, her blood will be on your hands.'

'My hands? You're the one who's bungled it. You're the incompetent bastard who's handed the Mafia all it needs to ruin all my efforts, to destroy the work of my committee . . .'

'Calling me names isn't going to save her, Senator. Do you want her alive or do you want her dead?'

'Yeah? Wait just a minute. How do I know you're who you say you are? I'll bet you're not Peter Congdon. You're the Mafia. You think you're going to make me give the witness away.'

'Room 306D in the Shoreham Hotel, right, Senator? Roger S. Desmond's the name, right, Senator? Mother's milk is good for babies, so says Doctor Spock, right, Senator? And if I'm the Mafia and I know all that, you're lost anyway and I wouldn't be phoning you in the first place, right, Senator?'

'All right, but how do I know if I give you this information you can get to her before the Mafia? The way you've bungled . . .'

'You don't know and I don't know but every minute you waste lessens the chances. The Mafia has had the key to the code about forty minutes now and it's a question of how long it'll take them to figure how the code works and then to decode your information. It's going to be touch and go, Senator, but I just might save her for you. What's her name and where is she?'

'I'm taking a big risk giving you this,' the senator snarled. 'If anything happens to that girl, you're responsible. Her life and her future are up to you.

Her blood will be on your hands. Do you understand that?'

'What's her name and address?'

The senator took a deep breath. 'All right,' he said unhappily, 'I have to take you at your word. It's on your head now. The name the girl is going under is Karen Halley. You got that?'

Peter had nothing to write on and nothing to write with. 'Karen Halley,' he said and pictured the name. 'And her address?'

'Sixteen Via dei Saponai. That's D-E-I. Dei. S-A-P-O-N-A-I. She's on the second floor, the apartment on the right—what I guess they call the first floor. Got it?'

'I've got it.'

'In Florence.'

He started. 'In Florence?'

'That's right. You don't think I'd send you to Rome if she was in Rome, do you?'

'I don't know what the hell you'd do, Senator.' Peter rubbed a hand over his face. Florence seemed as far distant as Siberia. 'What's her phone number?'

'She doesn't have a phone.'

'Oh my God. Bono's mistress and she doesn't even have a phone?'

'She's hiding out, you stupid idiot. Who's she going to phone?'

'All right, what's she look like?'

'She's blonde. She's young. I'd say twenty-five. She's pretty.'

'Blonde? I thought she was Italian.'

'There're blonde Italians and anybody can buy a bottle of dye.'

'She's a dyed-blonde Italian then?'

'She's not native Italian either. She's—well, never mind. Regard her as American. I've got her coming in on an American passport. Get used to her as an American.'

'All right, Senator. Karen Halley, phoney blonde, phoney Italian, phoney American passport. Does she know me by my own name?'

'Yes she does. Now it's up to you. And if you don't bring her back alive . . . say, are you in a night club?'

'What?'

'I hear music.'

It was from the Capriccio Night Club on the corner across the street, and the joint was jumping. Peter held the phone away from him towards the open window for a moment and then said into it, 'Senator, you kill me.'

He hung up, put the phone back on the table, then slumped and sat there, weak and trembling. His hands were wet and his head was splitting. He felt sick and he wanted to go to bed. He wanted to rest and sleep and get well.

After a little, he dragged himself to his feet, went to the window and looked down at the street. The music was loud and two couples on the sidewalk were laughing and joking and getting into a tiny car. None of the other cars seemed to be waiting for him.

He pushed the windows closed and turned the knob, but the music still came through. He stared at the welcoming bed but resisted the temptation to sit down again. He had the shakes and the sweats and he felt ill and pale. He had to stay erect.

He opened the door into the hall and the action made him think that it would have been a crowning irony had his assailants locked him in without a key. That, and killing him, were about the only things they hadn't done.

He held onto the rail with both hands going down the stairs and, in the elevator, he sank onto the little red bench before pushing the T for *tèrra* button.

WEDNESDAY 1:50–1:55 A.M.

Vittorio Del Strabo pulled up in a sleek black Mercedes-Benz 280SE convertible five minutes after Peter got out on the street. The top was down, though the night was chilly, and Del Strabo was wearing black loafers and dark slacks, a white wool turtle-neck sweater and a grey tweed jacket. He was a handsome man of thirty with a black pencil moustache and the look of a movie star on holiday. He leaned across to open the door for Peter and said, 'The Brandt Agency has a far-flung net.'

'And it doesn't catch enough fish,' Peter said, getting in gingerly.

Vittorio appraised him quickly. 'You look somewhat the worse for wear. I guess you'll want the aspirin first.'

'Please. And let me borrow a pencil and paper. I don't trust my memory right now.'

Del Strabo handed him a notebook and pencil without question, following it with the box of tablets when Peter tore a sheet from the notebook and tucked it in his pocket. Del Strabo put away his notebook and said, 'Where do we go from here?'

'Farther than I thought. I need the car to get to Florence. Can you put me on the right road out of this town and get home by yourself?'

'Florence?' Del Strabo laughed and started on. 'That's a long ways from here.'

'And I've got to get there fast.' Peter gulped down two of the tablets and pocketed the rest. 'Did you get the other stuff?'

'Oh yes. The passport's blank. It's a replica of an American one but you'll have to fill it in yourself. It's stamped with an entry into Italy and I've got a seal to impress on your picture. You happen to have your picture on you?'

'I don't have anything on me. I was slugged and robbed.'

'By some thieving countrymen of mine, or in the line of business?'

'Business. You got a receipt for me to sign for the money, the car, the gun and all?'

'Everything's in order. We'll take care of it in good time.'

'I'm in a hurry, Vittorio.'

'But of course. And I'll get you there in a hurry.'

'You?' Peter straightened. 'You're not going.'

'Oh, but I am. This is my own car and I'm very proud of it. I wouldn't let anyone drive it who looks as if he couldn't keep it on the road for two blocks.'

'Vittorio, your business with Brandt's is here. In Rome. My business is taking the risks. You can't go.'

'My dear fellow,' Del Strabo said, turning onto the Via Veneto and into the still-busy traffic, 'for four years I've been Brandt's Rome representative. I've been taking orders, collecting information, playing host to agents like you, fulfilling their needs, some of which are illegal—such as yours—taking all manner of risks and having none of the fun of the chase, which is what you have. This is my chance to stop being just a glorified travel agent for Brandt's. This is my chance to escape the dreadful dullness of the family business for a little while. When I heard the trouble you were in, I decided *here's* a man who needs some help. Here's a chance for me to have some fun. Sorry, old man, but if this car is going to Florence, I'm driving it.'

Peter said, 'Look, I'm not going to argue with you. This isn't fun, this is dangerous. I'm not letting you take the risks.'

'You're letting me take the risk of forging passports.

And I agree you shouldn't argue. You don't look in very good shape for an argument.'

'Listen, Del Strabo,' Peter said wearily, 'you don't know this business. You're only a contact. You're on the fringes of the payroll. You haven't had the training for the real work. You haven't been trained how to shoot, how to handle yourself in a fight. You don't have the physical conditioning, the reflexes . . .'

Del Strabo laughed. 'You're very flattering this evening. Really, at this moment I fancy myself a good deal less flimsy and helpless than you are. As for shooting, my good fellow, I hold medals. Trap, skeet, rifle, pistol. It's a family sport. I grew up with guns.'

'And an English governess too, I'll bet.'

Del Strabo enjoyed that one. 'Ah, but you are a good detective. But regard yourself, my friend. Could you find your way to the autostrada from here? Do you have an international driver's permit? Do you even know how to drive this car? If speed and safety are the considerations, I am an essential. With me at the wheel I should have you there by five o'clock. I know the way well.'

'You're a damned fool, Vittorio. You can get yourself killed.'

'And what of it? I regard the time of one's death as of no consequence. All that matters is how one lives. Come on. You can tell me what this business is about as we drive. Then you can sleep and arrive there refreshed. It's really the only way.'

'The business is about the Mafia. How does that interest you?'

Del Strabo only laughed. 'Unpardonable sinners, every one of them. A blot on Sicily and the Italian people. Are we going to shoot any of them? I fortunately brought a gun for each of us.'

'They may shoot us.'

'But of course. I wouldn't expect them to stand still while we took aim. This promises to be most stimulating. Now tell me about it.'

WEDNESDAY 5:10–5:35 A.M.

It was ten after five and the sky was a black overcast when Del Strabo's swift Mercedes came into Florence along the Via Donato Giannotti and flashed across the Piazza Gavinana. Beside him, Peter Congdon was sleeping. He had been asleep for two and a half hours, ever since they had worked their way out of Rome traffic to the autostrada and Peter had finished his tale of what the business was about and what the reception in Florence might be like. Del Strabo had found it fascinating. He said it was like an American movie.

Now, as the Italian turned along the south bank of the Arno, he reached over and shook the sleeping detective. 'Hey, friend Peter. We're almost there.'

Peter stirred once, then sat up quickly, his hand slipping inside his jacket to where a new automatic failed to fit well into his moulded holster. 'What? Where?'

'How dramatic,' Del Strabo laughed. 'Do you always wake up like that?'

Peter looked around at the empty, arc-lighted street, the buildings on Del Strabo's side, the trees, high walls and fences on his. The arcs gave a ghostly glow and everything was still and strange. A motor scooter crossing a bridge far ahead was the only source of sound or movement. Peter didn't answer Del Strabo's question and he didn't take his hand off his gun. 'Is this it?' he asked.

'This is beautiful Florence, the jewel of Italy. I thought you might want to watch the approach. The Arno is beside you, behind those walls, but you can't see it. It goes under that bridge up there.'

'You don't say?' Peter sat up straighter. The black roof of the Mercedes had been put back up when they reached the autostrada and he had to peer through the windows to get an idea of the town.

'On November fourth, a year ago,' Del Strabo said, 'the Arno was twelve feet over our heads right here. Now, though, it's very low. You know, it rained here this past November fourth and the Florentines got very nervous. But it's way down. And very muddy.'

Peter wasn't interested in the Arno. He was studying his surroundings, watching and listening for other cars. 'Yeah, I heard they had a flood,' was all he said.

Del Strabo smiled at him. 'We'll go over the river,' he said. 'But not at this bridge.' He bore left at the approach, fringed the grassy traffic circle and continued down the south bank towards the next bridge. 'By the way, how's your head?'

'Better. But I can still feel it.' On the thought, Peter opened the box and swallowed two more aspirins.

'You only just feel it? Bashed into insensibility and already up and at them. You must have a skull like a rock.'

'I have rocks inside the skull too.'

The wall beside the Arno was low now, with lamp-posts studding the repaired part. Peter put down his window and stared across the river at the shuttered buildings two hundred yards away, glowing a serene yellow in the reflection of hanging street lamps.

'Is that not a beauty to behold?' Del Strabo said, observing him.

Peter said, 'You're kidding. Do you think I'm concerned with beauty at a time like this?'

'What is there to worry about? I'm here.'

'That's one of the worries.'

'You sound like a man with a headache, friend Peter. Do you know where the Via dei Saponai is? Do you have a map of Florence? What would you do if you came here alone, which is what you claim you wish?'

Peter said sheepishly, 'Do you know where it is?'

'I do, but it's a tiny place and I only know because I love Florence.' He gestured. 'In some ways more than Rome and Rome is my home. Rome is for the mighty. It is for the flesh. But Florence is for the soul. So you see? I am thinking of your soul.'

'And I'm thinking of the girl's soul—and trying to keep it in her flesh.'

'And for that you need me. You agree?'

Peter sighed. 'All right, I agree.'

They turned onto the bridge called the Ponte alle Grazie and Del Strabo said, 'We are very near. But everything is very near in Florence.' They passed two policemen in dark uniforms and flat, visored caps, walking together to their posts, and Peter looked at his watch. It was quarter past five. He peered out at the blackness overhead. 'When does it get light around here?'

Del Strabo laughed. 'Do you expect me to know about sunrises, my friend? I haven't been up that early since I was thirteen.' He put a hand on Peter's arm coming off the bridge and his tone changed abruptly. 'Hah, now we're close. Up past this stone building and left. We're almost there.' He turned down a narrow one-way alley that the Mercedes nearly filled. On either side were tiny sidewalks and looming stone and plaster buildings which hung over them threateningly.

Then they were out of the alley in a small paved square containing a scattering of parked cars and a statue over by the Lungarno Generale Diaz, which bordered the north bank of the river. Far away there was the sound of another car but all else was still.

Peter kept his hand inside his jacket, fingering the comfort of the automatic's grip. He waited for Del Strabo to give some indication.

The Mercedes eased across the square and into the opposite alley. Del Strabo's tone was light but wary. 'And here we are, friend Peter. Via dei Saponai. And no enemy in sight.'

'Where's number sixteen?'

'It should be up ahead a little. We can park in front.'

'Not in front. Never park in front of the place you're going to. You might as well advertise.'

Del Strabo laughed. 'Forgive me. I am a beginner in these things.' He backed out into the square and drew up beside one of the standing cars. 'How is this?'

'O.K., but now let's move. And don't slam the door.'

'Relax, friend Peter.'

'When the senator gives me a signed receipt for this dame, then I'll relax like you never saw anybody relax. But not until then.' Peter got out of the car but, when he stood, he swayed so dizzily he had to clutch the door to keep Vittorio from noticing. He steadied himself, closed the door carefully, and started forward, walking resolutely. He crossed to the Via dei Saponai and was feeling sturdier. 'This is number two,' he said, indicating the first tall arched double door with a small number painted in a white square beside it.

'Are you all right, friend Peter?'

Peter clapped Vittorio on the arm. 'I'm great. Let's find number sixteen.'

He led the way with stronger steps and they went up the narrow street, their path lighted by large glass-shaded bulbs thirty feet overhead and the semiellipses of yellow light they cast upon surrounding walls. On the right were apartments with huge wooden doors and shops with metal roll-down shutters locked in place. On the left there was scaffolding against the large industry and commerce building and still-visible signs of flood damage.

Somewhere an alarm clock rang and was silenced. Two motor-bikes sounded in the distance and, with a nearer rattle of wheels, a man came across the Piazza dei Giudici at the end of the street pushing a pedlar's cart. The sky was as black as midnight but Florence was waking up.

They found the entrance to number sixteen and there was no need to ring bells to get in. The double doors were both new, both wide open, and the one on the left was fastened to a temporary stud. In the marble-floored corridor beyond, the flood had eroded the plaster on both walls to a height of five feet and the brickwork was showing. A single, unfrosted bulb lighted a three-step landing where the corridor widened and a staircase started at the left, doubled around and went up overhead. Beyond the stairs the landing dropped three steps to a narrow dark corridor that went through to a courtyard door. The front doors were eight feet tall and the ceiling height inside was another eight feet above that. Short of the landing, a fifteen-foot ladder was propped against the wall, with room to spare, and on the landing was a half-empty sack of Casal Bosca, a small pile of sand, some rubbish and some tools.

'Well,' Del Strabo said, indicating the open doors. 'That makes it easy for us.'

'And I hope only for us.' Peter sought to close them but they had not yet been fitted with hardware. He went on to the landing and took the stairs two at a time. On the next floor there was another unfrosted bulb and two apartments, left and right. The one on the right was by the stairs and there was a buzzer beside it, but no nameplate. Peter pressed the buzzer as Del Strabo caught up with him and he could hear it sounding faintly from somewhere inside. They waited and Peter nervously unholstered and reholstered his gun. He pressed the buzzer again, insistently, then put his ear to the panels and listened for sounds of movement. His headache was gone, everything was gone except his concentration on the sound of stirrings behind that door.

There were none.

Del Strabo, watching Peter and trying to listen too, shook his head. 'Not so good?' he whispered. 'Maybe we aren't first after all.'

'We've got to find out and I don't have anything to pick the lock with.' He rang once more, a long ring this time, and listened for half a minute. He tried the door but it didn't budge. He didn't think it would.

'There's nothing here,' he said and turned to the stairs again. 'Let's see what's out back.'

The door at the end of the narrow dark corridor opened into a moderate-sized courtyard surfaced with paving stones and planted with shrubs. There was no lights and with the black, overcast sky, it was, at first, impossible to see anything. All that was visible was the glint of light behind the shutters of a third-floor window across the way.

Then, as their eyes grew more accustomed, they could make out a tall shuttered window to the right of the door and, above it, twenty feet up, a shorter window with the shutters open. 'That's it, up there,' Peter whispered.

'Nice of her,' Del Strabo whispered back. 'She leaves the outside door open and now the window.'

'I'm told she's not Italian. Maybe shutters . . .'

'And we're not angels either. She leaves the window open, but how do we get up to it?'

'Let's try the ladder.'

'It won't reach.'

'Let's try anyway.' He went back for it and Del Strabo helped him carry it out. When they set it up, the top rested against the shutters of the gound-floor window. Del Strabo said, 'It's not high enough. I told you you wouldn't be able to reach.'

Peter, studying the situation, was unperturbed. 'I can if you're as strong as you tell me you are.'

'Oh. I'm to pitch you in?'

'No. You're to follow me up and then I'll stand on your shoulders and you'll ease up another rung or two . . .'

'I suppose that's what's called American ingenuity. Have you stopped to think what would happen if you fall?'

'Of course not. Come on. You wanted to be a part of this. Let's go—and be quiet.' Peter went up the ladder, climbing until he had to bend a little to keep hold of the top rung. Del Strabo came up behind him. 'Now what?'

'Now my feet on your shoulders. Hold steady.'

Del Strabo braced himself but wavered a little when Peter's foot, carefully placed on his shoulder, started to take weight. 'I should say one thing I'm not trained in,' he grunted softly, 'is acrobatics.' He adjusted to the pressure and Peter carefully set his other foot in place on Del Strabo's other shoulder, his hands holding tight to the top rung. 'All right. You got me?'

'Yes,' Del Strabo panted. 'But I wish you'd dieted.'

'Next time you'll know enough to stay home.'

'I wouldn't miss this for life or limb, and I suspect life and limb are both involved. Now what?'

'I'm going to let go of my rung and put my hands against the wall. Can you balance me and move up a couple of rungs?'

'All right, let's give it a try.' Del Strabo put one foot up and struggled to raise his body and Peter's evenly.

Above him, Peter clutched for handholds and found none. The window ledge was near, but out of reach.

Del Strabo started a second rung and his body moved closer to the building. Peter had to press flat to keep from falling backwards. He groped above him and started to lose all sense of up and down. He wavered and for a moment thought he'd send them both crashing onto the stones below, but a last desperate hand got hold of the window ledge. He swallowed and tried to shake off the pounding of his heart. 'I got it,' he whispered to Del Strabo.

'And you can give a man quite a turn in the process. But you do weigh less now and that's a blessing. What is the next step?'

'Come up higher and give me some purchase.'

'That's a word I don't know but I follow the thought.' He moved up a rung and Peter was able to get hold of the inside of the sill. He could do it himself after that. 'O.K.,' he whispered. 'Go on down.'

He braced his feet against the side of the building and pulled himself up till his head was through the window and his body doubled over the sill. The window was curtained and opened inward and he pushed the sections wider, but it was too dark to see and there was no sound to hear.

He straightened, raising himself like an athlete on parallel bars, and swung a leg over the ledge. In another moment he was all the way inside and standing, listening to the panting of his own breath. The room was as dark as the outside but his eyes were accustomed and he could faintly make out the lines of a bed and something in the bed. Closer was a lamp on a table. He reached out and turned it on.

The bulb was bright and its glare revealed the half-covered body of a girl in a filmy nightgown lying on her back with her arms spread. For a moment she lay motionless and then, shocked by the light, she was suddenly sitting bolt upright, staring at him with great wide eyes and open mouth.

She was blonde, as Gorman had said, and she was young and she was pretty. But what Peter had not anticipated was *how* pretty. The picture he had formed was of a girl with the brittle, coarse and painted prettiness of the common trollop. He didn't know Joe Bono but he could guess his taste and he could also guess, from what he had learned, the kind of girl he had taken up with: hard and world-weary, a girl who would use her position shrewdly and sell her information dearly. Right from the start he had determined that Bono's mistress wasn't ratting on the Mafia to avenge her murdered lover. She was doing it for a United States passport and a healthy grubstake in a new country. She would take her chances with the Mafia not for love, but only if the price was right.

But this girl's face was beautifully structured and the pale blonde of her hair was natural. If she didn't look fresh out of boarding school, and if terror softened her expression, her face still had nothing of the ruthless, flintlike quality Peter had expected. That aspect of her nature was carefully hidden.

Her body was as beautiful as her face, lithe, firm, full, and teasingly visible through the sheer and expensive nightgown she wore—an obvious souvenir of her past with Bono. It struck Peter, as he looked at her, that she could have done far better in life than sell herself out as shabby mistress to a Mafia hood. If villas were what she wanted, she could have married millionaires. But that was none of his business and none of his concern except that, because she could have done better and hadn't, his contempt for her was that much greater.

'What do you want?' she asked him in a terrified whisper.

She thought he was the Mafia come to kill her. She sat there, clutching the mattress, frozen with terror, wishing, perhaps, she had never met a man named Bono, or heard of a senator named Gorman. The villas didn't matter to her now, any more than the inadequate cover of her nightgown, since modesty—if she were, in fact, modest—earns no homage in the palace of death.

But, despite his contempt, Peter still had pity and he wanted to remove that stricken look from her face. 'Relax, kid,' he said. 'I'm not going to hurt you. I'm Peter Congdon.'

The name didn't register. She still remained frozen and he tried again. 'I'm the man Senator Gorman sent to protect you. Remember? You're supposed to be expecting me.'

Her eyes stayed wide and fixed. 'Not here I wasn't.'

He took a small, conciliatory step and she shrank away. 'What are you going to do to me?'

'I'm going to get you out of here. The Mafia is hot on your trail.'

The buzzer sounded and both turned to the open doorway and the dark hall beyond. She looked back at Peter and he put a finger to his lips. 'That's reinforcements,' he said. 'I'll be right back.'

He went quickly through the hall, threw on the overhead light in the sitting room and approached the door. 'Yes?' he whispered against the panels and drew away.

'Peter? It's Vittorio.'

'The Brandt Agency . . .' Peter said.

The other man laughed. 'Many fish. Many fish. You are a careful one.'

Peter slid back a pair of bolts, top and bottom, which, with the regular lock, formed the girl's protection against her lover's killers. He turned the key and opened the door wide enough to let Del Strabo through. 'See anyone?' he asked, rebolting the door as before.

'Nothing. Is the girl here?'

Peter nodded soberly. 'She's here.'

'Alive?'

'Alive. A bit frightened, perhaps, but after all . . .' He led the way back.

In the bedroom the girl had left the bed and covered her near-nakedness with a quilted robe from a clothes cabinet. She was standing against the wall between the cabinet and bed, her hands behind her, almost but not quite like an animal at bay, and her eyes darted first to Peter and then to Vittorio.

'Here she is,' Peter said to him. 'Alive and healthy. Miss Karen Halley. At least that's the name on her passport. Karen, this is your other benefactor, Signore Vittorio Del Strabo.'

Vittorio bowed with an old-world flair and said with Latin gallantry, 'The treasures of Florence have been exceeded by the beauty of a woman.'

Miss Halley did not reply in kind. She straightened a little and brought her right hand out from behind her back. In it she held a snub-nosed Colt revolver and she aimed it at the two of them. The soft, frightened-doe look was gone from her face. A hard, cold contempt was in it now and when she spoke her voice held the icy edge of authority. 'Put your hands on top of your heads,' she said. 'Both of you.'

WEDNESDAY 5:35–5:50 A.M.

The two men slowly obeyed and Vittorio said, 'Peter, my friend, you know the most charming ladies.'

'This one happens to be addled.' To Karen he said, 'Look, we don't have any time to waste. Every minute increases your danger.'

'You're the one who's in danger,' she replied. 'I'll kill you if you move and I'm a very good shot. I will also shoot you if you don't answer my questions. Who sent you here?'

The quality in her voice said she was capable of doing exactly what she threatened and Peter felt like a fool. He had been taken in by her helpless terror. He had thought her harmless and turned his back. He forgot this was the ruthless and materialistic girl who would sell such wares as were worth her life and charge such prices as made senators bleed. 'Senator Gorman sent us,' he told her coldly. 'You should be expecting me. At least he said you were.'

Her voice was colder than his. 'I'm expecting a man named Peter Congdon. Since I do not know what Peter Congdon looks like, I'm not about to believe that a man who climbs through my bedroom window in the middle of the night is Peter Congdon just because he says he is . . .'

'We rang your bell. We got no answer. I tried the windows because I thought you were dead or kidnapped.'

One corner of her mouth curled. 'You rang my doorbell at this hour? Even if I'd heard it I wouldn't have answered. What kind of a fool do you take me for? And who's your Italian friend? You slipped up there. Either you forgot or you never knew that Peter Congdon was supposed to come alone.' She turned her attention to Del Strabo. 'How high up do you rate in the Mafia, Mr. Del Strabo? Will you be missed if you're dead?'

Vittorio said, 'I really wish you'd believe my friend here. As for me, I am from Rome, not Sicily.'

'We'll find out very quickly who Mr. Congdon is,' she replied. She turned back to Peter. 'Senator Gorman gave you a password to identify yourself. What is it?'

Peter said helplessly, 'How about, "Mother's milk is good for babies"?'

'That won't do it. Now, whatever-your-name-is, you'll answer my questions. Who sent you, and don't tell me Senator Gorman.'

He tried again. 'Look, I never got the envelope that had the password in it. Believe me. The Mafia has the envelope. They're the ones who know the password now. They kidnapped the man who was going to give it to me.'

'Let me see your passport and be very careful how you reach for it.'

Peter swallowed. 'I don't have my passport. The Mafia robbed me too. Look.' He bent forward slowly and opened his hands to reveal the top of his head. 'See where they hit me?'

The girl was not impressed. 'I think you came here to kill me, the two of you,' she said.

'We came here to warn you,' Peter insisted. The girl was holding the gun very steadily and he tried to read her intentions. He suspected the itchiness of her trigger finger was proportional to her fears that he was a Mafia agent. 'Look, Angel,' he pleaded. 'If there's any chance I'm not lying, you'd do well to consider it.'

'There's that chance,' the girl replied. 'A pretty faint one,' she added contemptuously. 'I could shoot you and call the police, but just because there's the slight chance you aren't the Mafia, only some petty thief, or even Peter Congdon, I think I might let you go. But you're going to be taught a lesson, both of you. Take off your clothes.'

Peter stared at her. 'What?'

'Everything. When you're stripped I'll turn you out the door.'

Peter half lowered one hand from his head but put it back quickly at a threatening thrust of the gun. 'Look, Angel, fun's fun and all that, but this is going a little far.'

Karen stood firm and unmoved. 'You're going out on the streets naked—if you go out of here at all. You have the choice. And I'll tell you, it's against my better judgment to let you go at all. Take off your clothes!'

Vittorio said, 'The lady has very original ideas, friend Peter, but I think we'd better humour her. Her patience is wearing thin.'

'She's a nut,' Peter said and lowered his hands slowly in the face of the gun. He unbuttoned his jacket and started to peel it off. When his holster came into view the girl said, 'Hold it.' Then she said, 'Go ahead slowly.' She indicated Vittorio. 'You wait till he's through.'

Peter went on, slipping his left arm out of the jacket and, at that moment, the door buzzer sounded.

'The Mafia,' Vittorio snapped and the girl, shaken, turned her head.

Peter flung his jacket at her and leaped for the gun. It was neatly done and he had the weapon wrenched from her hand in a moment, but he had the uneasy feeling she could have shot him if she'd wanted.

Now, however, he was in control, holding the girl pinned, her gun arm behind her back. 'That's the Mafia,' he whispered. 'Do you get me? The Mafia!'

She was looking up at him wide-eyed and uncertain. Now she was the way he had first seen her, all feminine and vulnerable, the hapless, the helpless, the beautiful damsel in distress. But Peter knew better and he didn't play sucker twice.

The buzzer rang again, insistently. 'Is there a back

way out of here?' Peter asked, but he knew before she shook her head that there was not. Vittorio lowered his hands and adjusted his jacket. 'We seem to be in a bit of a trap.'

'They're going to be in the trap,' Peter answered abruptly. He threw the girl's gun on the bed and gripped her arms with both hands. 'If you play it right, nothing will happen. Come with me and say what I tell you to say.'

He walked her through to the sitting room and drew his own gun. 'Ask who it is,' he whispered to her. 'But don't stand in front of the door. They might shoot through it.'

He pulled her to the side by the knob and Vittorio stood on the other side by the shuttered front windows. He had his own gun out and his face was set, the twinkle gone from his eye. This was the kind of excitement he had been looking for and now his eyes were dark and glowing.

The buzzer rang a third time and when it stopped, Karen, who had been silent and unresisting, said, close to the panels, 'Who is it?'

From the other side a low male voice said, 'Peter Congdon. I've come to protect you from the Mafia.'

Peter felt a certain chill at the mention of his name. This was it and for real. Karen, without prompting, said, 'What do you want at this hour?' and drew back.

It was good—with just the right amount of annoyance in it, and Peter raised an eyebrow at her. At least she could pull her weight.

'Let me in. The Mafia's on your trail. We've got to get out.'

Karen looked up at Peter for her next cue. His grip was painful but neither noticed. 'Ask for the password,' he murmured.

She leaned forward obediently. 'What's the password?'

'The Battle Hymn of the Republic. Quick. Open up.'

She nodded to Peter and he whispered, 'Tell him to slide his passport under the door.'

'Let me see your passport,' she said. 'Slide it under the door.'

The man outside said impatiently. 'I gave you the password. Stop stalling. The Mafia will be here in a minute.'

'The password isn't enough,' she answered with the same ice-edged authority she had used behind her gun in the bedroom. 'I want more proof. If you're Peter Congdon, show me your passport.'

The man muttered and there was a small delay. Then a thin, blue-grey folder came through under the door and Peter snatched it up. It was his own passport all right. He showed it to the girl, pointing from the picture to his face, and she nodded.

Outside, the voice said, 'Hurry it up, will you? It's life and death.'

'Tell him it's all right,' Peter whispered. 'Then go back and get your gun. If they get past us, don't make them strip. Kill them.'

She said to the door, 'All right, Peter,' then tiptoed quickly away over the thin rug towards the hall. Peter indicated the locks and nodded at Vittorio. He flattened himself beside the door while Vittorio slipped the top and bottom bolts, turned the lock and, keeping well back, pulled the door open.

No more than a six-inch gap appeared before the man outside hit the panels with his shoulder and charged through. The door burst wide, striking Vittorio and knocking him back. Peter, having to rush his swing, didn't get a clean hit when he brought his gun butt down on the man's head.

It was good enough, however, to drop him on his face and Peter whirled to the outer hall. A heavily built, narrow-eyed youth with thick features and an ugly twist to his mouth was standing there with a gun in his hand, ready to back up the play. He had taken a step forward when his companion charged, but now he stepped back in shock and whipped up the gun by instinct.

It never went off. Peter's Italian automatic roared and burst flame and the heavy wallop of the bullet striking was mingled with the blast of the explosion.

The man's gun flew from his hand and went clattering down the marble stairs. The man himself crashed against the frame of the opposite door, spun around and landed on his back, his head striking the red-tiled floor with a crack that echoed against the walls.

Peter, flattening himself against the doorway, took a careful peek down the stairs as the gun bounced to a stop on the landing. In the dim light of the bulb a face was visible down there at the turn, peering around the corner, looking up. It vanished the moment it saw Peter and quick steps scurried down the rest of the stairs. It was the thin man with the dead eyes who had ridden the jet from New York and he was rushing to report.

Peter lowered his gun and turned back. The man he had felled had pulled himself to his hands and knees and Peter spotted him just as Vittorio smashed him flat with the butt of his own gun. Vittorio looked up and smiled. 'I thought I'd like to get in on things a bit myself, you know.'

Peter laughed shortly and there was a harsh note in it. He didn't like danger, he didn't like tension, he didn't like killing. He tucked the gun away and shivered. Vittorio stepped over his own victim and looked into the hall. 'Well, you have had quite a time,' he said. 'He's dead of course?'

'Very dead. That's a powerful weapon you gave me.'

'He's not bleeding very much.'

'Not in front. It's all inside or out his back.'

'Are these the only two?'

'There're more outside, so we can't waste time. And I expect somebody will call the police.' He gestured back at the sitting room. 'Clean that guy's pockets, I'll take this one.' He went out to the dead man, removed his wallet, keys and papers, anything that would identify him. He found the man was wearing his stolen wrist-watch and strapped it back on his own wrist. Throughout, his actions were deft and quick and he faced the stairs to watch and listen. There was no interruption. The Mafia didn't return and no one in the building dared to open a door.

When he re-entered the sitting room, Vittorio was still searching the unconscious man and Karen, gun at her side, was leaning forward watching. Peter locked and bolted the door and said to the girl, 'I thought I told you to stay in the bedroom.'

She shook her head. 'I preferred to back you up from the hall.'

She was a cool one, all right—lithe, lovely and capable. It had been a shoot-'em-up with murder and mayhem, and her the prize, and she hadn't greyed a hair.

Peter watched her for a moment. Maybe to the mistress of a Mafia leader this was nothing. Who knew what she had seen and done? Well, she'd be doing a lot more. He said to her, 'Get your purse and whatever you can carry. We're going out the window.'

'The window?'

'Right now. The Mafia's watching the front and the police will be coming. We're going out the back, across the court and into the next street. How about it, Vittorio? Do you feel athletic?'

'Oh quite. I must say the pair of you are the two most original thinkers I've ever encountered.' He got up with the loot from his search. 'Do we just, ah, leave him here?'

'I wasn't going to kill him if that's what you mean. You have his gun and everything?'

'His gun, his wallet, your wallet, your gun—I expect this is yours—plus a lot of papers I haven't had a chance to look at.'

Peter picked up the revolver. It was his. He put it in his holster, switching the automatic to a side pocket. He picked out his wallet and health certificate and Vittorio tucked the other things in his own pockets. They went back to the bedroom and Peter looked out the window. The sky was still black except for a lone star flickering between the clouds. Around the courtyard there was enought light from Karen's window to make the surrounding windows faintly visible. All still had their shutters latched, but eyes might be peering through the slats.

Peter pulled their own shutters closed, then seized the bedding and started to knot it. Karen, getting clothes from her wardrobe, said, 'What are you doing?'

'Making a rope that will get us down to our ladder.'

'I've got a rope.' She reached into the bottom of her wardrobe and pulled out a new twenty-metre coil of two-centimetre line. 'I got it just in case.'

'Angel, you think of everything.' Peter threw the blankets aside and shoved the bed to the window. He tied the rope about its middle and switched off the lamp. The room went dark but there was enough light coming from the sitting room for them to get around. Peter pushed the shutters wide again and pitched the other end of the line out into the night.

Karen came onto the bed beside him. 'Here's my purse,' she said, keeping her voice low. 'Give me a couple of minutes to get into some clothes.'

'Get into anything but make it fast.'

She went into the bathroom, but she had no sooner

shut the door when the wail of a far-off siren cut the air. Peter whirled. 'Karen.'

She had heard it too and she came out quickly with only her nightgown on.

'Grab a coat. Get on a coat. We've got to go.'

She ran and pulled one out of the wardrobe and Vittorio helped her into it. She climbed onto the bed where Peter was testing the rope. 'My purse?'

'I've got it.'

'What do we do?'

'Put your arms around my neck and hang on.' Peter straddled the window sill. 'Get on my back and put your feet out the window. There's a ladder down about five feet. If you can get onto that, it'll be easier. If not, hang onto my neck.'

She said, 'No, you go first. You find the ladder. Then I'll come down the rope after.'

'Can you. . . .'

'Don't you think a girl can hold onto a rope? It'd be a damned sight safer than hanging onto your neck.'

The sirens were coming close and Del Strabo said, 'I wish you two would get on with it. I'm going to be the last to leave, you know, and I don't really want to go down with the bloody ship.'

'All right, we'll try it.' Peter put Karen's purse strap between his teeth, slipped over the side, holding the rope, and eased his way down to the ladder. She came out next, straddling the sill and testing the line. She let herself over the side but, when her legs swung free, her hands slipped and she started down fast. Peter braced to try to hold her but she caught herself and stopped just short of him. 'Oh, God,' she muttered.

'You all right?'

'Now I am. Hurry up, your friend wants to leave the ship.'

Peter went down the ladder and she followed closely.

Above them, Vittorio climbed onto the rope and started his descent. Peter gave Karen back her purse and went to hold the ladder.

The sirens were loud and near now and one wailed to a stop out front. Vittorio stepped off the final rung and joined the pair, grinning. 'By the skin of our teeth, you might say. Shall we be off?'

They groped their way among the plantings and found an unlocked door on the other side of the court. Above, lights were on in three of the windows but no one pushed open the shutters to look down.

They went through the hall of the other building, unlocked the big front doors and looked out into another narrow street. A motor scooter and two cars roared through it together and then the street was momentarily empty. Peter led the way into it and they hurried after the cars. 'Now we're going to have to find a place to hide out,' he said to Karen. 'Who do you know in this town?'

She shook her head. 'No one.'

Vittorio said, 'Perhaps I can be of service. Did I not say I knew the route to Florence well? There is a young lady here who will be glad to assist us. Come, follow me.'

WEDNESDAY 5:55–7:50 A.M.

Vittorio took over, leading them the way they were heading. They came out by a movie theatre and entered another narrow street that ran along the side of the

Palazzo Vecchio. Vittorio crossed them to the palace side to get around a coffee shop crowded with laughing and talking labourers who had gathered for a cup before work. Ahead, at the entrance to the Piazza della Signoria, the Loggia dei Lanzi faced them, its ghostlike statues looming like young giants partying on an outsized porch.

When they reached it and entered the square, they stayed close to the steps of the Loggia dei Lanzi and hurried to the alley on the other side that separated it from the outdoor restaurants beyond. There, Vittorio stopped and touched Peter's arm. 'Look back,' he said and pointed.

Peter turned, his hand slipping inside the lapel of his jacket. But there were no approaching police, no onrushing cars or motorbikes. There was only the silent bell tower of the old palace, black against a near-black sky, with Venus high and Jupiter higher beside it. Below the tower, where the façade was lighted, the great statues shone pale and white in the yellow street-lights.

The two motor scooters came up the alley beside the palace and cut across the square away from the trio. 'You mean them?' Peter asked.

'No, no,' Vittorio chided. 'The palace. That lovely tower.' He shook his head. 'But for me, you would have crossed the square and never have seen it. Surely you would not want to visit Florence and not see the Palazzo Vecchio, would you?'

Peter stared at him. 'Say, what are you, some kind of travelogue? Do you know what we're here for?'

Vittorio laughed and led them down the alley. 'Just a little food for the soul. I fear for your soul, friend Peter.'

'And I fear for this girl's hide. I don't want to sightsee, I want to get her under cover.'

'Do not worry. We're almost there.' Vittorio led them out into a slightly wider alley, turned left a few steps and then right alongside the Uffizi towards the river. He turned them again into another narrow street, this one short, diagonal, and overhung with low arches. They went past the stench of an open urinal and Vittorio had them hug the wall. 'It's the Ponte Vecchio ahead,' he muttered. 'There might be traffic.' No sooner were the words out of his mouth than a green and black police car with flashing blue light streaked by the end of the street going up the Lungarno Generale Diaz along the river towards the Via dei Saponai. 'You see?' he said. 'The Florence police are active.'

They reached the road, crossed to the colonnaded walk on the river side and approached the Ponte Vecchio. A car turned the corner and the driver twisted to stare at Karen. Vittorio said, 'He has taste,' and shepherded the two across the intersection onto the Lungarno Acciaioli which ran along the river down to the next bridge. It was a barricaded street with wall repairs going on, and only a narrow lane for pedestrians was open. 'You see?' Vittorio said proudly. 'No accidental police cars can come upon us here. Is that not smart?'

'Very smart. Where does the girl live?'

'Right up near the end of this street.'

It was six o'clock when they reached the apartment. The sky was still a mottled collection of black patches and white-black clouds, but way up the river, beyond the Ponte Vecchio, a streak of sky was whitening under the clouds. Day was starting to rise.

The apartment building was near the farther corner and one of the big double doors was propped open with a wedge. Vittorio led them up two wide flights of stone stairs that doubled back around landings and fitted a key in the door at the top. He said, a little self-consciously, 'She's a very good friend of mine.'

They entered a small but luxuriously furnished sitting room with two front windows and Vittorio switched on lights and rebolted the door. 'Now if you'll excuse me for a moment,' he said, 'I'll explain our presence to our hostess.' He disappeared down a narrow hall and Peter was left with Karen.

She moved to the windows and went through the task of unfastening the swivel catches, pulling them open and pushing the shutters wide. The view was the Arno but it was a black river with only a scattering of lights showing in the windows of the wall of buildings on the other side.

Peter watched her, sizing up, for the first time, this mistress he'd been sent to fetch. And she wasn't just any old common garden variety of mistress, he decided. She was a super-special, sexy-as-hell mistress. She was, in fact, one sexy-as-hell female. It was the animal way she moved. It was the way she looked at you out of the corners of her eyes. It was her face and her figure. Just the way she was built spelled trouble.

Then add to that the cool way she could watch Mafia men get slugged and shot, the cold-blooded way she could point a gun, and the ice-hearted bargain she drove with Gorman and she spelled trouble in spades. He had assumed Bono had bought her for his slave, that she had sold herself for a villa on the Tiber and a cushy life of luxury, with payment on demand when Bono chose to come collect. Now he wasn't so sure. Maybe Bono had been the slave. Maybe she was the enticer and Bono the enticed, struggling to hold her attentions, keep her contented, and save her for himself. Maybe this was why Joe Bono told her everything. She had pumped him for it. She would have started laying the foundations for her future right from the beginning, gathering material for blackmail against the time—not when Bono would be murdered—but when he might try to leave her. She was a pretty girl, all right, the kind you'd just love to jump into bed with, but, Peter decided, that would be about the worst mistake a man could make.

However, she was Gorman's headache, not his. Let the senator worry about her. Peter's concern was getting her delivered. He went to a round, covered table with a large lamp on it and began laying out the articles he'd taken from the dead man. The haul was slight. There were only three letters, a wallet and a key ring.

Karen came over in curiosity. 'What have you got?'

Peter, without a word, gave her the three letters to read. He himself concentrated on the wallet. There was a card in it identifying the man as Antonio Marchesi. There were twelve 10,000-lire notes and four 1000-lire notes. In addition, there was a passport-sized photograph of Karen, the code key Peter had written out in Gorman's study, and a folded $8\frac{1}{2}'' \times 11''$ sheet of white paper containing Gorman's message. Under the five-letter groups had laboriously been pencilled: 'THE GIRLS NAME IS KAREN HALLEY YOU WILL FIND HER IN FLORENCE AT SIXTEEN VIA DEI SAPONAI UP ONE FLIGHT OF STAIRS THE RIGHTHAND APARTMENT SHE HAS NO PHONE GO TO HER IMMEDIATELY USE YOUR RIGHT NAME AND SAY BATTLE HYMN OF THE REPUBLIC FOR THE PASSWORD THE ENCLOSED PICTURE WILL IDENTIFY HER SHE SPEAKS ENGLISH BOOK PASSAGE ON FIRST AVAILABLE PLANE BACK TO STATES WIRE ME YOUR ARRIVAL TIME AND PLACE IN CODE AND I WILL MEET YOU WITH ADEQUATE PROTECTION TAKE CARE OF HER FOR THE MAFIA HAS PUT A HUNDRED THOUSAND DOLLAR PRICE ON HER HEAD GOOD LUCK R G GORMAN.'

Karen started reading the note over Peter's shoulder and he handed it to her. 'What're the letters about?'

'They're from his family in Sicily saying, "Why don't you write?" '

'Why doesn't he?'

'I don't know. Do you want me to read them to you?'

'Not if they don't say anything about you.'

'They don't.' She read the rest of Gorman's message

and said, 'So this is how they found me. How did they get hold of it?'

'They took it from the guy Gorman sent it to.'

'How?'

'They beat him up, of course. You ought to know. Isn't that standard operating procedure?'

She flushed. 'I mean how did they know who he was?'

'Gorman is supposed to have got him his job.'

'Oh. And then they caught you and injured you too? I mean your head. That was their doing?'

'They were just having a little fun. You know how it is with them. From now on, though, I think they're going to want some of my blood.'

Vittorio quietly closed a door and returned down the hall. 'The signorina will be out presently. She is a little surprised at the interruption but not at all resentful.' He took stock of Karen admiringly. 'Yes, and I think she'll have something you can wear, Miss Halley. You look about the same size.'

She gave him a nice smile and said, 'I'm really sorry I was going to make you walk the plank.'

'It would have been awkward,' Vittorio agreed. 'We may thank the Mafia for small blessings.'

Peter wanted to see what Del Strabo had taken from the unconscious man and Vittorio added his hoard to the items on the table. This included a gun, Peter's box of bullets, Peter's packet of travellers cheques, some $920 worth, and a loose wad of money—112,500 lire in notes and some change. There was no wallet and no identification.

'Quite a haul for an evening's work,' Vittorio said. 'Are you sure Brandt wouldn't like me for an active agent? I can't remember enjoying a night so much.'

'Brandt wouldn't buy you. He likes his agents to enjoy their work, but you revel in it. And besides that, in the middle of a game of hide-and-seek, you stop to sightsee.'

Vittorio laughed. 'But why, when one travels through life, should he not sit by the windows?'

Vittorio's ladyfriend came out then, a dark-haired, attractive and smart-looking girl. She was wearing a peach négligé and high-heeled mules, lipstick and freshly combed hair. Vittorio introduced her in Italian as Maria Botticelli and told Peter that she didn't speak English and that she was working in the Pitti Palace helping in the restoration of manuscripts damaged by the flood. 'Though she is very—shall we say, "All woman", she is also an expert on book bindings and the preservation of—what do you say, illuminated manuscripts?' He grew heartier. 'She is also a good cook and is delighted at the opportunity to prepare us some breakfast.'

Breakfast turned out not to be a cooking meal. Maria Botticelli only used the stove to brew a pot of coffee, heat a pitcher of milk and warm some croissants. The rest of the meal consisted of hard rolls, sweet butter and a jar of jam.

They ate it at a gate-leg table and, since Peter and Maria were totally unable to communicate and there was little to say, a transistor radio was set on the table, which gave them first some music and then the news. The news programme was only background noise to Peter but, as he poured another round of coffee, he became aware that his companions had stopped to listen. Karen was solemn-faced and Vittorio intent. Maria was watching them both in wonder.

The tone of the radio voice changed and Vittorio relaxed a little and smiled. 'Well, the cat's in the fire, if that's the expression. And I see our leader is puzzled.' He grinned at the girls and went on to Peter, 'It appears that a dead body and a seriously injured man have been found in an apartment on the Via dei Saponai. The apartment was otherwise empty but neighbours have identified the tenant as a Miss Karen Halley. Others, who are called "witnesses", claim that also involved is a man named Peter Congdon, an American. Police have been given a description of the couple and that has just been put on the air. The police want very much to talk to them.' He reached out to clap Peter on the shoulder. 'My friend, you are now famous.'

'You forgot about the reward,' Karen said.

'Oh, yes. They want you so much they are offering a reward of three hundred thousand lire. That, in American money, is close to five hundred dollars.'

'That, in any kind of money, is peanuts,' Peter snorted.

'It's more than they're asking for me,' Vittorio said. 'I wasn't even mentioned.'

'That's because the skinny guy didn't know you were there. He only got a look at me.'

Karen said, 'Now they've got the police on their side. How're we going to get out of here?'

Vittorio shrugged. 'Oh, along about the time Maria goes to work, I'll wander over and pick up my car. We shouldn't have much trouble.'

'I mean how do we leave the country? They'll be watching for our passports.'

Peter wasn't worried about that. 'Vittorio will get us false ones. We'll be Mr. and Mrs. Robert Gorman or something. How good a description did they have of us?'

Vittorio said, 'Moderately good of the girl, very good of you. The other tenants might not have seen much of Miss Halley, but the thin man you talk about obviously knows you very well.'

Maria was watching intently but the words meant nothing. Vittorio started speaking to her in Italian and Karen listened. From Vittorio's gestures, Peter gathered he was explaining how they'd climbed in and out of Miss Halley's window, bashed and shot people. Maria's eyes widened and she started talking back rapidly.

Karen said to Peter, 'She's afraid the police will come here. She's afraid she'll be arrested.'

Vittorio put a hand on her shoulder and spoke soothingly. He said to Peter, 'She's upset. She didn't know I was so virile. I'm assuring her that we'll leave just as soon as we can and I'm also asking if she can outfit Miss Halley with some clothes.'

The outfitting of Miss Halley was accomplished while Vittorio and Peter had after-breakfast smokes, a cigarette for Peter, a long, very thin cigar for Vittorio. Karen reappeared in a neutral print, quite tight and quite low-cut, the sort of thing Vittorio bought Maria to salvage manuscripts in.

Maria was also dressed and she was soberer now, almost politely distant from Karen and Peter and respectful but not loving towards Vittorio. Her mood had changed with the news broadcast and she was trying to go through the amenities without really proffering aid and comfort to wanted criminals.

Peter noted the change and read its reasons. While the girls were dressing he had nodded towards the bedroom and said to Vittorio, 'Just how safe are we here?'

'She won't talk,' Vittorio was quick to assure him, but he added, 'I'll leave with her and come back with the car. I think we ought to get out of Florence.'

Vittorio and Maria went off at quarter of eight, a good hour before she would normally depart. Conditions were awkward and uncomfortable in the apartment and there was no point in prolonging them. Good-byes and thank-yous were said and Maria wished Karen good luck and tried to mean it. Vittorio, who was the only one whose spirits refused to be dampened, said airily, 'Don't move till I return. In fifteen minutes, half an hour at the most, we'll be on our way back to Rome.'

Karen said, 'What about roadblocks?'

Vittorio laughed. 'That's easy, no? You may look like

Miss Halley, but I don't look like Mr. Congdon. So you ride with me and friend Peter can hide in the boot.' He nudged Peter. 'A smashing idea, what?'

Peter said dryly, 'I've got a better idea. I'll be a travel guide and you can be a sightseer.'

Vittorio roared at that one and went down the stairs laughing. Peter double-bolted the door and joined Karen at the window. Day had finally dawned in Florence and the sun was half an hour high, throwing low-angled rays on the solid phalanx of buildings sunk into the southern side of the Arno. The Ponte Vecchio was in shadow, the Ponte San Trinita in sunshine, and over its trio of arches cars, trucks and motorcycles moved in a noisy, constant stream. The river itself was low and lazy quiet, its colour a deep and unattractive brown. Across the way, on a little grassy spit, two swans slept.

Below, Vittorio and Maria appeared and turned left towards the Ponte Vecchio. The construction railings so hemmed them in on the narrow sidewalk that they had to walk single file. Vittorio turned to look up and gave a cheery wave. He had worked all day, driven all night, climbed ladders, fought Mafia assassins and eluded police dragnets, yet he looked as untarnished as new gilt and eager to tackle the next twenty-four hours. Peter hoped he would stay that way.

WEDNESDAY 7:50–8:10 A.M.

Karen's return wave to Vittorio, Peter noted, was outgoing and friendly. She seemed to like him and was less reserved than with Peter. But Vittorio, on his part, accepted her more readily. He appeared not to concern himself with her past nor share Peter's contempt for what she was and what she stood for. Vittorio, in fact, seemed to enjoy having her around. For Peter, just because she was such a sexy dish and made maximum use of the fact, her presence was an annoyance and a danger he had to guard against. He couldn't wait to get Bono's self-serving mistress across the Atlantic and into Gorman's hot little hands. And that moment would be before the day was out if he could possibly manage it.

She turned away when Peter closed the window, going back to the gate-leg table and another news broadcast. It was much the same, she told him when it finished. The unconscious man had a brain concussion and could not be questioned. There was, as yet, no identification of the victims and no understanding of what had taken place.

Peter accepted that report in silence. He had other things on his mind—mainly, getting prepared for their departure. Karen, with her own coat and purse, and with Maria's dress and shoes, could walk out the door, but he had organising to do. He retrieved the possessions he and Vittorio had taken from the assassins and which he had put away from Maria's sight. He emptied the money from the dead man's wallet into the pile Vittorio had taken from the other man, laid out the guns and ammunition and other items, and counted up. Including the 16,000 lire in his own wallet and the 25,000 Vittorio had brought him, he had a total of 277,500 lire in notes (or about $450 worth), a few hundred more in coins, and his packet of travellers cheques back of that. There was his jackknife, cigarettes and lighter, notebook, and a couple of pens. In the weapons department, he had his own gun and box of shells back, plus the automatic Vittorio had brought him and the revolver they'd taken from the unconscious man.

He concerned himself with the money first, stashing the larger bills in various hiding places in his clothes. There was the secret pocket inside his jacket for some, the hip pocket of his trousers for more, watch pocket, the waistband of his shorts, down inside his socks. If his wallet were lost or stolen, he'd have plenty left.

He worked in silence and Karen watched in silence. When he was through, he reholstered his own gun, pocketed the box of shells, and tucked the automatic in his belt. The spare gun and Marchesi's wallet he left on the table. He would do something about those when Vittorio got back.

Karen indicated his belt. 'You need two guns?'

He patted the extra. 'It might come in handy. You're a very popular girl. All your friends are after you.'

'They're not my friends.'

'Your ex-friends, then.'

'All right, my ex-friends, then. What do you want me to do, apologise?'

'Apologise? You mean for living off the Mafia?'

'I mean because they're after me and you're my bodyguard and that means you're in trouble.'

'Do you think I'm afraid? Is that what you think? Forget it. I'm not in trouble. They're in trouble.'

'You're mad about something. Is it because I pulled a gun on you?'

'No. I can only kick myself for that. It was stupid. I should have known you'd have a gun. I'm glad you know how to use it. It's one more plus in our favour.'

'You're mad, though. I've done something and you're mad. If it wasn't about the gun, what is it?'

'If you really want to know what the trouble is, I'm starting to get a headache again. Let's forget the questions and answers. This is a job. That's all. A job. I'm to get you to the United States in one piece. Let's just leave it at that.'

She wouldn't leave it at that. She followed him into the kitchen. 'It's because I'm going to testify. That's it, isn't it? In your American code, nobody tells tales—even against the evil ones, the criminals. You call it "ratting", "squealing", and by other unpleasant names.'

Peter put two pills in his mouth and gulped a swallow of water. He turned to her. 'Look, sister, it's all right with me for you to testify. I'm all in favour of it if you've got anything to say, and you apparently have. How you live your life and what you get out of that life is your business. You have your job and I have mine. Right now they overlap, but that's only coincidence. We're going to be together for a while but that's strictly because of our jobs. It's a business arrangement and nothing else.'

'Did I suggest it ought to be something else?'

'No, but we might as well have that straight in the beginning.'

She was leaning in the doorway, eyeing him, and she smiled slightly. 'You know, I think you resent the fact I was Joe Bono's mistress. I've heard you Americans are very moral. At least you *feel* moral even if you don't act moral. How many mistresses have you had, by the way?'

'Knock it off,' Peter snapped, stepping past her, back to the sitting room. 'You can be Bono's mistress or anybody's mistress. It's nothing to me. Your soul can be black, white or grey, it's all the same. All I'm supposed to do is get you to the United States and turn you over to Senator Gorman.'

Karen followed as he went to the window, pulled back the curtain impatiently and looked out. She stopped a proper distance away and said quietly, 'Joe was good to me. He wasn't a bad man. I would have married him but he already had a wife and his church doesn't permit divorce. Besides, we weren't the same religion and the Church wouldn't have let him marry me anyway. So what else would you have us do?'

Peter turned and leaned a hand on the window frame. 'Sure,' he snorted. 'Good old Joe. He treated you like a queen on money he got from dope smuggling and dope peddling, from gambling and prostitution and extortion, from murder and all the rest. All the dirt you're going to give Gorman about the Mafia, he was a part of it and high enough up to know it all. And you know it all too.'

'At least he was honest with me. He didn't pretend.' She shrugged. 'I won't say I liked what he did, but I liked him. I'm Danish, if you didn't know, and not from a wealthy family. I left home when I was sixteen so there'd be one less mouth to feed. I came down to Rome because it's warmer down there, like Miami to New York in your country. In my country, the Danes go south for the winter too, and I went with them, but to work. I worked in night clubs. You dance with the customers and they buy you drinks. And you get a commission on the drinks they buy you. And that was how I met Joe. He was over here in Rome on business at the time. And, well . . .' She gestured. 'I guess that's the story.'

Peter made a face. 'That's a great story. All it needs is a violin in the background. Is that the one you told Gorman?'

'That's what I told him, yes.'

'And he believes you?'

She flushed. 'Why shouldn't he? I've got proof.'

'Like what?'

She eyed him. 'What's the matter? Why should you think I would lie?'

'Why should I think you'd tell the truth? Say something in Danish.'

A corner of her mouth tightened. *'Dra til helvete.'*

'What's that mean?'

She lifted her chin. 'It means, "I think you're very pretty."'

Peter gave her a wicked smile. 'You're a cute one. You really are. You're fixing to travel a long way on Joe Bono's friendship and I wonder if you've got the money to pay the fare when you get there.'

She coloured again. 'What do you mean by that?'

'Where did you learn your English?'

'In high school. English is everyone's second language over here.'

Peter snorted. 'Sure,' he said. 'Sure you did. But that's Gorman's worry, not mine. All I have to do is deliver you.' He looked out the window again. 'That is, if Vittorio ever gets back here with that damned Mercedes of his.'

'But what is Gorman's worry? I can produce. And he knows I can.'

'I'll bet you can too, kid.' He looked out the window again.

'Then what've you got it in for me for? What am I supposed to have done that's so much worse than anything you've ever done?'

That brought him around fast. 'Worse than I've ever done? I'm at least fussy who I sleep with. But let's forget that. Let's say you did it for love. But there's more to you than that, sister. I've got the book on you. I know what you are and I know what you're up to and all I can say is, if you were my sister, I'd horsewhip you naked in the public square.'

She stood still and took it but she turned a deep red. 'So that's how it is,' she whispered.

'That's how it is.' He looked hard out the window again.

She moved away a little and toyed with a glass paperweight beside the table lamp. 'You shouldn't have taken the job.'

He turned and gave a short laugh. 'Why? My personal feelings don't enter into it. You'll get full protection. I'm even prepared to lay down my life for you, ironic as it might sound. Now what more could a girl ask?'

She tossed her head. 'Ironic as it might sound, I can assure you I would not accept such a sacrifice.'

'And I can assure you you won't have to. We're going to have you safe in Gorman's . . .'

He stopped and both turned as the music from the radio was interrupted by a news bulletin and Peter caught the name Vittorio Del Strabo. 'What is it?' he said when the voice ceased.

Karen's face was no longer red. It was white. 'They caught Vittorio. They were watching the Mercedes. It was from Rome and parked not far from the building. They found a gun on him with blood on it and they're holding him for questioning.' Her eyes were wide and deep. 'Safe and sound, did you say? Now what are we going to do?'

'How the hell did they know the car—wait a minute...'

'The licence plate has "Roma" on it. Florence plates have "FI".'

'Damn it, he's too new. He should have known better. I should have known better. I should have noticed the plates.'

'What will they do to him?'

'Question him. Try to make him tell where we are.'

'If he does, we're going to be in one bad spot.'

'I think he'll take some working over.'

'Will his ladyfriend?'

'What do you mean?'

'Quarter of eight they left. She can't possibly have to go to work before nine. Nine to three, or nine to one and three to six. Not before. Not for her. So where is she right now? Did she go with him? Did they arrest her too?'

'I don't know but I don't think she's the type to talk either.'

'Even so we're in a spot. What are we going to do? Now we can't get the false passports. We can't even walk the streets.'

Peter wasn't worried about that. 'We can get passports in Genoa. Brandt has a contact there. What I don't like is leaving Vittorio.' He paced the floor muttering curses. 'That's the trouble with jobs like this. That's why we try to keep it to one man. It lessens the risks. I knew I shouldn't have let him drive me here. If I'd been alone . . .' He stopped and looked bitterly at Karen. 'It's great. I've got to protect you and I'd rather protect him. Well, I'll have to do that later. I guess you're queen for today.'

The flush returned to her face. 'I'd rather somebody else had the job too, if you want to know, Mr. Congdon. But since it's yours, maybe you can tell me just how it is you plan to get to Genoa.'

'By train. It'll be fastest. Call the railroad station and see when the first train leaves.'

WEDNESDAY 8:10–9:05 A.M.

While Karen made the call, Peter rummaged through the medicine cabinet in the bathroom and through drawers in the kitchen. Karen poked her head in as

Peter came up with a bottle of glue and set it beside a bottle of liquid shoe polish. 'Just what we need,' he said. 'What did you find out?'

'There's a train for Genoa at ten o'clock. It's the Rome express to Nice.'

'Good. That gives us better than an hour and a half. That should be plenty of time.'

'What's the shoe polish for?'

'Disguise.' He slipped the bottle out of the box and said, 'What colour is it? Brown?'

'Yes. What are you going to do with it?'

'You're going to give yourself a quick rinse. From blonde to brown in five short minutes.'

'You mean you think I'm going to paint my hair with that stuff?'

'I mean we'll put some water in the washbasin, pour in some of this and then you soak your head. The police and the Mafia are looking for a blonde. We have to do something about that before we leave here.'

Karen made a face but she didn't protest. 'What's the glue for?'

'Me. My upper lip. I cut a lock or two of hair, stick it on and trim it and, behold, a moustache.'

'I'll bet.'

'Oh, it'll work. This isn't an original idea. This is part of Brandt's training programme—how to disguise yourself with what you find at hand in normal households. We all have to learn how to do things like this.'

Karen leaned a shoulder against the entrance. 'I don't want to appear unappreciative, Mr. Congdon, but after I make this mess out of my hair, then what happens? Dyeing my hair doesn't get us to Genoa.'

'It's very simple, really. After you dye your hair and I put on a moustache, we walk out of here as a husband and wife taking a trip to visit relatives in Genoa. We buy tickets at the station, get aboard the train, and there we are.'

'Of course there won't be any policemen in the railroad station. There won't be anyone wanting to see our passports.'

'We're Italians. We don't need passports travelling in our own country.'

'We're Italians, only you don't know how to speak Italian.'

'I'm an Italian with laryngitis.' Peter stepped around her and led the way to the bathroom.

She followed, her face stony, and watched while Peter drew two inches of water in the bottom of the basin. 'You're getting to sound like your friend Vittorio,' she said. 'You seem to think there's nothing to any of this. I'm not quite a fool, you know. Or maybe you don't know. Vittorio's now in the hands of the police and that's where we're going to be—or worse—unless you know what you're doing. And I don't think you do.'

Peter, carefully pouring the liquid shoe polish into the water, darkening its colour to mahogany, said, more seriously, 'Listen, Angel, I'm not a fool either. We can't hide out in this apartment very long. I don't know at what point Vittorio may decide playing detective isn't fun any more and bare his soul. And, as you point out, there's Maria and who knows what a woman is going to do? But we can't walk the streets of Florence very long either, disguise or no disguise. We've got to get out of town and hiking isn't a very good way—and for more reasons than just sore feet. Our best bet is to bluff our way through with brown hair, a moustache, and a big front. You'll be surprised what you can accomplish by sheer nerve.' He motioned to the basin. 'Here. Rinse your hair in this and see what you look like. Wait, there're some rubber gloves in the kitchen. Better put those on so you won't stain your hands. And you'd better take off that dress. It's too pretty to soil.'

'And what are you going to do, watch?'

'I'm going into the bedroom and find some scissors and get busy on the moustache.'

It took Peter just under half an hour to adorn his upper lip with fragments of hair from various parts of his head. Despite the haste with which he worked, it was a professional job. The hairs were carefully straight, the upper line curved, and, when they were well stuck to his skin, he trimmed the edges accurately and admired himself in the mirror.

Karen returned from the bathroom as he was finishing up. Her hair was a reddish brown now, partially dried, but still wet. She had her dress back on and that was clean, as were her hands, but stain marks were on her brow, parts of her face, and the back of her neck. She said sombrely, 'Well, I guess you did get a training course. You did a better job than I did.'

He studied her and nodded. 'Some of those stains have got to come out. We've got the time to do it right. How far is the station from here?'

'Only a few blocks.'

'It's a breeze then.' He brought her back to the bathroom, bent her over the washstand, and with a scrub brush and soap scoured the stain spots vigorously, ignoring her cries of pain. The stains weren't totally removed but they were well faded and he had to be satisfied. 'Powder your face, girl, go heavy on the lipstick and get that hair combed. Then we'll be set to face the dragons.' He hung up the towel she had dried her hair with and shook his head. 'We're going to owe Miss Botticelli not only for a new dress but a towel. Shoe polish is hell on everything but shoes.'

He went back to the bedroom, found one of Miss Botticelli's suitcases and threw into it Marchesi's wallet and the other man's gun, then added some bedding for weight and bulk. Karen came back from making up her face and said, 'What are you doing, stealing everything that poor girl owns?'

'Borrowing. We can't visit relatives without a suitcase.' He snapped the catches, helped Karen into her coat and took her by the arm. 'Your name is Maria Botticelli,' he said and pointed to the nametag on the suitcase. 'I'm your husband, Antonio. Think you can remember that?'

'I can remember, but what do you want to leave now for? It's nearly an hour till train time.'

'Why wait? If it's going to be bad news, let's find it out fast.'

'But we'd have to wait at the station. Out in front of people.'

'And who'd expect a fleeing couple to do that? Right? Besides, waiting around drives me up the walls. And let's not forget that staying here is dangerous. We can't be sure Vittorio won't break down.'

'I wish we didn't have to leave him. What will happen?'

'He'll be all right. He's better off than I am, no matter how things turn out.'

'Because he's not stuck with me? Is that what you mean?'

'No, I don't mean that. I mean because Brandt will get him out of hock as soon as he finds out about it. But Brandt will take the hide off me for letting him get in there in the first place. And who knows, maybe it'll convince Vittorio to stick to the leather goods business. Now, are you ready? Remember, we're husband and wife. We're going to Genoa to see your sister's family. We've been married three years. We're in love. Start getting yourself believing it.'

She said dryly, 'Including the love bit?'

'Sure. It's the test of a good actress. Pretend I'm handsome and dashing—like Vittorio.'

She gave him a look. 'I'll pretend you're Joe Bono,' she said and opened the door.

WEDNESDAY 9:10–9:40 A.M.

Outside they had no trouble at all. They turned the corner at the Ponte San Trinita and found a cabstand a short block north around a tall monument. They climbed into a yellow Fiat, the driver threw the suitcase into the rack on top, pulled down the meter bar and swung out into traffic. It was as simple as that.

The ride was short and fast, around sharp corners, down crowded streets, into the Piazza della Stazione where the broad, low lines of the railroad station showed ahead, and finally to a stop under the huge mottled glass portico. The driver leaped out, but it was to unload the suitcase, not to open the door for Karen. That courtesy was effected by a blue-uniformed man with white gloves, a squat, visored cap and a policeman's badge while, back against the entrance doors, three other policemen looked on.

Peter's heart stopped. He was certain that Karen, in shock, would blow the whole thing.

But he didn't know Karen. All she did was turn on her thousand-watt smile and give the policeman her hand as if minions of the law had been opening doors for her since she was ten. And when she got out, she not only thanked him, she gave him the eye. Karen Halley hadn't ventured into the open to avoid the police, she had come to chase. And with this policeman she was so effective he never even saw Peter climb out after her. He was too busy escorting this luscious bundle of sex to the doors.

The meter read 260 lire and when the driver set the suitcase down, Peter gave him three 100-lire coins. The driver only looked at them, said something, and waited. Peter didn't know what he wanted. He hesitated, then tried to bluff. He turned and started to pick up the suitcase. The driver gestured at it and jabbered something else and this time he was a bit louder. Peter felt trapped.

Then Karen was beside him, thrusting another coin into the driver's hand, giving the little man a big smile and a joking remark. She turned Peter around and led him towards the station. 'Fifty lire for the bag, you dumbbell. You trying to ruin everything?' She gave her waiting policeman the thousand-watt treatment again and, pointing to Peter, said something in a mocking voice that made him laugh. She muttered to Peter, 'Maybe we'd better pretend you've got encephalitis, not laryngitis.' She smiled at the three policemen by the doors and said something that made them laugh too. She took Peter inside, holding tightly to his arm as if guiding a dim-witted grandfather, and he seethed helplessly.

The polished stone waiting room was empty except for half a dozen people in line at the second and third ticket windows of the row under the big letters BIGLIETTERIA. A solitary policeman wandered around a large centrepiece display of potted plants and a grey-haired old man was changing movie posters on the sign stands beside four of the green marble pillars that supported the high, mottled glass roof.

Karen hardly gave the policeman a glance. She stopped Peter and held out her hand. 'Give me your wallet. I'll buy the tickets.'

'How will it look for the wife to buy . . .'

'How would it sound if you tried to buy?'

Peter gave her the wallet without demur and watched as she marched to the line at window two. She was good, he had to admit. She was a real pro. She didn't try to brazen her way through. She didn't force it. Instead, she behaved as if the idea she might be stopped and questioned about anything never occurred to her. She was a cool cat, that one. She was ice.

Above the BIGLIETTERIA sign, two large rectangles

spelled out the time as 9-22 and Karen was talking to the man behind the window, shoving money across. Then she came away smiling and Peter watched her approach, the swinging, easy walk, the nifty figure, the low-cut dress she flaunted through the open coat. To look at her was to want her and even Peter wasn't immune. That was what made her dangerous. You knew she meant trouble, but you wanted her anyway. The trick was to remain detached.

She said something to him in Italian while she was still far enough away so the strolling policeman could overhear. He was already watching her—with admiration, not suspicion—and she was playing to her audience.

When she reached Peter, she handed him his wallet with the tickets inside, took his arm firmly and directed him towards the concourse doors. Above them, on the *Treni in Partenza* board, the Pisa-Livorno; Genoa-Torino train was scheduled for ten o'clock on track eight.

The concourse itself was a broad area fronting on twelve tracks and six platforms, with exits far off left and right. This was where the people had congregated and they were busy wandering around the portable food and souvenir counters, making phone calls, or standing and waiting. There was another potted plant centrepiece, a huge, six-foot bowl encircled by seven smaller bowls, a duplicate of the one inside. There were also more policemen. Two guarded the distant exists and three others strolled among the waiting passengers.

Track number eight was near the middle but the train was not yet in, so Peter kept Karen away from the circulating policemen by developing a great interest in a huge model of the Italian liner *Cristoforo Colombo* on display in a fifteen-foot glass case. It was in the middle of the concourse but away from the souvenir and magazine counter, and away from people. Peter muttered in a low voice, 'Any trouble with the tickets?'

'No trouble at all.'

'What kind did you get?'

'First class, of course.'

'You should have got second. We'd fit in the crowd more.'

'When did you last ride a train in Italy?'

'Remember, you're supposed to be playing a role.'

'Stop worrying.' She switched suddenly, put a hand on Peter's arm and spoke Italian as a policeman strolled over near the display case. She left Peter, went up to speak to the policeman and, in a moment, was letting him guide her to one of the magazine stands where they started looking over the reading material together.

It was quite a show. She laughed with him, she gave him flirtatious looks, she put her hand on his arm in that flattering way that suggests to the man that the lady finds him most attractive, and she encouraged him to glance down the front of her low-cut dress.

By the time he had equipped her with reading material for the trip, he had one gloved hand half around her waist and the neighbouring minions of the law were paying more attention to their lucky comrade than to the hunt for runaway fugitives. Peter had to concede that, no matter what she did or was in other areas, in this particular one no one could touch her. And he didn't kid himself that she wasn't relishing the attention she got. She was eating it up.

The Genoa train had backed into place when Karen finally left her policeman friend but she was still playing to him and his companions when she got back to Peter. She put her magazines on the top of the glass case and rattled off Italian to him rapidly in an excited tone, illustrating the story of what the police were there for by gesturing in the direction of the Via dei Saponai, shooting herself through the heart with a finger and hitting herself over the head with the palm of her hand.

Then she took Peter's arm and led him towards the train, waving and nodding at the entranced policemen who, in turn, stared after her like children at a toy window.

They boarded the second coach at the first-class end and found one empty compartment. It had an *occupato* sign on the seat by the window, a glove on the seat by the door, and luggage on one of the racks, but it gave them temporary privacy and they took it. Peter threw their suitcase onto a rack and slid the door closed while Karen took the middle seat riding backwards. She stretched her arms above her head and gave him a superior smile. 'How was I, boss?'

His eyes dropped to the low V of her dress. He couldn't help it and he knew she was glad he couldn't. She really could stand the men on their ears, that girl. He looked back to her face. 'You're good, all right. You're very good. You're the best I've seen.'

'Don't sound so bitter about it.' She opened her purse and took out her cigarettes. 'You told me to be bold. Nothing like boldness, you said. Do you have a light?'

He gave her one, still standing over her. He snapped the lighter shut and returned it to his pocket. 'I can see I didn't have to worry about that. You're bold, all right. You climbed all over the whole police department.'

She stretched again, taunting him and grinning. 'And it worked, didn't it? I fooled them all, didn't I? So aren't you glad I'm the kind of girl you'd like to horse-whip in the public square?'

'I told you to play a loving wife.'

She laughed at him. 'I find it easier to play a mocking one.'

The door was pulled open by a slender and slightly distraught woman about Peter's age with a crying two-year-old girl in her arm and a four-year-old in tow. She picked up her glove and took the seat there and tried to stop the little one from crying. Peter sat down in the window seat beside Karen and got out a cigarette for himself. Karen had mocked him, all right. To every cop in the Florence station.

Across the way the little girl's crying was irritatingly loud. Women! Peter thought. The grown-up ones or the baby ones. They were all a headache. He exhaled an angry cloud of smoke and glowered out the window.

WEDNESDAY 10:05 A.M.–2:30 P.M.

By the time the train started moving silently and smoothly out of the station, all was quiet in the compartment. The mother had the two-year-old on her lap and was showing her pictures in a magazine called *Tempo* while the four-year-old, beside them, looked on desultorily. Karen was reading one of the magazines her policeman friend had helped her select and, since it and the others were in Italian, there was nothing left for Peter but to stare out of the window as they rolled past freight cars in the railroad yard, past apartment complexes in the outskirts of Florence, and finally open country.

The car had a gentle rocking motion and the only sound was the whirr of the wheels on the tracks, occasionally turning to a rattle as they went over switches. It was soothing and comforting and Peter was beaten and tired to exhaustion. He leaned back in the safety of his seat and let himself slide over the edge of sleep. He stirred once when Karen took the tickets out of his wallet and that was the last he knew.

He came to feeling refreshed, but with the simultaneous sense that something was wrong. The overhead lights were on in the compartment while outside it was black, the windows giving back only the reflection of the compartment itself. He sat up quickly, completely alert. All was serene. The woman in the corner seat was asleep while, beside him, Karen was showing a different side of her nature. She was telling a story to the four-year-old, who sat beside her, enthralled. The two-year-old lay asleep in her arms.

Peter looked at his watch. It read one-thirty. He held it to his ear and it was running. One-thirty was the time, but one-thirty when? How long had he been sleeping? How long had they been riding? Suddenly he wasn't even sure what day it was.

Then, just as suddenly, the train burst into daylight and bright, early afternoon. They were out of a tunnel and in a green valley with a patchy sky overhead. A small cemetery passed by close at hand, a tight little walled collection of tombstones on a hillside. Peter looked around, trying to orient himself. They were entering a town now. There were buildings and terraced hills and the train was slowing. 'Where are we?' he asked, interrupting Karen.

She turned away from the child. 'I don't know. Some stop along the coast. Would you like a sandwich?'

'A sandwich?'

She produced one from her purse, wrapped in paper.

'Where did you get that?'

'In Pisa.'

'In Pisa?'

She said patiently, 'While you were asleep. From a food cart they wheeled out onto the platform.'

'You got off the train? You shouldn't have.'

'And you shouldn't have let me, should you? I could have been kidnapped and you'd have slept right though it.'

He was already aware of that and chagrined enough. 'You'd better eat it,' he said and turned away.

'I had mine. And wine as well. Go ahead.' She put it in his lap and resumed her storytelling.

The train stopped and people got off, but it wasn't Genoa yet. A conductor on the platform called out, 'Sestri Levante.'

Peter munched the sandwich in brooding silence and glanced at Karen. Her back was to him and the enraptured child occupied all her attention.

The train left the town, ran by the sea, and entered another tunnel that took a minute to get through. Peter spent the time looking at the reflections in the window and what little he could view of Karen and the baby she held. He had seen Karen Halley, the terrified young girl, all feminine and vulnerable when she thought she was going to be killed. He had seen Karen Halley, the icy-voiced one, holding a gun and ready to kill. He had seen Karen the flirt, encouraging with her eyes and body the stares and desires of every male in sight. Now she was Karen the Madonna, cradling children as if motherhood were the be-all and end-all of existence. And in every case, be she terrified child, heartless goddess, bewitching siren, or devoted mother, you felt that this time you were seeing the real Karen. Yet the real Karen lay deeper still. The real Karen Halley was the mistress of a Mafia leader, a woman who lived off his money, entertained his accomplices, shared his secrets, and gave him her body. And now that the tides had turned and the currents ran counter to the old courses, she would expose the secrets and the Mafia and her lover and herself for a little ready cash, questionable protection, and the guarantee of American citizenship.

For Peter, the girl was disturbing. She showed so many contradictory facets. What he found equally disturbing was that he was thinking about it. She was a job. She was somebody to get aboard the first available plane and deliver to Gorman unscathed. Don't think about her, there's no rhyme or reason in it.

They came out of the tunnel and ran beside a long beach of grey sand, grey stones and a scattering of empty cabanas. On the other side of the tracks, homes climbed a gently sloping hill. They bridged a small river and came in for a stop in a town called Chiavari. From then on, for the next fifty minutes, the ride was nothing but a succession of tunnels, short and long, brief views of a grey, chill Mediterranean under a cloudy, sun-streaked sky, and a succession of stops as frequent as a commuters' local. From the way teenagers with books under their arms got off, it could have been a school bus. It looked as if it were being used for such.

At twenty-five after two, between tunnels, they came into an exposed view of the sea and Genoa was close. Two freighters were moving with the train on a beeline and another was sailing away on an opposite course. Out beyond, a liner was heading for the horizon.

The mother stirred into wakefulness and smiled at Karen. There was talk and the passing back of children. The mother started organising for departure.

Peter went out into the corridor and lighted a cigarette. Karen followed in a minute as he knew she would. She wasn't in Florence now and she didn't like being alone any more. She accepted a light and looked around. 'Do you think we've got away?' she said because she needed to say something.

He exhaled a lungful of smoke. 'We've got away from certain members of the Mafia,' he said, 'but you don't get away from the Mafia itself. Not all of it. Not when you're carrying a hundred-thousand-dollar price tag on your head. That buys them a lot of eyes and ears in a lot of places.'

'Yes,' she said thinly. 'I suppose it does.'

They came out of a final tunnel and were in the city proper now, riding on elevated tracks. Someone in the next compartment slid open the door and set out a suitcase. 'Don't worry,' Peter assured her. 'We'll make it. All I have to do is lose them once and they'll never get a smell of us again. I know too many tricks.'

She nodded but she didn't look convinced. The train was slowing now and the platform of the Stazione Brignole came into view. Peter winced. He knew too many tricks, did he? One of Brandt's rules for avoiding capture was: 'Change your transportation before your destination.' And this he had not done. He had bought a ticket to Genoa and he was arriving in Genoa. He should have bought a ticket to Turin or he should have got off the train in Nervi or Recco, or even back at Portofino, and come in by cab.

They returned to the compartment to pick up their luggage and Peter lowered a corridor window to look outside. There were only a handful of people on the platform and none of them were in uniform. At least the police weren't on hand, ready to seal off all cars and search them through. And it seemed pretty certain that the Mafia wasn't on hand either.

He hadn't been smart but maybe he was lucky.

WEDNESDAY 2:35–4:35 P.M.

They went down a flight of steps from the platform into a broad corridor under the tracks and headed for the sunlit street. The baggage counter was on the right near the exit, across from new construction around the waiting room, and Peter checked Maria's suitcase there, pocketing the claim stub.

Outside, they waited in line where the cabs came in and, in turn, climbed into the rear of a green Fiat. 'Vico Tacconi,' Peter told the driver and got out his cigarettes.

The driver turned around. *'Cumme scia disce?'*

Peter glanced at Karen. He tried again.

The driver rattled off more Italian and Karen told Peter, 'He doesn't know that place. What's it near?'

'Hell, how would I know? I'm a stranger here myself.' Then he said, 'There's another name. Shanghai Via Prè.'

'Via Prè?' the driver said. 'Ah.' He gave a grin and a nod, twisted the meter key and started off. They ducked around the electric buses, went across the traffic of the square towards the distant Monumento ai Caduti, then right onto the Via XX Settembre.

Karen said to Peter, 'Why are you looking out the back window?'

'Just seeing what else turned the corner.'

'I thought you said we left them behind.'

'I thought we did. I still think so.'

The ride was a short one, taking them past the big stores with their covered sidewalks, under a high-arched narrow bridge reaching for the hills above, right at the fountain in the Piazza de Ferrari, left at the floral designs surrounding the statue of Vittorio Emanuele II in the Piazza Corvetto, through a couple of tunnels under the hills, and finally into the Piazza Acquaverde, where the driver swung around and pulled in at the semicircular entrance to the Hotel Colombia Excelsior.

He gestured at a narrow, stone-paved roadway sloping down beside the hotel and explained matters. Karen translated for Peter. 'He says down there is the Via Prè. He doesn't want to go down because the car is a little big. The place we want is probably a side alley. The shops will open in five minutes, at three o'clock.'

Peter accepted that but he wasn't interested in going down there yet. He took Karen into the hotel instead, borrowed stationery, and had her write a note to Maria explaining about the suitcase, promising a return of the dress and shoes, plus restitution for the inconvenience. When she had done that, he put the luggage ticket in the envelope and addressed it to the girl at 24 Lungarno Acciaioli in Florence. Then he sent a cable to Brandt, clear, which said, 'DEL STRABO HELD BY FLORENCE BULLS STOP DO SOMETHING CONGDON.'

Then he took Karen down the ramp with him to the Via Prè. It was a narrow alley, twelve feet wide, crowded with people and lined with tiny shops selling anything from shoes to fruits and groceries, woollens, watches, clothing, meals, cold cuts, candy and fish. There were *albergo* entrances, camera stores, bars, and everywhere the atmosphere of a bazaar. Shoppers and wanderers jammed the streets while occasional little three-wheel trucks or tiny cars tried to edge through. It was a melting pot of people and cultures. The shabby and the nondescript rubbed elbows with the well-dressed and prosperous. There were men, women, tourists, students, and sailors from foreign ports. It was a meeting place, a public market, but it was also home, and washing hung like banners from lines stretched between windows overhead.

To the right, the Via Prè sloped downhill and ended in a small parking area and taxistand beside the wide and heavily travelled Via Antonio Gramsci. To the left was where it stretched, climbing and dipping and full of movement. To the left was where the crowds were. To the left was where Peter and Karen turned to seek the Vico Tacconi.

They found it right away, the first alley on the left

and the name painted on the corner of the building. It was a stone-paved path, seven feet wide, rough and uneven, with an upward slope, a scattering of tiny shops, and a stone staircase way at the far end leading up to the Via Balbi.

It was an empty alley with a slightly sour smell and Peter took Karen's arm as they went up it. In Maria's heels, it was rocky going for her.

Halfway along, on the left, was a cobbler's shop. It was the last door on that side and beyond there was nothing but overgrown foundation ruins and three small cars parked among the rubble.

There was no sign on the shop, nothing to indicate whose it was, but Peter didn't hesitate. He glanced around once, then led Karen inside through a grey wooden door with two horizontal panes in the top.

The building was stone and the room they entered was stone too, and tiny. There was a small counter with a display case on top offering shoe polish, brushes and laces for sale. Behind the counter was a seat, and a last and tools. Shoeboxes were piled on shelves against the whitewashed back wall. At the right, a burlap curtain covered a narrow door to a room behind. In front of the counter was a customer's chair and a rack with some shoes on it. On the wall above the shoe rack there was, strangely enough, a telephone.

The burlap curtain parted and the cobbler came out. He was a short and aged man with close-cropped grey hair, steel-framed spectacles, a bent and frail physique, a bushy moustache and a face that looked a hundred years old. He shuffled forth behind the counter and looked at both Karen and Peter inquiringly, saying something in Italian.

'Signore Celotto?' Peter saked.

The man said, '*Si.*'

'You speak English?'

The man nodded. '*Si*. Yes. A little.'

'Do you know the expression, "The Brandt Agency has a far-flung net"?'

The little old man blinked once behind his glasses and stared steadily at Peter. At length he said slowly, 'I think I have.'

'Do you know the rest of it?'

'And it catches many fish.'

Peter took out his wallet and put a calling card on the counter for the old man to read. The man bent close and murmured the name once or twice. He glanced out the door, then at Peter. 'In the back,' he said and turned to hold the curtain.

The room Karen and Peter entered was larger than the front, or store, section, but not by much. There was a bed opposite with a worn and ragged coverlet, a small stove in a corner, a rear door to a narrow alley that led out to the rubble. There was a sink, a little table, one comfortable chair and a couple of wooden chairs, a clothes rack and a water closet. With three people in the room it was crowded.

The old man gestured at the chairs, took a peek back into the store, and let the curtain fall in place. He shuffled by to slide a bolt in the alley door and came back to open a small cupboard over the stove. 'Are you hungry?' he asked. 'Can I give you eats?'

'No thanks.'

The man nodded, closed the cupboard door and let himself down on the bed. The food had looked unpalatable, the room was depressing, its owner appeared on the verge of collapse. He was supposed to be Brandt's contact in Genoa and Brandt was supposed to know what he was about, but this man looked as if he'd never ventured beyond the Via Prè and had seldom been outside his own alley. Peter was almost as surprised that he could read as that he could speak English.

The man rubbed a chin that needed shaving and looked at his visitors nervously. It was as if Peter were the first Brandt agent ever actually to call on him. 'I got word you were in Italy,' he said hoarsely and in low tones. 'You want something? You want I should help you?'

Peter nodded but he didn't feel hopeful. Vittorio Del Strabo, Brandt's Rome contact, was a man in high position, knowledgeable, capable of producing what was required. This man couldn't even produce a satisfactory bit of food. 'We need passports,' Peter said and waited for a look of dismay and a gesture of helplessness from their host. Instead, Giuseppe Celotto didn't so much as blink. 'What country?' he asked.

'America, if we have a choice. Anything that will get us out of Italy.'

'America?' the man mumbled, staring at the floor. He looked up. 'Are you going back to America?'

'That's where we're heading.'

'In that case, are American passports wise? They check your passport number against a list when you get to America. You can get into any country with a false passport except America.'

The old man's knowledge was impressive. Peter didn't know that himself. 'We don't need them to get into America with,' he said, 'only to get out of Italy. The point is, can you get us passports?'

The man coughed and retched a little. 'I can,' he said and cleared his throat. 'But it will take money.'

'We've got money.'

'It'll take American money.'

'We've got that too. How much?'

'I don't know yet. I find out.' He got to his feet and squeezed by the pair, digging a finger in his ear as he passed. 'I telephone,' he said. 'They tell me.' He pushed aside the burlap curtain and went to the wall phone.

The call was a long one with the old man mumbling along, his voice occasionally rising as if haggling over something.

'Price trouble?' Peter asked Karen. 'The guy wants the moon?'

'Time trouble. Your friend wants them right away and whoever he's talking to is protesting.'

There was more talk, a good deal of it, and the ancient shoe-maker's tone developed a ring of authority. He seemed to be giving orders and was not as enfeebled as he looked.

Finally he replaced the phone with a bang and re-entered the room. 'How soon you need them?' he said, sliding by and sitting again on the bed. 'It takes a little time. I said now, but he said he can't have them before six o'clock. I'm sorry. It's the best I can do.'

'Six is all right.'

'It will be five hundred American dollars for the two.'

'They do want the moon.'

'Huh?'

'Nothing. All right. Five hundred American dollars.' Peter got up. 'Where do we go?'

'Come.' The old man took them through the store and out into the alley. He pointed. 'Down there is the Via Prè. You turn left. That way. You go to the end. There is a street. It is the Piazza della Darsena. You see a big tower there. Like a castle. With an arch. It is the Porta dei Vacca. Go through the arch and you are on the Via del Campo. No? And you go and near the far end, on the right . . .' He gestured to indicate the right. 'There you find by a *barbiere* shop a door to a place for photographs upstairs. You go and say Giuseppe sent you. Then all will be—proper. Be—right.'

Peter said he understood and the old man smiled at him and shook hands. 'You will be fine.'

He took Karen back to the Via Prè and along its

length until they came out at a cross street shunting in from the nearby Via Gramsci. The tower and arch were opposite and they went through onto the Via del Campo. It was a counterpart of the Via Prè, yet it was distinctly different. There were the shops, the same paved alley, but in this section the crowds were only half the size and the spark was missing. This was the backwater area, the poor relation, the outskirts of the market, and the farther Peter and Karen went, the thinner became the crowds.

The studio was-two thirds of the way through. It was a door beside a barbershop and opened onto a flight of worn stone steps. In a cracked glass display case beside the door was a faded picture of a Genovese sailor with a girl on his lap. Hanging on a short iron bar over the door was a triangular sign with the single word, *Fotografia.* Peter pushed open the door and they went up.

Off the head of the stairs, in a narrow corridor, was a door with a marbled glass pane on which was lettered *Fotografia* and, beneath that, *Entrare.* Peter turned the knob and they found themselves in a dingy room equipped with a tripod camera, a bench and some crudely painted sets depicting, by a stretch of imagination, ships and the sea. Two tripod lights flanking the camera stared with deep dark eyes at nothing.

Since no one was in the room and no one came into it, Peter returned to the door and closed it smartly. That brought a response, and, after a moment, an enormously fat man with black fingernails, a worn and frayed pair of overalls and a tee-shirt that had never been washed, waddled through a doorway in the corner. He looked and smelled as unwashed as his clothes and the odour of garlic and other, less encouraging aromas, formed an aura around him that radiated six feet in all directions. He came closer than desired, towering over Karen and slightly taller than Peter, looked at the two with shrewd eyes that peeked from an otherwise dead and lacklustre face and mumbled something Peter couldn't understand. His teeth were broken and stained, his face covered with a grey bristle that was on the verge of becoming a beard.

Karen answered him briefly and the man slowly turned back to Peter. 'English?' he rumbled in hoarse tones that seemed to take an effort to produce. 'O.K. What you want?'

Peter said evenly, 'Giuseppe sent us.'

'Yeah,' the man said heavily. 'You got dollars?'

'I've got travellers cheques.'

'Same thing. Five hundred American dollars.' He reached in a pocket of his overalls, stuck a cigarette in his mouth and held out a hand.

'When we get the passports.'

'In advance,' the fat man rumbled. 'Got a light?'

Peter was tempted to say no, restrained himself and produced his lighter. The man puffed, took a drag that ate up a quarter of the cigarette and pulled it from his mouth with his thick fingers. A half inch of the end was wet with saliva and he didn't exhale, he merely went on talking, letting the smoke issue forth from nostrils and mouth as he did. 'Five hundred American dollars in advance,' he said slowly and huskily, stressing the point with his cigarette hand, almost but not quite thumping Peter's chest.

'I'll pay you half now,' Peter said. 'The other half on delivery.'

'In advance,' the man repeated. 'Always in advance.' He took another huge drag on the cigarette and ash fell off.

'Forget it,' Peter told him and turned Karen around to the door. He had it opened and Karen in the hall before the other man stirred. 'Wait,' he growled.

Peter turned around. 'Yes?'

'You got five hundred American dollars?'

'I told you I did.'

'Come back.'

Peter stepped in and Karen followed. They stood waiting in the open door. 'So,' the man said. 'For a friend of Giuseppe's?' He shrugged hugely. 'Half now. Half later.' He held out his cigarette hand for the money again.

Peter took out his folder of cheques and tore five fifties out of the back. He went to the window where open shutters and ragged curtains let in some light, and signed them on the ledge. The big man followed, looked over his shoulder as he wrote and, as they were handed to him, examined each cheque like a teller looking for counterfeits. 'So,' he said and smiled for the first time. 'Now you want a passport.' He tucked the cheques in a pocket of the overalls, took a final drag on what was left of his cigarette and crushed it underfoot. 'First I take your picture.'

He sat Karen, then Peter on the bench, moving it in front of a blank space on the dirty wall near the window. He swung the camera around, adjusted the lights, went over to close the shutters, came back, aimed the camera and snapped the pictures. When he was through, he pushed open the shutters and turned off the lights. 'What names do you want?' he said.

'Greer,' Peter said and spelled it. 'Charles Greer.' He spelled the Charles and the man wrote it down laboriously on a pad from a hip pocket.

'The lady?'

'Evelyn Greer.' Peter spelled that and the man got it down.

'Birth dates?'

Peter made up a pair of reasonable ones and gave New York City as their place of birth.

The fat man wrote that, recorded Peter's hair as brown, eyes brown, and Karen's hair as brown, eyes brown. He asked their height and said, 'All right. That is enough. What date do you want for the passport?'

'September fifteenth of this year.'

'Italian entry stamp?'

'October twenty-seventh at Rome airport.'

The big man nodded. 'You wait here.' He turned and went back the way he had come, closing the door behind him.

It was a long wait. Fifteen minutes went by and Karen and Peter took it in silence, shifting their feet impatiently, wandering here and there in the dim room, looking out at the scattering of people in the shadowed alley below. Finally the big man came back, closing the door behind him, his face solemn. He halted just inside and looked the pair over. 'All right,' he said. 'They will be ready at seven-thirty o'clock. You will get them from Giuseppe at seven-thirty o'clock.'

'Giuseppe?' Peter said. 'We're supposed to get them at six o'clock from you!'

'No.' The fat man shook his head. 'Impossible. I take the pictures. There is more. Much more. It is a special typewriter your country uses. Another man has to print like your typewriter. There are seals and punches. These are very difficult to copy. It is a work of art to copy. When they are done, they will go to Giuseppe. You will pay the rest of the money to him. That is all.' He moved around a piece of scenery and opened the door for them.

WEDNESDAY 4:45–7:30 P.M.

Giuseppe was behind the counter heeling a shoe when Peter and Karen got back and he wasn't disturbed about the change in plans. 'So why be unhappy?' he said. 'It is a small delay. An hour and a half, no? And he is no doubt right. There is much to do.'

'I don't like it all the same.'

Giuseppe shrugged. 'So it comes here. So I close at seven-thirty. It's all right. I stay open. There is no trouble.'

'I hope not.'

They left him, starting down to the Via Prè again and Karen said, 'What are you worried about? I don't get it.'

'I had to sign my name to those travellers cheques.'

'And you think the Mafia is going to track you down because of that?'

'It's a calculated risk, one I didn't have much choice about taking. So the moment I sign those cheques, the plans get changed.'

'I'm sure there's no connection. As the man said, there're a lot of things to do.'

'Probably, but I'm going to feel better come seven-thirty.'

'And what do we do meanwhile?'

'Figure how to get out of Genoa. If there's an airport, we'll see about planes. If not, we'll see about trains.'

There was an airport. Karen found it out from a cab-driver down at the end of the Via Prè and they rode with him out to it. It was a large field a fifteen-minute ride away, projecting into the water so that it was surrounded on three sides by the Mediterranean. The terminal building was a long, one-storey temporary structure made of glass panes and sheets of construction material in a random assortment of colours. It was a modest-sized, intimate place where the scream of Viscount turboprops stopped conversation even with the doors and windows closed.

When Peter and Karen arrived it was quarter past five and all that was left of the sun was a faint edge of pink on one high cloud. The sky was white but shadows were deepening on the ground. Beyond the hedge along the water's edge, lights gleamed on the loading derricks and distant freighters. In back of the city the darkening hills were sprinkled with lights. Beyond them was the ebony ripple of mountains.

Inside, Peter and Karen booked passage to Nice. There was a plane out at nine the next morning, laying over nearly three hours in Milan and arriving in Nice at one-fifteen in the afternoon. The clerk made out tickets and confirmed seat reservations for the Milan part of the journey. There was a delay, however, getting confirmation for the second leg and he offered to phone verification to Peter's hotel. 'Unless, of course, you'd rather wait.'

Peter said they'd wait. He paid for the tickets, tucked them in an inside pocket below his holster and felt better about things. He'd feel even better when the verification came through and when he had the false passports to show in Milan, but things looked good on the whole. Nice was all but home.

They ate in the snack bar while they waited, for restaurants wouldn't open until seven. Karen said, 'That clerk mentioning hotels made me think. The plane leaves at nine tomorrow morning. We get the passports at seven-thirty this evening. How are we supposed to spend the intervening thirteen hours and thirty minutes?'

'Getting a good night's sleep is how I'm going to spend it.'

'And where is this good night's sleep going to take place?'

'In an hotel. We'll be Mr. and Mrs. Charles Greer with brand new passports to show. We'll be able to get a room without any trouble at all.'

'Two rooms, *MIS*ter Greer. Consider me your sister-in-law.'

Peter laughed. 'Now what do you think I had the

passports made out to Mr. and Mrs. for? Just so we wouldn't need two rooms.'

'I've got news for you. It's going to be two rooms.'

He shook his head. 'If you think you're sleeping in one room and I'm sleeping in another on this trip, Mrs. Greer, you haven't learned anything about my business. I'm to get you to Senator Gorman all in one piece, remember? So the only time I let you out of my sight is when you visit the powder room and then I'm going to be waiting outside the door.'

'And what if I don't like strange men sleeping in my bedroom?'

'Complain to Gorman when you get to Washington. All I can tell you is old man Brandt wouldn't have it any other way.'

'Old man Brandt doesn't happen to be the one in the room. It's young man Congdon.'

'Who will protect your precious hide with his life.'

'You're repeating yourself. You read me that one before. Remember?'

'Listen, if you think I've got ideas about you . . .'

'Not you. That's right. I'm beneath contempt. You've already said so. All you want is to take a whip to me. But I've heard that one too. I know all about the self-righteous, holier-than-thou prigs who look upon the fallen woman with loathing—all the while they're tearing the clothes off her back. Somerset Maugham had you moralising bastards pegged. He pinned you in his spider collection when he wrote *Rain*.'

Peter flushed. She'd hit him closer than he liked. It wasn't that he had designs on the girl but, dammit, he did notice her. And he noticed the stares she got wherever she went—not just when she put it on for the Florence policemen, but going through the crowds on the Via Prè when she wasn't putting on anything. And he had enjoyed the envious looks he'd been given because he was with her. And maybe to jump into her bed was to receive the kiss of death, but hadn't the idea crossed his mind? He wouldn't do it, not for a king's ransom, but damn it, didn't she make him want to as no girl had since Stephanie?

He said to her briskly, 'Listen, you can think anything you like, but I wouldn't touch you with lead gloves. Even if you begged me.'

And she said back, 'Beg you? After Joe Bono?'

The confirmation came through at half past six and Peter and Karen thanked the clerk and went out to seek transportation back to town. A cab came out with passengers fifteen minutes later and they returned in it to the Colombia Hotel. When they started down the ramp again it was just seven o'clock and Karen said, 'We'll be early.'

'That's right. For appointments like this, that's the aim of the game.'

The Via Prè was crowded and noisy, full of lights and movement, with everything in full swing. They pushed through the throngs, Peter leading the way, and then they turned the corner into the Vico Tacconi and it was a different world. The alley was quiet and empty and with little light. And when they went up its rough paving stones to the cobbler's shop, they found the front room dark and the door locked.

Peter looked around sharply. In the butcher's shop across the way two men were cutting up a carcass of beef. In the rubble, among the broken foundation walls, two empty cars were parked. Nobody was on the steps to the Via Balbi. Nothing seemed out of the ordinary. Except that every other shop in the area was wide open, but not the shop belonging to Brandt's Genovese agent.

Peter rapped and peered through the horizontal panes. There was a dim light back of the burlap curtain. The curtain moved, the back light went out and the shop light came on. Then a man came to the door and looked through the glass. It wasn't Giuseppe; this was a young man with a good-looking face, carefully combed hair, and dark, well-cut clothes. He unlocked the door and looked out at them, first to Peter, then to Karen, and back to Peter. When he spoke, it was in English. 'Yes?'

'I want to see Giuseppe.'

'He isn't here.' The man left the door open and moved back to the end of the counter. 'He had to go out. I am taking his place.'

The muscles in Peter's jaw tightened. 'Where is he?'

The young man gestured ignorance. 'I do not know. I only know he asked me to wait for you.' He smiled a little. 'You are Mr. Congdon?'

Peter looked at him sharply and the man's smile widened an inch. 'It's about a passport, is it not? He asked me to help.'

Peter's eyes darted. He turned for a look into the alley but no one was there. He closed the door and moved ahead of Karen. 'What about a passport?'

'Giuseppe said you were to get a passport.' The man was mollifying. 'That is so, is it not, Mr. Congdon?'

Peter came a step closer. He had two inches on the well-built youth and he fixed him with a steady gaze. 'Who are you?'

The man expostulated. 'A friend of Giuseppe's. The son of a neighbour. He asked me to help. He said you would come for passports. One for you and one for the lady.'

'Where are the passports?'

'In another place. I will take you there.' He started to move forward from the end of the counter. His hand reached to guide Peter's elbow. His hand didn't find Peter's elbow. Peter's hand, instead, caught him by the lapel of his jacket, stopping him. 'The passports are to come here.'

'No.' The man did not lose his poise. He made no attempt to disengage himself. 'Giuseppe said that is not the way. Something has happened. They can no longer be delivered. You have to get them. It is a place I know.'

'What place? Where?'

'Some miles from here. I have my car. Just outside. It is to take you in.'

Peter jerked the man by the lapel. 'Where's Giuseppe?'

'I tell you. He did not say. He called me and begged me to help him. He said . . .'

Peter pushed the young man aside and started for the curtain. The man leaped back and blocked the way. 'Please. You cannot go in. We must hurry. The passport!'

Peter seized him with both hands and thrust him from the doorway. He stepped into the room behind the curtain and switched on the light. The bed was rumpled but everything else was in place. It was almost an empty room but it wasn't quite. Peter took two steps and stopped. Against the side wall by the water-closet door, Giuseppe lay dead, his sightless eyes turned to the ceiling, his mouth open and slack. Sticking out from his chest was the handle of a long, thin-bladed knife and the blood it drew formed a little circle of stain around the cut in his shirt. Giuseppe had soled his last shoe, had eaten his last poor meal, had lived his last dreary day in his hovel-like room. His body was still warm but it no longer belonged to Giuseppe.

Peter wheeled and reached for his gun, but he was too late. The young, dark-haired lad came into the room holding Karen with one hand, aiming an automatic with the other. Peter stopped and stood still. He was looking at death and he knew it, but overriding the throb of fear was rage, rage at the youth for what he had done to Giuseppe, at himself for seeing the trap and still falling into it, at his own helplessness and his own failure. 'Pig,' he spat at the man.

'He refused to betray you. He refused to help. So you die here instead. You and this girl.'

The youth got no further. Karen, who had been struggling with seeming futility, was suddenly transformed. Her free hand shot out and seized the gun. It went off, firing wide of Peter's shoulder at a corner of the ceiling. At the same time, she swung around and butted the man in the face with her head and brought her knee up hard for his groin. She didn't quite fell the youth but she drove him back and made him let go. He backhanded her across the face with his fist and wrenched his gun hand free, shoving her aside for clearance. His nose and mouth were bleeding and he was half doubled over, but he had what he thought he wanted, a clear shot at Peter.

He couldn't even start. Peter's gun was on him and Peter's gun roared. A .38-calibre slug hit him in the chest slamming him back into the doorway. He bounced off and clutched for the curtain. His gun fell out of his hand and he tumbled into the shop in a slow turn that tangled his feet so that he crashed full length on his side and rolled over face up with his head against the customer's chair.

For a moment neither Peter nor Karen moved. Both stared at the pair of well-shod feet and silk socks and knife-edged trousers that projected into the room around the quivering curtain. Then Karen sank slowly onto the bed shaking her head.

'You all right?' Peter asked.

She nodded but her face was white and scared. One corner of her mouth was swollen and bleeding where the youth had smashed her with his fist. She gave Peter a wry smile. 'I think I'm getting the shakes.'

'Thanks for saving my life.'

'Yeah.' She laughed a little. 'We make a good team.'

Peter stepped to the door and flicked the light switch

on the other side, throwing the shop into darkness. He wished he could lock the shop door but he didn't dare. People were already gathering outside in the alley, jabbering with questioning voices. He turned off the inside light and the blackness of the shop was instant and complete. He peeked around the curtain at the shop door and waited. The voices were loud outside and silhouetted heads appeared against the panes as people tried to see inside.

'Peter?'

'Yes?'

'Can they get in?'

'They can but they don't seem to want to.'

'I know. I can hear them. They don't know what the noise was but they don't dare come in and find out.'

'Let's hope they stay chicken.'

The bedsprings creaked and there was a sound as Karen groped her way to Peter. 'What are you going to do?'

'I'm going to hope to hell nobody sticks a head in here. Then, when it quiets down, we'll go out the back way.'

She was close, her body just brushing his. 'Do you mind if I stay beside you? I don't like the dark.'

Stay beside him? She could do anything she wanted. She could be mistress to the whole Mafia; she could sell her mother into slavery, she could cheat, lie, steal, or murder. She had saved his life and she was golden.

'Sure,' he said, and was highly conscious of the contact, her body against his, lightly brushing, but always touching.

'I don't like to be a bother, but two dead people—and in the dark . . .'

'Ssh.' Peter heard a sound at the door. It was the knob turning. He pushed Karen back and leaned across the dead youth's legs to see into the shop past the edge of the curtain.

Slowly the door opened and the figure of a man appeared, waiting and listening, while other people stood out beyond. The man took one careful step forward, his silhouetted head turning left and right. Then he paused and his lighter flared, showing his face in its glow. It was the face of the thin man with the empty eyes who had ridden the plane to Rome and ducked down a staircase in Florence.

He was by the counter, leaning forward, peering intently, and the first thing he saw was the upturned face of the dead man. He froze as motionless as the corpse and only the flame on the lighter moved. Then his eyes shifted. They went to the curtain and the black gap at the end, where Peter watched. They darted in other directions but his head stayed still. His left hand slowly reached out to the counter for support and very slowly and very quietly he took a small backward step and then another. He retreated into the doorway, let the lighter snap shut, and very carefully pulled the door shut after him until it latched with a quiet click.

Several questioning voices sounded outside but there was no answering response from the thin man. Peter seized Karen's arm. 'He's the Mafia,' he whispered. 'He thinks we may still be here. We'd better go out the back fast.' He fumbled his way among the chairs, groped for the side wall, and his foot bumped Giuseppe's legs.

He opened the back door and peered into the alley but no one was there. It was a cramped space, two and a half feet wide, ending to the left against a blank wall, extending on the right in back of the room they were in and opening into the area of rubble and ruined foundations.

Peter, gun ready, flattened himself against the wall and edged his way to the mouth of the alley. Karen, with a hand on his arm, moved behind him. The view from there included the whole of the rubble-strewn area, the two parked cars, the shops on the other side of the alley, the buildings beyond the rubble, and all of the Vico Tacconi from Giuseppe's shop to the stone staircase at the end.

Three of the curious bystanders were returning to other shops and a butcher was re-entering his slaughterhouse. But they did not interest Peter. His attention was drawn to the stairs where two men stood in quick conversation.

One was the thin man and he gestured with more animation than Peter had seen him show before. The other was the beefy man with the black front tooth and the carnation in his lapel.

WEDNESDAY 7:30–8:00 P.M.

The talk was brief, then the two men came down the steps and as far as the start of the rubble. They conferred again for a moment and the carnation man started moving in among the broken foundation walls, picking his way over the bricks and stones, sticks and broken glass. It was dark there and when he got in among the standing sections of wall, he was hard to see. The thin man, meanwhile, came slowly down the pavement and the whole action was an encirclement. The thin man, moving down the Vico Tacconi, would soon pass from sight and then he could either sneak up on Peter's dark alley along the side of the building or, worse yet, he could come through Giuseppe's shop.

Peter edged Karen back into the blackness. He found the door again, took her back inside, then shut it and slid the bolt in place. He got on the bed and tested the shutters, making sure they were fastened. 'Karen?'

'Here.'

He reached out and touched her. She was in the middle of the room and she had a gun in her hand. 'Over by the curtain,' he whispered. 'In case the skinny guy comes in the front door.'

'Why don't you lock it?'

'Then they'd know we're inside. I'm hoping they'll think we've gone.'

They found the doorway and Peter got down on the floor beside the dead youth, where the gap in the curtain was. Karen stayed on Peter's other side. He said, 'If anything happens to me, don't fool around. Shoot to kill.'

'Don't worry about that.'

They listened then. Across the alley there was the rattle of an overhead metal shutter coming down. Another clattered down beside the first and two men passed a remark. In the distance, other shutters rattled. It was seven-thirty and the Via Prè shops were closing.

Karen sat pressing against Peter's legs. She shuddered and whispered, 'I'm scared.'

'Don't worry. If they try to get in here, I get first shot.'

'I'm not scared of them. It's being in here. With dead men.'

He touched her arm and squeezed it. 'It's the live ones you have to watch out for.'

One of the cars parked in the rubble started up and drove slowly past the front of the shop. Then there was another sound at the rear, stealthy and soft, with an almost disembodied quality to it. It was the delicate moving of the handle on the back door. Karen clutched Peter's arm with her free hand and her nails dug in.

The sound came again, a little bolder this time. Then

there was a soft but heavy thump as a shoulder tested the strength of the latch. A low, muttered remark followed and another responded, both too soft to catch. Silence fell and then there was a scraping noise at the shutters. At almost the same time, the knob on the front door turned and the door came open.

Peter, on one knee, could see the top of the opening over the counter and the black outline of a man's head. It was the thin man again.

Peter aimed his gun through the gap in the curtain and waited.

The thin man didn't come in this time. He remained in the doorway for a long moment as if sniffing the air. Then, very slowly and quietly, he backed out again and relatched the door.

There was one more sound, that of someone walking over the broken mortar and bricks around the side of the building. After that, there was nothing.

Peter waited without moving and the minutes went by. Karen's hand groped for him and touched his leg. 'Peter?'

'Yes?'

'What are you doing?'

'Waiting.'

'For what?'

'For them.'

'Don't you think they've gone by now?'

'They may be lying in wait. It depends on whether they think we're here or don't think we're here.'

'Peter, I can't stand it. I can't stay in here any longer. I'll go mad.'

'We've got to stay.'

'Oh, Peter.'

'Give me your hand. I'll hold your hand.'

'No. I'll be damned if I'll have my hand held.' She moved away.

'However you want it.' He went back to waiting and listening.

'Peter?'

'What?'

'How did the Mafia find us?'

'I suspect it was our photographer friend. The word's out and he recognised my name on the travellers cheques. That's why there was that long wait and the change in plans. He was phoning somebody, and those two men you saw outside, they came up full speed from Florence. They probably got here just after we did—right after the shooting.'

'How long do we have to stay?'

'Suppose you were hunting for us and you thought we might be in here. How long would you watch this place before you'd decided you were wrong?'

'Fifteen minutes maybe.'

Peter sighed. 'The impatience of women.' He looked at the radium hands of his wristwatch. 'It's nearly eight o'clock now and we've already been in here half an hour. We'll give it an hour more.'

'Another hour? In here with . . .'

'That's right. Because I'm itching to get out of here already. Because I hate sitting around doing nothing. So we're going to fight it and we're going to wait so long that anybody outside is going to be certain we couldn't possibly be here. Because we wouldn't have been able to stand it.'

WEDNESDAY 8:40–9:45 P.M.

'Peter. Where are you? Peter?'

'Right here. I haven't moved.'

'Did you hear it?'

'Hear what?'

'He's alive.'

'Who? What?'

'Giuseppe. I can hear him over there. I can hear him breathing.'

'Stop it, Karen. He's dead.'

'No. I can hear him move. He's trying to crawl.'

'Stop it. It's your imagination.'

'Oh, Peter, Peter, let me out of here.'

'Not for twenty more minutes.'

'Now. Please, Peter.'

'At nine o'clock.'

'You sadist! I hate you. I hate you!'

'Karen, I have to protect you. I have to do what I think is best and I can't let anybody talk me out of it.'

'I don't care if the Mafia is outside. Let them kill me. I don't care. I can't stand it in here with these bodies. I keep thinking they're moving. I keep thinking they're trying to get up.'

'They're dead. They can't move. They can't ever move again.'

'I hate you.'

At the precise moment that the hands of his watch reached nine, Peter stirred. 'All right,' he whispered. 'Time's up.'

Karen, after whimpering and pleading, had been silent for ten minutes. Now she said bitterly, 'Is it really? At long last? I'm never going to forget you, Mr. Peter Congdon. I'm never going to forget or forgive.'

'What am I supposed to do, weep? I've got a job and I'm doing it. All I expect from you is that you give me as little trouble as possible.'

'Don't worry, Mr. Congdon. I won't give you any trouble. I won't give you a God-damned thing.'

Peter didn't answer. He pushed the curtain aside and moved silently around the counter to the door of the shop. After the inner darkness, the outside alley seemed almost bright through the window. Karen rustled the curtain and then came after him, waiting a step away as he looked through the glass at all angles. He opened the door with his gun in his hand and slipped into the alley. It was empty. He put the gun away, signalled Karen to come out, took her arm and walked her quickly down to the Via Prè and around the corner. They had cleared the trap and were free.

The Via Prè had a different and more sinister look to it now. The shops had closed and the shoppers had gone but the bars were still open, the pizza places, the beaneries and bakeshops, and a different kind of person roamed those grey paving stones. Now the only women were young and shapely ones who stood alone by doorways and talked to each other while they waited. Now a different kind of hawker was selling wares. These were hard-faced, gravel-voiced men or slender youths and they showed off cigarettes or transistors, electric shavers, and other hard-to-get items in cardboard display boxes set up in the middle of the alley on orange crates.

Peter stopped and smoked a cigarette in a doorway while he looked around. Karen, tight-lipped, let him light one for her and waited beside him in silence. Across the alley a man was spieling a line to twenty others as he laid out cards on a blanket and had someone draw a number out of a paper bag. Peter didn't know the game but he could smell a come-on.

Beside him, Karen smoked impatiently and finally

broke the silence. 'Well, Mr. Congdon, do you have any plans for our future, or do we just stand here and pollute our lungs?'

'I've been giving it thought,' Peter said. 'The first step is to finish the pollution bit.'

'What's the second step?'

'We paid a man two hundred and fifty dollars for passports. We're going to see this man and get the passports.'

'He won't have any passports.'

'But if we stick a gun at his head, what do you want to bet he won't get some for us?'

'And what about your friends? Those two men. You think they've stopped looking for us?'

Peter shrugged. 'All they've seen is me without a moustache and a picture of you when your hair was blonde. The chances are the photographer didn't phone in any description, he only told them they'd find us at Giuseppe's. And you'd be surprised how different we look, especially to people who don't know us well.'

'We could walk right by them on the street and they'd never know it, I suppose.'

'I'd give you odds they wouldn't. Especially with you giving them the eye.'

She dropped her cigarette under her foot and muttered, 'You bastard.'

Three soldiers in khaki with C.A.R. patches on their sleeves came by and one stopped and spoke to her. She answered, shaking her head and laughing and indicating Peter. Then she nodded and laughed and he looked pleased and went away.

'And what the hell was that?'

'He wanted to go to bed with me. He thinks I'm in the business. So I told him I had to go to bed with you first but you were so inept it always took half the night and he should come back at twelve.'

She could have been lying, but she probably did it just that way. Certainly, in that dress showing under her open coat she could pass for any of the other girls standing around by doorways—a hell of a lot more attractive than any of the others, a hell of a lot sexier. He took her by the arm. 'Come on,' he said. 'Before you forget why we're here.'

They followed the Via Prè back and through the arch onto the Via del Campo where the people were fewer and seedier and more dangerous. When they got to the last section of the street there were no more vendors, no prostitutes, almost no people. Peter walked boldly beside Karen. They were a couple passing through, minding their own business, but Peter was watching the stragglers they passed, the one with the limp, the curly-haired youth with the too-tight trousers looking furtively around before coming out of an alley, the man slumped in the doorway with his head lolling.

The window over the barbershop beside the *Fotografia* sign was tightly shuttered and the staircase behind the glass-paned door was dark.

'I don't think he's home,' Karen whispered.

'If he isn't, we'll wait.' Peter moved in beside the door, turned the knob with a small sound and pushed. The door opened into the black chasm of the staircase. In there was the silence of the dead and Peter froze in the doorway, one hand still holding the knob, the other against the frame.

Then, as if belatedly fleeing, he backed out quickly, relatched the door, and pulled Karen away against the barbershop window. 'It's a trap.'

'A trap?'

'Nobody would leave a door open like that. Not in this place. Not without lights. They're in there waiting for us.'

'Who?'

'Those two men. And their friends. They lost us and

they're hoping we'll come back for the passports.' He grabbed her arm. 'Come on. We're getting out of this damned hole.'

He led her away fast and suddenly the man who had been lolling in a doorway was up in front of them, blocking the way. He staggered like a drunk and he was mumbling some kind of question which could have been for lire for a drink. But he was too much bigger than Peter, his feet were too set, his position too much in the way, his arms too octopus-like.

Peter hit him with a left uppercut to the stomach and a right cross to the jaw. The man went down but he didn't go out and he yelled as Peter pulled Karen around him.

Peter ran with her then, dragging her by the hand and drawing the automatic from his belt. Out of the *Fotografia* two men came flying and the big drunk, lying on the stones, pointed. The men had guns but they saw Peter's and held back.

Peter pushed Karen ahead of him and ran behind, shielding her, keeping his face to the enemy, forcing the two men to keep their distance. They spread out, hugging the sides of the buildings, hiding their guns back in their pockets, but following as close as they dared, keeping the pressure on.

Karen ran on and on, panting, stumbling in her heels, tiring with the pace, but forced to keep going by the goading of Peter's presence behind her. They came out at the end of the Via del Campo, onto the crossroad from the Via Gramsci, and her legs started to sag. 'Peter . . .'

'The Via Prè,' he told her. 'Keep going.'

'I can't. They're going to run us into the ground.'

'No they aren't. Not on the Via Prè.'

They crossed and started up its winding length. The other men came out of the Via del Campo and crossed over after them.

'I can't run any more,' Karen panted.

'Get over to the side. Go slow.'

She moved nearer the doorways and looked back fearfully.

'Relax,' Peter told her. 'They won't come so close I don't have to aim.'

She kept going, half running when she could, just walking when she couldn't. Where there were people, she slowed and felt safer. Peter kept his gun in his belt now and stayed three or four feet behind her. The pursuers, now that no guns were showing, moved out into the middle of the alley, keeping their distance, but moving more boldly.

They stayed like that, just out of easy range, playing it safe. They had the game in the bag and were content merely to run their quarry to earth.

Peter had other ideas. 'The taxis,' he muttered to Karen as they ducked in and among the occasional passersby, around the hawkers with their orange crates. 'Down at the end. We're going to get a taxi.'

And Karen nodded without speaking. It took all her breath to keep going.

The Via Prè was long—almost endless—and it seemed to Karen as if they had jogged forever before they passed the ramp beside the hotel and started down the slope to the Via Gramsci and the taxi area. They were past all the people now and their pursuers pulled out their guns again and started to close the distance. Peter had the automatic in his hand too but the dark, swarthy men weren't cowed by it now. They looked willing to move into shooting range.

The range was almost short enough when Peter and Karen reached the end of the ramp and the corner of the last building. In the area beside the curving Via Gramsci, two cabs were parked, the drivers talking idly. 'Go for the near one,' Peter muttered and made a bluffing move at the oncoming men. 'Get in and keep low.'

'What about you?'

'I'll hold them at bay till we can get away.'

The men weren't bluffed. They spread out on both sides of the alley, taking advantage of available cover, and moved closer.

'Run for it,' Peter said. He gave her a lead, then turned behind the corner of the building and sprinted after her. Behind him, heels clattered as the men broke into a race down the ramp.

They came around the corner cautiously, guns ready, but Peter and Karen were behind the nearest cab, on the little island separating it from the roaring traffic of the thoroughfare. The men halted and Peter said to Karen, 'Tell the driver to get us out of here fast.'

She was panting, trying to open the door and, at the same time, keep low. But she couldn't tell the drivers anything. They had seen the guns and were fleeing for cover.

Peter cast about for an alternative move, and that's when he discovered the approaching sedan. It was still far down the Via Gramsci, only coming around the last bend, and it wasn't its size that caught his attention, it was its crawling pace, the way it hugged the side of the road, the way it slowed at every alley off the Via Prè while everything else on the highway roared by. No wonder the two punks were content to let Peter run his own course. It was into a cul-de-sac.

He had to move fast. Across the Via Gramsci, under the *sopraelevata*—the elevated highway that ran through Genoa—a heavy wire fence separated the narrow sidewalk from a twenty-foot drop to railroad tracks and, beyond them, the warehouses, trucking areas and ship-handling facilities of the old Porto Vecchio. It was a dead end except for one break in the fence where steps led up to a walkway over the tracks and down a broad, well-lighted staircase to the warehouse area.

Peter didn't ponder the matter. He grabbed Karen's arm and pointed. 'Run for it. Run like hell . . . NOW!' He dragged her across the street through a break in traffic and they made for the steps.

Behind, the two gunmen raced to the cabs and raised their guns but a bus got in the way. Then Peter and Karen were up on the walkway, dodging a departing seaman and running for the stairs.

The big sedan sped forward, jumped to a halt beside the gunmen, and a man leaped out of the back. The car roared on, cut across traffic five hundred feet ahead, and started down the ramp that led to the dock level. Back on the avenue, the three men gave chase on foot.

The staircase was wide and long with a landing break and it ended in a broad roadway between warehouses where twenty cars were parked. Peter, loping down the steps behind a flying Karen, was halfway past the landing when the three men reached the head of the stairs above him. His gun was out and ready and they scrambled back in a wild mêlée at the sight of it. They returned to the top stair on their bellies, but now Peter and Karen were hiding behind the first car.

At that they leaped up and started down. Peter coolly aimed the automatic and fired. He was trying for a body hit on the middle pursuer but it wasn't his own gun and the bullet whined a half-inch past the man's chin. That drove them back again. The outside men dashed for the top of the stairs, the middle man dived.

Peter took advantage of the scramble. He grabbed Karen's hand and pulled her behind another car and then another, moving them away towards the end of the warehouse. It was what Brandt liked to call the 'cock-roach manœuvre', pointing out that the reason a cock-roach was so hard to trap was because he ran behind something not to hide himself, as a mouse did, but to hide his tracks and thus keep secret where he ducked to next and next and next. Brandt's orders on the subject of flight were, 'When you get under cover, move!'

At the corner of the other warehouse a watchman came out of a small shack, looked around for the cause of the explosion and walked around the corner. Peter retreated with Karen behind still another car and, at the top of the stairs, one of the gunmen signalled the sedan for help.

Beyond the warehouses was a broad open area for trucks and trains. Beyond that, the huge, shedlike operations building and the brightly lighted Stazione Maritima fronted on the water. Peter moved Karen two cars farther from the stairs but he was running out of hiding places.

A train whistled and a small steam engine started up, pulling a string of twenty creaking and rattling four-wheeled freight cars. It passed across the open area just as the big sedan appeared from the other direction. The sedan swerved and cut in front of the train, swung between the two warehouses, roared past the place where Peter and Karen hid, and came to a stop near the stairs where the first cars were. Men with guns leaped out on the far side, took cover behind it and looked for someone to shoot.

Peter moved Karen behind the last car and indicated the corner of the warehouse, fifty feet away. 'Keep low,' he whispered. 'Let's go.'

They crouched and ran together. But their luck didn't hold. Just before they got there a man on the stairs shouted.

Then they were around the corner out of sight and Peter dragged Karen full speed behind the last car of the moving train and into the shelter of its other side. They ran with it but it was gaining speed. A tank truck towing a tank trailer lumbered by in the direction of the operations building and they ducked behind that. Peter tried to get Karen a handhold on the trailer but it started drawing away and she fell. He pulled her to her feet but their shields had been stripped away. They were all alone in the open and there was an immediate shout of discovery.

But the cockroach manœuvre had been effective. Pursuit had become disorganised. The nearest man was a hundred yards away; the sedan, a hundred yards farther and heading in the wrong direction.

Now, however, the quarry was sighted and the hunters homed in. The first man started for them, a second yelled, and the far-off sedan screeched into a tight turn.

Peter and Karen made for the operations building, around its side, and to the front. But that was as far as they could go. The great building overhung a railroad track and was open at each end. Its loading doors were closed and the big pillars supporting the overhang were flush with the concrete sides of the dock where water lapped eight feet below.

The Stazione Maritima building was fifty yards off to the right, with the white passenger liner *Augustus* moored at its pier, but the lights were too bright and the distance too great for Peter and Karen to escape there unseen. Freighters were berthed at a pier off left but that was beyond the other end of the building and unreachable. Close at hand, two boats were moored with stern anchors and bow lines but there was no time to pull them in. A large scow was tied against the dock in the corner but it had nothing on it but a flat deck, flush with ground level, and there was no place to hide. As for the doorways and pillars, they offered the couple only temporary refuge for, in a matter of moments, men with guns would advance along the track from both ends of the two-hundred-foot building and flush them out.

Peter pulled Karen to the side of one of the posts, just

past the prow of the flat-decked scow. 'Can you swim?'

'Yes.'

He shoved her off the top of the pier, tucked his automatic in his belt and jumped after her.

WEDNESDAY 9:45–10:35 P.M.

She was sputtering when he came up beside her but she didn't protest. 'In here,' he whispered and guided her to the narrow gap between the concrete wall of the dock and the sloping wooden side of the scow.

They waited, treading water and seeking what handholds they could manage where the concrete had become eroded. They were out of sight and they could keep themselves afloat but they couldn't change the temperature of the water. They were cold and getting colder.

At first there was nothing but the distant sounds: the squealing and puffing of the train, the rumble of trucks on the Via Gramsci, the purr of cars on the *sopraelevata*. Then a shoe scraped on stones almost directly overhead. A voice all but in their ear said something and another voice, only slightly farther away, responded. Someone jumped onto the deck of the scow, crossed to the water side and spoke again. Then from the other end of the building came other voices. Men were moving in carefully, sure their prey was caught in a vice.

The search was post by post, doorway by doorway, and the voices grew bolder, louder, more frequent and more plaintive. The hunters were growing bewildered. The fugitive man and woman weren't there. But where could they have gone? Not aboard the boats—they hadn't been touched. And there was no sign of them in the water. Flashlight beams reflected only gentle ripples.

It went on like that for fifteen minutes and then the distressed and angry voices went away. A car motor started, doors slammed and the sound of the engine died away.

'Thank God,' Karen said. 'I'm freezing. Let's get out of here.'

'Not yet.'

'They're gone.'

'It may be a trick.'

'Oh, damn it, Congdon, I heard them. They said we must have got over to the liner or to the steamship building.'

'Of course. They'd say that to make us feel safe.'

'God damn it, I heard the *way* they said it. It wasn't any trick. They're stumped. They don't know we're anywhere around where we *could* hear them.'

'But we wait—because it might be a trap. And the way you avoid traps is by bearing the unbearable and enduring the unendurable.'

'Like at the cobbler's shop.'

'That's right. Just like the cobbler's shop.'

'And we didn't have to! You made me sit there for an hour and a half with my flesh crawling. I had to sit there imagining I could hear them breathing, hear them gurgling, hear them moving, until I thought I would faint. And now you want me to freeze to death, you God damned sadist. I won't. I damn well won't.'

'I thought you boasted you wouldn't be any liability to me.'

She clenched her teeth. 'You son of a bitch. You would say that.'

'I'm responsible for your welfare. Can you get that through your head? Stop trying to make me take chances.'

'My welfare? There are other ways of dying besides being shot. Like pneumonia for instance.'

'Stay angry. That'll keep you warmed up.'

She turned away in the darkness and endured in silence, bearing the numbing cold for three more minutes. Then she whispered, 'Peter, please,' and her teeth rattled. 'I can't stand it. I can't stay up any longer.'

Peter, who had a Spartan fortitude about such things, was numbed himself. 'All right,' he conceded, 'but go carefully. I don't know if our guns will shoot any more.'

'Oh, thank God. Where are we going? How are we going to get out of here?'

Peter swam out from behind the scow, saw no waiting guns above him, and continued close to the face of the wall. When Karen followed, he indicated the nearer of the two moored craft, a twenty-five footer with a small cabin and a tall wheelhouse the size and shape of a phone booth. 'You see that funny red boat there?'

She, moving stiffly beside him, said, 'You mean we're going to board her?'

'Board her and hide.'

They swam to it quietly through the dark water and Karen grabbed its stern, but she could do no more than that. Her fingers could hardly close and grip and she had no strength. Even Peter barely had the ability to pull himself up onto the canvas cover that protected the open back. He took Karen's hands, braced himself, and together they managed to get her over the edge and aboard, and she lay on the canvas, shivering and spent.

Peter took out his knife and hacked through the lines that lashed the canvas in place. He pulled up a section and they struggled under the gap and, in the blackness beneath, groped their way to the ugly little wheelhouse. There was no chance of putting to sea, however. Not only was there no key in the ignition, but the wheel was chained and locked.

Below the wheel, he found a doorway down two steps into the cabin, and that was open. In there he encountered a small sink and counter on the starboard side, a navigation table and chart shelves on the port. Forward were two bunks with worn woollen blankets folded on top.

'Blankets,' he said to Karen. They couldn't set sail but they could get warm.

She squeezed by him, her teeth chattering, and climbed onto the starboard bunk. He took the other and both worked in silence trying to get out of sop-sticky clothes with frozen fingers. It seemed to Peter he'd die of the cold before he got stripped to his shorts and wrapped in the two blankets there. And even with the blankets around him it would be a long time before warmth returned. Karen, however, was still struggling in the darkness, her teeth still chattering. Peter said, 'You having trouble?'

'Yes.'

'You want some help?'

'Don't you come near me.'

'Just trying to be of assistance.'

'Assistance,' she answered bitterly. 'Keeping me in icy water till I'm so numb I can't stay afloat.'

'The water really wasn't that cold.'

'It was like ice. And if it had been less cold, you'd have kept me in longer.'

'I told you why I did it.'

'I know what you told me. I also know why you really did it.'

'I did it to protect you.'

A hunk of wet cloth dropped on the floor from Karen's bunk and she said through her chattering, 'Protect me? Do you call this protection? I've been running since five o'clock this morning. Running, running. You keep saying we've got away but they're always on our heels. You let them take the key to the code away from you. Then you tip them off with travellers cheques. And for what? For passports we aren't going to get. Our plane's going to fly to Nice tomorrow morning and we aren't going to be on it.' She wrapped blankets around her. 'I'm tired and hungry and frozen. I don't have any clothes. I don't know how we're going to get out of here. And you say you're giving me protection! God, what would it be like if you weren't?'

'I can tell you what it would be like,' he said, his pride stung. 'You'd be dead.'

'I'd rather be.'

'Don't talk nonsense. I'll get you out of here.'

'How?'

'Never mind. I'll do it.'

'Sure you will. What's your plan? Stay here till we get a little bit warm and then get back into our wet clothes and swim over and stow away on that big liner over there? That ought to be a nice torture chamber idea for you.'

'I'm not trying to torture you.'

'You are. You don't like what I am and you're going to punish me for my sins. Peter Congdon is God and Karen Halley is dirt and God is going to put dirty little Karen through his own special hell. He's going to scar her for life to show her what's what.'

'You're talking like a fool. I'm not sitting in judgment on you. I'm not even thinking about you. I've got a job to do and I'm doing it and that's all I'm doing. I don't give a damn who you are or what you are. You're just my job.'

'Like hell I'm just a job,' she whispered fiercely. 'I'm the girl you want to horsewhip in the public square. Remember? And that's what you're trying to do!'

'Don't flatter yourself. I said it was my sister I'd horsewhip. Not you. Not anyone like you. You're not my sister, so the statement doesn't apply. Me punish you? Me bother? That's a laugh.'

'Sure it's a laugh. So is your excuse for keeping me in freezing water or shut up in a black room with two dead bodies. And the men you killed. That's pretty funny too, isn't it? And how clever you are at eluding the Mafia. That's the biggest laugh of all. I can't wait for tomorrow. Tomorrow ought to be great for laughs. Tomorrow we die.'

'Sure,' he answered. 'We make a great team. Isn't that what you said? Too bad you saved my life. Think what you could have been spared.'

She didn't reply to that and silence fell. Peter looked at his watch. It was twenty-five of eleven. A long, bitter day. He was feeling warmer and that helped a little. He could move his fingers better. He peeled away the remnants of his moustache, reached out for his gun and pulled it from the holster. He wished he could bathe it in oil, or even fresh water. Lacking that, he did the next best thing. He disassembled it and dried every part thoroughly. Then he put it back together again.

When he was through, he stretched out with it in his hand and went to sleep.

THURSDAY 6:15 A.M.–4:15 P.M.

Peter awoke in pre-dawn blackness to nearby voices and a slight motion of the boat. There was the clump of someone jumping onto the deck, then someone else, and the boat drifted. Foot-steps and sounds went over the cabin roof and side gunwales past the tiny oblong portholes.

'Peter?' It was Karen and she was frightened.

He was lying on his stomach facing the cabin entrance, his gun lightly held, his condition relaxed. The sounds weren't unexpected, though, at quarter after six, they might have been earlier than he had anticipated. 'Yes?' he whispered back.

'We're trapped. What are we going to do?'

Peter cocked and uncocked the gun, easing the hammer gently back against the shell. The gun seemed to be working all right. 'We're going to sit tight,' he said.

Outside, lines were loosened and remarks passed as the newcomers began removing the protective canvas.

Karen said, 'They'll know we're here. You cut the ropes.'

'It's all right. They're going to take us for a boat ride. You're going to tell them.'

There was a stir of excitement at the stern of the boat. The cut line and raised canvas had been discovered. The two men jabbered at each other and seemed to argue.

'What is it?' Peter whispered.

'They think somebody's inside. One wants to find out, the other wants to call the police. But they've untied the front rope and they can't get back to the dock without taking off the cover to start the motor anyway.'

'Which is just what we want.'

There was grumbling and talking and the canvas was unlashed. Finally a section was raised and in the lighter darkness of the gap, Peter could see the crouching silhouette of a young, well-built man trying to peer inside. The man said something and the pair pulled more of the canvas aside, finally stripping it away from the tiny wheelhouse and pulling it down onto the stern deck. Now the other man was visible, grey and lean in the dim light, and both started folding up the canvas, but with wary and nervous eyes on the low black opening under the wheel that led to the cabin.

Peter, his gun on the two, got to his feet and discarded the blankets. All he had on were his still-wet shorts, and the early morning air had the breath of rawness in it, but he was unaware of climate. 'How do you say "Hands up" in Italian?' he whispered.

'*Mani in alto.*'

Peter repeated it softly three times.

The two men finished folding the canvas and hesitated nervously. What to do: try to stow the canvas in the hold, which meant finding out once and for all if anybody were in there, or leave the canvas on the deck and put to sea without investigating? There was more discussion and, with the younger man leading the way, the two started dragging the canvas over to the gap.

'*Mani in alto.*'

The two men stopped in momentary paralysis.

'*Mani in alto!*' Peter said again, moving to the opening so they could see the gun.

They stared at the apparition of the nearly naked man and his naked gun and slowly raised their hands.

'Ask them who they are,' Peter told Karen.

Karen, who had come up so that he could feel her blankets pressing against his back, said, '*Chi siete? Como vi chiamate?*'

The men acted for a moment even more aghast at the sound of a woman's voice coming from the darkness. They looked at each other and peered at Peter more closely. They were not so alarmed now as curious. '*Umberto,*' the younger of the two said and pointed to himself. '*Mi chiamo Umberto.*' He pointed at the other. '*Questo è mio padre. Lui si chiama Luigi.*'

Karen said to Peter, 'The young one is Umberto, the old man is Luigi, his father.'

'Ask them if they'd like to earn a hundred thousand lire.'

'A hundred thousand?'

'That's right. Ask them.'

'Quest 'uomo vi pagherà centomila lire se fate quel che vi dice?' she said.

The two men, still with their hands raised, looked at each other for a long moment. Both started speaking at once and the younger deferred to the elder.

'Luigi asks what you want them to do,' Karen translated.

'Take us to the coast of France.'

'You mean across the border?'

'That's right.'

She explained that and reported that father and son doubted that this unclothed man had a hundred thousand lire.

'Tell them it's wet, but it's there.'

She did and they wanted to see the money.

'You tell them,' Peter said irritably, 'to get this tub under way and out of this harbour or I'm going to get mad and shoot somebody.'

She spoke to them in stern tones and they grumbled but started to obey. The old man asked, through Karen, about the hundred thousand lire and Peter let it be known that if the two men co-operated, he would give them that amount. If they gave him trouble, they would get nothing. In either case, they were going to sail to France.

They complained that they had no charts and Peter said they would do it without charts. They complained that their fuel tanks were nearly empty but, when Peter demanded that they show him, they remembered that they had had them filled the preceding afternoon.

Meanwhile, grudgingly and suspiciously, they pulled

in the stern anchor and got the engine started. The young man took the helm, turning the boat around and starting it out of the harbour. In the pre-dawn darkness, the great cruise liner *Augustus* was a ghostly white as they passed. It was a ship of comfort and luxury but Peter was, at that moment, satisfied with the old, but sound craft they were riding, with its smell of oil and the sea.

By the time the sun came up, the mountains behind Genoa had already sunk low on the horizon and the boat was rocking over gentle swells at a steady twelve knots. Umberto, the son, was at the wheel, his legs athwart the cabin exit. He was curly-haired and dark, with flashing eyes, a gold earring in his left ear, a moustache, white teeth, and a gypsylike, devil-may-care air. He had long since ceased to protest against this misuse of a boat geared for selling household wares in small towns along the coast and seemed to enjoy the idea of the trip for its own sake, quite apart from the promised reward. If the gun made him go, he might as well make the best of it.

The old man was another type. He was thin and wiry, with a lean, lined, weather-tanned complexion and close-cropped grey hair. There were no earrings in his ears, no moustache, no devil-may-care attitude. If he had learned to smile, it had been in his childhood, before the cares and vicissitudes of adult life drove merriment to the wall. He was shifty-eyed, suspicious of all things, and an unwilling believer in hundred-thousand-lire bonuses, the seaworthiness of ships, or the value of life. He was the eternal pessimist and he kept a far distance from Peter's station, staying back by the low stern rail, or moving up to the forward deck where Peter could not see him.

As light grew and the boat continued paralleling the shore at nearly the limits of visibility, Peter relaxed a little. They were far enough out now to be in a universe of their own, three men and a girl aboard a small craft making a southwestward course off the coast of northern Italy.

When the sun got warm enough, he left Karen in her blankets and took a new post on the cabin roof. There he spread out their belongings to dry and had the men produce a can of crankcase oil for him to wash his guns with.

Umberto was especially intrigued by the articles Peter laid out and weighted down. They included all the undergarments of the unseen woman, which indicated she must be down in that cabin with nothing on. It was a fascinating proposition but Umberto, under Peter's narrowed eye, didn't seek to verify it.

When enough of her things were dry, Peter, who had dressed on the cabin roof, took them down to her and returned to his solitary lookout. She got into them and primped as best she could. Then she came out, dressed but barefoot, her dried passport and papers restored to a still-damp purse, her low-cut dress spoiled but wearable. She had combed her hair and put on lipstick and when Umberto, stepping aside to let her through, got one look at this gorgeous creature, he so rushed to assist her that he forgot the wheel and the boat heeled badly, almost pitching the two of them overboard in each other's arms. He stabilised the craft and showered her with profuse apologies, and she acted almost as dazzled as he. Meanwhile, the two witnesses to the occasion were considerably less entranced by the romantic encounter. In the stern of the boat, the old man hacked and spat as loudly as he could. Peter, soaking his disassembled automatic in the crankcase oil, glowered in disgust.

If Peter found the meeting revolting, what followed was worse. The pair was an instant twosome and Karen's interest in the cocksure, arrogant young buck was sickening—especially since she ignored Peter completely, and she looked even sexier in the ruined dress than when it was new.

But it was Karen and Umberto and they were like leeches together; especially when crammed into the narrow confines of the pilothouse, she learning how to steer, he paying more attention to the bared curve of her bosom than the heading of his compass.

There was food on board, a basket of bread, cheese and wine under the stern seats, and half an hour after Karen appeared on deck, Luigi produced it. Father and son split the piloting duties, the old man eating while Umberto conducted his steering lessons. Then Luigi took the wheel and the young people ate together, laughing, talking, and sitting very close.

It wasn't until they were finished that Karen remembered Peter. She came up around the side of the cabin to where he still sat on the roof, fitting a clip into the newly oiled and assembled automatic.

'You want something to eat?'

He pitched the can of oil overboard. 'A little cheese would be fine.'

'You want it here?'

'Yes.'

She shrugged and stepped back. He said, 'And see if they have a spyglass or something.'

There were binoculars under another of the seats and Karen handed them and a chunk of cheese and the nearly empty wine bottle up to Peter. Umberto was with her, keeping her safe with an arm around her waist, and she gave him an appreciative look when she stepped back.

Peter ate in solitude and studied the distant shoreline through the glasses. He was not sure how far Genoa was from the border nor how far they had come and he sought some indication from the coastal towns they passed.

It was close to two o'clock when his spying brought some reward. That pretty harbour with the palace overlooking it, and homes on the terraced hills behind, that had to be Monaco. Wherever, from now on, they put in, they could show their passports without fear of arrest. They had left Italy behind.

He thought of calling Karen to show her the joyful sight but she and Umberto were steering the craft, she with her hands around the wheel, he with his hands around her waist and his cheek against her hair. Let her go to hell.

They left Monaco behind and the coastal heading was west. Karen was handling the boat herself now, taking her through the swells. The old man was down below and Umberto was lifting a hatch in the stern deck to check the fuel tanks. Peter pointed at the coastline and called, 'Head in there. Aim for that point.' Karen nodded and turned the wheel. Umberto rejoined her and got a fix.

They drew closer and gradually a point of land grew out from the shore, lushly dark and green, with here and there the gables of fine homes showing through the trees. On the right, now only a couple of miles away, were the barren, sandy cliffs of the southern coast of France, the scrubby hills, the grey-blue dots of vegetation. Zigzag roads coursed their sides and the arches of a high bridge spanned a chasm. Dwellings huddled on the shore in clusters but climbed the steeps in scatters. Farther back, they seemed randomly thrown into the hills and valleys behind.

The sun was low on the left now but the water was still blue and calm and there were no clouds in the sky. It was close to four o'clock and the boat was heading for a round white building with tall windows which stood on a hill. Below and to the left, Peter, through the binoculars, picked out the beacon tower on the white travertine wall of a marina. He directed Karen and Umberto to it and in another fifteen minutes they turned through the narrow opening into a tiny circular basin crowded with boats.

It was a quiet, out-of-the-way harbour with little activity. The big boats were fender to fender just inside the sea wall; the small boats were clustered in the shallows on the beach side. The gas pumps, hoist, and service area were on the right, where the land came out, and the only people about were a couple of men mending nets. No sirens sounded, no whistles blew. No one paid any attention as the old, red, ugly Genovese boat hove to at the mouth of the marina, and under Peter's directions, edged in against the walk by the steps to the beacon platform.

Peter leaped ashore with a bowline and hitched it around a large rusted iron post, holding the boat clear of a black, fity-foot sailboat which was first-moored by large white cabin cruisers. Karen, meanwhile, gave Umberto Peter's hundred thousand lire and he accepted it, all grins. He helped her onto the shore and gestured eternal gratitude to Peter.

Peter tossed back the bowline, the old man set the engine in reverse, and the boat backed off. Karen, with her still-damp purse and coat over her arm, gave Umberto a warm final wave and blew him a kiss. Peter looked away. 'I wonder where the hell we are,' he said irritably.

She turned from Umberto and gestured at a small stucco office with a sign on it on the other side of the basin back of the gas pumps. 'The sign,' she announced, 'says International Sporting Club de Saint Jean Cap Ferrat. Does that tell you anything?'

Peter stared but the sign was too far away. 'Who told you?'

She shrugged. 'I read it through the binoculars while

you were doing all the landing. I wanted to make sure we weren't still in Italy.'

'Thanks for the vote of confidence. Do you speak French?'

'No. Do you?'

'I had two years in high school.'

'So did I. What's that prove?'

'It proves you went to high school for two years.' Peter took her arm. 'If you can forget your friend on the boat, let's go find somebody who knows enough English to tell us where the nearest airport is.'

THURSDAY 4:20–5:05 P.M.

'What's the matter?' Peter asked, for Karen was limping.

'The shoes. They must have shrunk or something. And they weren't mine to begin with. There must be a place to buy shoes in this town.'

Peter said, 'You're out of your mind.'

Karen stopped dead in her tracks. They were rounding the back side of the marina now, where the shallows showed the pebbly bottom. Ahead and to the left the hills rose steeply and homes were sparse. Behind, the hotel La Voile d'Or looked down on the harbour from the bluff, and across the way Umberto and Luigi guided their boat in at the Total and Shell gas pumps.

They waved and Karen waved back, a vigorous, regretful wave. She said to Peter, 'What do you mean, I'm out of my mind?'

'Do you think we're going to stop to buy shoes? We're getting the hell out of here as fast as we can.'

'Get out of here as fast as we can? I've got to get some clothes.'

'Gorman will buy you a wardrobe trunk full when you get back to Washington.'

'I mean now.' She kicked off her shoes hard. 'I'm not going to wear those shoes. I'm not going to wear these clothes. Look at me. A dirty mess of a dress, salt-caked, shoe-polish hair . . .' She flipped the coat onto the iron rail that ran along the sidewalk. 'And a wet, filthy coat. It can rot there.' She stuck her hands on her hips and faced him. 'Look at me. Do you think I can go around like this?'

'Look at me. I'm going to.'

'You're not a woman.'

'No, I'm a man who's responsible for getting a woman safely to the United States and I'm not going to worry about how she looks or how I look en route.'

'That's more of it, isn't it? The torture test. Like back rooms and freezing water. Now you're going to make me ride an airplane barefoot in a wretched dress . . .'

'Put the coat on . . .'

'I don't want the coat. The coat is wet. I'll get pneumonia if I wear the coat. All I want is a new coat, something cheap, to cover this dress, and sandals or something for my feet. Is that so much?'

'It is when I don't know plane schedules or how far it is to the nearest airport. There's a price on your head and just because we've crossed a border doesn't mean we've gotten away.'

'That's right. I forget that, don't I? I should remember how they've tracked you before. You, who are supposed to be so damned good at eluding people. Let's run to the airport. Let's get there just as fast as we can. The Mafia is probably hot on our heels.'

'It's simple logic, lady. First things first. First we look

at plane schedules. Then, if there's time, we can see about clothes.'

'Stop talking so much. Let's find that airplane you're so hot about, before the Mafia gets us.'

They went on and the road forked, one branch circling back to the gas pumps, the other going up the hill to a higher road. The sign for that one said 'Nice–Monaco', and they went up on a narrow pavement lined with shops.

At the top was a bus stop, a little park with a high view of the marina and, across the street, a car with a *taxi libre* placard in its windshield. Peter and Karen got into it and told the driver, 'Nice airport.'

The ride was along a high road terraced into the mountainside which, except when it wound through towns, looked down upon the sea. Then the harbour of Nice appeared below with a long arm of breakwater reaching to a beacon far across the entrance. The road dropped rapidly into the town and when the breakwater appeared again, it was at eye level far out to sea.

They went through the heart of the city, riding each to his own side, looking out of the windows in silence. The route was along the Promenade des Anglais, beside the long stony beach pounded by the aquamarine breakers of the Mediterranean. The sun was low on the horizon ahead, glowing a deep hazy yellow, and a rising jet came out of its fading glare, paralleling the shore.

The sun had dropped lower and was a red ball ready to sink when the taxi swung off the highway, looped underneath, and came in to a halt under the blue corrugated-glass marquee of the terminal. Peter converted his lire at the *Caisse-Cash* counter inside to pay the driver and took Karen to the Pan Am desk in the corner to ask about flights to the United States.

The clerk, a blond man with an English accent, watched them come. Hippies he had seen—but this pair?

Karen, however, walked with her head held high, looked him straight in the eye, and opened the ruin of a purse on the counter for her make-up. The clerk looked at the low V of her dress and then told Peter there was a flight out at ten thirty-five the next morning, stopping at Barcelona, Lisbon and JFK. It would cost, he took care to add, $281·40 apiece.

Peter wasn't concerned about prices. He was concerned about time. 'I want it sooner than that. What about the other airlines?'

'Air France has a Paris flight at ten-oh-five this evening. I'll see if there are connections.' He went into the office behind the counter for schedules.

Peter lighted a cigarette and, beside him, Karen uttered a low, animal sound that made him turn. She was digging through her purse with increasing frenzy. She pulled things out onto the counter top, even her gun, and tore at the lining. Her face was chalk.

Peter snatched up the gun and stuffed it in his pocket. 'For God's sake, what are you doing?'

'My passport! It's gone. My passport and my wallet!'

'You mean you left them . . .'

'No. No. I put them in the purse after you tried to dry it. I put everything in. I made sure.'

'Nice friends you've got. Your pals Umberto and Luigi.'

'But they couldn't—I never put it down. I—Oh, God. When I steered.'

'Sure,' Peter said sourly. 'The cute one holds your hand and the old one robs you blind.'

'Oh God. But they couldn't. Why wouldn't they take the gun too?'

'Because then you'd find out. They don't want the gun. They're not going to shoot it out with me.'

'But why? We were . . . They were . . .' She put her hands to her cheeks. 'My wallet—if they wanted to steal. But why my passport?'

'To keep you here. They knew who you were. It's obvious. The word was spread that we'd last been seen around the docks. So who else would we be? And, remember, the reward is in dollars, not lire. I'll bet they weren't just getting gas when we left them. I'll bet they were making phone calls.'

The clerk came back, flipping the pages of the schedule book.

'Forget it,' Peter told him. 'We've lost a passport.'

'Your passport? Oh I *am* sorry.'

'Where's the American Consulate in this town?'

The man pulled out a phone book to see. He didn't know if this strange pair were straight or not but he played it that way. 'I rather fear they close at five,' he said, glancing at his watch, 'and it's just five now. But I'll give them a ring if you'd like.'

'Please do.'

He made the call from the office and it was quick. He slapped down the receiver and came back. 'Five-thirty is closing,' he said. 'You *are* in luck. You should just be able to make it. I told them you'd be coming. Number three Rue Docteur Barety. Here.' He scribbled the address on a slip of paper and tore it off for them.

THURSDAY 5:30–5:55 P.M.

The consulate building was square, two-storied, and cream coloured. There were high first-floor windows, green shutters, a railing around the roof, and it was in mid-block off the Boulevard Victor Hugo. Traffic en route was impossible but the cab got Peter and Karen there with two minutes to spare and Peter breathed a sigh to see in the growing darkness that its windows were still lighted.

They went inside and hurried up marble steps to a reception room where a girl sorted cards at a desk under the United States seal. On the side wall, the portrait of Lyndon Johnson was flanked by the American and consulate flags. The wall opposite the desk bore a large abstract painting which hung over a low visitor's couch and magazine table.

A grey-haired woman came out of a door at the end of a short hall directly ahead of the steps as they came up and she strode forward as if she'd been waiting with her hand on the knob. 'You have the passport problem?' She took in their appearance without comment, led them to the visitor's couch, and told the receptionist she could go. 'Here, my dear,' she said, turning a comforting smile on the chalk-white Karen, drawing her down onto the couch beside her while Peter took the other end. 'Now what seems to be the trouble?'

The answer was simple. The young lady had lost her passport.

Lost it, how?

It appeared to have been stolen.

The small, grey-haired lady compressed her lips. 'I see. Have you reported this to the police?'

'No,' Peter answered.

'That's the first thing you should have done. You should have done that before you came here.'

'The point is,' Peter replied, 'what are we going to do about it? How can we get back into the country?'

'That's quite simple. It's a matter of issuing her a new one.'

'How long would that take?'

'A day or two, depending on how busy they are.'

'A day or two?' Karen moaned.

'Of course, in an emergency . . .'

'This is an emergency,' Peter said.

'Then it can be done faster.' She smiled at Karen comfortingly again. 'You needn't upset yourself, my dear.'

'Could we get it in time to catch a ten-thirty plane tomorrow morning?' Peter wanted to know.

The woman pondered uncertainly. 'Well, that doesn't give us much time, especially starting this late. Things are closing up, you know. And since Armistice Day is Saturday, we'll be closed tomorrow. I forgot that. Really, before Monday I don't see . . .'

Peter said, 'It's not just an emergency. This is critical. It could be life and death.'

'I see,' the woman said soberly. 'I can't promise anything, but I'll try to do what I can.' She held out her hand to Karen. 'May I see your birth certificate?'

Karen started a little. 'I . . . ah . . . don't have it with me.'

'Oh.' The woman paused. 'Your driver's licence?'

Karen said, 'It wasn't just my passport. My wallet was stolen too.'

'Oh dear me. You mean you don't have any identification?'

She shook her head.

'Nothing at all? You can't give me any proof of your identity?'

'I'm afraid not.'

'Oh, I am sorry. Then there will be problems, I'm afraid. We'll have to get in touch with the State Department to verify the issuance of the passport and all that sort of thing. That, I'm afraid, will take a little time.'

'How long a time?' Karen asked weakly.

'Two or three weeks if it's done by mail. Of course, by phone . . .'

Peter stood up. 'Forget it,' he said. 'That's not going to do any good at all. Look, are there any hotels nearby?'

The woman glanced once again at Karen's garb, the bare feet, the low-cut and rather strange-textured dress, that awkward purse. And she looked up at the man accompanying this strange woman. What was there about his clothes? The two of them looked as if they might have been shipwrecked together. Both were definitely suspicious. He seemed to be American, all right. He seemed in no worry over his ability to get into the United States. It was all about this woman. Frankly, the girl's credentials were highly suspect. In fact, her background was much too suspicious. Did the man, American as he might be, really believe that all he had to do to get an alien mistress into the country was to pretend she was a native-born citizen who had lost her passport? Really . . .! The unflattering ignorance some Americans had about their government!

'The Albemar Hotel is not far from here,' she said sweetly to the American. 'Turn right on the Victor Hugo Boulevard and it's on the right-hand side about five or six blocks up.' Then she added, with just a touch of malice because she was suspicious, 'But I'm afraid it won't be much help to the young lady. You can't get a room without the concierge filling out a police card and this must be done from the passport.'

Peter ignored the barb. 'Are there any clothing stores in the neighbourhood? And when do they close?'

Shops, she told him, were on the Avenue Medecin en route to the Albemar, and they stayed open till seven.

Peter thanked her and said he'd take it from there. He led Karen around the rail to the steps, down and out the front door, down the side steps from the stoop and out the front gate. It was completely dark now and the street was quiet, cars lining both sides. Karen stopped and leaned against the iron fence and buried her face in her hands. 'Fool,' she sobbed wretchedly. 'You utter, utter fool!'

'Forget it,' Peter said. 'Kicking yourself isn't going to do any good.'

'You were right,' she answered bitterly, her head against the fence. 'You didn't trust them. You didn't let them near you. I thought they wanted the hundred thousand lire. They sell goods to towns along the coast and they don't make much. And now I've done it.' She stared down at her bare feet on the cold sidewalk. 'Now I'm trapped and the Mafia knows it. And they know where I am. Now it's just a question of time.'

'Don't talk nonsense.'

'It's true.'

'They knew where we were last night and it didn't get them anywhere.'

She shook her head. 'I'm tired. I can't go through another night like last night. I can't run any more. I can't hide any more. We had the chance and I blew it.' She gave a short, bitter laugh. 'And I accused you of giving us away. That's funny, isn't it?'

'You couldn't help it.'

'I could have stayed in the cabin. I could have kept away from them the way you did. But no. I had to make a play for Umberto. Handsome, dashing Umberto and his slit-eyed old man. And the girl got taken for a ride. God, did she ever get taken for a ride!'

Peter touched her for the first time, putting a hand on the back of her shoulder. The bare skin of her arm was cool. The night air wasn't cold but it wasn't meant for light dresses and bare arms. 'Stop kicking yourself,' he said. 'You can't help the way you're made.'

She gave a little, hollow laugh. 'You really believe that too, don't you?' She shrugged. 'Well, why not?' She pulled away then. 'There's only one thing. I'm not going to expose you to any more danger. You've got a passport and you're going to use it.'

Peter laughed. 'You mean, go back and tell Gorman I quit?'

'I mean, go back and tell Gorman that the lady blew the assignment.'

'And his investigation along with it? I have a feeling I'd be safer facing the Mafia than going back to him without you.'

She shivered and clasped her arms. 'Well, make up a story. Tell him I'm dead. Tell him anything you want, but just go and get out of here. It's not your fight any more, so let's at least have one of us get home.'

Peter looked her over from her shoe-polish-and-sea-water hair to her dank, moneyless purse, her thin, skimpy dress, and bare cold feet. He put his hands on his hips and grinned at her. 'And what would you do if I did leave you?'

'Peter, I mean it. If you could give me a little money.' I can get by just fine.'

'Sure you could. What would you do?'

'Buy some clothes.'

'And then what? Become a streetwalker? You don't even know the language.'

She lifted her chin. 'I'd get my passport back. I'd have them call the State Department. It's a valid passport. It's not a phoney real, it's a real real. Senator Gorman fixed it so it's a real passport.'

Peter laughed at her. 'You don't really mean it's a real one. You only mean he's *told* you it's a real one. You might find the State Department has different ideas about it. That is, if you could prove you're Karen Halley. But you can't. And even if you could, and even if the passport was real, you couldn't prove you're the same Karen Halley, because you aren't. And, of course, there's the problem of where you'd stay while you're waiting to find all this out. Where are you going to register? What hotel? What inn? As the woman in there told you, you have to show a passport.'

Karen said, 'Don't worry about it, will you? Give me what money you can spare and go. Please, will you go?'

He took her arm. 'Come on, it's cold and we're wasting time.'

'Peter, I said . . .'

'You said a lot of stupid things. Forget it. The reason I was sent to fetch you is because you don't have enough sense to get to America on your own. Which is why we're going to do things my way.'

'But the Mafia,' she said as he propelled her towards the Boulevard Victor Hugo at a good pace. 'You'll be in danger.'

'That's all right. I'm developing a taste for it.'

'What are you going to do?'

'First we're going to buy ourselves those clothes you want so badly. Then we're going to get a room, then we're going to eat some dinner, and then we're going to call the senator and tell him it's his turn to pick up the ball.'

THURSDAY 6:00–9:15 P.M.

The shops on the Avenue Jean Medecin were expensive, especially those where the Boulevard Victor Hugo became Boulevard Dubouchage. Some of the men's suits cost more than the 861 francs in Peter's wallet and clothes in the women's stores were equally frightening. Farther down the street, however, below the Rue Pastorelli, was a big department store where dresses sold for as low as 18·95 francs, rather than 189·50, and Peter and Karen did their shopping there.

He had been spending money without counting heretofore, but 135,600 lire blown on unused plane tickets and a disastrous 100,000-lire boat ride, to say nothing of $250 for undelivered passports, was bringing him down to the narrow edge. His total assets now were $670 in soggy American Express Travellers Cheques and the 861 francs left of the 903 he got for his lire at the airport. And fare to the United States would eat up close to $600 of it. It was time to economise.

By seven, when the stores closed, both he and Karen had complete, if inexpensive, new outfits, including a light coat for Karen, and a sweater as well as a jacket for Peter. They had purchased a few incidentals too—a suitcase, toothbrushes, a razor and some blonde hair-dye to remove the curse of the shoe polish. And Peter still had 274 francs left in his wallet.

They hunted up the Hotel Albemar then, on the Boulevard Dubouchage. It was a five-storey cream and salmon building on a corner, with a little drive in front. The lobby was small and up half a dozen steps on the left of the entrance, and the only people in it were the grey-haired desk clerk and a dark-haired woman in the office behind.

Peter had worked it out with Karen in advance and she took a chair by the stair rail while he went to the desk. A single room was Peter's inquiry—for himself, that was—and could he have a guest for dinner?

The clerk spoke only fair English, but he could handle that much. Guests would be twenty francs, a single with bath would be sixty, which included *petit déjeuner* and one other meal.

Peter went up to see the room. It was large and

pleasant with a separate toilet off the entrance hall, a big double bed, the customary writing desk, clothes cabinet and chairs, and a shiny pink bathroom with shower stall, basin and bidet. Two tall windows with tufted curtains looked down on the little drive. It was just what he wanted and he left the suitcase.

Back in the lobby, Peter let the clerk fill in the *fiche de voyageur* card from his passport and took Karen through a small lounge-television room into the dining room beyond, where a scattering of the other guests ate.

The meal was simple and tasty and they ate it leisurely, washing down *noisettes d'agneau poëlées* with a half bottle of wine. While waiting for fruit, cheese and coffee, Peter passed Karen the room key under the table. 'Thirty-eight *bis*, whatever that means,' he said. 'It's on the fourth floor, the room right back of the elevator. Push the key in till it stops, turn it ninety degrees and it'll go in the rest of the way.'

When they went back through the television room, half a dozen of the other guests were watching an anti-American programme on the Vietnam war. Since it was off-season and Nice was a haven for the retired, the guests were all elderly, a mixture of sexes and nationalities, none of whom paid attention as Karen and Peter passed behind their chairs.

Outside the room was the connecting hall and service pantry from the lobby to the dining room. Across the hall, out of view of the desk, were the stairs. When no one was looking, they simply crossed to them, Karen going up, Peter going down. He went through the kitchen in the basement and out the back service door into a small parking lot behind the building.

He wandered the streets till nine o'clock and then walked back boldly into the building through the front door, up the steps and to the desk. The clerk, the woman and an elderly, uniformed night clerk come to relieve them were all on hand to witness his solitary entrance. He smiled at them like a man who has just seen a young lady home, and said he'd like to put in a collect transatlantic call to the United States.

The woman handled it, writing down Gorman's name and numbers, telling Peter the post office would let her know how long it would be. He said he'd take it in his room—38 *bis*.

'*Oui*—yes.' She turned towards the rack. 'Your key?'

Peter patted a pocket. 'I've got it.' He opened the heavy elevator door, bade them all a good night, and pushed the next to top button.

When he got out, he went around to 38 *bis* and knocked two shorts and a long. Karen's voice said softly, 'Peter?'

'Yes.'

She let him in, pulling back the slide that worked the latch.

'Anybody see you?' he asked, shutting the door and following her.

'One of the maids almost did. She came in to turn down the bed but I got into the bathroom and turned on the shower.'

The phone buzzed and the woman told Peter he could expect the call to go through in forty-five minutes. Peter relayed that to Karen and said, 'Now we'll let him earn his pay.'

'Yes,' Karen said. 'Gorman. Not Brandt. Gorman.'

'Sure. Gorman's got better strings to pull. Why not?'

'Why not indeed. There wouldn't be a Brandt agent in Nice, would there? I mean like Rome and Genoa and places like that.'

'Yes, he does have an agent in Nice, but that agent is in West Germany right now.'

'Or you *say* he's in West Germany, which amounts to the same thing.'

'What's the matter with you?'

'I'm surprised you haven't noticed.' She gestured at the bed. 'The sleeping arrangements. One bed. No couches.'

'It's a single room. You're lucky it's not a single bed.'

'Yes, I'm very lucky. I'm penniless and helpless and without a passport. Everywhere else, Brandt has agents who can get you passports, who can give you shelter and protection while you wait. But not here. Not in Nice. The Nice agent is out of town, so there's nothing to do but bunk in with Peter Congdon while Gorman goes through governmental red tape three thousand miles away.'

'Oh my God, do you really think I'm trying to stage a seduction scene?'

'My mistake, I'm sure. Not virtuous Peter Congdon. He's never seduced anybody in his life.'

'Look, if I were going to make passes at you, I would have done it in the boat last night.'

'Not last night. Not after keeping me in freezing water. You owed me too much. But tonight, I owe you. And don't tell me it hasn't passed through your mind that I was a guy's mistress and I therefore ought to be a pretty soft touch.'

'If you've got any ideas . . .' Peter came close. 'Listen, sister, I'm going to sleep on this half of this bed. Facing that door. Where you sleep or how comfortably you sleep is up to you. But I'll tell you this. Your questionable virtue is safe. I don't mix pleasure with business in the first place and, in the second, if I wanted a woman, I'd go get one. But it wouldn't be you. It wouldn't ever be you!'

'Oh it wouldn't?' she answered hotly. 'You try, but you don't hide it. I've seen you look at me. I've seen your eyes. You may hate me. You may look down your nose at me, but you want me. You hunger for me. I've seen that look too many times.'

He denied it fiercely. 'Want you? Hunger for you? I couldn't even touch you without thinking of the money you got paid for being touched by Joe Bono—money that was bled from prostitutes and drug addicts. Money from slaves. So they could stay slaves. Because they think it's better than being dead. Me touch you? You'll never have the satisfaction.'

She tossed her head. 'And you'll never get the chance.'

'Good. We understand each other. So now, if you're going to bleach your hair, get at it, will you? I want to shower and shave.'

THURSDAY 10:05–10:45 P.M.

The call came through at five after ten, by which time Karen was a blonde again, though not a natural one, and Peter was clean-shaven and refreshed.

'What are you doing in Nice?' Gorman asked before Peter could even start to talk. Peter explained. They'd had a run-in with some Mafia members. They'd got away but they had to leave Karen's passport behind.

'What do you mean you had to leave it behind? I don't understand you, Congdon.'

'I mean they took it from her and getting mixed up with them to try to get it back isn't my idea of how to get her safely over to you.'

'What *is* your idea?'

'I was thinking the best thing would be if you could get her another passport.'

'Oh, that's what you think? Just like that, eh?'

'Senator, she's got to have a passport.'

Gorman said testily, 'God damn it, Congdon, first the Mafia takes your code key away from you, now they've taken her passport. Any God-damned agent with any capability would have had the girl home here by now. Instead, you're stuck in some God-damned foreign country because you don't have a passport. Of all the things to be stuck for!'

Peter didn't want to tell the senator it was his fault the Mafia had got onto him in the first place, for he couldn't blame the senator for their subsequent problems. 'I'm sorry, sir, but that's the way it is. We're also short on money too.'

'You're short of money, too. I'm surprised you've still got the girl. Or maybe you don't have.'

'I do, Senator. She's alive and in good health. And I can deliver her to you just as soon as she can be equipped with a passport.'

'And money for the tickets, I gather?'

'I still have enough, but I'd like another five hundred. The Mafia knows we're in Nice and if we have money troubles . . .'

'All right, but what're you coming to me for? If you have problems, call your boss. He's the one who's responsible. He picked you, I didn't.'

'My boss doesn't traffic in passports, and Miss Halley tells me you managed to work it in some kind of way so that her passport is for real. That means the State Department can issue a duplicate, except that Miss Halley cannot convince the consul's office here of her identity. So, Senator, since you arranged about her passport in the first place and since you can vouch for her identity in the second, what would be more natural than for me to turn to you to replace the passport that was stolen?'

Gorman muttered and swore. 'All right,' he said. 'It's obvious that if anybody's going to save you from the Mafia it's got to be me. I'll have to see what I can do. Call me up at my office here at four o'clock tomorrow afternoon.'

'Four o'clock your time or my time?'

'My time, of course. How do I know what time it is where you are?'

Peter said he would do that and Gorman said, 'And for God's sake, don't get caught. I need that girl!'

Peter said he wouldn't, said good-bye and hung up. He got off the hard bed and lighted a last cigarette. He was stripped to his waist, wearing only his trousers and shorts. Karen, with a towel around her head, was in her slip and both were barefoot. Peter put his automatic on the bedside shelf below the phone and hung a *Ne Pas Déranger* sign on the outside knob of the door. He set one of the chairs under the inside latch, switched off all but the double gooseneck lamps over the headboard, stripped off his pants with his back to Karen, hung them over a chair, then slipped under the covers. He took off his watch and wound it, laying it on the glass shelf top. 'Good night,' he said. 'You'll excuse me if I don't keep you company, but I need my beauty sleep.'

She had stood on the far side of the bed watching the whole process. 'Don't mention it,' she said, but she still watched without moving. He stretched out on his side, facing the six-foot hallway and the barricaded door, flinging back the blankets and keeping only the sheet over him. He didn't look at her at all.

She watched him for another minute but he didn't stir. She went into the bathroom, locked the door, took a shower and washed out her four-hour-old underthings, hung them on a hook over the bidet, got back into her slip, and brushed her teeth. Then she cautiously unlocked the door and peeked out. He was as she had left him, still on his side facing away from her. She came to bed silently, turned off the gooseneck lamps and slid under the covers herself, keeping to the far edge of the bed, a good foot beyond contact with him. He was breathing evenly and she relaxed. The strains began to ease. Gorman and Peter, between them, would save her.

She was soon asleep but she wasn't the last to drop off. Peter, though he had lain motionless through it all, did not relax his vigil until the heavy rise and fall of her breathing told him that she was secured for the night.

FRIDAY 10:00–10:10 P.M.

Peter and Karen spent the whole of the next day in the room. By calling the desk that he was indisposed, he kept the maids away, but he did have meals sent up.

In normal circumstances, a healthy young male and female, locked up together in an hotel room for twenty-four hours, can have themselves quite a ball. In fact, Peter had once done just that with Stephanie. They'd spent a weekend in a motel room, only leaving it to eat, and it was a memorable, if exhausting, occasion. If, however, the expected type of entertainment is unavailable, that same period in an hotel room can be a rugged one. And when the girl in question was the sexiest female Peter had laid eyes on, a free and easy type who made a play for, and gave the eye to, every male in the universe except Peter himself, and when he had the hots for her as he hadn't had them for any girl since Stephanie, the twenty-four hours in room 38 *bis* were pure hell.

He and Karen scarcely spoke to each other, they scarcely looked at each other, but the more they tried to ignore the other, the more aware they became. Peter had a Paris edition of the *Herald Tribune* sent up, but reading that and eating meals was all the two of them had to do. By the time Peter's call to Gorman got through at ten o'clock on Friday evening, both were so nervous and edgy they were ready to eat holes in the walls.

When the phone buzzed at five after ten, Peter almost dived to snatch it up.

Gorman's voice had its usual sharp edge but it didn't contain despair. 'Congdon? Are you still there? How's the girl?'

Peter said she was fine, they were both fine and, no, the Mafia hadn't located them. He waited.

'Well that's something anyway,' Gorman said. 'I want you to know you've put me to a great deal of trouble. You and your sloppy handling of this matter.'

'It couldn't be helped.'

'It should have been helped. Now I'm going to tell you something. You're a damned lucky man. I'm bailing you out but it's only by accident that I can do it this soon. It's a series of fortuitous circumstances.'

'I appreciate that, Senator.'

'I got you . . . the girl rather . . . another passport and was lucky in being able to give it to a courier who flew with it to Paris last night. He gave it to a friend of mine there who happens to have a villa in Antibes, which isn't far from where you are. This friend's name is Pierre DeChapelles and he's in Antibes right now. He flew down this afternoon for the weekend. And he has an envelope for you. I called him not an hour ago and he is waiting for you. Have you got all that?'

'Yes, sir. Pierre DeChapelles in Antibes. Whereabouts in Antibes?'

'I'm coming to that. Now here's what you're going to do. You're going to get a taxi and go to Antibes tonight. To find his villa, you go along the main road by the beach that goes past the hotels—the Hotel Royale is one. That road then turns inland, away from the beach. Very soon after, there's a road off to the left which has a sign saying Cap d'Antibes. You take that road. The houses there are numbered. DeChapelles' house is number thirty-seven. Got that? Thirty-seven. It's just a little before you get to an intersection, as I recall. Anyway, if there's any trouble, his phone number is 88.89.55. Got that?'

'I've got it.'

'All right, good. Now, you should be flying back here tomorrow sometime. Wire me what plane you're taking —what time you'll arrive. I don't think we'll need code on this because it's not going to matter who knows it. I'll have plenty of men on hand to take you off the plane and rush you to safety.'

'You'll be one of them, won't you, Senator?'

'Oh yes, I'll be on hand.'

'Then, see you tomorrow.'

'Watch out for yourself, Congdon.'

'I'll watch out for the girl too. Good night, Senator.'

FRIDAY 10:20–11:15 P.M.

All the ancient-vintage guests had gone to bed and Peter had no trouble sneaking Karen out of the hotel through the basement. He returned to wake the grey old night clerk and ask for a cab.

The ride to Antibes was just under half an hour and directions were easy for the town was too small to get lost in. They passed through the centre, went down by a small formal park and then along the water's edge where the closed and shuttered Hotel Royale was undergoing 'modernisation'. They turned inland up the curving Boulevard de Cap and the juncture Gorman had mentioned was well marked, the arrow 'Cap d'Antibes' pointing left, 'Cannes' and 'Juan-les-Pins' straight ahead. They made the turn and the road was a narrow two lanes between walls and shrubs and homes of various sizes—the farther from the road, the larger.

The DeChapelles residence had the number 37 on the gatepost and a short driveway took them to a large two-storey home with high windows on each floor and a three-storey tower on the left corner. The main entrance was beyond the tower but a porch serviced the middle sets of french windows at the rear and connecting balconies served the windows above.

The cab stopped by the broad stone steps at the side of the villa where the bright lights were and before Peter and Karen could disembark, the tall double doors at the top were thrown open and a greying man in his early fifties, wearing knife-edged trousers, a white, fine-wool turtleneck sweater, and a burgundy satin jacket, appeared. He had something of the dash and charm of Vittorio Del Strabo but the years had forced him to make concessions to a swelling waistline and a slower pace. However, between corsets and *esprit de vie,* the inroads of time were slight in appearance.

He came down the steps as Peter paid off the driver, switched a highball glass to his left hand, and shook Peter's right. 'You are?' he said, and waited for Peter to give the name. Then, when Peter gave him the one he expected, he pumped the hand still further. *'Et Mademoiselle Halley, non?'* He said some more things in French, watching responses to see just how much she understood. It became immediately apparent that, whatever it was he said, she comprehended none of it. Satisfied with that, he then brought the couple up the stairs and into the house as if visiting royalty had descended. Whatever else Senator Gorman might lie about, he seemed to be right regarding his friendship with Pierre DeChapelles.

DeChapelles, with one arm tucked through Peter's and the other around Karen, brought them into a sumptuous living room whose tall windows looked out at that moment on darkness but could, in the presence of the sun, sight ships on a horizon twenty miles away.

The room was not empty. At a gaming table by the windows two people played backgammon on a leather board. One was a handsome woman in her middle thirties, gowned and stately, with long black hair done in a bun. The other was a grey-haired man in his seventies who was bowed, enfeebled, thin and translucent. A large brandy and soda was beside him and he sipped it constantly.

DeChapelles made introductions, explaining that the backgammon players were the Count and Countess Benedetto di Gravura who were very dear friends, and that Peter and Karen were friends of a very important United States official he had come to know well when he was serving in De Gaulle's cabinet.

They had come on a matter of business and would the count and countess please excuse them?

DeChapelles pulled a bell-cord and brought Peter and Karen over to a couch and a couple of chairs around a small table. A servant appeared and DeChapelles offered refreshments. Something to drink, perhaps?

Peter said he'd rather have a sandwich.

'You haven't eaten?'

'We haven't eaten much.'

'By all means then, but not a sandwich. Soup, perhaps? Then an omelet. Perhaps breast of chicken and a sauterne to go with it?'

'No, really. A sandwich would be fine. We don't want to keep you and we should be getting back.'

'Back where?'

'To Nice.'

'But not at this hour. Surely you don't have midnight business in Nice. Tomorrow would be time enough. Meanwhile, you are, of course, my guests.'

They tried to protest but DeChapelles wouldn't have it any other way. Peter and Karen were to spend the night. He gave a string of orders in a rapid French that showed an accustomed handling of guests, expected and unexpected.

The servant left and DeChapelles made small talk. Time enough for business. The count and countess finished their game and spoke to each other in a totally unfamiliar tongue. The count tried to get up but the brandy and sodas had had their effect. He lost his balance and fell onto his knees, upsetting the table. The countess made an ugly face, then took his arm and tried to help, speaking to him in soft cradling tones in the same strange tongue. DeChapelles leaped to assist and together they got the count onto his feet again, well supported on both sides. The count, his head sunk forward, muttered now in French and they answered him in French. DeChapelles said something to the woman' calling her Julia, and a secret look passed between them. He patted the rocky count on the shoulder and gave him a hearty, *'Bon soir, Benedetto,'* and watched the countess help him from the room. He returned to the couch and said, 'The count is a little under the weather this evening. The plane ride down to Cannes was quite bumpy.' He opened a cigarette box on the table and passed it around, then lighted both Peter and Karen with a heavy table lighter.

The servant brought in a tray with two glasses of pinaud for the guests. He started setting places at the little table. Peter said, 'Look, we shouldn't plan to stay. You have guests . . .'

'I always have guests. Many guests. Ten, twelve.'

'But we don't have anything with us—pyjamas . . .'

DeChapelles laughed. 'What is that? I have plenty. I am a bachelor, you see. But I must have people. So I am a host. That is my avocation—being a host. But to be a good host, one must be prepared. The house is well equipped for whatever might be the case.'

Peter sipped the apéritif, which was sweet and delicious. 'Senator Gorman,' he said, 'tells me that you are going to solve a problem for us.

DeChapelles shrugged. 'Let us say I am to give you something which, I hope, solves your problem, whatever it may be. I am not a problem solver myself. I am merely a courier.' He reached into the inside pocket of his dinner jacket and produced a small manila envelope with his name on it and the address of his Paris business firm. Inside was a smaller envelope with Congdon's name across the front and he passed it over.

Peter ripped it open and withdrew five hundred dollars in American currency and a crisp new passport made out to Karen Halley and identical to the one she had lost. Peter showed it to her and she tucked it into her purse and held the purse tightly. 'Believe me, thank you,' she said to DeChapelles.

'Don't thank me, it is your friend Robert Gorman whom you thank. All I know is when I arrived home last evening—to my apartment in Paris—my man told me there was a call from the United States awaiting me. It was Robert. He asked my plans. Was I coming down here for the weekend? I was. Would I deliver an important envelope to a Mr. Peter Congdon and a Miss Karen Halley if they should call for it? I would be delighted. I gather he was able to use the services of a State Department courier of some kind. In any event, the courier delivered it in a diplomatic pouch or something chained to his wrist, all very impressive. I presume this has a connection with the investigation he's conducting. He refused to comment on that but I follow his exploits in the press and I would be forced to conclude that anything to do with Robert these days has to do with the Mafia. In fact, though it's admittedly a wild guess, I suspect that you, Miss Halley, are the secret female witness he's promised to produce and that you, Mr. Congdon, are some sort of escort for her.'

Peter said, 'I'm sorry, but business ethics won't permit me to speak on the matter. I hope you'll understand.'

'I understand perfectly. But one more thing Robert told me. You'll be returning to the United States as quickly as possible. And anything I could do to assist you—to speed things up—he asked me to do. Am I right in my belief that you wish to go immediately to the United States?'

Peter conceded that that was the idea.

'Do you have plane reservations?'

'No. Not yet.'

'There's a plane for New York out of Nice tomorrow morning. Would you like me to get you seats on it?'

Since the Mafia could be presumed to have the Nice

airport under surveillance, Peter favoured other possibilities. 'What about Cannes?' he asked. 'How far is that?'

'A little closer than Nice but the airport won't do. It's small and deals only with local flights along the coast.'

'But you flew in there from Paris.'

'That was in a private company plane.' He smiled at Peter. 'You are reluctant about Nice, no? You would rather fly from somewhere else?'

'If possible, yes.'

'Would Paris be a good point of departure for the United States? If you do not want to go to Nice, I can fly you to Paris from Cannes.'

'When would that be?'

'Whenever you wish. Tomorrow morning if you would like. The plane is there, no? It waits for me to fly it.'

'That would be great, but I'm afraid it would be an awful imposition.'

'It would be a service. It would be one of the few things we French might do for you Americans. We have not been properly appreciative of what you people have done for France. Or, perhaps, I should say those in positions of influence have chosen to bite the hand that has fed and supported us. De Gaulle is not popular here. There is little we can find good about the man. He has stayed too long if, indeed, he should ever have come at all.'

The servant brought in the soup at that point and DeChapelles went to phone his co-pilot and have the plane made ready.

SATURDAY 12:15–12:30 A.M.

Peter's watch said twelve-fifteen when he tied the sash of his bathrobe and took the watch off to wind and set on his bedside table. His bedroom and bath were adjacent to Karen's at the rear of the house, overlooking the drive, the wall, and the shrubbery which protected them from the view of the neighbours. It was a well-appointed room, like the rest of the rooms he had seen, and even if the house were not the largest in the exclusive part of Antibes, it still bespoke a man of considerable wealth. Especially when one recognised that this was but one of Pierre DeChapelles' homes.

DeChapelles was, likewise, as courteous and considerate as he was wealthy. Peter might almost call him 'gallant', were it not for his choice of houseguests for the weekend. One had but to see them to realise he suffered the count for the friendship of the countess. She had reappeared while Peter and Karen were supping and she and Pierre had drawn aside and done their talking in French, which Peter caught enough of to get that the count was now in bed and dead to the world.

When the meal was finished, DeChapelles had shown him and Karen to their respective rooms and a servant had brought them night clothes. There were good-nights and Peter and Karen were disposed of like unwanted chaperones. However, Peter thought, lighting a cigarette, he could hardly complain. The sweat and strain were far removed now. The blow on the head, even the dunking in the Porto Vecchio seemed far in the past—mere unpleasant memories that, one day, might even be an amusing and suspenseful tale for his grandchildren. ('Tell us the story of how you saved the Mafia

leader's mistress, Grampa.'—'Grampa, what's a mistress?'—'Was she beautiful, Grampa?' . . .)

Yes. She was beautiful.

He opened the french windows to the balcony and stepped out. The rain that had lingered throughout the day had stopped near suppertime and now the clouds were gone. The moon was bright and close to full, the night air cool but not unpleasant, the noises faint and unobtrusive. A car went by in the road with only the reflection of its lights indicating its position. Off to the right, its jets purring, a plane descended on the approach leg to Nice. Peter took a drag of the cigarette and blew out a cloud of smoke. He could really like it here. It was a surcease from the cares of the world. He could leave his gun in his bedroom, he could lean in his doorway, breathe fresh-scented air and bask in moonlight.

A sudden sound on the balcony made him start. A catch scraped and the other french windows opened and Karen came out. She didn't see him and took a short step to the rail, which looked down a high drop to the ground. For a few moments she stood against the rail sampling the texture of the evening like Peter. She was robed in a white dressing gown that hugged her trim, full figure. Her hair would be a while returning to that soft white-gold sheen it had had for those two short hours Peter knew her before he dunked her head in diluted shoe polish, but it was well brushed and arranged in a casual but fetching way. Joe Bono had really been gone on the girl and Peter could believe it.

She sensed him looking at her and turned, slowly at first, then quickly. 'Oh.'

'Admiring the view?'

'Yes.'

'What do you think of our host?'

'He seems very nice.'

'I think the countess thinks so too.'

She shrugged. 'What of it?'

'Well, now, that's the beautiful part. You get an old man like the count and you wonder. Does he know he's being used? Does he really think it's his ancient charm that lures such an attractive young wife to his side?'

'She's not so young.'

'Not compared to you, lamb. Not even compared to me. But compared to him? There must be forty years' age differential there. So what does he have? A title. He might even have some money; though, of course, in cases like that you can't be sure whether he's got money or she's got the money or neither of them have it and the title carries them through. A title is usually equal to a certain amount of cash in the bank. How much, of course, depends on what the title is and where it is and where you are and who cares how much for it. Take this case, for instance—I mean, Julia and Benedetto being guests of our friend Pierre. Do you think it's Benedetto's title or Julia's charm that accounts for their free weekend here—private plane trip and all that?'

'I wouldn't know and I couldn't care less. What does it matter?'

'How much it matters depends on who you're talking about. Now, to you, I can see it wouldn't matter one bit. If Pierre bails us out, what does it matter who he is or what he is? But suppose you're the count. He drinks quite a bit, doesn't he? And he's pretty old, too. And he's not a well man. And he sits there playing backgammon with his wife and pulling heavily on brandy and sodas. This is when he's a guest in another man's house. And we're not talking about some poor slob who's never read Emily Post. This is a man who knows right behaviour. So why? Why does he drink so much? Why does he let his wife tuck him into bed alone? Why does he break bread with such an attractive host? Why does he hold his head so low that he can never catch the signals his wife and that host are constantly passing? Doesn't it make you wonder how much he knows, and how much he doesn't want to know and how much he wants to pretend he doesn't know? And why is it important to him? Does he get drunk because he wants his wife to put him to bed —or does he get drunk because she puts him to bed?'

Karen looked at him levelly. The balcony was only four feet wide and only long enough to cover both windows and they were close together. 'You can't leave it alone, can you?' she said.

'Leave what alone?'

'Me and Joe Bono.'

'You and Joe Bono?'

'It eats you, doesn't it?'

'Eats me? You must be kidding. I couldn't care less.'

'You couldn't? You get all excited about the friendship of two people you've never set eyes on until less than two hours ago, who will pass out of your life forever in another eight hours, most of which time you'll spend sleeping. And then you expect me to believe that you couldn't care less about the behaviour of a girl whose life and existence has been your responsibility for better than fifty hours and will be for another eighteen at least, a girl you've slept in the same bed with, been dunked in the same water with, been hit on the head over, have risked your very existence to protect? This is a girl you just can't wait to throw the moral code at, to sit in judgment on—and believe me, I'll bet you never sat in judgement before. You're not the type. But you sit in judgment on me. All the time I was flirting with the policemen in Florence and all the time on the boat with Umberto, you were sitting scowling your disapproval like God on high. You have no morals but you throw morals at me as if you invented them. You know what the trouble with you is? You're jealous.'

'Jealous?' Peter exploded. 'Of you?'

'Of Joe Bono. You can't stand it that he got to me first It eats you because you want me for yourself and your puritan ethic says you can't have me now because I'm tainted. And you're going to torment me and make me suffer because you're suffering.'

'Me want you? You must be out of your vain little mind.'

'You don't think I see the way you look at me? You think a girl doesn't know what a man is thinking from the way he looks? I dare you to tell me you don't want to kiss me right here and right now.'

'Kiss you? You'd love me to, wouldn't you?'

'You bet I would. Because then you're finished Because then you're no better than Joe Bono and you're no better than I. Because you gave in and you gave in with your eyes wide open and you won't ever be able to open your mouth about me again.' She stood there challenging him. 'Go ahead. I dare you. Joe Bono did right? And so does everybody else who comes along right? All except Umberto. He didn't get a chance, did he? You wouldn't let him out of your sight. You couldn't stand the idea of what might go on.'

'Shut up.'

'You make me.'

He grabbed her and kissed her hard. And in that moment, he forgot Joe Bono and Umberto and all the other men and all the other loves who had ever existed for her or for him. It was the Fourth of July with sky rockets and roman candles and cannon crackers all going off at once. And they went off for both of them. One kiss and suddenly they were straining at each other, kissing uncontrollably and holding on as if for life itself.

It was a runaway train with both of them on it. Their kisses were desperate, their clutches instinctive. His hands coursed up and down her back, caught and held her face pushed down inside the front of her robe and the frai nylon of her nightgown and roamed over soft full breasts and erect, excited nipples. She only embraced him harder. He undid the sash of her robe and pushed it open. His lips coursed over her cheek and nibbled at the smooth lobe of her ear. He pushed the robe off one shoulder, off both shoulders, and she let it fall at her feet. He caressed her ear and almost whispered into it, 'I love you.'

He didn't quite. Something nudged the back reaches of his consciousness—a tiny, insignificant recollection that suddenly swelled and engulfed him, blotting out the love, the passion, and the desire. He froze for a moment, clutching her bare shoulders as if hanging on. He drew back, shaken, and looked at her and drew back farther, staring in shock at her face. Her eyes were glazed, her lips parted. She was the most overcome girl in the world, the most helplessly devoid of resistance. That much was real. But for him, desire had fled like an extinguished flame. He gripped her shoulders, fingers, digging into her flesh. 'Who are you?' he whispered through clenched teeth.

'What?' She shook her head dazedly.

He thrust her away. 'Who are you?'

She went against the frame of the door, clad in a sheer green nylon gown whose pale hue tinted the flesh tones beneath. Her eyes came wide now with just a thread of fear in them. 'Peter,' she whispered back. 'I don't understand.'

'Neither do I. But believe me, I'm going to.' He seized her arm and thrust her roughly through the doors into his bedroom. She stumbled and lost a green satin mule, she turned at the side of the bed and stared at him with still-disbelieving eyes. One strap of her nightgown was half down her arm and she slid it into place.

Peter followed and shut the doors behind him, locking them deliberately. 'All right,' he said, advancing on her.

'I don't know what the game is but it's ending right now. What's your real name?'

She sat down slowly on the edge of the bed. 'But you know my name. It's Karen Halley.'

'I said your real name. And where are you from and why?'

'But that's my real name. You saw my passport.'

'That's the name Gorman got you a passport under—but not you. That's the name he got Joe Bono's mistress a passport under.'

'But that's who I am. I told you. I came down from Denmark and I got a job in a night club and I met Joe there . . .'

'Listen, Sweetheart, I am not a fool. I knew that one was a lie the minute you told it to me. But I figured if you fed Gorman that line and he wanted to buy it, that was his business. My business was to get you over the seas and into his grubby little hands and he could match wits with you from there. So far so good. What I didn't tumble to . . .'

'Just a minute. What do you mean, you decided I was lying? I ought to know where I was born and raised . . .'

'You sure as hell ought, Sweetheart, and it wasn't in Denmark. It was in the good old United States of America. It's America's version of the English language you speak.'

'I learned it from Joe.'

'Save it,' Peter snapped. 'I knew you were American the minute I climbed through your window. I don't care how many damned languages you may know, when you get startled out of a sound sleep and wake in peril of your life, you're going to start off in your native tongue. Either that or, just possibly, if you've been in the country long enough, that tongue. You didn't start out in either Danish or Italian, you started in American and that makes that starving little Danish girl bit a lie.

'But, as I say, no matter what stories you told Gorman and tried to tell me, at least I thought you were the girl Gorman sent me for. After all, you were at the address he gave me, you knew the password, you fit the description. Even the picture I took off the Mafia guy was of you and so was the photograph in the passport. So I was really suckered in on that one. All your talk about Joe Bono. You really had me believing you were his mistress. Right up till a minute ago.'

'But I am. Really . . .'

'Save it. Like waking up speaking English, you tripped up again. You're an impostor, Sweetheart. You're taking her place . . .'

'How can you say impostor? Didn't you admit—the passport picture? The picture of me . . .'

'How can I say it?' He took her by the arm and pulled her to the mirror. 'I'll show you how I can say it.' He pushed her hair away from her ear and turned her head. 'See? Take a good look.'

She said. 'I don't understand. At what?'

'Sweetheart! You mean you didn't know? You seem to know everything else. Joe Bono made a set of earrings for his mistress from a handsome pair of cuff links. His mistress sent one of those earrings to the senator to authenticate her story. I saw that earring, sweetheart, and it's made for pierced ears. Show me the hole in your earlobe, Sweetheart. Go on, where is it?'

She pulled away. 'That doesn't mean anything.'

'You slipped up on that one. You thought you had the role down letter-perfect, didn't you? But you didn't know about the earrings. Nobody told you about those earrings, did they?'

'Peter, you've got it all wrong . . .'

'That's right, Sweetheart. And you're going to set me right.'

'I mean you misunderstand.'

'Kid, Joe Bono had a mistress and she got in touch with the senator and offered to testify against the Mafia. And I come across the ocean to pick her up but I pick you up instead. She isn't there, you're there. So the question is, what happened to her? Because I'm not supposed to bring you back, I'm supposed to bring her back. So you're going to tell me where she is.'

'Peter, Peter,' she said, sitting down again on the bed, her face white and drawn, 'you've got it all wrong. I'm the one you're supposed to bring back.'

'Let's not go into that again.' He stepped over to her and took her wrist. 'I don't want to have to get rough with you but I'll get just as rough as I have to. And I want you to believe me. I've been sent to carry out an assignment and I'm going to do whatever I have to do to carry it out. And that requires you telling me where this woman is, how you managed to take her place, why you're doing it, and who's behind the whole thing. Four questions. We'll start with the first one first. Where is this woman? The real mistress.'

Karen shook her head and looked away. 'I don't know.'

He jerked her around so hard that her breasts bounced. 'Come on, kiddo. You took her place. You know why you took her place, so you're going to know what plans were made for her. Is she alive or is she dead?'

Her face was very white now. 'Please. You're hurting me.'

'I haven't even started. I told you you're going to answer my questions. If I have to inflict pain to persuade you, then I'll inflict whatever amount is necessary. Is she alive or dead?'

'I don't know.'

He applied more pressure to her wrists and she gasped. 'She's alive as far as I know,' she whispered. 'I think she's alive.'

'Where?'

Karen shook her head. 'I don't know. I really don't.'

'Kiddo . . .' He let the word hang for a moment. 'Remember. You're in this up to your neck. You know what it's all about. Tell Poppa like a good girl?'

'Peter, please. I can't stand it. My wrist.'

'Where is she?'

'Peter, honest to God I don't know. They wouldn't entrust me with that kind of information.'

'Who's "they"?'

She shook her head, gasped at a little more pressure twisting her wrist, and whispered, 'It's not a they, really. And it's not what you're thinking.'

'What is it "really"?'

'It's a "he".' She turned. 'Please, Peter. Don't ask his name. He'd kill me if I told. He made me promise.'

'What's his name, Karen?'

She gave up and the tears began to fall. 'It's Senator Gorman,' she said in despair.

SATURDAY 12:30–1:15 A.M.

Peter was so startled, he let go of Karen's wrist. 'Gorman?' he said. 'You mean Senator Gorman put you up to this?'

She nodded and cradled the arm Peter had been hurting. The strap of her nightgown had slipped down again but this time she ignored it.

Peter said to her, 'Why?'

'He wanted a decoy.'

'With me playing sucker! No wonder he made you promise not to tell.' Peter laughed harshly, took cigarettes out of the pocket of his robe and lighted a pair. He handed one to her and she nodded thanks. 'All right,' he said. 'Let's have the whole thing. How did you get involved in all this, and what the hell is Gorman trying to prove?'

She hugged her arms. 'I'll tell you, but could I have my robe? I'm cold and practically naked.'

He unlocked the french windows and brought the robe to her, helping her into it. She tied the sash, took a shaky drag on the cigarette, and said, 'Well, I guess it's a long story. Are you sure you want to hear it all?'

'In all its glory.'

She shrugged. 'Did Senator Gorman mention a man by the name of William Clive to you?'

Peter nodded. 'He was a private detective who was found murdered.'

'Yes. Murdered by the Mafia.' She had a last drag and put out the cigarette. 'I was his sister,' she went on. 'Actually, his half sister. Karen Halley is really my name, which is why my passport is valid. It's the real thing. Anyway, our mother is Norwegian, so I really am Nordic. And she married an Englishman named Clive, who was killed in the war in the spring of 1940. Bill was born then and they were living in England. Then the Americans came over and she met and married my father and I was born over there and spent my first two years in England until my father was sent home. Then we moved to America.'

She started on another cigarette and said, 'Bill had this detective firm in Washington. Just a small operation. He and I alone. I was his secretary, bookkeeper, accountant, and everything else.

'Then the senator hired him for the job you've got but

he was caught and killed. He had a wife and three young children, which didn't make it easier to take.

'Then one day I got a call from the senator. He wanted to talk to me and there was this elaborate system of getting together which he made me follow so that we wouldn't be seen by the Mafia. We met and we had this talk. He's quite a talker, the senator. He can be very persuasive. Not that I wasn't interested without persuasion, but he was very good at bringing in all the reasons I should want to do the job he had in mind. The job was to pretend I was Joe Bono's mistress. He was going to set me up in a small cottage in an English village and he was going to make a thing about hiring another detective to do the job Bill had been killed on, and he'd send the detective over to bring me home, the idea being that if the Mafia caught on, they'd be following the wrong lead.'

Peter said, 'And maybe killing the wrong girl.'

'Well, there was that,' she admitted. 'But he played that part of it down. What he played up was the chance to uncover my brother's killers. The next detective would be well warned so if they managed to pick up his trail, things would be different. And, of course, there was the patriotic bit—helping the Senate of the United States of America. And helping to uncover the evil Mafia conspiracy, that was in there too. And I suppose that's the one that affected me the most. All I had to do was look at Doris—that's Bill's wife—and what she was left with: widowhood, three mouths to feed, having to find a job in order to feed the mouths—and my blood would boil. And I would wish there were something I could do to get back at the people who killed him. So, I guess I was easy prey. If I could help Gorman get Bono's mistress onto the witness stand, believe me, I would. And there was the monetary angle, of course. Let's not overlook that. Five thousand dollars I was paid for this enterprise—or I should say Doris was paid, because I gave it to her with some story about an extra insurance policy Bill had forgotten to make over to her when they married. And, of course, I got a subsistence allowance plus the chance to travel and see a bit of the rest of the world.

'So that's how it came about. Of course the picture was paintcd a little differently than it actually turned out. I was assured—all but guaranteed, in fact—that there would be no trouble. It would be nothing more than a very profitable vacation and I'd be making a contribution to society in addition. It sounded like something I couldn't afford to turn down.'

She paused and reflected for a moment and Peter waited quietly, watching her, listening. Then she said, 'Of course it didn't turn out to bc England after all. He found out I was fluent in Italian, so he immediately changed it to Florence instead. Italy seemed a more likely place to send a detective to pick up a Mafia member's mistress.

'So, over I came to take up residence and wait. It wasn't supposed to be for very long, and I could do pretty much what I chose—go to art galleries, see all the points of interest. And I guess there isn't much in Florence that I missed, including the doves on the ceiling of Elizabeth Barrett Browning's bedroom.' She smiled faintly and went on. 'I was given a password and, when it was decided, the senator sent me a cable with nothing on it but your name. And then you came. Only the way you came terrified me. I think I'd been getting gradually more and more nervous living alone there, just waiting for a detective to come and take me away. You can't help, after you go to bed at night, thinking about some of the things the senator didn't tell you. The Mafia killed your brother and they certainly won't hesitate to kill you either, not if they believe you're going to betray them. So I'd lie there and work up a fine case of the chills imagining the wrong man coming, and finding myself in the Mafia's clutches. But then I'd tell myself that it was all ridiculous. In the first place, the Mafia wouldn't find me and, in the second place, if they ever got a look at me, they'd know I wasn't his mistress. As the senator said, after all, the Mafia people would know what she looked like and they'd know somebody made a mistake.'

She laughed wryly. 'But I guess I forgot all that when you came in the window. I thought the wrong man had come that time all right. And then the wrong men did come and suddenly I realised this wasn't quite what Senator Gorman had in mind. This was ugly and real and for keeps. And from that moment on, everything has been wrong. Even the big love scene, out there on the balcony, where the hero and heroine go into a clinch, even that went all wrong. The lady forgot to get her ears pierced.'

She snubbed out her cigarette but if she were issuing invitations, Peter's mind was on other things. 'And what were his plans when I brought you back—if I brought you back?'

'It would all be very hush-hush, of course, and meanwhile he'd sneak in the real mistress. He wouldn't tell you I was a decoy, if that's what you mean. You wouldn't find that out until the real mistress started to testify.'

'And I suppose nobody knows what you're doing or where you are—meaning not your mother or your sister-in-law. So, if we don't come back, Gorman gets his witness but nobody can start making embarrassing inquiries.'

'Well he did have me promise not to tell anyone where I was but that was only because it had to be so secret. After all, there wasn't supposed to be any trouble. What's been happening to us wasn't supposed to happen.'

Peter's mouth tightened and he looked at her.

'What makes you so sure what's been happening to us isn't exactly what Gorman expected to have happen to us?'

She blinked at him. 'What?'

'He told you it would all be fun and games, but of course that's what he'd have to tell you to get you to take the job. That doesn't mean he thought it *would* be himself.'

'But he wouldn't have done it if he thought there really were serious risks. He told me he felt personally responsible for Bill's death, that he'd have cancelled the investigation rather than have Bill harmed if he could have known. He told me over and over that it was only because he was certain no risk was involved that he'd let me undertake the job.'

'He tells a lot of people a lot of things, Karen. I suggest that he was snowing you. I suggest he not only thought the risks would be great, he *hoped* they'd be great. And I'm further willing to bet you that, contrary to his assurances that practically everybody would know what Bono's mistress looks like, practically nobody does.'

'Oh, Peter. You're being unfair.'

'Am I? Those two men Vittorio and I tackled in your apartment had your picture with them and they were coming to kill you anyway. That tells the story right there. They didn't know Bono's mistress on sight or any other way. They took their cue from the senator.'

Karen sobered and chewed a lip. 'You said he *hoped* it would be risky. He hoped we'd have trouble. Why?'

'Because he wants Bono's mistress to testify. Whatever his ambitions, whether it's to crush the Mafia or to get into the White House or both, he's got to put this witness on the stand. She's all he's got. So getting her over to the States is all that matters to him. He doesn't care about you or me or anybody else. He only cares about that woman. So, as part of his strategy, he decides to set out a decoy and go through a very realistic attempt to save the decoy. Now think about that. A decoy won't do him any good if everybody who sees her knows she's a decoy. Regardless of what stories he may tell us, he must have reason to believe very few people can identify the mistress. He thinks the decoy is going to fool everybody.

'Now, suppose I go flying over to Rome, pick you up and bring you back, and do it so slickly the Mafia never even knows it happened? What good is that going to do Gorman? The Mafia will still be watching for the mistress. In other words, a false trail isn't any good if nobody follows it. Therefore, he's going to want the Mafia to find out he's sending a particular man—me—to bring back the mistress. I thought it was because of his stupid arrogance, his certainty that he was too smart for the Mafia, that got him followed when he gave me the papers I needed. That's how they got on my trail. Through him. But I see now he *wanted* them to pick up my trail. They didn't see him meet you. They weren't supposed to. But they *were* supposed to see him meet me. That son of a bitch is cleverer than I've been thinking.'

She scowled. 'He could have got us killed.'

'That's right, he could. In fact, I think that's what he might want.' He grabbed her arm. 'God, if I'd only known about this before . . . Get dressed. We're getting out of here.'

'What? What are you talking about?'

'That's exactly it! It's to his advantage if we get killed. Don't you see? It'll make it safer for him to bring in his real witness if the Mafia thinks she's dead. They won't be looking any more. As long as we're alive, every move he makes is monitored. Bringing in his witness will be a risky business under those conditions. And, if we get back safely, the Mafia is still going to be riding tight herd on everything he does, trying to stop you and him from getting together—which would stop the mistress too.'

'But why should we leave here?'

'Because, if he's allowed the word to leak that he's rushing you a new passport, the Mafia might figure out who his contact is in Nice—the way they did in Rome—and start nosing around to see who Pierre DeChapelles is entertaining this weekend. I may be all wrong on this, but we're not going to stick around to find out.' He started her towards the french windows. 'Get ready as fast as you can.'

'But he'll fly us to Paris first thing in the morning.'

'That's eight hours from now. That's too long to be sitting ducks.'

'What are we going to do then?'

'Borrow one of DeChapelles' cars and drive to Paris.'

Karen took only a few minutes and they crept down the stairs together at ten minutes past one, left a note for DeChapelles, and went out the french windows at the rear of the house and down the porch steps. Only the night lights were on in the main portion of the house and one window glowed in the servants' quarters in the cellar.

Two cars were parked out there; a big maroon and cream Citroen, the other a small, sporty, bright red Sonnet Saab, low to the ground. The Saab had an ignition key in it, which made it their choice. They got in and started and slammed the doors and didn't worry about noise. The gear shift diagram was pasted on the windshield and Peter threw the car into reverse, backed around into the drive, and headed out. They turned right at the road, crested a slight rise, and then their headlights picked out a large sedan directly ahead, blocking the way.

Peter hit the brakes hard and the little Saab screeched to a halt. At the same time, headlights went on in a blacked-out car that had materialised behind them, and two men leaped from the bushes on either side of the road.

Peter and Karen never had a chance. Their doors were torn open and they found themselves staring into the enormous muzzles of very close guns.

SATURDAY 1:15–2:35 A.M.

They were dragged from the little car and roughly searched. Weapons were the object but the brutal young Italian searching Peter discovered Gorman's five hundred dollars in his wallet and appropriated that, as well as the automatic and revolver. Karen had her ·32 taken but that was all.

It was dark on the road with only the headlights of the Saab and the car behind for illumination and Peter wasn't sure how many men there were. At least six, it seemed, and they talked Italian.

A door slammed in the big car behind and a voice gave orders. Men obeyed, moving the Saab in by the stone wall, swinging the roadblock car around. Another voice, back of the headlights, muttered in English, 'What'd you let them get out of the car for? Whyn't you leave 'em in? We could push the car to the side.'

The hard-voiced man who had given the orders answered in English. 'Because we don't want to leave them here.' They both came forward and the headlights caught them. The complainer was the thin, tubercular man and the boss was the man with the black tooth and the carnation. Peter was not surprised.

Mr. Carnation didn't gloat over Peter, talk to Karen, or even acknowledge their presence. His concern was the disposition of the Saab and he pointed and gave more orders in Italian. The thin man did cast his gaze on the prisoners, but his attitude was clinical, like a scientist about to inject a guinea pig. When the Saab was parked, he gestured. 'You,' he said to Peter and Karen. 'Back inside the car.'

Peter tried to talk to the big man. 'Listen, Mac, I know what you think this is all about . . .'

The man ignored him and turned to his thin companion. 'What do you want them to do?'

'Get back in the car. It's the best place. You don't want to leave them in the road, do you?'

Peter said, 'This girl isn't the girl you think she is.'

Carnation ignored that. 'Not here,' he said to his friend. 'We're not doing anything here.'

The thin man said coldly, 'It's here, now, in the car.'

The big man pointed to himself. 'I am Vico Barbarelli and Vico Barbarelli gives the orders. And I say we are not going to kill them here.'

'You got a better place?'

'You're forgetting something.'

'I'm not forgetting anything. I'm ignoring.'

'That is not wise.'

The thin man's lip curled. 'You want to run it? You run it. You want the job done? I'll do the job.'

'But part of the job . . .'

'I tell you you don't mess around. You want them dead, right? We kill 'em. Right here. This instant. We make sure.'

'But the order . . .'

'The order is to get that girl. That's the only order that counts. The order is to see she don't open her mouth.

There's one way to keep it shut. Only one. So you don't fool around. Let her stay alive one extra minute and that's one unnecessary minute when something could go wrong. You decide what your goal is and you decide the best way to get to it and you forget everything else. And you know what this goal is, so don't talk about no other orders.'

Barbarelli glowered. 'I don't need you to lecture me. How you do your business is your business. How I do my business is my business. And this is my business. I got my orders and I'm giving you yours.'

The thin man made an ugly face. He spat in the road. 'All right,' he snarled. 'Give your goddam orders. But I quit on it. If something goes wrong from this minute on, you're the one to blame.'

'Nothing's going to go wrong, I'm telling you.' He left the thin man and approached Peter, 'All right, Congdon. We're going to take a ride.' He pointed at his car. 'You and the girl get in the back seat.' He gave other orders in Italian and men marched them off.

The car was an American Cadillac with jump seats. Barbarelli got in front with the driver, Karen and Peter in back, and two men with guns took the jump seats. The thin man and the others rode in the second sedan.

They returned through Antibes and picked up the road to Nice, the captors riding in silence. Barbarelli was the only one who spoke English and Peter tried to interest him in Karen's true identity. 'I know what you want her for,' he told the man earnestly. 'But you've got the wrong girl. She wasn't Joe Bono's mistress.'

'Shut up.'

'She's a plant. It's a trick of Senator Gorman's to fool you.'

Barbarelli said something in Italian and the nearest man hit Peter in the mouth with the muzzle of his gun. It stunned him and brought the blood flowing. Karen gasped and pulled his head against her breast. 'Don't talk any more,' she said, cradling him. 'Please don't talk.'

They came back into Nice along the Avenue des Anglais and turned left down the service side of the empty and shuttered Hotel Ritz. It was a large, block-sized building facing the sea, seven storeys high, with windows in its rounded corners and in its almost vertically sloped roof.

The cars stopped on the narrow empty street beside a door under the sign Ritz Bar. They all got out and Barbarelli opened the door with a key. They went inside, where he relocked the door and led the way by flashlight through the stale-smelling room. Other men had flashes and their beams caught the lustre of the polished counter, the stacks of tables and chairs against the wall, the carpeted hall outside, where arches revealed a spacious colonnaded ballroom and a glass wall looking out on a dining terrace and the sea.

'Fermatevi!' Barbarelli said and the group halted. Peter and Karen were stood against the wall in the glare of two flashes and Barbarelli went across the hall, through a wide door to some inner room.

An uneasy five-minute wait followed and Peter squeezed Karen's hand to give her courage. He wished he could give her hope as well, but Gorman had done his job to perfection. The senator was getting everything he wanted. His decoy had been trapped—and who in the world would believe she was a decoy? She and her guardian would be quietly slain and their bodies, in all probability, would remain unrecovered for a long, long time—Peter could see that it was Barbarelli's scheme that their remains not be left carelessly at the side of the road for the glare of the resultant publicity. Peter and Karen would disappear and nobody would ever know. Except Gorman would know. When he heard no more from them after their nocturnal disappearance from

DeChapelles', he would know what had happened and he would then quietly bring in his real witness and then, one day, there would be great headlines and Gorman would pose and posture and the witness would blow the whistle on such as Barbarelli and maybe somebody—Barbarelli himself perhaps—might even go to jail. And maybe, just maybe, in four and a half years, in some convention city, the name of Robert Gerald Gorman just might be placed in nomination as candidate for President of the United States of America. Only Karen Halley and Peter Congdon wouldn't know anything about any of that. Karen Halley and Peter Congdon would long since have been eaten by worms and nothing but their bones would remain to remind the senator of the price of ambition.

Barbarelli reappeared at the distant doorway and waved imperiously. Karen and Peter were marched across the hall to enter what was a night club room. Again chairs and tables were stacked against the wall and covered with sheets. At one end was a raised platform, on which a pair of folding screens had been placed close together.

Peter and Karen were brought across the floor to the foot of the platform and halted. There they stood facing the screens while torch beams played on them.

Finally, a heavy voice from behind the screens said, 'Turn around.' Peter started to obey, but the voice snapped, 'Not you. The girl.' Karen turned slowly, doing a three hundred and sixty. The voice said, non-committally, 'Again.' She repeated the performance. 'That is not the girl,' the voice said.

Barbarelli stepped forward. For the first time he was less than the arrogant master of the situation. 'But that cannot be.'

'Don't tell me what cannot be,' the voice snapped. 'I said that is not the girl.'

'But, but—signore, she is the girl he came to get. There is no mistake about that. The picture! It is the picture the senator sent.'

'You are a fool, Barbarelli.'

Barbarelli wheeled on Peter. 'So that's it,' he said. 'A trick.' To whomever was behind the screens he said, 'I'll find out where she is.' He snapped an order in Italian and two men seized Peter's arms. Barbarelli swore at him and swung a heavy fist to the body which made Peter grunt. 'You trick me,' Barbarelli growled. 'Now you tell me where she is.'

'I don't know what you're talking about,' Peter muttered.

Barbarelli struck him a swinging, hammerlike blow on the side of the head and Peter sagged. 'Where is the girl, you pig?'

Karen leaped on him, grabbing his arm. 'No, no,' she cried. 'Don't hit him. He doesn't know.'

He threw her aside and a man seized her. Barbarelli hit Peter with two savage blows, putting hate and frustration into them. 'Stop it!' Karen shrieked, and Peter's head lolled drunkenly.

'Who is it?' Barbarelli shouted in increasing rage and hit Peter another sledge-hammer blow that drove him to his knees despite the efforts of the two men to hold him up. 'Who is it?'

Peter, half retching, said weakly, 'I don't know.' Barbarelli kicked him in the ribs and sent him groaning to the floor. In two other men's arms, Karen struggled and cried out to Barbarelli to stop. 'He doesn't know, he doesn't know. The senator wouldn't tell us!'

Barbarelli ignored her. His anger grew greater. 'Tell me,' he raged, seizing Peter by the jacket, dragging him to a half-sitting position. 'You tell me,' he said again and slapped Peter across the face. 'I dunno,' Peter mumbled. 'Tell me!' Barbarelli screamed. He swung to the side of Peter's head and Peter hit the floor, slid two feet, and lay there. 'Oh, Peter, Peter,' Karen sobbed.

'Pick him up,' Barbarelli yelled at the guards, but they didn't know English and didn't move. 'Pick him up,' he yelled again and threw a punch at the nearest man that almost knocked him down.

The voice behind the screens cut in sharply. 'That will be enough, Barbarelli.'

The man swung around. He was panting and sweat stood out on his face. 'I'll make him talk,' he gasped. 'Don't worry. I'll make him talk.'

'You are a fool, Barbarelli,' the voice said. 'He doesn't know anything. Even you should be able to see that. He and the girl are only pawns in the whole affair.'

'They know something. They must know something. Just let me work on them some more.' He turned to where the two men were getting the groggy detective to his feet. 'Are you gonna talk?'

'Desist,' the voice snapped. 'I've let you have your fun, but we don't have any more time now. We must go quickly if we want to get the real girl.'

Barbarelli gaped at the screens. 'You mean you know who she is?'

'Yes, I know who she is. I am not, like you, a fool, Barbarelli. I make allowances for the senator's cleverness. There are two girls, Barbarelli. The question we had to answer was, which onc was the impostor and which one was the real one. I thought I knew. But the senator is very smart and he made me follow the wrong trail. But we have found our mistake in time and now we must go after the right girl.'

'You know where she is?'

'I know where she is.' The voice took on a tone of dismissal. 'Remove those two and hold them outside.'

Barbarelli gave the order, remembering to put it in Italian this time, and the guards took them out into the broad hall again, marching Karen, half dragging Peter. There, Peter leaned dazedly against the wall and Karen held him, putting her head against his chest, crying quietly.

After a bit, one of the other men came out, gave orders, and led the way with his flash. The guards seized the couple and marched them behind. They went to the main staircase in the lobby and climbed it in the dim light of the torches. They reached the mezzanine, then the second floor, and continued, floor after floor, until they were nearly at the top. Then the leader brought them down a dark hall and fitted a key into one of the doors. Peter and Karen were pushed inside without a word being said. The door was closed after them, the key turned in the lock, and the footsteps went away.

SATURDAY 2:35–4:45 A.M.

Peter lighted his lighter. They were in the entry hall of one of the suites. There was a bath on the right and a good-sized room beyond with a big brass double bed and a plain cotton coverlet spread over the mattress and pillows. The room also included a writing desk in the corner, breakfast table in front of the shuttered windows, a clothes cupboard, and an assortment of chairs.

He tried the light switch but there was no power. There was nothing. There never was anything. He felt weak, tired, battered and sick. Beside him, Karen was weeping. He didn't know she could cry. 'Whassa matter?' he asked thickly.

'You. What they've done to you.'

The lighter was getting hot and he snapped it shut, groped his way through stygian darkness and fumbled with the windows. He got them open and pushed out the shutters. The moon was still above the rooftops shining full on him and it threw light into the room. They were, Peter discovered, looking out on the inner court of the hotel and shutters covered every window but their own.

When he turned away, he swayed a little and Karen was there to hold him. 'Oh, Peter,' she cried. 'They hurt you.'

He put an arm around her. 'Just bruises,' he muttered. 'I'm all right.'

'Lie down. Please.'

'In a minute.' He took one of the straight chairs into the hall and tucked it under the doorknob. He went into the bathroom and turned a faucet but the water had also been shut off for the season.

He came out again and sat down on the bed heavily. Karen climbed on it and knelt beside him, pulling his head against her breast. She kissed his hair and pressed her cheek against it. 'What will they do to us?'

'Kill us, I expect.'

She slipped down beside him and put her face in her hands. 'And it's all my fault. I'm so sorry.'

'It's Gorman's fault.'

'No, it's mine. I let them steal my passport. I'm to blame. If I hadn't let them steal it, we'd be in Washington now, Gorman or no Gorman.'

'You can't blame yourself. You couldn't know he was going to take advantage of you.'

'But that's the terrible part,' she wailed. 'I only played up to Umberto to get you jealous. And now it's going to get you killed.'

He stared at her face in the moonlight. 'Jealous? What are you talking about?'

'You. Me. You hating me. All the contempt you had

for me and what you thought I was. You said you wanted to horsewhip me. Naked in the public square was the way you put it. You know what that did to me? It was just as though you had. A girl can't stand being looked at with contempt like that. It cut and hurt and made me furious. Because I couldn't tell you I was better than that. I had to pretend I was worse. And I knew that when you delivered me into the senator's hands that would be the end. You'd leave me, forever believing I was the mistress of some Mafia gangster, and I didn't want to be that to you. And I hated you, for that's just what I would be. So then I decided I didn't want you to know the truth. I could feel that you were attracted to me despite your contempt and I went to work on that. I set it up as my goal to make you say to me, "I love you." I was going to make you say that to a girl you wanted to horsewhip, all the while believing the worst about me, that I was Joe Bono's mistress and the biggest flirt on the block and the cheapest tart and all the rest. I should have been working with you, and, instead, I was working against you. You were trying to save my life and I was trying to make you fall in love with me. The senator hired me to do a job and I didn't do it. I did something I had no business doing and I ruined it for everybody. I should have sat up on the cabin of that boat with you and kept my purse in my lap. Instead, I made eyes at Umberto and teased him into putting his arms around me, and he and his old man stole me blind. And now I've killed you. And myself as well, only I deserve it. You don't.'

She brushed a tear away and gestured helplessly. 'Stupid, stupid girl.'

'I almost said it,' Peter mumbled.

She looked at him. 'Almost said what?'

'I almost said, "I love you," the way you wanted me to—believing what you wanted me to believe.'

'When?'

'At DeChapelles'. Only I discovered your ears weren't pierced.'

She put her hands over her face. 'Oh, Peter,' she cried. 'I should be happy and I feel so sad. I didn't deserve it. I'm worse than I ever pretended.'

'But I didn't say it then, so I'll say it now.'

She came to him on one knee, putting her fingertips to his lips. 'No,' she whispered, and kissed the tip of his nose and his eyes. 'I love you. It's all right for me to say it, but not for you. It's not right and proper.'

'Who cares what's right and proper?'

'All right, darling. Say it. Say it once so I can hear it. You don't even have to mean it.'

'I love you so much I ache all over. And I do mean it.'

She put her arms around his neck and stared into his eyes. She nodded her head at the door behind. 'Can they get in here?'

'Not without fire axes.'

On her knees she had a height advantage. She smiled down at him and edged in closer. 'Good. Because until they do, you're going to be loved like you've never been loved before. Like nobody's been loved before.'

It was a long time after, when they were lying together, that he thought of it. 'What did you really say that time?'

'What time?'

'When I told you to talk Danish and you did.'

She laughed. 'That wasn't Danish, it was Norwegian. I said, "Go to hell." Literally, "Drag yourself to hell."'

'I deserved worse than that.'

'Oh, that was bad. That's about as bad as you can get in Norwegian. They don't have four-letter words.'

'If you're a case in point, it doesn't seem to hamper them in the activities those words describe.'

'Flattery is only going to get you more of the same.'

'Consider yourself flattered.'

SATURDAY 6:45–8:15 A.M.

Peter stirred at early morning light coming into the room. He felt chilled for he was nude and, though he partook of the warmth of a slumbering and equally nude Karen, their only covering was the thin cotton coverlet that had been spread over the bare mattress of their bed.

When he sat up and looked at his watch, Karen stirred, turned over on her back and blinked sleepily. 'Whazza?' she mumbled.

'It's morning.' Peter slipped out of bed and went around to the hallway. The chair was still in place, jammed under the doorknob. He held still and listened but the old building was as silent as an untenanted mausoleum and gave off the same empty feeling.

Karen struggled onto an elbow but she didn't really know what day it was, what month, or what year. It was quarter of seven in the morning and she and Peter had been making love to each other desperately and almost unceasingly from three o'clock until less than an hour before when, in a state of total exhaustion, she had slipped unwillingly over the edge of sleep. 'We're still alive,' she said witlessly, for it was the largest and most comprehensible thought to come to mind and, therefore, the easiest to grasp.

Peter removed the chair and tested the door. It was still locked. He put his shoulder to it a couple of times but it was a solidly built hotel. Nothing even rattled. He went back into the room and Karen had already gone off to sleep again, sprawled most unconsciously and indecorously under the haphazard cover.

Peter yawned and looked out of the window, above and below. The top floor, the one whose windows were gabled into the roof, had balconies and one might climb from one to another. The Mafia, however, had been careful not to provide Peter with a similar means of escape. His window opened onto the blank sides of the hotel, a six-floor drop to a concrete bottom and no handholds within reach. He pulled his head back in and started to dress.

Karen woke again, dragging herself out of the depths with great effort. She pulled herself to a sitting position and shook her blonde head, trying to clear her eyes. Finally she was able to focus and grasp the idea that Peter was dressing. 'Where are you going?' she asked vaguely.

'Nowhere. The door's locked.'

Reality stabbed her sleepiness and her eyes wakened perceptibly. 'What time is it?'

'Ten minutes of seven.'

'And we're locked in?'

Peter nodded and tucked his shirt into his trousers.

'Then they aren't coming back for us?'

'I think they've gone.'

Karen leaped from the bed and went to the window. Peter watched her pretty, bare body but at that moment he was incapable of more than academic interest in it. She turned. 'We're on a court. Nobody could hear us shout.'

'No.'

'They locked us in and left us? Left us and nobody will come until they open the hotel six months from now?'

'I think that's what they had in mind, yes.'

She ran to the door, twisted the knob and tugged, then pushed. She turned, wide-eyed. 'Peter. What are we going to do?'

He laughed. 'Relax. They're not going to keep us in here.'

'No? How are we going to get out?'

'There are a number of possibilities. The man behind the screens who decided Barbarelli was so dumb isn't exactly perfect himself. They took our guns and that five hundred Gorman sent us, but they didn't take anything else. You've got your purse and passport, I've got all my things, including my travellers cheques . . .'

'They probably figured we wouldn't need passports and money if we couldn't get out of this hotel.'

'But they made the mistake of leaving us some tools to get out with. A plastic card in my wallet, which is very good at opening doors, and, if that shouldn't work, there's the screwdriver blade on my jackknife which can take the knob apart, or the blade, which I could use to cut out the lock. And there's my lighter, which we could use as a last resort to burn the door down. So relax.' He kissed her and slid a hand over her body. 'We won't be in here any longer than it takes you to dress.'

She began to relax and the desire for sleep came back in strong. She yawned. 'Maybe we shouldn't hurry away. Maybe we should sleep some more.'

'You can sleep on the plane. We're going to be on that ten thirty-five jet to New York if they've got a pair of seats available.'

She brightened. 'Peter! We're going to be saved! I'm not going to kill you after all.'

'No, you're not going to kill me.'

She came close and put gentle fingers on the bumps and bruises of his face. 'Oh, but poor Peter. Look what I did do to you.'

'You made up for it. Now get dressed.'

She laughed gaily. 'And there's no more Mafia!'

'What would they want with us now?'

Peter went to work on the door while Karen got back into her clothes. The door didn't yield to the plastic card since the catch wasn't the kind that could be forced back. However, it did succumb to the screwdriver blade of his jackknife and Peter, disassembling the knob section, was able to get the blade in there and turn the lock.

They left the door open to throw light into the otherwise black corridor and, with the aid of the lighter, found their way to the stairs and down. They went out the way they had been brought in—through the bar door, which had an inside snap lock, and into the narrow side street. It was only a few minutes after seven and the street was empty.

They looked carefully around, walked quickly back to the corner and crossed over to the broad, tiled promenade above the beach. There, Peter sought to oricntate himself. 'This way,' he said, starting east.

'Where are we going?'

'Back to the Albemar for my suitcase and a telephone and maybe a bite of breakfast.'

'Who are you going to telephone?'

'The senator, of course. Don't you think he'd like to hear we're on the way home?'

'I don't think so, especially since it'll be about two o'clock in the morning where he is.'

Peter laughed maliciously. 'All the more reason. Besides, though I'm not exactly eager to see his plans work out, Bono's real mistress is in danger and I don't want to see her get killed if a word of warning can save her.'

'You don't think it's too late?'

'I don't think we ought to take it for granted it's too late.'

They walked hand in hand through the gardens between the Hotel Ruhl and the Casino Municipal, found the Avenue Jean Medecin, and wended their way back to the Albemar by twenty minutes of eight. There, Peter called the airport and got two seats on the ten thirty-five jet to JFK. He asked the night clerk about the transatlantic call and breakfast. The call would take a while. As for breakfast, the dining room didn't open until eight, but they could have a little something in the lobby.

They did and a young waiter served them. The old clerk got on the phone and, when Peter and Karen were finished with a cup of coffee and a bun apiece, he reported that the transatlantic call should go through in another half hour. He finally acknowledged Peter's battered face. 'Could I get you a doctor, sir? You have had an accident?'

'An accident,' Peter agreed. 'But I don't need a doctor. I'm healing.'

'You should rest, sir.'

'I'll try to get around to that.'

'Will you be taking the call in your room?'

'Yes, on condition that I don't have to leave the young lady down here.'

The old man pursed his lips in a moment of thought and then said, 'Well, sir, I think it would be all right for her to go up with you under the circumstances. You won't be too long?'

'Only long enough for the call.'

They went up to 38 *bis* with the clerk's blessing and opened the door. Peter hung out the *Ne Pas Déranger* sign and fastened the inside lock so an outside key couldn't open it. He took Karen in his arms and started to undress her.

'Peter! Haven't you had enough?'

'I won't ever have enough.'

'We don't have time.'

'Let's see how far we can go.'

She laughed. 'I should have suspected an ulterior motive in your bringing me up here.'

'So should the clerk, which shows how unaware some people can be.'

'I suppose we really should do right by this room. We didn't the last time we were here.'

'Which is why I wanted you to come up. It's too warm a room to leave as frigidly as we left it.'

SATURDAY 8:40–8:50 A.M.

They had more than enough time and when the phone buzzed beside the now rumpled bed, Peter and Karen were in the shower together soaping each other down. He came out drying his hands, spread the towel to sit on and picked up the phone. The operator was on and made the connections and then an irritable and tired voice said, 'Damn it, Congdon, do you know it's twenty minutes of three in the morning?'

Peter was feeling in gay spirits. 'Is it?' he said. 'It's twenty minutes of nine here.'

'What do you want anyway?'

'I want to thank you for the passport, Senator, and tell you when we'll be coming home.'

'Oh, you got the passport all right?'

'We got it and we've booked passage on the ten thirty-five plane out of Nice, which gets us to JFK at four-fifteen this afternoon. That's New York time.'

'All right,' he grumbled.

'Are you writing that down, Senator? You sound rather sleepy and I don't want you to forget.'

Karen came out of the bathroom and over beside Peter to listen. She dried herself idly with a towel.

'Yeah. Four-fifteen,' he growled. 'I'm not going to forget.'

Peter winked at Karen. 'That's good, Senator, because, remember, we're expecting you to meet us.'

'All right, all right.'

'You don't sound very happy, Senator.'

'You didn't have to wake me up with this, Congdon. You could have sent a wire.'

'Oh, I'm sorry. I thought you'd want to know just as soon as possible.'

'You've been lucky so far. You're taking a chance on the Mafia tapping my phone line. A wire is safer.'

'That's all right. We don't have to worry about the Mafia any more. I meant to tell you. We straightened it all out with them.'

Gorman's tone took on more focus. 'You straightened it all out with them? You straightened all what out with who? Have you seen the Mafia?'

'Yes. We saw them.'

Gorman didn't sound sleepy now. 'I want to know what the hell you're talking about. What's happened?'

Peter smiled. He said into the phone, 'We saw the Mafia and they told me I had the wrong girl. They said she wasn't Joe Bono's mistress at all.'

'They said that?'

'That's what they said. It was the first time they got a good look at her, you understand—the first time somebody who really knew Bono's mistress was brought into the case. So he took one look and said she's not the one, so it must be the other girl.'

Gorman picked that one up fast. 'What other girl?'

'I don't know.'

'Come on, Congdon! This is vital. Just what did they say?'

'He said there were two girls and the question was, which of the two was the real mistress. And he said that you had worked it so cleverly that they had all been tricked into thinking Karen must be the one. But now they've found out in time that she isn't. So they're going after the other one.'

Gorman said in alarm, 'How could they know?'

'I don't have any idea, but I thought I should tell you so you can warn whoever's protecting her.'

'Oh my God,' Gorman shrieked. 'When did this happen?'

'About six hours ago.'

'Six hours?' His voice became a raging, hysterical scream and he called Peter a string of violently filthy names. 'Six hours! What have you been doing? Why didn't you call me?'

'Because they didn't want me to. What do you think—that they told me they were going after the other girl and then turned us loose? They left us to rot in a locked room if you want the truth and if we hadn't managed to get out, you'd never know what the Mafia was up to.'

'Oh my God. Six hours.' He was almost babbling now. 'It's the end. We're washed up. It's the end. We're finished. We're finished. Congdon, listen. Maybe it's not too late. Congdon, do you hear me?'

'Yes, I hear you.'

'Maybe it's not too late. Are you sure it's six hours?'

'All I know is they locked us up at three o'clock this morning. I suppose they started after the girl right away. I can't swear to it.'

'Maybe there's a chance. Maybe they haven't got there yet. Congdon, listen. Save her. You've got to save her.'

'Save her? You mean Bono's mistress?'

'The real mistress. Don't you get it? They're after her. Only you can save her.'

'I can't save her. Whoever's guarding her . . .'

'Nobody's guarding her. That's the point. Like Karen. She's alone. She's hiding and waiting. Congdon, they'll kill her. You don't know the Mafia. They'll kill her. You've got to do something. A woman's life is at stake.'

'I can't do anything, for Christ's sake. They've got a six-hour head start on me. Call her and, if they haven't got to her yet, tell her to hide.'

'Yes, but I can't—I can't lose track of her, I've got to know where she is. You've got to know where to go.'

'I?'

'You've got to go to her. You've got to protect her and

bring her here. Never mind the other girl, you've got to save this one. She's got all the information on the Mafia. We can't let them get to her. You've got to get her and bring her home. I'll tell her to expect you.'

'Senator, they've got a six-hour head start . . .'

'Never mind. There's a chance. She's in Paris and if they drove they wouldn't be there. We can still save her. The police. She'll call the police. I'll have her call the police to protect her till you arrive. Then you'll protect her from there. We'll get her, Congdon. We'll save her yet.'

'Listen, senator, I've got a girl to protect already. She's been through hell and I'm bringing her home while the bringing is good. Don't try to keep me here any longer. I've been here long enough.'

'She'll help you. Karen's a detective herself. She's capable in judo. She's an excellent shot. She's—she'll help you. Put her on. Let me talk to her.'

'Like hell. You've sweet-talked her enough.'

'Congdon, forget about her. Think about the other girl. Her safety is vital to the welfare of our country. And her life is in your hands. If you don't care for her life, you must care for your country! What is it, man? Are you sore because I made you risk your life for a decoy? I'll make it up to you. I'll pay you ten thousand dollars cash bonus if you can bring her back.'

'You can take that up with Mr. Brandt. He handles the financial . . .'

'I don't mean Brandt. I mean you. Brandt wouldn't have to know a thing about it.'

'He would from me. He's got regulations about that sort of thing. All right, I'll see what I can do, but I'm not doing it for any reward, nor as any favour to you, but strictly because I might be able to save a life. But what you tell me had better be true.'

'On my honour as a senator it's the gospel truth.'

'All right, give me the dope. Name, address, passwords, everything.'

'Her name is Rosa Scarlatti. Her address is 30 Rue Chanoinesse, Paris, and it's in the fourth section or division or whatever they call it.'

Peter wrote it on a piece of hotel stationery. 'O.K.,' he said when he had the spelling right, 'any password or identification?'

'No, because I wasn't going to try to contact her yet. I'll just tell her to expect you.'

'All right, Senator. I'll see what I can do.'

'Don't see. Do it. I want that woman brought back unharmed. And I'm going to call your boss on that right now.'

The senator hung up and Peter whispered some unpleasant words into the mouthpiece of his own phone before putting it down. To Karen, he said, 'If that son of a bitch ever gets to be President, democracy isn't a fit form of government.'

'I gather he wants us to go after the real mistress?'

'He wants *me* to go. He wants you aboard that ten thirty-five plane to New York.'

Karen shook her head. 'Whither thou goest, darling. Only there will I go.'

'Karen, listen . . .'

'Where you go, and everywhere you go. Forever and ever.'

'There may be danger . . .'

'And I'm not going to stop sharing it with you now.'

Peter sighed. 'What am I going to say?'

'How about "welcome aboard"? Where is the woman?'

'Paris,' he told her. He called the airport then to lay out a new flight plan. There was, he was told, a 9:35 A.M. Air Inter flight to Paris. Space was available but passengers were supposed to be checked in by now.

Yes, they'd change his reservations and hold two seats but they could not hold the plane.

Peter told the man to hold the seats and not to worry. They'd make the plane all right. And they did, with four minutes to spare.

SATURDAY 9:35 A.M.–12:25 P.M.

The Air Inter flight to Paris was made in an Air France Caravelle and took place almost entirely between layers of overcast or in haze. It wasn't until the descent was started and candy passed out that ground finally came into view between patches of cloud. Then there were glimpses of the Seine, a few villages, a cathedral, and touchdown was made at Orly at five after eleven.

Karen and Peter caught a cab outside the terminal and the driver, after looking up Rue Chanoinesse in a guide-book, set off along the divided highway at a little better than the 100-kilometer-per-hour speed limit. They sped by flat, undeveloped land with high-rise apartments in the distance, then down the slopes into the city and traffic. They picked up the Boulevard Raspail, cut over behind the guarded Palais du Luxembourg, left onto St. Michel, and across the bridge onto the Ile de la Cité, the driver making good time despite those two banes of prosperity, cars and construction. Traffic in Europe was like New York in rush hour and construction caused bottlenecks everywhere Peter had been. They squeezed past some now, on the Quai du March Neuf, and found that the Place du Parvis, in front of the Notre Dame Cathedral, was excavated to a depth of fifteen feet.

They went single file between rows of parked cars, turned in front of the char-black, age-grimed face of the cathedral, turned again down its equally dirty side to a narrow street that went off to the left. It was the street they wanted and the address was a short distance ahead, at a bend in the road. The number thirty, white on blue, was painted on an arch leading into a stone-paved alley that faced the end of the street and the side of the cathedral.

They paid off the driver, went into the alley, and found themselves surrounded by connected apartments, three to five storeys high. Two entrances were there, one to the first-floor rooms of the concierge, the other to stairs to the other dwellings. Ahead, the roadway went through an apartment-covered underpass to an inner court, where there were more attached apartments, one doorway, some garages, and a few parked cars. There was no sign of trouble nor of any police but it was unquestionably the number thirty that was supposed to be the location of Rosa Scarlatti.

Peter looked first for nameplates or a directory but there were none. There were no names anywhere. He tried the concierge next, but got no answer. A woman came through the arch with a small shopping bag and he asked her, saying, 'Scarlatti?' and indicating the dwellings with a broad sweep of the hand.

'*Connais pas,*' she muttered and strode doggedly on.

He started knocking on doors then and got to the third landing before a woman indicated, as best Peter and Karen could understand her, that no one of that name lived in the building and perhaps they should try the court.

They went through the underpass to the inside court, entered the doorway there and tried again. On the ground floor an old man winked at the name and pointed to the floor above. He went into a discourse they could not understand, but they smiled and said *'Merci'* a few times and walked up the narrow, wooden steps to the landing on the other side and then back to the next floor.

Peter rapped on the door there twice without reply but small sounds indicated someone was just inside. Karen leaned closer. 'Signorina Scarlatti?' she said, and then, encouragingly, *'Noi siamo Peter Congdon e Karen Halley. Ci manda il senatore Gorman per portarvi in America.'*

From behind the panels a voice said in English, 'What is the name of your brother?'

Karen looked at Peter and at the door. 'What?'

'You have a brother, no? Tell me his name.'

'His name is William Clive. Is that what you want to know?'

'That is what I want to know.' The key turned and Rosa Scarlatti opened the door.

She was five and a half feet tall, with black, naturally wavy hair and a coarse, peasant face which her large eyes would have made very becoming except for the shrewdness in them. She had doubtless been trimmer and more curvaceous when she was seeing Joe Bono, but she had never been slim and now she was dumpy and old-looking and there were hard lines in her face. Her voice had a slightly raucous note and her manner bore the arrogance of a petty tyrant. 'I saw you from the window,' she said, looking them over. 'I decided to myself, "those are the ones".' She shrugged. 'I would not have bothered with asking about your brother except that the senator—he tell me to ask that. He is afraid of the Mafia. He is much afraid.'

Karen and Peter stepped into the narrow hall. 'He has reason to be afraid,' Peter said, closing and bolting the door. 'Where are the police?'

She snorted. 'I did not call the police. I am not afraid

of the Mafia like the senator. Besides, the Mafia does not know where I am.'

'They do know where you are. That's why you should have called the police.'

She snorted again. 'I do not fear them. Pigs. They are pigs. They killed my Joe. You know that they kill my Joe?'

'Yes.'

'Pigs.'

'I want to use your phone. Are you packed? We're taking you to America just as soon as we can get seats on a plane.'

'I shall be fond to go to America.'

'The senator will be fond to have you. Where is the phone?'

Rosa showed him an adjacent doorway into a study and the phone was on a battered desk. He called Orly Airport and found just the thing. It was the four-thirty daily flight to Washington and he went about the process of reserving three seats.

The desk was in the middle of the room but Peter did his phoning by the window looking down at the garages, the parked cars, the other apartments, and the underpass to the outer alley. Thus it was that he found himself looking down at a man who suddenly appeared in the underpass, looking up. This was a Frenchman who wore a beret and who had a long scarf knotted around his neck. He was someone Peter had never seen before and nothing about him looked in any way suspicious. The only thing that attracted Peter's attention was that the man, looking up at the windows, saw Peter at the same time Peter saw him, at which point he hesitated, looked at every other window in that face of the building, turned around and, with a little too much nonchalance, walked out of sight again.

Peter, hanging up, didn't mention the man. Instead,

he said to Rosa, 'I hope you have some money, because I don't have enough to buy us all tickets.'

Rosa's suspicious eyes got hard. 'I don't pay my money,' she said.

'This would only be a loan.'

She gazed at him warily. 'For how long?'

'Till we get you to Senator Gorman.'

'At what interest?'

Peter's lip curled slightly. 'That's something you'll have to work out with the senator.'

'I will not work it out with the senator. Let him buy my ticket.'

'He will. It's a question of not having the money on hand right now.'

'Let him send the money.'

Peter rolled exasperated eyes at the ceiling. 'We don't have time. The plane leaves at four-thirty.'

'We get another plane.'

'And the Mafia gets us.'

She laughed harshly. 'You are afraid of the Mafia too. Like the senator. Poof.' She snapped her fingers. 'They are nothing. They cannot ever find me. They don't know anything.' She indicated the phone. 'Make the arrangements.'

'What arrangements?'

'We go tomorrow's plane. We wait for the senator to offer us money.'

Peter said, 'Listen, Miss Scarlatti, the Mafia already has found you. I saw one of them down there'—he indicated the courtyard—'just a minute ago.'

Rosa went to the window and looked with a glowering eye at the empty courtyard. 'Nobody's there.'

'He went away.'

She gave Peter a contemptuous look. 'Do you think by telling me each person whom you see is the Mafia, that will frighten me? That will not. I do not become frightened and upset.' She pointed to her head. 'I keep my thinking cap on.' She gestured with both hands. 'Besides, I have not yet done packing.'

'Packing?'

'Absolute. I have many things to be transported. The senator said he would give me time. He calls and gives me no time. He is the fault, not I.' She left the room, went down the hall and around the corner. Two doors opened off left into two sitting rooms overlooking the Quai Aux Fleurs and the Seine. The corridor doubled back then, revealing a small kitchen with a narrow window looking into the court and, to the right of that, a small sit-down bathtub which had been installed beside a sliding bedroom panel.

Miss Scarlatti strode purposefully through the corridor which, in effect, went around the study. She slid the thin panel back, squeezed past the tub, up a step and into the bedroom. It was not a large room and there was barely space to get around a fourposter and a clutter of furniture covered with knick-knacks. A suitcase was open on the bed and one dresser drawer was pulled out, but that was as far as the packing had gone.

Karen and Peter, crowding into the bedroom after her, all but filled it. 'You see?' she said, indicating the host of photographs, memorabilia, and senseless items on display. 'These must all go. The movers must—be telephoned. The movers must put these things in boxes and boxes.'

'Miss Scarlatti,' Peter said, 'we don't have time.'

'And all the furniture.' She pushed past them both, squeezed into the narrow hall, and went back to the first of the sitting rooms. A lot of the furniture was salvage from junk yards, covered with drapes and cushions to make it serviceable, but many of the things were of some value. There were a lot of oriental items: Chinese screens, lacquered tables, inlaid chests, teak and mother-of-pearl boxes, Japanese paintings, incense burners and silks. Miss Scarlatti was quite determined that those would all go to America with her and not only those, but the pieces of junk furniture as well. If she thought she could take the plumbing fixtures and the stove, it was a fair bet she would have included them on her must list.

Peter said, 'Well, that's fine. When we arrive, you tell the senator you want the whole apartment picked up and moved.'

She paid no attention to that. 'Now in the other room,' she said.

He caught her arm at the doorway. 'I know, I know. But right now let's see the bedroom and what you've got there. The rest we can worry about later, but you're going to want a coat . . .'

She went back to the bedroom and they all crowded in again. 'I'm not leaving,' she announced, 'until all things are cared about. The senator said all things would be cared about.'

Out in the court two men were in the open garages beside the underpass while, in the underpass itself, a man was talking to a woman, both looking at Rosa's windows. Peter took Rosa by the arm and turned her to where she could see through the curtains. 'Those people out there. Do you know them?'

Rosa squinted. She pulled glasses from the pocket of her housecoat and held them to her eyes. She went closer and parted the curtains a little. The woman and the man were both indicating that very window. Rosa said, 'She's the concierge.'

'Who's that with her? And who are the two men by the garage—one of them's in the garage so you can't see him.'

'I don't know them. I don't like their looks.'

'What would the concierge be telling them about this place for?'

'I don't know,' Rosa said and backed away very quickly. 'Concierges aren't supposed to tell people things. That's why people don't have names on their doors and why the concierge is supposed to be there all the time. People are supposed to be safe!'

Karen went close enough to get a good view. 'They look French,' she said.

Peter nodded. 'Local thugs, I except. Except for the one in the garage—there, just coming out. He looks Italian.'

Rosa leaned close and peered through her glasses again. She shrieked and staggered. 'I know him! I've seen him! He drove for Joe!'

Peter said, 'I guess they want to make sure they have the right girl this time.'

Rosa let out a long wail and backed against the wall, white and sweating. A rosary had materialised in her hands but she couldn't make her fingers move. 'It's the Mafia, it's the Mafia,' she blubbered. 'They will kill me. They will kill me.' She lapsed into Italian and stared at Karen and Peter with rolling eyes.

SATURDAY 12:25–12:45 P.M.

Peter turned back to the window. The concierge was gone now and the man was conferring with the Italian Rosa had recognised. He was fiftyish, had a small Van Dyke, and seemed to be in charge. The man with the green beret reappeared through the underpass.

He gestured back at something or someone out of sight and the bearded man waved in a 'cover the front' manner. Beret-and-scarf ran off quickly.

'Looks as though they've got us bottled up,' Peter said sourly.

Karen, who had been soothing Rosa, came for a look. 'The enemy forces are gathering,' she agreed. 'I wonder how many they've got.'

'I wonder what took them so long.'

'I wonder what we're going to do about it.'

'We'll stay put for now. I don't think they'll try to take the place by storm.' Peter left the bedroom and returned to the sitting room. The view of the Seine was over the slanting roofs of attached apartments. The roofs were but a short drop below the window ledge and escape looked easy. However, a man was out on the river wall watching the windows and that took care of that.

Peter went on around to the front door to check the locks. Karen joined him and Rosa, sobbing and jabbering Italian hysterically, came flying after.

'What's her problem?' Peter asked as Rosa seized Karen and hung on.

'She was afraid we were going to leave her.'

Peter took the woman's arms. 'Come on, get hold of yourself.'

She sobbed and jabbered beseechingly and he shook her. 'Speak English. And do as I say. First, answer my questions. Do you have a gun?'

She nodded.

'Get it for me.'

She started back, pulling Karen with her, and they all returned to the bedroom. The gun was in the bureau under the underwear. It was a small nickel-plated ·32 automatic and it didn't have any bullets in it. 'Where'd you get this?' Peter asked, sliding out the clip.

'It's from Joe. Long ago.'

'Where are the bullets?'

'No bullets. I don't have bullets.'

Peter made a face but stuck the gun in his belt anyway. 'How much money have you got?'

'No,' she shrieked. 'You're not going to take my money!'

'If you want to get out of here, give me your money.'

'Thief. Thief. You can't have my money.'

'Listen, Rosa. I've got money for her and for me. I don't have any for you. If you want to come with us, you have to pay.'

She turned around reluctantly and, lapsing into Italian cursing, took her purse off the bureau and opened it, dumping it upside down on the bed. Besides the heavy assortment of cosmetics she carried, there was some change and a flock of loose bank notes. Peter picked them up and counted them quickly but the total was less than fifty francs. It would not make up the difference for plane tickets. 'You must have more than that.'

'Yes.' She nodded. 'In the bank.'

Karen said to the ceiling, 'And today is Saturday and the banks are closed.'

Rosa said to her earnestly, 'But how I know you come today?'

Karen turned to Peter. 'But does it really matter? We're not going to be taking any planes out. We're trapped.'

Peter, at the window watching the two visible men deployed in the courtyard below, said, 'Brandt has an agent in Paris. It's a question of getting hold of him and seeing what he can do for us.'

Rosa came up and grabbed Peter's lapels. 'You have friends who can save us?'

'Save you—maybe. But not the apartment.' He waved a hand. 'Not all this stuff. Just you.'

'Just me. Just me. The senator. He will pay me for this, no?'

'That's between you and him.'

Peter led the way back to the study and the phone. He hunted up a number in the directory and dialled. He said, 'Monsieur DeSaulnier, please.' Then he said, 'I don't speak French. *Je ne parle pas français. Comprenez-vous?* I want Mister DeSaulnier. It's important. *Très importante.*' He made a face at Karen and blew her a kiss.

She laughed. 'Your French is so good.'

Peter made another face and put his hand over the mouthpiece. 'God only knows where this guy DeSaulnier is. He's got a construction firm. He's probably out digging up that park in front of the cathedral.' Into the phone he said, 'Tell him, Brandt of Philadelphia . . . Philadelphia. P-H-I- . . . Brandt. B-R-A-N-D-T. In the United States. Tell him that and tell him it's very important.'

Peter grinned at Karen again and shrugged his shoulders.

She said, 'Are they calling him?'

'I don't know what they're doing. Their English isn't any better than my French.'

'What do you think he can do—if you can get him?'

'Maybe talk the police into giving us an escort. If not, maybe he can machine-gun the opposition.'

'The head of a construction firm is Brandt's agent in Paris? Why?'

'Why a cobbler in Genoa or a leather goods dealer in Rome?'

'That's what I want to know. Why?'

'You mean, why do they have occupations? They have to make a living. They don't make it being Brandt's contacts. Giuseppe, for instance, would have his phone paid for by Brandt—he certainly wouldn't have a phone in his shop otherwise—and he'd get a small monthly stipend and if and when he was called upon to do some work for the agency, then he'd get extra pay. The same with Vittorio. Except, with Vittorio, it wasn't money that interested him, it was the bizarre, and hopefully exciting, connection it gave him.'

'But how would he get somebody like Giuseppe—and in a place like that?'

Peter said, 'You don't understand the old man. He wants listening posts. He's got a network set up all over the world and don't ask me who or where, because only he knows the extent of his operation, but it's big. And it's fluid. He's got part-time agents all over the United States and all over the world. That's how he does it. For a small monthly fee, these people obligate themselves to the organisation and express a willingness to do a job when called upon. The agent in Paris—and Brandt may have more than one for all I know—is named Paul DeSaulnier and he owns a construction company and, presumably, is quite well-to-do. It's my guess Brandt likes his contacts wealthy when possible. They can't be bought easily if they're in it for fun and games. Anyway, this would be the man in Paris who Brandt has decided meets the agency requirements.'

'You think he can do anything? Or will if he can? How much does he want to risk?'

'God only knows, but I hope Brandt can pick them.' Peter looked out the window where two sinister figures lounged together in the underpass and passed the time of day.

Finally a voice came on the wire identifying the owner as DeSaulnier. Peter said, 'The Brandt Agency has a far-flung net,' and waited. After a bit, the other said slowly, as if trying to remember, 'And it catches many fish.'

'And I am a Brandt fish who someone else has caught. The name is Peter Congdon.'

The name didn't mean anything to DeSaulnier but he said politely, 'What's the problem?'

Peter gave him a quick rundown. He and two women were penned by Mafia agents in the second-floor apartment off the court at 30 Rue Chanoinesse. They were scheduled for a four-thirty take-off to the U.S. and the Mafia agents didn't want one of the women to make the flight, or to make anything else for that matter. What Peter was after was some kind of safe conduct aboard that plane, plus the loan of enough francs to pay for the tickets.

DeSaulnier listened to all this and remarked that it was interesting and what he found particularly interesting was that a Brandt agent would be coming into the territory without Brandt giving him a word of advance notice. He called it interesting but he meant it was, despite the fish-net business, suspicious.

It wasn't supposed to be in this area, Peter told him. It wasn't really supposed to have gone outside of Rome and Florence but a certain amount of mobility had been acquired by those involved and the affair had got pretty far afield. 'Of course it would be a simple matter to put in a call to Brandt to verify it. In fact, he might like to know where I am, since I haven't been able to get a report off to him in the last couple of days.'

'Well, I just might do that.'

'Do, if it'll set your mind at ease. Also, tell Brandt that the client pulled a fast one and sent me after a decoy and I had to come to Paris to pick up the real McCoy.'

'I don't quite understand that.'

'It's all right. If you say that to him, he will.'

'And you are at present on the second floor of the rear apartment overlooking the court at thirty Chanoinesse Street? And there are two men in the court waiting for you to come out?'

'Two who are visible. There's another watching our front windows and at least two more out of sight. And there may be a back-up team behind them.'

'And what evidence do you have that these people are waiting for you?'

'Chills up and down my spine.'

'I don't understand English well. What does that mean?'

'It means, Mr. DeSaulnier, that there is that quality about their manner, their appearance, their interest in this particular apartment, plus their not seeming to have anything else to do but hang around this courtyard, that says to me that it would be most unwise for us to walk out of that door downstairs.'

'I see. All right, I shall decide what to do.'

'Don't forget the plane we have to make.'

'I shan't. Be patient.'

SATURDAY 1:30–4:45 P.M.

For the better part of an hour, conditions in the little courtyard remained static with the two men lounging around, keeping themselves available. At one point the man with the beret and scarf reappeared to give them containers of coffee and sandwiches wrapped in paper. It was a homely touch sufficiently ludicrous to draw wry smiles from Peter and Karen. The feeding of hatchet men while they waited to do their hatcheting.

Rosa spent the time in the bedroom, alternately crossing herself and going through the beads, praying aloud in a rocking, moaning singsong to God for deliverance, and praying with almost equal fervour to Peter for deliverance. He tried to persuade her to pack a suitcase to get her mind on something constructive but it was no use.

The sight of Joe Bono's ex-driver had reduced her to quivering incoherence.

Then, at a little after half past one in the afternoon, it happened. Peter was just returning from a check of the sitting rooms, where he periodically made sure no one was coming over the roofs after them, when there was a roaring, chugging sound out back, and he hurried to the bedroom window. Below, in the court, the hatchet men had turned and were staring in shock as there hove into sight a huge six-wheeled dump truck with a blue cab and a yellow dumper. And in the dumper stood twenty men, all with yellow work jackets, yellow helmets, and blue work pants.

It was a tight squeeze coming through the underpass and the men had to duck, but the truck squeaked in, passed the astonished thugs, and rumbled up to the door. There, twenty jacketed and uniformed workmen jumped out and a good ten of them burst through and piled up the stairs. The other ten moved around the yard, shoving the thugs back as if a construction job were going to start on the spot, and the truck itself started the arduous and tight job of turning itself around.

Peter had the door open at the head of the stairs when the crowd of workmen came up. The leader was six-four and two hundred and forty pounds, with black curly hair and a plump, good-natured, ruddy face. He said in good English as he came onto the landing, 'You the Brandt fish who's caught in the net?'

'I'm the one.'

'And I'm DeSaulnier. Good to be of service.' He held out a big paw and shook Peter's hand hard. 'You got two women, right?'

'Right behind me.' Peter stepped aside to expose Karen and Rosa.

'And we got outfits.' He turned and snapped his fingers. *'Voilà, donne-moi ces vêtements.'*

A man crowded up beside him carrying extra jackets and pants and helmets. DeSaulnier gave them to Peter. 'They won't fit but it doesn't matter. Just get them on.'

The girls climbed into the pants in the study with the door closed. Peter pulled a big pair over his own trousers in the hall. When the girls reappeared, swimming in the pants, with the cuffs turned way up, Karen was laughing and even Rosa was able to behave rationally. They donned the big yellow jackets and put on helmets and went downstairs in the middle of the group of grinning and jabbering workers. 'I got money,' DeSaulnier said. 'Three tickets for America?'

'For Washington D.C.'

The truck in the court was now backed up to the door and the two frustrated Mafia men were inside the garage, where they could see the group troop out and climb aboard, but where they were hemmed and watched and powerless to act.

Up in the dumper, the girls were made to sit down below the level of the sides. Other men clambered aboard and the monstrous vehicle started into motion. It inched its way through the underpass, gained speed in the outer alley, and turned right onto Rue Chanoinesse. Waiting for them out there, Peter discovered, were two more identical trucks, with another thirty men aboard. There were cheers and waving and laughter as they started up and fell in behind.

Chasing after came the two little men. There was a car in the alleyway and the car swung out into the road in pursuit.

The pursuit never developed. The last truck in line came to a stop at the corner, blocking off everything behind it. And there it stayed while the other two trucks went on. By the time the men in the sedan realised they were being blockaded, two other motorists were behind them, beeping their horns. It was the last Beret, Van Dyke and Associates ever saw of Rosa.

The ride to Orly was a merry one with laughter and rollicking songs. Then the two trucks pulled up under the long marquee of the 'Aéroport de Paris' and forty yellow-jacketed workmen climbed down and went inside. And no one noticed that two of the party were female or that one of the males knew no French.

As they started through the doors, Peter saw something that made him blink and catch DeSaulnier's arm. Between each set of double entry and exit doors in the long building was a glass niche holding two open telephones. Standing beside this particular niche was the sallow, tubercular, dead-eyed man who had chased Peter across a continent. At one of the phones, obviously just arrived from Nice and making contact, was the brutal, black-toothed carnation-fancier who had battered him by flashlight in the night club room of the Ritz Hotel. 'Don't look yet,' Peter muttered, 'but right there, at the phone, are the two guys who are after us.'

'Eh?' DeSaulnier said. 'Here?' He gave a hard look as they went through the doors. 'What do you want us to do?'

Peter didn't have to think hard about that one. 'Get the girls out of the way and give me a cover. Have your guys fence those two off so nobody else can see.'

DeSaulnier issued the order and nearly forty yellow-jacketed figures surrounded the niche, outside and in, sealing off the whole entrance, blocking off public view through the glass.

The encirclement only attracted bland interest from the thin man at first, but as the lines grew defined, with him in the middle, he started looking quickly, his eyes at first puzzled, then darting with the sudden fear of the hunted.

Peter moved in and the thin man turned, not recognising him, not understanding any of this. Peter hit him one quick, hard hook to the solar plexus and followed with a karate chop to the side of the jaw and neck which brought the thin man down as if hit by a safe.

At the phone, with his back turned, Barbarelli was so engrossed in conversation he was only vaguely conscious of the gathering host of yellow jackets and he only turned around at the sound of Peter's blows. He too failed to recognise his erstwhile prey and his first reaction was one of astonishment at the attack. Only after the man fell did his own reflexes react enough to drop the phone and reach for the inside of his coat. Peter hit him three successive blows to the head and face with the heels of two very powerful hands. Two of the blows broke bones, one his nose, the other his left jaw, but he did not know anything about this—or anything else—for quite some time.

The encircling workmen gave gasps of astonishment. They had not seen the sort of damage a karate expert could inflict in such a swift matter of moments. They did not know that their boss was contact for a man named Brandt, or that Brandt was the sort who required his active agents to work very hard on judo and karate.

DeSaulnier, who was a much larger man than Peter, was the most impressed. 'I don't ever want to fight with you,' he said. 'Now what?'

'Keep me covered.' Peter knelt beside both men, found a gun on each and a passport apiece. He got up, gave the guns to DeSaulnier, and kept the passports. 'Can you get them aboard those trucks and give them a ride back to town?'

'Yes. We can do that.'

'Maybe take the big one to a hospital? From the way he's bleeding I think he's kind of hurt. I smashed his nose, I'm afraid, and I felt his jaw give.'

'Sure. I send one truck back with them.'

'Brandt will take care of all expenses.'

'I know. I called him to check on you.'

Peter started stripping off the work clothes. 'What'd he have to say?'

'He wants very much to hear from you. He wants to know what you're doing in Paris, what you mean getting Rome agents arrested in Florence. He told me to do what you wanted, but he didn't sound pleased with you. He said you weren't sending in reports and he doesn't like being kept in the dark.'

Peter muttered under his breath, finished changing, and said, 'I think the girls had better give you back your things now—if the men can keep a circle here so the girls can change.'

DeSaulnier grinned. 'The men will like that very much.' He turned and explained it to them and they all laughed. The women were ushered into the select circle and Karen stared at the unconscious men. 'You?' she asked Peter.

'Revenge,' he said.

'For my brother too, if they are the ones.'

'They're in it—whether they killed him or not—up to their necks.'

The girls got off their work clothes and returned to femininity in front of an appreciative audience. DeSaulnier's construction crews were getting unusual treats this day—karate chops and costume changes. Then they got busy on Peter's victims, putting jackets and helmets on them. The two were regaining consciousness but were ill-equipped to resist. They still did not know their assailant or why these things were being done to them.

Meanwhile, as a blind, four or five of the construction men started measuring things and setting up sawhorses to block off the area. Large construction projects were going on in other parts of Orly Airport and none of the constant stream of travellers entering and leaving paid more than passing attention.

Finally, with the two Mafia men loaded aboard, one of the trucks and all but half a dozen of the men went off. DeSaulnier and the others remained with Peter, Karen and Rosa as protection. As DeSaulnier put it when he accompanied them down to the Pan Am counter at the end, 'Don't let Brandt say Paul DeSaulnier does not do the job.'

'I'll tell him right now and you can send it to him.'

'What's that?'

'He's beefing about not getting a report, is he? As soon as we get tickets and I wire my client, I'll write him out a detailed report—and I mean detailed—while we're waiting for the plane. And then you can cable it to him for me—collect.'

Which is what, after seeing Peter and his charges off into the setting sun, DeSaulnier did.

SUNDAY 12:00–1:00 A.M.

Senator Robert Gerald Gorman himself poured the drinks: Scotch and water, short, for Peter, bourbon and water, long, for Karen. They were in his study on the second floor of the house at 2250 Kalorama Road, Northwest, a room Peter had last seen only seven days before, though it felt like aeons. It was midnight Saturday, but that was Washington time. In Paris it would be six o'clock Sunday morning, which made it far too many hours for Peter and Karen to have been up. Add to that the fact that Rosa had been safely delivered to the senator at Dulles Airport and spirited away to a secret destination under heavy guard, and it was no wonder the young couple's heads were drooping. The pressure was off, the mission accomplished. The mission had, in fact, been so successfully accomplished that no trace of the Mafia had appeared at the airport. Its power élite did not yet know that the star witness had been safely delivered.

'Magnificent, absolutely magnificent,' the senator chuckled, giving out the glasses and toasting the visitors. 'The hearings will start Monday and, of course, you two will be my houseguests until then. And seats in the front row when Miss Scarlatti does her stuff.' Gorman couldn't keep the glee out of his manner. The investigation was Big Time now. He'd announced the arrival of the secret witness and promised her appearance at the very next committee meeting and that story was getting nationwide newspaper coverage. The hearings would be on television Monday afternoon and Gorman could expect a greater audience than Joe McCarthy drew against the Army. (Admittedly, it wasn't that interest was greater, only that the number of sets was greater.) But whatever the reason, Gorman was guaranteed broader exposure than any other senator had ever achieved in a hearing room. It was his launching pad for a national reputation and high public office and he owed it all to the man and woman right there in the room with him. Should he get to be President, and at that moment it did not seem to him a remote possibility at all, he could truthfully say that an unknown young man named Peter Congdon and a very pretty but totally undistinguished girl named Karen Halley put him there, and right then he was inclined to be grateful. By the time the wheels of the years should actually turn to such an event, he would, of course, be more disposed to attribute his election to the selfless dedication of his public-spirited nature and the perspicacity of an enlightened electorate: but now he could lick his lips and savour that future and he needed someone to enjoy the feast with him. 'Yes, sir,' he said. 'I want you both front and centre when she struts her stuff. Because, if it weren't for you, she wouldn't be there.'

Peter mumbled an unintelligible comment and sipped some of his drink. If there was one thing he thought would make him physically sick, it would be watching a woman he found repulsive doing a job that was unpretty, giving momentary notoriety to an evil group of parasitic cannibals who fed on their own species, and a more lasting reputation to a double-dealing committee head who was equally cannibalistic. What galled Peter was his being the instrument that brought it about and that he had no choice. The senator might be willing to let him and Karen die; but he could not leave Rosa to the same fate.

Gorman took Peter's mumbling for acceptance and babbled on. Peter reached for Karen's hand. At least there was Karen. He could forgive the senator for setting him up as a decoy chasing a decoy, for his decoy had been Karen. For eight hours, while Rosa sat at the window and looked down on the Atlantic, he and Karen had held hands and looked at each other. It was as if they'd never been in love before. And they never had—not like this. It was as if they'd always known each other, and talk of marriage as fast as they could find a preacher was as natural-sounding to them as if they'd planned for it since childhood and ached for it since puberty.

Gorman concluded his babbling and raised his glass. 'To Rosa Scarlatti.'

His guests raised theirs and Peter said an abrupt, 'Cheers.'

Gorman finished off his straight bourbon and he

wasn't sure how many shots he'd had. But then, on a night like this, who wanted to keep count? He looked at his guests, at the slumped position of the detective, the almost lackadaisical air. Congdon was a man of fatigue. He had been driven and pounded and held sleepless until he had reached the point of near collapse. It was an unkindness to intrude upon him further. And the girl; she looked fresher but it was obvious she too needed rest. And Gorman would enjoy being free to turn in himself and lie awake for a while, sipping a few more ounces of bourbon and savouring the presentiments of glory. 'I forget,' he said to the couple. 'You may be in Washington but you're still on Paris time. You have your rooms. Just across the hall, yours on the left, Miss Halley. You're on the right, Congdon. So I'll let you turn in.' He went past them to the door and turned. 'I almost forgot, Condon. Your boss asked that I have you call him just as soon as you got in. He said it didn't matter what time of night.' He gestured. 'You may use that phone.'

Peter had struggled to his feet. 'Thanks,' he said and managed a 'good night' to follow it.

The senator went out, closing the door behind him. Peter took a drink and pointed with his glass. 'That's civilisation,' he said. 'That son of a bitch wanted us to die painting him with glory. We paint him without dying and the result is he can entertain us in his study and give us seats to his damned coronation. Since we didn't die for him, we can cheer for him.'

Karen was more philosophical, or less resentful. She had come closer to death than she had anticipated but she had gone in a lonely, bitter woman, stripped of a brother, and she was coming out with a new life, with love and marriage and fulfilment for all the needs that lay deep within her. 'We can sit and watch,' she said. 'We don't have to cheer.'

Peter picked up the phone and said to Karen, 'Maybe Brandt can make it worth our while. He owes me the moon after this job.'

She went into her room while he put a collect call through. After a bit Brandt was on the line, his voice snappy and brisk. 'You made it then? The girl? She's all right?'

'Yes, sir, she's fine. At least she was when I delivered her to the senator and got a signed release. She's his problem now.'

'Any trouble on the flight back?'

'No, sir. There was some before. Did DeSaulnier wire you?'

'I got that report. And it was wordy enough. What were you cabling me all that crap for when you could have put it in the mail or reported to me on Monday in person? Do you think cable messages go free?'

Peter was well aware of how costly they were but he pretended the purest of motives. 'I only wanted to let you know as soon as possible that the woman was safe. In fact, the Mafia won't know until they read the papers that Gorman's got her.'

Brandt's voice was acid. 'What do you want to do, take a bow?'

Peter sobered. 'No, sir. Why?'

'You're sounding pretty pleased with yourself.'

'Well, we did accomplish the mission, sir.'

'If I had thought you wouldn't, I wouldn't have sent you on it.'

'Well, as you might note from my report, we did encounter a few difficulties.'

'I note a great many things from that very lengthy cabled report of yours, and most especially I note your many difficulties. Which difficulties, I also took pains to note, you brought upon yourself.'

'I'? Peter was tired and he wanted to be appreciated,

not tormented. 'Was it my fault the Mafia got on my trail? Was it my fault I got sent to the wrong girl?'

'Who the client sent you to does not concern me. Nor do your suspicions as to how the Mafia got on your trail. How Senator Gorman handles this kind of a matter doesn't concern me either. But how you handle it does. And if your report is as accurate as its great and detailed length make me presume it to be, you get no medals for this job. So take that smug note out of your voice. This was as sloppy and mismanaged an assignment as any agent of mine has produced in the last five years!'

'A sloppy, mismanaged job?' Peter exploded. 'It was the senator's fault that the Mafia picked up my trail. It was his fault that they learned who his Rome contact was . . .'

Brandt's voice took on additional sharpness. 'I said I don't blame you for the Mafia picking up your trail. I'm not a fool. But when they stay on your trail, I do blame you! When they can jump you in your own hotel room, I regard the job as mismanaged. They're not supposed to know where your hotel room is! And because of that, they get the key to the girl and the only way you can save her is by the use of firearms.'

'I saved her, didn't I?'

'A good agent wouldn't have had to save her. A good agent wouldn't have endangered her in the first place. And if that isn't bad enough, you let another agent get captured by the police. That is really abominable. I don't want to tell you what kind of problems I've had cleaning up the results of your shooting spree—getting Del Strabo freed and keeping from having to hand you over to the Italian police. You only just missed becoming an international incident, if you want to know.'

'Look, I couldn't help . . .'

'Don't interrupt me. I'm not through. So you and the girl got out of Florence and on to Genoa . . .'

'And we avoided the police and the Mafia.'

'You did? How great. But the next thing we know, they're on your trail again and have killed my Genoa agent in the bargain. Are you going to blame that on the senator or was it you who gave the play away that time?'

'I had to sign those travellers cheques to get money for passports . . .'

'Now that is smart thinking, isn't it? It cost a man his life. But I suppose you're going to call that good management, eh?'

'No, sir. I'm not.'

'I'm glad of that, at least. So on you flee to Nice so you can bring the girl home, except her passport has been stolen. I suppose you're going to blame *her* for that?'

'No, that's my fault.'

'That's right, that's your fault. Some bodyguard. It's a good thing they only wanted her passport and not her life!'

'All right,' Peter said defensively. 'All right, maybe I did make a few mistakes . . .'

'A few? I don't know how anybody could have made more. You ought to be sent back to school.'

'Now wait a minute, Mr. Brandt. You're overlooking one important fact which, as far as I'm concerned, makes up for the rest—except for Giuseppe.'

'Oh,' said Brandt. 'And what, pray tell, is that?'

'I saved Rosa Scarlatti.'

Brandt said with mighty disdain, 'I beg your pardon. Would you repeat that, please?'

'I said I saved Rosa Scarlatti. If it weren't for me, she'd be dead.'

'You mean if it weren't for Paul DeSaulnier she'd be dead, don't you? You're not the one who saved her, you're the one who endangered her.'

'Endangered her?' Peter's voice came up. 'I endangered her?'

'Come,' Brandt snapped. 'I didn't pick you for this job because I thought you were bright, but please show at least a modicum of intelligence. When the Mafia said they knew the whereabouts of the real mistress, didn't you stop to wonder *how* they knew?'

'How the hell would I know how they knew?'

'You knew how they found your girl, didn't you? Through you. Right? And why were they chasing you? Because they thought she was the one they wanted, right? Meanwhile, the real mistress was lying low, wasn't she? So how would the Mafia know where she was?'

'I don't know and what does it matter, so long as they knew?'

Brandt sighed. 'All I've got to go on is that report of yours but it says enough so that even I can read the obvious. Think a little. Why the hell do you suppose the Mafia people told you they knew where the real mistress was?'

'They didn't tell me. The man behind the screen told it to the others.'

'In your presence. Now, why would he say it in your presence?'

'Because he didn't think it mattered.'

'Think big, Congdon. Sometimes the number of motives is greater than one. He said it in your presence for either of two reasons, Congdon. Either he *wanted* you to hear it or he, as you say, didn't think it mattered. Why wouldn't it matter? Because you wouldn't be able to do anything about it. Why? Because you would be dead. Isn't that right?'

'Yes. That's exactly right.'

'But they didn't kill you, did they? They let you live.'

'They tried to kill us. They locked us up in an empty hotel . . .'

'Please, Congdon, please. Do you really think those people are so careless they'd leave you with that vital piece of information in your possession and trust to luck you'd die—when they could just as well put a bullet in your head and make sure? Not only does this faceless man behind the screen stop the beating you were getting while you were still ambulatory, he puts you in a room with money in your pockets, passports in hand, and all the tools of your trade in your possession. How did you get out of that locked room, Congdon? How did you manage it?'

'I unscrewed the lock,' Peter said sourly.

'With the jackknife they *didn't* take away from you. They must have wanted to make very sure you wouldn't have any trouble escaping.'

'Now look, just because I got out doesn't mean they wanted me to.'

'If they hadn't wanted you to get out, do you really think you would have? I do give the Mafia enough intelligence to know that Brandt agents are trained in such subjects as how to escape from locked rooms without keys. Really, Congdon, do you expect me to believe they had a six-hour head start and you still beat them to Bono's mistress? They were *following* you, you idiot. I'll bet you didn't even turn around to see if anyone was behind you on that whole trip.'

'Now wait a minute, Mr. Brandt . . .'

'Come, come, Congdon. It's so obvious. All the details in your detailed report spell it out so clearly. Before they kill Miss Halley they want to make sure she's the right girl, so they bring her to some high-up who can identify her as Bono's mistress. And when it's discovered that she is not Bono's mistress, then they're as much in the dark about where the real mistress is as you are. So how are they going to find her? By telling you they know where she is, locking you up in a room a child could get out of, complete with all your papers and money so you'd be as unhampered as possible. Then they follow you and watch you do exactly what they hope you'll do—tell the senator what they told you. And the senator did exactly what they hoped he'd do—sent you flying to her side to protect her. And that's how they found her. And it's only because my Paris contact happened to be available that you, Miss Scarlatti and Miss Halley aren't lying on a slab in the Paris morgue right now.'

'Yes, sir,' Peter said bitterly.

'So you keep that in mind the next time you get any ideas that you might be a pretty good detective. Now, are you through there? Do I see you bright and early Monday morning?'

That was an idea that held even less charm for Peter than attending Gorman's hearing. He said, 'I don't know, sir. The senator seemed to think I could be of further use . . .' He hesitated and quickly changed it to the senator wanting him to stay over Monday. He didn't want to have to listen to any cracks about how deluded the senator must be to think he could be of any use.

'All right,' Brandt said. 'I'll expect to see you Tuesday.'

'Yes, sir.'

As Peter hung up, Karen came into the room in a négligé. She took one look at his face and said, 'What's happened?'

'The old man,' Peter said bitterly, 'just chewed me out over this whole affair, telling me I made a hopeless fool out of myself.'

'You didn't. You were wonderful.'

'I know him, the bastard. He lathers you with it so you won't dare come in to him and ask for a bonus. And he's getting even with me too, for sticking him with that expensive cable. But the trouble is, the son of a bitch is right. The son of a bitch is *always* right.'

Karen put her arms around his waist and laid her head against his shoulder. She smelled good and felt even better. 'He got to you, didn't he?'

'He's very bad for a man's ego.'

'Come to me. I'm very good for it.'

Peter put his arms around her. 'He'd have dragged me back to work on Monday, but the hell with that. I figure we're going to take advantage of the senator's hospitality and his hearings until we can get a small wedding taken care of and maybe even a honeymoon. Then I'll go in and see if he really thinks he's got any detectives in his damned agency who are better.'

She nodded and lifted her head. 'I'm a detective too,' she said. 'You know what I found out? There's a connecting door between our rooms. Locked, of course, with the key on my side. The senator doesn't know that the side doesn't make any difference because I'm just as eager and uncontrolled as you are.' She looked up at him appraisingly. 'Maybe more uncontrolled.'

'Not really. It's just been my long, hard day.'

'A very long day. Do you realise it's now almost twenty-four hours since we last went to bed together?'

He smiled at her as his mind began to swing around to the direction she was following. He kissed her. 'That was on French soil, too. Under De Gaulle's auspices. I think we ought to see if it's the same under LBJ's.'

EPILOGUE

The Senate Investigating Subcommittee hearing room was on the third floor of the New Senate Office Building and by two o'clock on Monday, the thirteenth of November, the third-floor corridor was a beehive. Television men were everywhere, senators congregated and spectators rubbernecked.

The hearing room was large, with metal and leather doors and a thirty-foot ceiling. A curved desk with eleven chairs behind it was on a raised platform at the front, with tables for witnesses, assistants, and members of the press between it and the hundred or so spectator seats. Bronze sconces decorated the walls and television floodlights decorated the sconces. Heavy electric cables crisscrossed the inlaid stone floor and three cameras on dollies were being aimed and adjusted.

By two-thirty the seats were filling. Admission was by ticket only and the lucky holders included one Supreme Court justice, fifteen senators, a number of important party members from Gorman's home state, a few constituents of other committeemen, and a select group of influential columnists whose support could mean much. Lastly among those present were Mr. and Mrs. Peter Congdon, so newly wedded that the first threshold they crossed as man and wife was that of room 3302 on the third floor of the NSOB.

By quarter of three nearly all the spectator seats were filled, the working press was on hand getting organised at the front table, and four of the committee members were fiddling with papers and microphones at the big curved desk. Four uniformed guards with revolvers on their hips were posted inside the room and more patrolled the long corridors outside.

At five minutes before the hour, Senator Gorman himself came through a connecting door under the bronze U.S. seal behind the desk. By then the ten other chairs were occupied and he took the one in the centre. He looked capable and confident as his narrow eyes darted, sizing up his audience, the setting, the mood of the press. He nodded to various nearby acquaintances but he did not smile.

When he stood in front of his chair the other committee members rose and so did the spectators. At the press table the reporters were a little more reluctant but they went along.

Gorman rapped with a gavel and all sat down with him. He checked with the cameramen and held a brief whispered conference with the TV director. The programme was scheduled for three o'clock, so there were only a scant couple of minutes to test equipment and get the witness out and sworn so that the nationwide viewing audience would find things ready to pop, crackle, and snap the moment the commercial was over. He said to the sergeant-at-arms, 'Call the witness.'

The sergeant-at-arms obeyed and Rosa Scarlatti came through the same connecting door on the arm of the committee attorney, Charles Weidemann, two guards preceding her and one following. She and the attorney sat at the small table on the platform in the curve of the desk, her back to the spectators, her face towards Gorman and two of the cameras. Her dress was a demure black that fitted well enough to round her figure and make her believable as Bono's mistress, but sufficiently discreet to give the illusion that she wasn't really that kind of a girl.

Weidemann murmured to her and she rose and he swore her in. She sat again and the TV producer pointed a finger at Gorman. The red light on the camera aimed at his face was glowing. The show was on. 'This afternoon,' Gorman said, acting as if he didn't know 65,000,000 Americans were hearing his words, 'our witness is Miss Rosa Scarlatti of Italy, who has graciously consented to appear before this committee and reveal to us certain information she has relating to the Mafia.'

Gorman paused and shuffled papers to let the cameras have their time with Rosa. Then, at the exactly proper moment, he spoke again. 'I have warned the people. I have called the Mafia conspiracy a conspiracy of evil. It is a conspiracy as vast and as diabolical as any that the world has ever known. You are going to hear, now, a report on some of the sins that this filthy organisation, that its hideous members, perpetrate against civilisation. You are going to hear this from one who has been exposed to their councils of crime and who knows these men for the beasts they are.' He turned to the witness and the fervour left his voice. Now he was the gentle prosecutor handling a tender witness. 'Miss Scarlatti, would you tell this committee exactly where you lived in Italy?'

'I lived in a large villa about thirteen miles north of Rome.'

'And did you know a man named Joseph Buonoveneto who went by the nickname of Joe Bono?'

Rosa nodded at Gorman. 'Yeah.'

'Did you know him well?'

'Yeah.'

'Was he a frequent visitor at your villa?'

Rosa frowned. Then she shook her head. 'No. Most of

the time he's in America. But when he comes to Italy, then he comes see me.'

'And how often would that be?'

She shrugged and gestured. 'Three, four times a year.'

'And how long would he stay?'

'Oh, it depends. Three, four, five days. A week. He go away on business and come back. You know.'

Gorman permitted himself a faint glow of interest. 'Ah, yes. Business. Do you know what business he was in?'

'Yeah. He was in the Mafia.'

'And what does that mean?'

She looked at him uncertainly. 'Huh?'

'What is the Mafia?'

'Oh.' She gestured. 'It is like a gang. An evil gang. They rob, steal, kill. All for the gang. It is a very bad gang.'

Gorman nodded and waited for that to sink in thoroughly before he went on. 'Did Joe Bono ever bring anybody to the villa with him?'

Rosa nodded. 'Lots of times.'

'Can you tell us the names of some of these people who came with Joe Bono to your villa?'

'Sure.' She counted off on her fingers carefully, going through a list of fifteen names of people who had been identified in the course of the investigation as top-ranking members of the Mafia.

Gorman looked around. That ought to impress those 65,000,000 viewers who hadn't been interested in the Mafia conspiracy before. He said to Rosa, 'And did you meet these people?'

She nodded. 'Yeah.'

'Did you know who they were?'

'You mean their names? I just told you.'

'I mean what their business was.'

'Yeah. They were in the Mafia.'
'How do you know?'
'Joe told me.'
'I mean, how else do you know?'
'What do you mean?'
'I mean, did you ever hear them talking about their business?'
'Oh,' she said. 'Sure. All the time.'
'All the time?'
'That's what they came for a lot of the time. They would meet at my villa. They were always talking about business, about gambling and women and making them pay. What you call it? Prostitution.'
'And drugs?'
'Oh, yeah. And all the time about drugs too.'
'Your villa was a kind of meeting place?'
'You bet. It was like a—headquarters. When Joe was over in Italy, when there was business in Italy, they all met there. Everybody came to my villa. They hold all their meetings there. They make all their plans.'
'And did you ever overhear any of these plans?'
'Oh, sure. All the time. I sit in the room with them. I sit with Joe. Or they talk to me after. They tell me what they plan. Joe tells me. They all tell me everything.'
'Now, that's interesting, Miss Scarlatti. Mafia leaders are notoriously close-mouthed, but they talked to you? Not just Joe, but the others?'
'You bet. They may keep still other places but not to me. They like to have me listen. They like to talk in front of me. They like to brag.'
'How, for example?'
'Like Midge Rennie telling me he stole three million dollars out of the Mafia treasury and then he blamed it on Peanuts Piccolo, who was his enemy, and had him shot. And not even Joe Bono knew Midge stole that

money, so he couldn't have told you that if he was here himself.'

There was a pleasing stir in the room but Gorman carefully did not smile. 'Anything else?'

Rosa was warming up. 'Lots of things,' she said. 'Like, for example, Mike Valdi. He told me one time he killed six people himself. All by himself.'

Gorman, of course, had already elicited this information from the witness in private and was unreeling it now for public consumption. And the public should eat it up—and the Mafia as well. These names were two of the biggest.

One of the other senators was impressed too. He said, 'Valdi admitted this to you himself?'

'You bet.'

'When was this?'

'When he was at my villa.'

'I mean, can you give us the date?'

'Oh sure. March of nineteen hundred sixty-five. The last week in March. Joe was over that whole month.'

'Of nineteen sixty-five?'

'That's right.'

Gorman went on. 'So they liked to tell you things and they talked about dope and prostitution and gambling? Now then, I'm going to ask you to tell us what you know of the setup of these operations, who's behind what, how widespread these operations are, how much money is involved, and, most specifically, the names of the people in the various positions.'

Another senator interrupted. 'Just a minute,' he said. 'I'd like to question the witness about this—about the way they liked to brag to her. Brag, I think, is the word you used, Miss Scarlatti?'

Gorman came in with his giggly chuckle. 'George, I think it is quite obvious that one only need to look at the witness to realise that she is just the kind of girl men do brag to.'

'Oh, I'm not questioning that. Quite the contrary. I'm only raising the point that when someone brags in front of a girl, it's to impress her. And, in the effort to impress, a man is often likely to exaggerate. I'm wondering if Miss Scarlatti had any way of determining the truth of the statements made in front of her.'

'They're all true,' she said abruptly. 'I ought to know what's true.'

'I'm sure you think you know, but how do we know?' He turned to the other committeemen. 'I mean, I think I understand bragging as well as the next man, but when Mike Valdi brags about killing six men . . .? I mean, I wonder why he wants to tell her that. I may be old-fashioned, but I ask myself, is this the way a man goes about impressing a girl?'

Gorman said, 'Well, I really don't expect we'll be arresting Valdi for murder on that kind of hearsay evidence, but . . .'

Rosa said, 'Well what am I talking for if you aren't going to arrest somebody?'

'We're building up a case against them, Rosa. That's what you're doing for us, helping us build a case. Hopefully we'll be able to take action against some of the members when we've heard all you have to tell us.'

The senator called George said, 'We have to authenticate the things you tell us.'

She said to him, 'I don't know what all that means but if you think I don't have enough on them for you to execute the whole bunch, I haven't even started. I got stuff to tell you I haven't even told him yet,' and she gestured at Gorman. 'I mean sensational stuff.'

'Like what?' the senator asked.

She looked around with fire in her eye. She was going

to show them but good. 'Like robbing the Vatican and kidnapping the Pope,' she said triumphantly.

For a long moment there was nothing but dead silence in the hearing room as eleven senators stared at her with open mouths and sagging jaws. And no jaw sagged more than Robert Gerald Gorman's.

The senator who had asked the question was the first to recover. 'Would you say that again?'

'Like I told you. Talking about robbing the Vatican and kidnapping the Pope and holding him for twenty million dollars' worth of ransom. Twenty million dollars. I guess that's pretty big, huh? I guess maybe you'll fix them good for that, huh?'

Gorman had recovered but his eyes looked sick. He said to the senator, 'I think we'd better call a recess, George.'

George was having none of it. 'Recess, hell,' he snapped. He grabbed an 8″ × 10″ photograph from in front of him. 'Show this to the lady,' he ordered, and Weidemann leaped to oblige. 'Now,' said the senator when she had the photo. 'Would you tell us who that is?'

Rosa was white now. Her hands began to shake and the photograph vibrated violently. 'I think—I think . . .' She looked at the senator helplessly. 'I am not sure. My eyes. They are not so good.'

'Does it look like Mike Valdi?'

The eyes that were not so good saw a flicker of hope and seized on it. 'Yes. I remember now. That is Mike Valdi.'

'It is like hell Mike Valdi,' the senator roared.

'Describe Mike Valdi,' another demanded. 'What does Mike Valdi look like?'

Rosa looked ready to faint. Weidemann said, 'Gentlemen, perhaps I had better question the witness.' Gorman was frantically signalling the TV producer to stop the telecast and the producer responded by turning the cameras on him. The senator who had first asked about Valdi stood up with a thick book open in his hand and he quoted from the record. A lawman named White had testified before the committee that on the twenty-seventh of March, 1965, Mike Valdi flew from California to New York and attended a meeting of twenty-four suspected Mafia leaders at Midge Rennie's estate near Phelps.

Weidemann, raising his voice over the pandemonium in the room, said to the woman, 'You will stand in contempt of this committee and we will take legal action against you for perjury if you do not answer my questions truthfully. Did you ever meet Mike Valdi?'

She didn't move but stared at the tabletop as if comatose.

He leaned closer and said it louder. 'Did you ever meet Mike Valdi? You will answer the question.'

She swallowed, sitting shrunken and sunken, and shook her head.

'Let the record show the witness answers in the negative,' he said to the recorder. 'Did you ever meet any friends or associates of Joe Bono?'

She shook her head again.

'Let the record show negative. Everything you've told this committee is a lie. Is that right?'

She nodded and murmured a yes.

'Joe Bono never told you anything, never introduced you to anybody. You don't know anything about the Mafia and you never have. Is that correct?'

'Yeah,' she muttered.

'Why did you come here and lie?'

She looked up desperately. 'I got no money. Joe didn't didn't leave me no money. I did it for the money.'

At the head of the table, Gorman was on his feet pounding wildly with the gavel. 'This is the way the Mafia works,' he shrieked against the din. 'This shows you the corruption the Mafia breeds. This investigation will go on. This investigation will not be stopped. We will uncover the evil—the terrible evil . . .'